Pr...

Not W...

"Brilliant, poignant . . . and just p...
— Courtney Milan, *New York Times* bestselling
author of *Unraveled*

"Intense, sexy, and emotionally satisfying."
— Jennifer Ashley, *USA Today* bestselling author of *Wild Cat*

Praise for the novels of Carolyn Jewel

"For the reader who wants fresh settings, for the reader who likes traditional Regencies, for the reader who likes character-driven stories, and for the reader who likes adventure and a larger scope in Romance . . . A wonderfully satisfying read." — *Dear Author*

"I cannot wait to see more historicals from [Jewel] in the future." — *All About Romance*

"Very entertaining . . . Hard to put down."
— *Night Owl Reviews*

"Dazzling." — *RT Book Reviews* (Top Pick, 4 ½ stars)

"A fast-paced, attention-grabbing, action-packed hell of a ride." — *Romance Reviews Today*

"Utterly radiant . . . and [the] characters are so bloody brilliant!"
— Deborah MacGillivray, award-winning author of
One Snowy Knight

"A wonderfully emotional story . . . packed with adventure and danger . . . This is one of the best books I've read all year." — *Fresh Fiction*

"A unique take on historical romance; it is an unusual and pleasurable tale." — *The Romance Readers Connection*

Not Proper Enough

CAROLYN JEWEL

BERKLEY SENSATION, NEW YORK

THE BERKLEY PUBLISHING GROUP
Published by the Penguin Group
Penguin Group (USA) Inc.
375 Hudson Street, New York, New York 10014, USA

Penguin Group (Canada), 90 Eglinton Avenue East, Suite 700, Toronto, Ontario M4P 2Y3, Canada
(a division of Pearson Penguin Canada Inc.) • Penguin Books Ltd., 80 Strand, London WC2R 0RL,
England • Penguin Group Ireland, 25 St. Stephen's Green, Dublin 2, Ireland (a division of Penguin
Books Ltd.) • Penguin Group (Australia), 250 Camberwell Road, Camberwell, Victoria 3124, Australia
(a division of Pearson Australia Group Pty. Ltd.) • Penguin Books India Pvt. Ltd., 11 Community
Centre, Panchsheel Park, New Delhi—110 017, India • Penguin Group (NZ), 67 Apollo Drive,
Rosedale, Auckland 0632, New Zealand (a division of Pearson New Zealand Ltd.) • Penguin Books
(South Africa) (Pty.) Ltd., 24 Sturdee Avenue, Rosebank, Johannesburg 2196, South Africa

Penguin Books Ltd., Registered Offices: 80 Strand, London WC2R 0RL, England

This is a work of fiction. Names, characters, places, and incidents either are the product of the author's
imagination or are used fictitiously, and any resemblance to actual persons, living or dead, business
establishments, events, or locales is entirely coincidental. The publisher does not have any control over
and does not assume any responsibility for author or third-party websites or their content.

NOT PROPER ENOUGH

A Berkley Sensation Book / published by arrangement with the author

PUBLISHING HISTORY
Berkley Sensation mass-market edition / September 2012

Copyright © 2012 by Carolyn Jewel.
Cover art by Jon Paul. Hand lettering by Ron Zinn.
Cover design by George Long.
Interior text design by Kristin del Rosario.

ISBN: 978-0-425-25097-6

BERKLEY SENSATION®
Berkley Books are published by The Berkley Publishing Group,
a division of Penguin Group (USA) Inc.,
375 Hudson Street, New York, New York 10014.
BERKLEY SENSATION® is a registered trademark of Penguin Group (USA) Inc.
The "B" design is a trademark of Penguin Group (USA) Inc.

PRINTED IN THE UNITED STATES OF AMERICA

10 9 8 7 6 5 4 3 2 1

ALWAYS LEARNING   PEARSON

To my son for being wonderful and amazing.

Acknowledgments

As ever, a big thank-you to my agent, Kristin Nelson, for all her help, advice, and assistance. Another thank-you goes out to my editor, Kate Seaver, and the entire team at Berkley. My thanks as well to Nyree Belleville, Jacquie Yau, Julie McDermott, and Robin Harders for everything done over dinners and European Sipping Chocolate. You guys keep me sane.

Chapter One

GRENVILLE FOXMAN TALBOT, MARQUESS OF FENRIS and eldest and only son of the Duke of Camber, always slept the sleep of the innocent.

As a child, he'd never had nightmares, because even then he'd possessed the power to stop any terrifying developments that appeared in his dreams. If there were dragons about to roast him in flames, he slew them. He vanquished monsters with one stony glare, sprouted wings and flew off high cliffs, and conjured swords or other weapons when faced with threat of attack. He transformed enemies into slugs or simply stopped an unpleasant dream entirely.

He was dreaming now, and it was one of those dreams in which he was both participant and observer. As was so often the nature of dreams, the subject was both fantastical and sexual. He was naked, and in front of him, her back to him, was Robert Bryant's widow. The part of him that was observing his depravity commented that this was absurd. Eugenia Hampton Bryant would never consent to be alone with him and certainly never in his private quarters. This observation was followed by the suggestion that it would be a thunderingly good thing to discover where this dream would take him.

On no account would he wake up until he knew. He fell into his dream in a way that he had not before. Not in any dream. He was immersed. Submerged. Colors were more intense, his senses exquisitely acute. In the context of a dream that involved his most frequent sexual fantasies, this was an excellent development.

She wore blue and gray silk, sumptuous and cut like something from the previous century. The gown or robe or whatever it might be called was open at the back, all the way to the top of her derriere, and sliding off her shoulders. Because she wore no undergarments, which was not at all ludicrous to him, he feasted on the sight of her bare skin, the curve of her shoulders, back, and hips. Her hair was unpinned and swept over her right shoulder. Her head was turned to the left, as if she were about to look at him.

He walked to her, stopped behind her, and trailed a finger along the top of her deliciously bare shoulder and then the length of her spine. A sigh escaped from her lips. He slid his palm to her lower back, then underneath her gown and over the swell of her bottom. In his other hand, he gathered a handful of her bodice and watched while he pulled the fabric down to expose her breasts.

Beautiful. Luscious. Delectable. His body, already tense with desire, went taut. He released her gown so that it fell, with a rustle of lace and silk, to the floor. She leaned back, and he cupped one of her breasts in his hand. She sighed again and whispered something too low for him to hear.

What did it matter whose name she whispered so long as she was soft and willing in his arms? But it did matter. He wanted Eugenia to moan his name when he slid into her. He needed her to long for him, to cry out his name when he brought her to her crisis, which his irritating, observing self pointed out she never would do except in this dream. In which case, he had damn well better enjoy this, hadn't he?

With her back pressed against his front, he caressed her, drew a fingertip along her hip to her rib cage, along the top of her shoulder, down her upper arm, and then slowly from the top of her thigh across her stomach. Such smooth, soft skin. He kissed the side of her throat, and she melted against him.

In his dream, she did not hate him.

"So beautiful," he whispered. "My beautiful Ginny."

She turned in his arms and clasped her hands behind his neck. Her eyes caressed him, and when he cupped her bottom and drew her closer, she let out a trembling sigh of desire.

He carried her to his bed, pushing aside the heavy red curtains around it, and placed her on the mattress. Eugenia wore nothing but a gold medallion on a ribbon the same shade of azure as her eyes. He joined her on the bed, touching, his fingers gliding over her, his mouth and lips tasting. Beneath his hands and fingers, her skin was soft, so soft. She lifted one knee, and his pelvis settled between her legs. He took her nipple in his mouth, swept his tongue over the peak, and she arched toward him on the end of a soft moan. He did the same to her other breast with a similar, satisfying result.

By the time he pulled himself over her, he was halfway to climax. She parted her thighs, and he slid inside her. Her body accepted him, soft and slick around him. Ready for him. Eager for him as she would never be in reality. Their eyes met, connected, knew each other. In his dream, she knew what he liked and wanted that from him. True, he could be tender and gentle. He often was. But there were times he wanted an edge, and right now he wanted that edge with her. Hadn't he always?

She wore a wedding band, but it wasn't the one Robert had given her. No, this ring was one he'd put on her finger himself. They were married, he realized. She was his wife now. Not Robert's.

Eugenia, God, so willing and passionate, put her arms around his shoulders, holding him close, moving with him exactly as he needed. Hard. Fast. Pushing them both to surrender. Her breath came in short bursts, and he was both masterfully making love to her and aroused almost beyond his endurance.

"I love you." She gazed into his face, besotted, trusting, while he thrust into her. Her fingertips slid over his skin. "Fox. Oh, Fox, I love you more than life."

"I love you, too," he said, and his heart dissolved into her. "Forever."

His observing self remarked, "You are deluding yourself." To which his dreaming self replied, "Sod off."

Eugenia wrapped her legs around him, and his body wound up tighter than ever. She whispered his name and then encouragement. *More. More, Fox. Please.* His climax shattered him to pieces.

Immediately, even before his orgasm had faded, she was asleep beside him, sated, and there was Robert at the foot of the bed where he and Ginny lay tangled in each other's arms. Had he been there the entire time? Fox slid out of her embrace and gazed at his best friend. Robert stood unevenly, as he always did, one hand on one of the bedposts so he would not lose his balance. His hair was shorn close to his head. He'd never been a handsome man, but no one who met him cared. Intellect, that beady-eyed genius, burned in him fever-bright.

"Robert." The apology he'd owed Robert from nearly the day Ginny had entered their lives paralyzed him. The words were too big, yet they must be said even though it was too late. He wanted to apologize, to confess what a damned fool he'd been to allow their friendship to founder, but the words remained jammed up in his throat. In any event, Robert lifted a hand to stop him from saying something else he could never take back. Eugenia's medallion, or one very much like it, dangled from his fingers.

"You're to take care of her, Fox."

He sat up, naked, one arm wrapped around his upraised knee. His other hand held a lock of Ginny's hair. "You know I will."

Robert leaned forward with that crooked grin of his. "I miss you, you old fool."

"I, too."

"There's nothing you could have said that would have

stopped me from marrying her. You understand that, don't you?"

"Yes."

From the moment Eugenia met Robert, she'd not cared about anyone else. Robert, whom Fox had always assumed would never marry, had fallen just as fast and just as hard. The connection between Eugenia and Robert took root so quickly there hadn't been a damn thing he could do to stop it. Not that he hadn't tried.

"Good." The medallion slowly turned in Robert's upraised hand.

"That's no excuse for the things I said to you."

Robert glanced at Eugenia. "She is the love of my life, Fox."

"I know."

"Keep her safe." Robert let go of the bedpost and took an uneven step back. The shape of his body wavered. "Make her happy. If it takes your last breath, see that she's safe and happy. Swear it."

He swallowed hard before he could manage words. "I swear it, Robert."

Robert's body wavered, thinned, then vanished as if he'd never been there. Which, seeing as this was a dream, he had surely never been.

Fox came awake, momentarily unsure of where he was. Wherever he was, he had no company. A chill permeated the air. A damn arctic wind.

He was at home. Not at Bouverie, but at his private residence. The one his father had never been in and never would be in. He pulled the linens and covers over his chest. London in October could be bitterly cold. His bedroom was silent, but his heart raced, and Robert's voice echoed in his head as if he'd really been here, speaking to him.

Make her happy.

He'd made Robert a promise.

Oddly enough, even though he had sworn to do so in a dream, he intended to keep that promise.

Chapter Two

The next day. London.

JUST WHEN EUGENIA THOUGHT THINGS COULDN'T GET any worse, they did.

He was here. That *awful* man, the Marquess of Fenris. Awareness of his arrival jumped through the room like a pestilence picking off the weak and unwary. The orchestra played a few more notes then petered out, bringing a lively country reel to a halt. No one, Eugenia included, could believe the Marquess of Fenris was here at a ball given by Mrs. Wilson. Plain Mrs. Wilson, who was merely gentry, who had no connections one might research in the peerage. The man did not attend any parties but those given by the very upper reaches of the British aristocracy, yet here he was.

Whatever the reason for his appearance, his timing was impeccable. The room fell silent as guests realized he was here, and that meant everyone in the room heard the tail end of Mr. Dinwitty Lane's comment, uttered in horrified tones as Lane stood not five feet from Eugenia.

"*Another* country chit? My God they're coming out of the woodwork this season."

The remark, though not intended as a direct insult to

Eugenia, nevertheless hit a glancing blow on its way to its intended target, which was the young woman standing beside her. If Mr. Lane had been within arm's reach, Eugenia would have slapped him, she was that angry. It was fitting, horribly, awfully fitting, that Lane's barb was universally heard because of that man.

One of the members of Dinwitty's band of supporters laughed, and that, too, carried through the nearly silent room. That man, Fenris, remained near the door, expression cool because there was nothing but ice in his veins. Eugenia was unnaturally aware of him even as she turned her attention to the odious Mr. Dinwitty Lane.

A great deal depended on her reaction to Lane, and she fought her temper. No good would come of anything she said in anger. She could not afford to give Lane or the Marquess of Fenris ammunition against her.

Fenris's social standing went without saying. Only son of a duke, after all. The Lane family had a page in Debrett's, and this particular Lane was not without influence. He fancied himself the Beau Brummell of the sporting world, and Eugenia had hoped to avoid meeting him until Hester had made a few friends. He had questionable taste in clothes but was held in awe by many for his ability to ride, race a phaeton, and shoot the dots from a playing card. As far as Eugenia was concerned, he'd wasted his time at public school and at Oxford. An intellectual giant, he was not. He was, however, one of the Essex Lanes. More, he was wealthy and generous with a loan. Friends and debtors of Dinwitty Lane were legion.

Miss Hester Rendell, whom Eugenia had agreed to guide through her first London season, gazed at Mr. Lane with placid calm. She was not a beauty by any stretch. In terms of her looks, she did not impress upon first glance and possibly not even upon the second. She was quiet and slow to warm to people she did not know, a reserve too easily mistaken for a lack of spirit. Anyone who troubled to know her soon learned she was kind, generous, sensitive, and shockingly intelligent.

Lane was a good-looking man, not as tall as Lord Fenris, but heavier through the shoulders, with legs like tree trunks. His waistcoat was mauve with embroidered pink dots, his trousers the absolute crack of fashion, his coat dark green. Half a dozen fobs dangled from his watch chain, which, in Eugenia's opinion, was five fobs too many. His cravat was a confection of linen so thoroughly starched he could not move his chin without danger of slitting his throat.

Hester turned to Eugenia, completely poised as Eugenia had discovered was her nature. Very little upset or perturbed her. "I believe I should very much like some lemonade. Shall we?"

"Observe," Mr. Lane said. He lifted a hand so as to alert his companions. "It speaks."

One of his friends barked. Deliberately. The room was still silent, and this little scene, this deliberate and cruel destruction of Hester's social hopes, was center stage.

Eugenia's head snapped toward Lane. She wanted to eviscerate the man. She wished him a hundred, no, a thousand painful deaths. If Lord Fenris followed Lane to his doom, all the better.

"Observe," Hester said with perfect serenity as she put her arm through Eugenia's. "It's forgotten its species."

And that was the beauty of Hester Rendell. Eugenia did not expect Hester to make a splash in the Ton, but Eugenia had, until now, been confident that by the end of the season, short as it was, some discerning gentleman would have fallen in love with her. That Eugenia managed to keep her temper in the face of Dinwitty's insult was nothing short of a miracle. "Yes. Something to drink would be delightful."

Arm in arm, they walked away from Lane, who had only begun to suspect one of his friends had been insulted and that, perhaps, he himself had just been summarily dismissed as unimportant. Perhaps, just perhaps, this encounter might not mean the utter ruin of Hester's social hopes.

"I believe," Hester said when she and Eugenia stood with glasses of what might more properly be called lemon water, "I do not like that man."

"Nor I."

"He's not kind."

Eugenia nodded her agreement.

"People ought to be kind."

The orchestra had begun playing again, and those who'd been dancing when Lord Fenris arrived and brought everything to a halt took up their pattern again. No one had yet asked Hester to dance.

Eugenia returned her attention to her nemesis, though at the moment she disliked Mr. Lane a good deal more than the marquess. Mrs. Wilson hurried to greet him, but she did so by walking the perimeter of the room as she must do now that the dancing had begun again.

Lord Fenris noticed Mrs. Wilson's approach and waited by the door, looking extremely forbidding and completely at ease at the same time. Eugenia was quite sure Fenris had not been invited to the Wilsons' ball. He kept to a very small and exclusive circle of friends. Mrs. Wilson would have been aware of the hubris of sending the Marquess of Fenris an invitation to any event she might sponsor. Yet here he was. Of all the bad luck to have.

The commotion occasioned by the marquess's arrival continued, albeit in less public fashion. Ladies who did not stare outright did so surreptitiously. Some of the younger ladies were not as circumspect as they might have been. They giggled or fanned themselves with too much energy. The whispers started.

There he is.

Oh, lud, isn't he handsome?

Now, I don't like a dark man, but I like it in him.

Honestly, he was only a man, and not a very pleasant one at that.

Lord Aigen, one of Fenris's few friends, slung an arm around his shoulder and spoke into his ear. Whatever Aigen said in such private tones, Lord Fenris's expression did not change. He remained by the door, surveying the room with a condescending eye. The ballroom, which was really two salons that had been opened into one room, wasn't large.

Good. He'd need the space of twenty seconds to see he had no business here. He'd done quite enough damage already.

Even from across the dance floor, she could see Fenris was exquisitely dressed. He always was. He was well made enough that anything he wore looked good on him. Nevertheless, unlike Lane, he dressed with a conservatism that prevented one from calling him a Corinthian or a dandy. His nose was a trifle large, but that was, alas, a part of his physical appeal. She wasn't so petty as to deny him his due in terms of his appearance.

Mrs. Wilson arrived at his side and curtseyed to him. To his credit, he greeted her with cool respect.

Hester followed Eugenia's gaze. "Ah. Lord Fenris."

There was such a familiarity in Hester's words that Eugenia said, "You know him?"

"He visited us once when I was a girl." Hester continued in a low voice. "With your husband. They came to see Charles." Charles was Hester's brother, and a childhood friend of Robert's. "Long before you and Robert met, of course."

"Indeed?" Her heart dropped to her toes. Disaster. This could only mean disaster. Hester didn't know what Fenris was like. Sweet, sensitive Hester didn't know that one well-placed word or contemptuous gaze from Fenris would prevent Hester from the sort of social acceptance she deserved.

She hated Fenris. She really did.

Hester put a hand to her heart, eyes open wide and fixed on Eugenia. "Have I given you a sad reminder of your loss? Oh, Lady Eugenia, I'm so very sorry if I have."

"No, my dear." She gave Hester's hand a reassuring squeeze. "You have not." Robert had been dead for nearly four years now. She would never recover from his loss, but, as she had discovered, time passed no matter what one did. She endured because there was nothing else she could do. "It's just I had no idea you'd any acquaintance with Lord Fenris."

"I was thirteen." There was so much one noticed about Hester eventually. Her complexion, in just one example, was flawless. Another was her figure. Men eventually noticed her figure. Hester was not, however, particularly graceful. "Naturally, I fell desperately in love the moment I saw him."

"In love with Robert?" She maintained an innocent expression and in return earned a rare smile from Hester. Her smiles never failed to improve Eugenia's mood.

"We all loved Robert." She took a drink of her watery lemonade, but Eugenia noted the way Hester's eyes darted in the direction of Lord Fenris.

"Thank you for saying so." Eugenia clutched her lemonade. Her sense of impending doom increased. Her skin crawled with the certainty that Fenris would find a way to cement the effect of Lane's unpleasant remarks. Unfortunately, it seemed that would happen sooner rather than later, for Fenris had left Mrs. Wilson and, with Lord Aigen beside him, was now moving farther into the room.

"I had the most awful spots at the time of his visit." Hester had no notion of what was about to happen and how badly an encounter with Fenris might turn out. Eugenia reached for calm. She must be calm if she was to have any hope of facing down that horrible man. "I was clumsy and already as tall as I am now."

"Hester, dear. Let me fix this." Eugenia put her lemonade on a nearby table and adjusted the bodice of Hester's gown, not that any adjustment was necessary. Her bosom was more than up to the task of impressing a gentleman. Was not Lord Fenris a man? Perhaps he could be distracted by the perfection of Hester's figure. Thank goodness he was a tall man, for Hester was taller than average.

Several times, Fenris was interrupted in his apparent intention of reaching the opposite side of the ballroom. Each time he was stopped, he was engaged in animated conversation. He did not appear to be in a hurry, and he had not, she realized, looked even once in their direction. His friend Lord Aigen wasn't in any hurry, either. No, the two men weren't going to reach this side of the room anytime soon. Thank goodness. Some of her tension bled away with what appeared to be the increasing likelihood that Fenris would ignore them entirely.

"He's still very handsome."

"I suppose." If the worst happened, and he did acknowledge them, Hester's reserve would serve her well. She hoped. She prayed. Fenris, as Eugenia well knew, wore his charm like a coat, to be removed when no longer needed. He'd been kind to a starry-eyed thirteen-year-old, and plainly, disastrously, Hester had not forgotten that kindness. The danger was that Hester would not, as she so often did, see through his pretense.

"I'd wondered if he might have gone to fat."

Eugenia clenched her jaw. No. Lord Fenris had not gone to fat.

"My love for him was more serious than anything you can imagine. It always is at that age." Hester, perfect skin and all, was one of those pale-complected brunettes who blushed easily. She blushed a little, now. "He was always polite to me. For which I was very grateful, I promise you."

"Ah." Her stomach hurt.

Hester looked in the man's direction again. "He must have known how I felt, yet he was always unfailingly polite. Despite my clumsiness, my alarming height, and mooning glances."

"You're not thirteen any longer."

"Thank heavens, no." Hester laughed, and this was another of those things about her that took one aback. Eugenia wished Hester had laughed when Mr. Lane was there to see it. That might have changed his opinion of her. At the very least he might have been stupefied into silence.

The interrupted set ended and couples parted at the edges of the ballroom. The noise of conversation increased as new partners were found and previous ones discussed. No one approached Hester, and Eugenia momentarily forgot about Lord Fenris. Were there no well-mannered young gentlemen at this ball? Eugenia began to harbor some ill will toward Mrs. Wilson. She had a son who was, at this very moment, lounging against the far wall, hands in his coat pockets. Not seeking out a partner with whom to dance, when there was Hester, the only young lady who had not yet been invited to dance. And that was the case even though there were more gentlemen in attendance than ladies.

Men. They were dogs. Every one of them. Every blessed one. Especially Lord Fenris.

Hester tugged upward on the bodice of her ball gown. Eugenia frowned. She stepped in front of Hester and adjusted her bodice again. "You have a bosom, dear. You'll simply have to accept that. Believe me when I tell you that trying to hide it only makes matters worse."

"Yes, Lady Eugenia." Hester looked away. "He's coming our way."

"Mr. Wilson?" She sincerely hoped someone would ask Hester to dance, even if it was the elder Mr. Wilson rather than their host's son.

"No, Lady Eugenia. Lord Fenris."

Hester was right. Fenris was mere yards distant. Eugenia stepped away from Hester, adjusted her shawl over her shoulders, and waited in silence. She had no desire to speak to the man. Ever. For any reason. Not even by an accidental meeting. Let him pretend he did not see them. Let him not recognize Hester. Let him, she prayed, simply leave them alone.

Lane, blast the man, was now looping around to intercept Fenris, henchmen following him like a pack of starving dogs. Her bad luck continued. Fenris was now so close there was no point pretending she didn't see him. She could cling to a hope that Fenris would ignore them, but Lane, she knew, would do no such thing.

No one else intercepted Fenris or otherwise diverted him from a trajectory that would bring him within feet of her and Hester. There were murmured greetings as he continued walking. Several mothers poked and prodded their daughters into better posture. Somewhere during his promenade, he'd lost Lord Aigen. A pity. Lord Aigen was quite handsome. And unmarried. Doubtless, Fenris would have poisoned Aigen against her, too.

Eugenia took Hester's lemonade and set it next to hers. "Come along."

Too late. She was too late. The marquess stopped. Directly in front of her and Hester. He smiled, but he didn't mean it. Not really. She prepared herself for a cold acknowledgment. An icy dismissal.

Hester curtseyed to him, though not with much grace. In fact, Eugenia had to catch her elbow to steady her when the heel of her slipper caught in the hem of her gown. Fenris's attention flicked to Hester's bosom. She couldn't blame him. She wanted to, but she couldn't.

Eugenia curtseyed, too. She would be polite if it killed her. For Hester's sake. "My lord."

"Mrs. Bryant." He took her hand even though she hadn't offered it to him. "A pleasure to see you, as always."

Liar. She drew her hand free of his. She was a liar, too. "Likewise."

"How is Mountjoy?" Mountjoy was Eugenia's eldest brother. He did not care for Fenris, either.

"In good health, thank you."

His gaze flashed over her. "I hope Lord Nigel and his bride are well." Lord Nigel was her youngest brother, and, like Mountjoy, recently married. As Fenris well knew.

"They are." She plastered on what she hoped was a friendly smile that was not, actually, quite friendly enough. "Thank you for asking."

"And Lily?" He meant his cousin Lily, Eugenia's dearest friend in all the world, and now Mountjoy's wife. "Have you had letters from her recently?"

Lord, would he stop this inquisition? He knew Eugenia did not like him, and he knew exactly why, too. He ought to *want* to let her alone, no matter their family connection. "Blazingly happy, my lord."

"I have no doubt of that, Mrs. Bryant." He pointedly glanced at Hester. Hester gazed back. So calm. As if one encountered a wealthy, handsome future duke every day of one's life. Honestly, you'd think she was forty-two not twenty-two. With a sideways look at Eugenia, Fenris cleared his throat.

"You are already acquainted." If he insulted Hester by

not remembering her, she'd make it her mission in life to see him suffer.

"I don't believe so." Fenris looked only mildly interested, but that, Eugenia reflected, was better than outright disdain.

"Miss Rendell, may I introduce Lord Fenris?"

"Rendell?" Fenris tilted his head an infinitesimal degree. She hated that habit of his. Behind him, she saw Lane working his way toward them, and her sense that only ill would come of this encounter increased. What if Fenris was one of Dinwitty Lane's nasty pack of dogs? What if he made some hateful dig at her? Eugenia tensed, prepared to defend Hester to the very ends of the earth.

"It's Hester, my lord." Hester spoke just as naturally and easily as you may. She held out a gloved hand. Her smile appeared, warm and soothing. How could anyone not wish to know a woman of such poise? "Captain Charles Rendell's sister."

"Charles's sister?" Fenris's eyes opened wide. "Miss Rendell? Good Lord, it is you." He took her hand and bowed over it. Eugenia remained tense, for she did not trust him. Not at all. "Well. You've certainly grown up."

"It was inevitable, sir."

On the ballroom floor, couples had begun to line up for the next dance. Mr. Wilson, the son, pushed off the wall he'd been holding up and made his way to a young woman with vapid good looks. The orchestra played some preliminary notes.

Lord Fenris grinned, a genuine smile, and he was quite unfairly more handsome than any man had a right to be. "Miss Rendell. I am both delighted and astonished to meet you again. Are your parents here?" He placed his other hand on top of hers so that he held her hand with both of his. "I know Charles isn't, as I've just had a letter from him, but where are you staying? Why haven't I heard you're in Town? Why wasn't I told?"

If she hadn't known he couldn't possibly mean it, Eugenia would have thought he was serious. None of that charm was real, as she well knew. Not genuinely. All the same, she was glad, burningly glad, at his effusive and out-of-character greeting because it mattered. Fenris's opinion mattered a great deal. Mr. Lane imagined he set fashion. Fenris actually did, and if he paid attention to Hester, well then, so would others.

"Mama and Papa are at home. I'm staying with Lady Eugenia while I'm in Town."

"That's splendid." He continued to hold Hester's hand but glanced at Eugenia. "May I say that you have a most amiable hostess?"

"You may, for it's true."

"Are you engaged for the next dance?" When Hester did not reply, he said, "Am I too late? Are you free for any?"

"I should hate to break my streak, my lord."

He lifted his eyebrows in a query. "What would that be?"

"The number of consecutive dances I've sat out." She spoke with such serenity that Eugenia held her breath, expecting Fenris would misunderstand. "I'm at five right now, and my record is seven." She leaned in and, in a confidential tone, said, "I've high hopes of reaching eight."

Fenris said nothing. Taken aback? Appalled by Hester's dry wit? Eugenia swore she'd kick the man in the shins, but then he looked Hester in the eye and said, "Mr. Dinwitty Lane has wagered you won't be asked to dance. I do not wish for him to win that wager."

"You've asked. Ergo, Mr. Lane has lost."

Fenris bowed, only slightly but enough for others to take note of his interest. "The proof would be in you actually dancing."

"A fine point, if you ask me," Hester said.

"Most wagers rest upon a finer point than that." He looked over his shoulder at the couples lining up. "Will you?"

He was fully capable of playing a deeper and more sinister game than Lane, and that possibility could not be discounted. While Eugenia debated the wisdom of encouraging Hester to dance with Fenris, Hester put her worries to rest.

"I think not."

His austere expression lightened. "Why? If I might inquire."

"I had rather not be danced with for a wager." She was completely earnest, as if the decision to dance or not were for her nothing more than an intellectual consideration. A mere calculus with no emotion involved.

Eugenia tried not to beam her approval, but Hester turning down Fenris—really, could anything be more deliciously awful for him?

"No, my lord," Hester said. "I had rather wait for someone to have a more usual reason for asking me to dance."

Eugenia saw no sign, yet, that Fenris was angry or insulted. Indeed, he looked bemused.

"Your beauty? Your lovely smile?"

Eugenia narrowed her eyes at Fenris. She hadn't imagined Fenris's glance at Hester's bosom. But was there a dig there, an insult implied about her looks? To her astonishment and consternation, she had to conclude that no, he had come about as close as any man to making Hester a compliment.

"Mm." Hester tipped her head to one side. "Those would be a more usual reason; you're correct in that. But I was thinking of my modest fortune."

"Were you?" Fenris grinned, and while he did that, his gaze swept over Hester. "I assure you I would dance with you for reasons that have nothing to do with wagers or modest fortunes."

Good God. The man was flirting. Flirting with Hester!

"Until then," Hester went on, "I am happy to be here, watching the ladies in their beautiful gowns and jewels. And the gentlemen, too. So elegant. I do enjoy watching the gentlemen."

Dinwitty Lane was now nearly upon them, his dogs in tow. "Please." Fenris held out his hand again. "Dance with me? So that I may do all that I can to make you smile at me."

"I don't care, you know," Hester said evenly. "What men like Mr. Lane say or do. 'Told by an idiot, full of sound and fury . . .'"

"'Signifying nothing.'" Fenris cocked his head. "You ought not care. I, however, do. It's a fault of mine."

Lane and the others stopped within arm's reach of Fenris. He ignored them. Eugenia couldn't decide where to look, at Lane and his hateful friends, for she quite hated them now, or at Fenris, who was giving the performance of his life. He could have made a living on the stage, he was that convincing in portraying himself as kind and thoughtful.

Lane put a hand over his heart and shook his head. "Is this possible?"

His query caused instant silence for a radius of some ten feet. Lane removed his gloves with an awful deliberation. He slapped them against his open palm to a collective intake of breath. The half of the room that could not see probably thought he'd slapped Fenris.

Fenris half turned. "What is that noise?"

Thwap, thwap, thwap, went the gloves against Lane's palm. "Fox. Do mine eyes deceive? Gentlemen," Lane addressed his companions, "did you not hear his lordship ask the girl to dance?"

To this there came a chorus of agreement. Eugenia tensed.

"To be sure," Fenris said. "I'm begging for the honor."

"The man who stole away the Incomparable is reduced to begging for dances?" Lane snorted. "I thought you were over your penchant for blowsy girls."

Fenris went perfectly still. "I don't know what you mean."

But he did. Of course he did. Some years ago, Fenris had leveled just that insult at her. He'd called her blowsy, a remark that spread through the Ton like fire and refused to die out.

"If your sensibilities were nice in any respect," Lane said, his hand still over his heart, "you would not be here pleading for yet another blowsy country girl to dance with you." He winced, but whether his pain was metaphorical or physical, Eugenia could not say. "Where's your pride? You're to be a duke, one day, man."

Fenris looked him up and down. "If you had the brains

of a lobster, you would possess twice the intelligence you've displayed tonight."

Lane frowned. "Brains?" He opened and closed his mouth several times and squinted as if thinking pained him. "Twice the intelligence?"

"I fear it's not a compliment." Hester shook her head sadly.

"Mr. Lane." Eugenia felt sick to her stomach as she stepped off the cliff with no protection but the hope that she was right that Lord Fenris's regard for Hester was sincere. "I believe Lord Fenris is suggesting that in a contest of mental acuity between you and a large crustacean, the crustacean would win."

Dinwitty gaped. "Of a . . . lobster?"

"Yes," Fenris said. "A lobster. As Mrs. Bryant so helpfully explicated, a large crustacean."

Lane's eyes widened. He tipped his chin downward until it collided with his cravat, which spoiled his attempt to look down his nose at Eugenia. She would gladly accept the man's blistering scorn as long as he let Hester alone. His lip curled as he turned his attention from her to Fenris. "You go too far."

"On the contrary, Mr. Lane." Fenris sounded bored. Bored beyond anyone's capacity to endure such tedium. "I did not go far enough. I cannot fathom why a gentleman would behave as you have this evening."

One of Lane's companions, Eugenia did not see who it was, barked again, to the general hilarity of the rest of Lane's followers.

Lane gestured at the men behind them. "Give his lordship your condolences, men." He spoke over several sotto voce mutterings behind him. "I believe his lordship has forgotten himself. My God." Lane glanced toward the heavens. "Save us from watching him dash his reputation to shreds on such inferior shores as these. You should not, sir, seduce in so poor a country."

"I beg your pardon," Fenris said in sharp tones.

Lane slapped his gloves on his palm again. "None shall be given."

"You would be wise to have a care what you imply about me," Fenris said so coldly she could practically see snowflakes dancing in the air around him. If you don't, it will be your mistake to rue. I shall not, however, permit you to imply anything untoward about me and any lady in this room."

Hester, Eugenia was aware, watched Lord Fenris with a sharp gaze.

"I'm sure," Lane said, "that I've heard more than enough insults for one night."

The world was perverse. Eugenia had long dreamed about serving Lord Fenris the ice-cold revenge he so deserved. Since the day she'd learned of Fenris's campaign against her she had imagined all manner of ways to make him pay. She had never, not once, imagined she would align herself with him or feel in any way compelled to defend him. "What insult do you imagine you've suffered, Mr. Lane, when, in fact, Lord Fenris has insulted not you but lobsters everywhere?"

Chapter Three

A few days later. No. 6 Spring Street, London.

EUGENIA DIDN'T REALIZE SHE WAS STILL HOLDING FEN-ris's calling card until he walked into her front parlor on the heels of Keyes, the butler Mountjoy employed at the town house.

"Shall I bring refreshments, milady?"

"That won't be necessary." Lord, no. The sooner Lord Fenris departed, the better. Keyes bowed and made his silent departure.

She ended up staring at Fenris as if she hadn't a thought in her head. She reminded herself she despised the man and wished him gone. Except, he'd been so wonderful about Hester. Asking her to dance and then defending her to that awful Mr. Lane. In front of everyone.

Fenris had come far enough into the room to allow Keyes to depart, and no farther. Now, he bowed, though the motion was more a curt nod of his head. "Mrs. Bryant." There was that vaunted reserve, that innate disdain she so despised him for. "Thank you for seeing me."

She lifted her hand, saw she was holding his card, and walked, slowly, to the fireplace mantel where she kept the calling cards people left. His coat of arms was engraved on thick cream paper, with the Fenris arms to the left and a smaller engraving of the Camber arms in the lower right corner. She pushed his card underneath all the others, to the very bottom of the pile, a silly and ridiculous thing to do, to metaphorically bury the marquess. But then he must be used to people displaying his card in pride of place, and she was *not* about to do that.

"It's early," she said. "Not even eleven o'clock."

"The very break of day," he murmured.

She turned from the mantel. His expression was unreadable. "Oh, do come in."

He walked away from the door. The years that had passed since she first met him had turned him from an attractive young gentleman into an appallingly handsome man. He was bigger now, and none of the additional size appeared to be fat. His skin fit close to the bone. She knew now, as she had not in the early days of their acquaintance, about men and their bodies. Their needs. She understood far too well the difference those years had made in him. The things a man wanted from a woman.

"Thank you."

She gazed at him until she realized she risked him misunderstanding the reason for her silence. "I presume you are not here to inform me my brothers have been killed or injured or of some other disaster that's befallen me."

He recoiled, and when she saw how she'd shocked him, she considered leaving the comment unexplained. She owed him nothing. Less than nothing. He had no right to understand why she would say such a thing. Nor was he entitled to the power an explanation would give him over her.

She closed her eyes and wished him gone. His arrival, unwelcome and unexpected, had frightened her, and while she waited for her dread to recede she realized she would have to offer him an explanation. When she opened her eyes, he was still there, and the remnants of her fear continued to echo through her. Softly and only after another long pause, she said, "I was not home when Robert fell ill."

He gazed at his feet. Her heart beat once before he looked at her again. He knew that Robert had died suddenly. She refused to accept what she saw there was anything real.

"I'm sorry for that." He gave a quick shake of his head. "No, Mrs. Bryant. I have not come here with sorrowful news."

"Then why are you here?" She touched the medallion she wore around her neck, a gift from Lily that, according to Lily, possessed the power to unite the wearer with her one best love. She'd teased Lily about the medallion's magical power and then watched Lily and her brother fall hopelessly in love.

Fenris stood in the middle of her parlor, his hat and his riding whip under one arm. She wasn't receiving yet, so she presumed he'd either bribed his way past Keyes or told the man his relation to her meant her not being at home did not apply to him. Sadly, this was true. Lord Fenris was Lily's cousin. She loved Lily to death and would for all the rest of her days, but she would have been very happy if Lily's cousin were anyone but Fenris.

"Come now. We have a family connection." He took up too much room in here. Eugenia moved away from him. Nearly to the fireplace. He gave her a smile that, if she were eighteen again, would have devastated her. She was a much wiser woman these days. "Am I not permitted to call on you?"

"Must you?"

"Suppose Cousin Lily asked me to look after you?"

"She wouldn't." She thought about that and decided she'd only got that partly right. "She might ask, but she'd tell you not to be so obvious."

A smile flashed on his mouth, but not in his eyes. "Clumsy of me, then."

"Go away."

"Am I wrong that Miss Rendell is here to find a husband?"

She only just managed not to roll her eyes, but she shot back with, "Are you here to find out if you'd like to be her husband?"

"What do you think?"

"I think Hester has a very full social calendar." She waved at the cards piled on the mantel. There weren't as many as there might be, but the number wasn't by any means a disappointment. Her brother was the Duke of Mountjoy, and that meant something here in London. "I'm not sure she'll have time to see you." She smiled brightly and insincerely. "I make no promises, but I'll ask if she's a minute or two to spare for you."

"I am not here to see Miss Rendell."

But while he was saying that, she'd already called for a servant and given the instructions. When she faced him again, he tilted his head very slightly. "Mrs. Bryant." A line appeared between his eyebrows. "Ginny."

"Don't call me that. We don't know each other well enough for you to take that liberty."

"I think we do."

"You are not correct." His clothes were lovely. Nothing gaudy, everything perfectly tailored to fit his form. A bright yellow fob hung from his watch and offered a pleasing relief from his sober dress. She didn't care for the whimsy, because it made him seem less unpleasant than she knew him to be. "You always wear that fob. It's not fashionable at all."

He shrugged. "I don't wear it for reasons of fashion."

"Then why?"

"For sentiment."

"You?"

"Even I, Mrs. Bryant, have my moments of sentiment." The man gazed at her with his ridiculously beautiful brown eyes, not a common brown but a lighter chestnut brown. Of course the Marquess of Fenris could never have common brown eyes. The world might end if his eyes were merely brown. Could any man be as perfect as Fenris? It wasn't fair for anyone to have the best of everything life offered. She looked him up and down, examining him for flaws, and found none. "If you aren't here for Hester, why are you here?"

"I should think that's plain enough."

"Well, it is not."

"For you."

She lost her battle for restraint and rolled her eyes. "Was it Lily or Mountjoy who put you up to this?"

"Neither." He walked to the table where Keyes always placed a vase of flowers. Hester would know their names. All Eugenia could identify were the roses and carnations. The man took over her parlor simply by standing there. No one ought to have that sort of effect on a room. He breathed in the scent of the flowers. "I've long been of the opinion that a beautiful woman ought to always have flowers to hand."

"I'll tell Hester you said so."

He turned. "Please don't imagine I'd insult her like that."

Behind her back, Eugenia made a fist. "She's not bad looking."

"No. Actually, she's not." He rocked back on his heels. "I daresay she's got something a good deal more dangerous than beauty."

"A bosom?"

He stared, and while he did, she felt herself flush. With no change in expression he said, "Is it difficult keeping that chip balanced on your shoulder?"

She'd insulted him, and now she felt terrible because she hadn't been kind, when the truth was, at Mrs. Wilson's he'd publicly come to Hester's defense. "I'm sorry, my lord. That was an awful thing for me to say. I wish I hadn't said it, for it's not true."

He nodded. "Not entirely untrue. She possesses a bosom." His smile flashed again, and this time there was an echo of that in his eyes. "An admirable one. You are correct that I noticed this." His fingers flexed around his riding whip. "But I also observed that she is wickedly amusing. Two words, by the way, I use with great deliberation. A lovely bosom isn't so uncommon, however delightful it is for a gentleman to encounter. But her sort of cleverness? That's decidedly rarer. That's the danger to which I referred."

She licked her lips and hated that she'd lost the keen edge

of her dislike. How awful if she had to forgive him. How utterly galling. "The truth is, I'm grateful for the way you defended her against Mr. Lane. I know *you* saw what makes Hester unique, astonishing as that is." She shook her head. "*You*, of all people, saw what a good nature and fine mind she has."

He tilted his head, and God, the silence. Horrible. She wished him gone. She did. He said, "That was a compliment. I'm sure of it. And lo, you've not been struck dead."

Eugenia sighed. "I suppose there's no way to convince you I don't know what you mean. Or that I didn't intend to offer you praise."

He smiled. "No."

"I could have kissed you for it, you know. For Hester, I mean."

There was another awkward pause during which the image of her kissing Fenris took root in her mind and blossomed, and it shook the very foundation of her existence. My God. Fenris?

With no trace of a smile, he said, "I wish you had."

"You ought to marry Hester." The words came from nowhere, shocking them both. She babbled on, desperate to move the conversation away from her kissing him or him wishing she had, because that was unthinkable. There could be no world in which she would ever, ever want to kiss Lord Fenris. "She's exactly the sort of girl who'd do you good."

He scowled again, but smoothed his expression so quickly she now doubted she'd seen it. She'd not touched a man since Robert died. Not kissed one, nor held a man in her arms, nor wanted to, either. But Fenris, he reminded her of all that, and she was swamped, positively overwhelmed, by the fact that Fenris was a man, not a boy. A man.

Her brain disconnected from her mind. "According to you I am a blowsy girl." She hadn't been, not even in the days when he'd made the observation. When she'd first heard what he'd said, her heart had felt the cut. What woman wouldn't upon hearing such an insult from a man she admired and found handsome? She hadn't believed anything except that the insult represented his opinion of her. Even after the comment had been repeated to her, or repeated within her hearing, she had only believed in the truth of his words when she was in a despairing mood. Was she a beauty? No. But she wasn't an unattractive woman. Not then, and not today.

Kiss Fenris? Never.

But here she stood, looking at Fenris, and, my God, how delicious it would be to have a man's strong arms around her.

Again without the slightest smile, he said, "You were never blowsy."

Laughter burst out of her, tinged, alas, with an edge of hysteria. "I know very well what you think of me. There's no point pretending otherwise. It's insulting to think anything else."

He frowned again. "I never thought you were blowsy."

She couldn't help laughing again. "How strange that you told everyone you thought so."

"It was . . . a remarkable error in judgment on my part."

"My lord." She put her hands on her hips. Just so, she was released from the past. She wasn't that girl anymore, and after all this time, who cared what Fenris had thought of her then? She'd met the man she loved, and had the great good fortune to have him love her back. She'd married him, and Robert had taught her to love herself better because he loved her. Fenris had only the power she gave him, and she chose to give him none. "Let us agree that you need not attempt to flatter me. We both know you are not sincere in it."

He bowed, and there was more than a hint of the infamous Fenris disdain in the motion. "As magnanimous as you are lovely."

"Do you trot out such double-edged tripe whenever you are compelled to make conversation with a woman as mentally inadequate as I am?"

His scowl reappeared, and she took a rather vicious satisfaction in it. Robert would disapprove of that, but no one was perfect. Not her. Not Robert. And certainly not Fenris.

"No, Mrs. Bryant, I do not trot out double-edged tripe. It wasn't that, by the by."

She snorted.

"Nor do I find you inadequate in any way. Quite the opposite."

"Insupportable." She paced the far side of the room and glared at him while she did. She might have put their past behind her, but not, after all, all of her resentment. "Death by a thousand cuts. Contrary to all that you believe, I am quite capable of discerning an insult when one is leveled at me. Even exceedingly clever ones. Tell me, my lord, have you a list of such things to say? Memorized for moments such as this?"

"An entire novel of them."

"Have you?" She watched him while she paced. He watched her with an expression that spoke volumes of his irritation. She liked that she'd discomfited him. "Pray tell me another, sir."

"The shape of your mouth puts me in mind of Titian's *Salome*."

She stopped pacing. "My mouth reminds you of a Venetian courtesan?"

His fingers tightened on his riding whip. Obviously, he hadn't expected her to know that about Titian's model. "I misspoke. I meant to say the world changes for the better when you smile."

She laughed at him again. "You don't say those things to other women, I hope. Lord, don't say them to Hester. She'll think you addlepated."

"I'll say them only to you." The man was a monument to sangfroid.

"Oh, please." She threw herself onto a chair and leaned one elbow on the arm. She was at a loss. How on earth had things between them so rapidly degenerated into trading cuts? And why, oh why, was it so amusing to trade them? "Let's not insult each other if we can help it. Inevitably, I'll win, and I know how you hate to lose."

"Very well." Fenris glanced at a chair, and she took a

perverse delight in not noticing and even more in not inviting him to sit. He looked at her gravely. "Having disposed of my primary aim in calling on you, I wish also to thank you for your support of me the other night. Against Mr. Lane."

She remained slouched on her chair. Was it possible he'd changed? Become a better man than he'd been? The not very admirable part of her hoped he hadn't. She did not wish to forgive him. "Did you expect me to lie?"

"No." He shifted the position of his hat. "However, I would not have been surprised if you'd been silent."

"Is that different from a lie?" Oh, damn. Was he going to mend things between them with an honest apology?

He let out a short breath. "Perhaps not enough to make a difference."

She rolled her eyes.

"It kills you, doesn't it, to find yourself beholden to me on account of Miss Rendell?"

"No, it does not." She waved a hand, then caught his eye and saw his amusement. "Oh, all right. Yes. It does."

His smile was appallingly triumphant.

She pointed at him. "This very moment thousands of lobsters are crawling out of the sea to exact retribution from you."

His smile became a grin, and that did something to her, seeing that change of his expression. "I will apologize the next time my chef serves me one."

She couldn't help it. She laughed. "With luck he'll plan that menu too late to save you from death by lobster pinches."

Fenris held her gaze. Was there something on her face? A stain on her frock? Did her shoes not match her gown as well as she'd thought when she dressed this morning? He must be offended by her careless manner of sitting. Her back was not straight, and her feet were not placed just so. Doubtless he was totting up all the ways in which she fell short of his idea of a proper lady. Doubtless, he was mentally calling her blowsy.

The quiet continued. She hoped he drowned in it. But, Lord in heaven, he was handsome.

"Mrs. Bryant . . ." He quite visibly struggled with some thought. "Ginny . . ."

How fascinating that he should be at a loss for words. "My lord?"

"I—"

Hester came in, fussing with the skirts of a frock of sea mist green that had got wound up in her legs. She nearly tripped but saved herself with a hand to the table between Fenris and the door.

"Miss Rendell." He bowed and took the hand she extended to him. "How lovely to see you."

Hester curtseyed and, with the same coolness as ever, said, "My lord." She withdrew her hand from his and walked to Eugenia. "I hope I haven't kept you waiting, Lady Eugenia."

"Not at all," she said.

Hester took a seat and kicked at the hem of the skirt until it was disentangled. "Do sit down, my lord. I'm afraid Lady Eugenia and I have an engagement this morning, but we should be pleased to spend a few moments with you."

"Thank you." With a graceful sweep of his coattails, he took a seat near Hester. His clothes remained perfectly aligned. "Where are you ladies engaged for this evening?" He set his hat and whip on his lap. "Lady Edmon's ball, perhaps?"

"No, my lord." Eugenia gave silent thanks that she had not accepted that invitation.

Fenris's eyebrows shot up. "No?"

"Hester did not arrive in Town in time for us to be prepared for an outing such as that."

"We have calls to make this afternoon, and we're to meet Miss Orpington at the British Museum." Hester smiled. "An afternoon to which I am very much looking forward."

"You have a full social calendar, I'm told."

Hester cocked her head, and it was a twin to the way Fenris did. Before Eugenia could interrupt, Hester brought down disaster. "Not at all. In fact, I don't believe we're engaged anywhere tonight."

Fenris looked unaccountably smug. Why? Because he'd caught her in a lie? Or because she and Hester were to spend a quiet evening at home? "Camber complains he is bored." He smiled at Hester. "Since you ladies are not otherwise engaged tonight, I hope you and Mrs. Bryant will agree to dine with us at Bouverie and so explode my father's expectation of a night of tedium."

There was a moment of profound silence.

"Well . . ." Hester smiled with just the edge of her mouth. "Lady Eugenia and I were talking just the other day about how lovely it is to spend a quiet evening at home. Or at the home—"

"Yes," Eugenia said. "A quiet evening—"

"—of friends such as you."

"Hester, dear—"

"You did say that. And Lord Fenris is a friend."

"Yes, but—"

Then Hester threw her to the wolves. Or, rather specifically, to the wolf sitting across from her. "Lord Fenris, I know Lady Eugenia would love to see Bouverie."

Chapter Four

Bouverie, London residence of the Duke of Camber.

"HESTER. THERE'S SOMETHING WRONG WITH YOUR skirt." Eugenia put a hand on Hester's shoulder while they climbed the stairs behind a white-haired and very proper butler.

"What?" Hester turned to look. "I'm sure not."

"Slow down. Let me look."

Hester swiped at the back of her gown and managed to get the upper portion of the satin ribbon meant to flow down her back twisted wrong side out. She missed a step, and only a grab at the banister saved her from a fall.

The butler, hearing the thunk of Hester's slipper-shod foot against the stair, looked over his shoulder at them. Hester waved. The butler, who walked with a stoop, and none too quickly, continued up the stairs.

"When we get to the top of the stairs, stop and I'll have a look."

At the top of the stairs Hester duly paused, and Eugenia shook out the white silk of her skirt before she adjusted the trailing end of the bow at the back. Hester's evening gown made the most of her considerable physical assets. The gown had a modest train, and she looked quite the thing in it. But now Eugenia wondered if a train had been a wise decision. Unfortunately, the skirt refused to fall elegantly to her feet but persisted in a sideways pull that quite ruined the line. Neither would the bow lie flat as it ought.

Eugenia bent for a closer look. "What is this?"

"What?" Hester craned her neck to look.

"Someone's sewn the ribbon to your skirt."

"I thought it was clever of me."

"But it's crooked, Hester. No wonder your skirt won't lie straight." She glanced at the butler who had not yet noticed they weren't following. He'd not got very far, and given his turtle's pace, Eugenia doubted he'd make it out of their sight. She opened her reticule and dug out the tortoiseshell etui that contained needle and thread and a tiny pair of scissors. She snipped the thread that fastened the ribbon to Hester's skirt. This time when she shook out the fabric, the bow straightened and the skirt took on the intended graceful drape. "There. Now you're perfect."

They hurried after the butler and arrived, not even slightly out of breath, at the doorway to an enormous saloon. Hester put her arm through Eugenia's, and they went inside. The walls and outer ceiling were white and gold. Vermillion curtains drawn for the evening covered the tall windows that lined the long side of one wall. Gilt-framed mirrors reflected light from the two massive chandeliers required to light the room. All along the walls were portraits of men in armor or astride rearing horses, a thematic complement to the vividly painted battle scenes in the center of the ceiling. She would not have been the least astonished had blood been dripping from the bodies to the Axminster carpet beneath their feet.

Like Hester, she pulled her shawl closer around her shoulders. The air was frigid. They continued to follow the butler through the saloon and, thankfully, in the direction of the fireplace. It was at this point Eugenia realized the room was not empty.

Two men rose as they approached. One of them was Fenris. The older man at his side could only be his father, the Duke of Camber. Her first thought was, no wonder people held the Duke of Camber in awe. In her mind, she'd pictured someone who looked more like the butler than the unsmiling, youthful man facing her now. The duke was in his early to mid fifties at the very most, with only a touch of gray in his dark hair. He was imposing and, unsmiling though he was, undeniably handsome. Like his son, he was slender, though he was not as tall as Fenris. The resemblance was marked. All in all, they made a formidable pair of gentlemen.

The butler stopped and cleared his throat. "Lady Eugenia Hampton Bryant, Miss Hester Rendell, your grace, milord."

Lord Fenris took a step or two ahead of his father. He wore fawn breeches, navy blue coattails, and a waistcoat the color of mist. A diamond stickpin sparkled in his cravat. He walked to them, hand outstretched until he took Eugenia's hand. He kissed the air by her cheek. "Welcome to Bouverie." Then he whispered just loudly enough for her and Hester to overhear, "Be forewarned. He's in a cantankerous mood tonight."

Hester snuck a glance in the duke's direction. "He's nothing on *my* father, my lord, I promise you."

Eugenia's heart sank to her toes. She fingered the medallion Lily had given her and took comfort from the habit. Lily, she had no doubt, would meet the duke with calm and poise. She hoped to do the same.

When Fenris released her hand, Eugenia curtseyed to him and Hester did the same. He curled a palm around Eugenia's elbow and then Hester's, too, and walked them to the duke.

"Camber," Fenris said, "this is Lady Eugenia. Mrs. Bryant."

Eugenia curtseyed again, feeling the weight of the duke's silent gaze on her. "Your grace."

Fenris brought Hester forward without letting go of Eugenia's arm. "Allow me as well to present Miss Hester Rendell of the Exeter Rendells. You've met her brother, Captain Rendell of the Second Dragoon Guards. He dined here once when he was on leave."

Hester was, of course, admirably serene, but then her family hadn't a history of ill will with the current Duke of

Camber. Or the future one, for that matter. The present duke examined Hester from head to toe, and Eugenia swore she could feel him totting up all of her flaws. Plainly, the man did not, as Fenris had, see past her modest looks. Eugenia was prepared to do battle with the duke, if need be, and damn the consequences.

"Captain Rendell is a handsome fellow as I recall." Camber, like his son, had a gift for putting more than a hint of boredom in his drawl. Such ennui.

"Oh yes, your grace." Hester smiled, and the duke narrowed his eyes. "Charles is handsome indeed."

The duke looked her up and down and frowned. No doubt he was used to young women quailing before him. Hester never would. "You don't look like him."

"Nor my father much, but for the color of my hair, your grace. It is my great good fortune to look like my mama." She lifted her chin. "The most excellent woman there ever was."

Camber firmed his mouth and stood before her, studying her, hands clasped behind his back. All this time Eugenia had thought Fenris the coldest man she'd ever known. Obviously, he'd learned the trick of his freezing gaze from his father. Camber's attention moved between her and Hester and settled on Eugenia. "You." He gazed at Eugenia with the same chill. "Robert Bryant's widow."

"Yes, your grace." With Camber's attention on Eugenia, Hester took a few steps away, drawn first to a painting of a soldier that hung just above eye level. Fenris remained at Eugenia's side.

"Mountjoy's your brother."

"Your grace."

"Told him I'd speak for his membership at White's. Fool boy joined Brooks's. Did it to spite me. Opposes me on nearly every issue."

"Does he?" Eugenia glanced at Hester. She'd moved closer to the painting and stood with her chin tilted up as she examined it.

"All that talk of reform." He pointed at Eugenia. "Mark

my word, reform will be the ruin of Britain. I'll lay the blame at your brother's feet, and you can tell him that from me."

"Mountjoy doesn't talk about politics much when he's home."

"I suppose he talks about farming."

Eugenia kept her smile. "Sometimes we talk about sheep."

Fenris cupped his hand around her elbow and gently squeezed. "Camber," he said. "Perhaps it's best we avoid talk of clubs and politics when there are ladies present."

The duke nodded and even, she thought, looked just the tiniest bit abashed. "Extraordinary man, your late husband."

"Yes, your grace." Her anxiety eased, for this was a subject that was familiar and safe. "He surely was."

"No one was more surprised than I when Robert up and married you." He looked her up and down the way he had Hester. Fenris did strongly resemble his father. Both were handsome men, but Eugenia liked the son's looks better. There was a hint of gentleness about Fenris that his father lacked. "Shocking thing. Very sudden."

"Perhaps it seemed sudden to you."

Camber stiffened. "It was so, madam."

"I don't deny that it was. To you." Fenris's fingers tightened around her elbow. She pulled her arm forward, but he didn't release her. He was right to have warned her. His father was difficult, and she would wager her last shilling that the duke knew that was his reputation and that he traded on it. As her elder, the duke deserved her respect, and more, because he was Camber. One did not antagonize a duke. Fenris continued to hold her arm as if he didn't trust her to keep her temper. He was wise to be cautious. "I only know I fell in love the moment we met. To me, an eternity passed before I knew my feelings were returned."

"He dined here often, your husband did, when he and the boy were younger."

"So my husband told me." The duke looked surprised at that revelation. Did he think Robert hadn't talked to her about his life, his boyhood, and, even, past friendships? "You're exactly as he described you to me."

He looked down his nose at her. "What did he say?"

Fenris pressed her arm again, a gentler warning this time than last. She wanted very much to tell him that she *did* know how to behave.

"That you mean to be intimidating and generally succeed at it." From the corner of her eye, she saw Hester had left off her perusal of the painting. She was now before a table on which there was an outrageously large vase of flowers. She studied the arrangement with some fascination. "My husband said you were unable to resist his charm, and that he became the only one of your son's friends to gain your unreserved approval."

The duke guffawed. "That sounds like Robert. Full of vinegar." He sent a glower in Fenris's direction. "Pity he stopped coming to dinner."

"Yes, Camber." Fenris's voice had that smoky edge to it that made Eugenia want to close her eyes and simply listen to him speak. "It was."

"If only you'd—"

"Your grace?" Hester remained standing before the flowers, none of which Eugenia had any ability to identify.

Camber turned his attention to Hester. She didn't think it was her imagination that Fenris relaxed. "Miss Rendell."

"Pray tell me, where did you acquire these?" She indicated the flowers. "These ranunculus are gorgeous. And the peonies. I don't believe I've ever seen a peony quite this color."

"There is a conservatory at Bouverie. They come from there."

Her eyes widened, and she raised clasped hands beneath her chin, the very picture of amazed excitement. "Oh, do you mean that? I should like to see that. And meet your gardener. If he's responsible for these lovely blooms. Is he?" She gave the duke a sideways look. "Is it you who cultivates these? In this color?"

Fenris touched a hand to the small of Eugenia's back.

The contact sent a shiver through her. She could have moved away. She didn't. No, instead she allowed him to guide her to a chair. He put his mouth by her ear and murmured in a voice of velvet and silk, "Do sit, Mrs. Bryant."

Meanwhile Camber gave Hester what could only be described as a sly smile. The effect on his appearance was remarkable. The duke's smile utterly transformed him. "I might dabble."

"Dabble." Hester touched one of the larger blooms and looked at Camber from under her lashes. "Unless I am greatly mistaken, this, sir, is *Paeonia suffruticosa*. Am I correct?"

"You are."

"You could only have obtained this from Kew Gardens. I suppose you know Sir Joseph Banks." She lifted a hand and stopped Camber's reply. "Unless, of course, you sent your own men to China. Did you?"

Any moment, Eugenia expected the duke to return to his terrifying oh-so-dignified manner, but it did not happen. Incredible as it seemed, Hester might have actually made a friend of the duke.

"I might have done." Camber strolled to the table and tapped the flower Hester had said was a ranunculus. "However, it is also true that Sir Joseph is an acquaintance of mine."

"Confess all, your grace. You've been experimenting with grafting, haven't you?"

"I have." He touched another of the flowers. "By chance, is your father or brother a gardener?"

"Not in the least, I fear. Have you had any success? I have a theory about grafting, you know. At home, I've produced a hybrid rose that gives a most spectacular blossom. It greatly resembles a peony. Alas, my rose lacks the intense scent of its Gallica ancestor."

"You garden, Miss Rendell?"

"Good God," Fenris murmured. "She's ensorcelled him. We're in for it now. We'll have no conversation now except about plants."

"Botany is my passion, your grace." Hester lifted her

eyebrows, animated in a way Eugenia had never seen from her. "How do you feel about cross-pollination?"

Camber regarded Hester with an assessing gaze. "A strange interest for a young lady."

"Ask anyone who knows me. I am peculiar. I freely confess it." Hester pressed a hand over her bosom. "Now. Your opinions on cross-pollination, if you please. I won't tell anyone. On my immortal soul, I shan't." She looked at Eugenia. "Neither will you, Lady Eugenia. Swear you'll hold close any secret his grace might reveal to us tonight."

Bemused, Eugenia lifted a hand. "I do so swear."

"Lord Fenris?"

"I am already sworn to the utmost secrecy, Miss Rendell."

"Well, your grace? You may speak freely."

Camber tapped a finger on the tabletop. "I am attempting to cross the herbaceous peony with my tree peony."

"Never say so." Hester was so enthralled by the notion that her voice fell to a whisper. Eugenia had a strong suspicion that she had forgotten she and Fenris were here. "Have you had any success?"

"A little."

Hester's eyes went wide and her breath hitched. "Never say so. Is it true?"

The duke held out his hand. "Come sit by the fire with me, Miss Rendell, and we'll see what secrets I may tell you."

She followed him to the fireplace, talking the entire way. "What success have you had attempting that cross? Oh, and I should like to hear of your progress with your tree peony. It's thrilling to know someone who has one. I wish I had. Have you seen the one at Kew? I saw an etching." With an aplomb that was completely careless of Camber's consequence, Hester sat on the sofa facing the fire, the duke beside her. "But first, will you tell me what you did to produce that color of pink?"

Camber regarded Hester with a critical eye. "It is a closely held secret. I don't tell just anyone who comes along."

Fenris put his mouth by Eugenia's ear. "If you haven't already guessed, my father is mad about flowers."

"As is Hester, it seems."

Camber and Hester were now deep in a conversation featuring such words and phrases as *soil content*, *pruning shears*, *propagation*, and *breeding true*.

"Did you know about his interest in the subject?" Fenris asked.

"No. Nor hers, either. Her mother or father ought to have warned me, don't you think? 'Do not allow her to discuss plants.' That might have been something to think of telling me." So immersed were Camber and Hester in their discussion that Eugenia didn't worry at all about being overheard. "All they said was she doesn't like cooked carrots. I grant you that's odd, carrots are a perfectly wonderful vegetable, but a dislike of them is nothing insurmountable. But this?"

"Are there plants you'd like to have in London?" Camber was asking.

"Some orchids Papa obtained for me. He spoils me terribly, I admit it. Cattleya primarily. A phalaenopsis as well. They were very dear, I promise you." She leaned into the duke, hands on her lap. "I very nearly refused to come to London for fear they'd not get the proper care. I write to Papa every day and ask him if they're still in good health."

"And?"

"And." She sighed. "Papa is not the best correspondent. They were alive a week ago. That's all I can tell you."

"Perhaps you'd like to have them sent here? I could find you space in a corner of the conservatory. I've had good luck with my phalaenopsis."

"Would you?" She put a hand on his arm. Eugenia was quite sure Hester had completely forgotten that the man beside her was a duke.

Camber seemed to have forgotten that, too. "It would be my pleasure."

"Oh." She gazed at him with shining eyes, and that smile was nothing short of enchanting. Hester was at her best when she was intellectually engaged. "You are magnificent."

Fenris choked back a laugh, and Eugenia glared at him. "Come now, Ginny. Admit you were thinking exactly what I was."

"Whatever do you mean?"

"I hope you'll say that to me one day. With just such an expression on your face." He lifted his voice an octave and pretended he was overcome with emotion. Sexual emotion. "*Oh, Fox. You are magnificent.*"

She hit his upper arm with the back of her hand.

"I assure you I am."

"Stop."

"I'll send my gardener with your letter," Camber said. "He'll see that your orchids and another specimen or two make it safely to London."

Hester had yet to look away from the duke. "Thank you, your grace."

"Write to your brother as well, Miss Rendell. I'll frank the postage."

Fenris bent over her, his breath warm against her cheek. Eugenia froze. He lowered his voice another notch. "Have I told you how lovely you look tonight?"

She twisted to look at him. "Have you gone mad?"

"Breathtaking." His eyes, those beautiful, chestnut brown eyes, sparkled. "Dare I say, magnificent, even."

Eugenia stared straight ahead. He was doing this on purpose, trying to disconcert her.

"What are you two whispering about?" Camber, on his way back from fetching a portable secretary, sent a hard stare in his son's direction. He placed the box on a nearby table and opened it. He gestured in Hester's direction. "Come, Miss Rendell. Write your letters and you'll have your plants with you before you know it."

Fenris composed himself. "Nothing that would interest you, sir."

While his father set up the writing surface and brought out paper for Hester, Fenris put his hand in the middle of the back stretcher of Eugenia's chair. His knuckles brushed her shawl just enough that she felt the fabric move against her skin.

Camber helped Hester to a seat at the table then reached over to select a pen for her. "Tell me what you said to the boy, Lady Eugenia."

Lord, but that voice wasn't anything but sharp as steel. He had the coldest eyes she'd seen from anyone but Fenris. "I told him I don't know a daisy from a violet."

The duke gave Fenris a sharp look. "Is that what she said?"

"Yes."

"It's true, your grace." Hester put an elbow on the table and looked at the duke. "Whenever I talk about horticulture, which isn't often, given the result, her eyes glaze over." Camber handed her the pen. "Thank you." Hester began writing. "Two cattleya and a phalaenopsis, is that agreeable? You're sure you've room?"

"Anything you wish to have with you in London."

"I've a special mix I use for my soil. I'll ask for some of that to be sent on. We can compare composition." She bent over the page. "Perhaps we might experiment. Your soil preparation versus mine."

"What makes you think I've a special soil?"

Hester picked up a sheet of blotting paper and laid it over her letter. "You dabble, your grace. Of course you have a formulation for soil. If you don't I should be very disappointed in you."

"I might have," Camber said. "Will you write your brother, Miss Rendell?"

The back of Fenris's hand brushed Eugenia's shoulder. When she looked, his face was all innocence.

"Thank you, I shall. That's very kind of you." Hester took out a clean sheet of paper. "Charles will be so annoyed when I tell him I've dined at Bouverie. All these years he's been boasting that he's dined with a duke." After a bit, Hester looked up from her letter. "There now. I think he'll be properly jealous of my adventures. Lord Fenris, Charles is a friend; will you add a line or two?"

"Yes, thank you, Miss Rendell." He sat in the chair Hester vacated for him and jotted down several lines. When he was done, he turned on the chair, pen in hand. "Mrs. Bryant? A word for Charles?"

Eugenia left her chair and took her place at the table to write a line or two to Hester's brother. She did not know him, but he had known Robert, and Robert had spoken fondly of all the Rendells. Fenris stood behind her as he had before, a hand on the back of the chair. She wished he wouldn't. He distracted her.

Hester headed to the table where Eugenia, having finished her note, had just put down her pen. "Charles will be so pleased when our letter arrives." Rather than retaking the chair, she turned to the duke. "What about you, your grace? Is it wrong of me not to ask if you'd like to tell Charles hullo? Or is it an awful presumption to ask if you will?"

There was a moment of silence in which Hester gazed at Camber with a guileless smile. Eugenia held her breath, and she rather had the thought that so did Fenris. Camber said nothing. Hester sat and prepared to direct the letter. "I always wonder such things." She glanced over her shoulder. "I had rather have you angry with me than feeling left out and that's a fact. If you had rather not, I shan't be hurt."

Camber bowed stiffly, but to Eugenia's astonishment, he walked forward and held out his hand for the pen. Hester gave him the chair. The letter was directed and needed only the franking when the butler announced that dinner was served.

They dined in a room that was every bit as overawing as the saloon. Squares of carved oak covered the walls and ceiling, and the chimney glass over the fireplaces at either end of the room reflected light throughout the room. There were discreet entrances and exits for the servants such that they seemed to appear and disappear by magic. The food arrived quickly and hot. The first course was a rather indifferent fish soup, the second a tolerably good ox tongue.

Fenris picked up the glass of wine one of the liveried footmen had just poured for him. There were six of them serving dinner, and as near as she could tell they were each of them precisely the same height and coloring. "This is the Regina dining room, so called because Queen Elizabeth

herself dined in this very room with one of my father's pre-
decessors. We've a state dining room, suitable for a hundred
and fifty guests." He leaned back to allow a footman to place
a plate of venison before him. "I thought this smaller dining
room was a better choice for us tonight. I don't know about
Camber." He glanced at his father. "When I am at Bouverie,
I much prefer dining in here."

"Thank goodness." Hester glanced around the room with
its gilt-framed mirrors, tall chimney glasses, and branches
of candles. "I don't know that I'd survive a formal affair. A
hundred and fifty, you say?" She shook her head. "I don't
believe I know even ten people I'd invite to dine. Just as
well, I suppose, for sixteen is the most Mama has ever had
to dine with us and I hardly know how she managed that."

Camber patted her hand. "There, there. I warrant you'll
do fine when one day you preside at just such a table as this."

Eugenia looked up in time to see Fenris lift his napkin to
his mouth. He had been watching her, though; that was plain
enough. As the meal was served, Hester did a splendid job
of diverting the duke. She possessed an innate art for gazing
at the man with her eyes open wide, so innocent and with
such fascination for any subject that even Camber sometimes
forgot to be unpleasant. More often than not, however, he
and Hester were engaged in yet another discussion of plant
arcana. His temper had mellowed considerably.

A wonderful braised chicken came next, though Fenris
barely touched his. A footman deftly removed her plate
while his veritable twin swooped in to deliver the next.

Which was—

Lobster.

She stared at the tail on her plate for a moment before
she raised her eyes to Fenris. He was in the act of lifting a
forkful of lobster to his mouth. "What a pity," she said.

He cocked his head. He didn't smile. Not even a hint of
a smile. He might as well be as innocent as the dawn. "A
pity, Mrs. Bryant?"

"That you survived the attack."

Chapter Five

Two weeks later. The Conservatory at Bouverie.

"MY GOD, FENRIS, LISTEN TO THEM. THEY'RE TALKING about dirt." Eugenia stood with Fenris at the conservatory window that overlooked the rear garden at Bouverie. The garden area wasn't large; this was Mayfair, after all. Outside there was a coating of frost on the grass and along the top of the walls. A groundsman carrying a burlap sack walked the perimeter because, so Fenris had told her, people had the unfortunate habit of throwing trash over the walls.

Behind them, Hester and Camber were deep in a discussion of the plants that had been brought from Exeter. She had, for a while, stayed beside Hester, pretending she wasn't bored out of her skull with all the talk of plant phyla and genera. She was actually grateful when Fenris took her aside.

Fenris glanced over his shoulder then back out the window. "They seem quite happy with the subject."

She groaned. "Imagine the letter I'll get when she writes to her parents and tells them she spent an entire afternoon with the Duke of Camber. Discussing the proper proportions of composted manure to soil. I shall be disgraced. Her mother will post to London to rescue her from me. There will be unhappy letters to Mountjoy, and he will give them to Lily, and I'll never hear the end of it. And rightly so. I've failed her."

"You haven't. Any young lady who captures Camber's interest is sure to be a social success if only for her connection to him."

"How galling." She stared out the window because otherwise she would have stared at Fenris and there was nothing right about that.

"What?"

"That I pray you're correct." She bent her head.

"Poor Mrs. Bryant. A bitter pill indeed."

"How much longer do you think they'll be at it? If I hear another Latin name for a plant, I'll go mad." Like Fenris had, she looked over her shoulder at Camber and Hester, and then out the window again. She lowered her voice. "It's as if they mean to see how long they can go without speaking English."

Fenris laughed. "I propose we leave them to it. I doubt they'll even notice we've gone."

"Gone where?" She grabbed his arm, and never mind it was an overly familiar gesture. "I don't care. If you've a collection of pencil shavings, I should love to see it."

"As a matter of fact . . ."

She tightened her grip on his arm. "I have spent the last twenty minutes listening to a conversation about dirt. I was seriously contemplating asking if I might assist the groundsman with the trash removal."

"Alas, I only just disposed of my pencil shavings." He touched a hand to his heart and looked heavenward. "To think I had the finest such collection in London." He shook his head sadly, attention on her. "There is a secret staircase in the library. It's a poor substitute for pencil shavings, but might you care to see that instead?"

"You know I would."

"I know no such thing."

"Don't leave me here another moment, you beast."

"I am yours to command."

A shiver went down her spine at those words, even though she knew he'd spoken them in innocent jest. "To the library, then."

They left Camber and Hester in a spirited discussion about the design of an experiment to determine whose soil composition was best. Hester waved at them as they left. Camber didn't even look.

She and Fenris walked arm in arm to the library, which she knew was famous both for its beauty and the number of titles it held, reputed to be in excess of twenty thousand volumes.

"Oh," she said when Fenris led her inside. The interior was two stories high with nearly every wall lined with shelves and shelves of books. The upper floor had a railed walkway all the way around, with three separate staircases leading to the second level. At each landing, top and bottom, was a chair or sofa as well as a table for reading. There was a grand fireplace with a marble mantel and floor-to-ceiling columns on either side. "This is lovely." She faced him, and felt another chunk of her resentment of him fall away. "Thank you for bringing me here."

"Of all the rooms at Bouverie, I confess this is my favorite." He cocked his head in that annoying way, except this time it wasn't as annoying as usual. "Just as Camber has given Hester permissions to the conservatory, so I grant you permissions to the library. Come here whenever you like."

His invitation was genuine, without the least hint that he intended anything but that she be able to enjoy the library whenever she liked. She found it disturbing and, yes, flattering, that he understood she was as book-mad as Hester was plant-mad. She curtseyed her acknowledgment. "Thank you."

"You are more than welcome."

She took a step toward the shelves. "I warn you, I might never leave."

"We'd find a way to make do, I suppose." He gave her a lopsided grin. "I'd have the servants throw in a bone now and again. Leave a bottle of wine outside the door for you."

"So gracious a host." She'd stopped mistrusting his charm, and that was yet another disconcerting change in her feelings about him. Then again, Robert had admired him, and that would not have been the case if there were nothing to the man but his future title.

Fenris took her arm again and walked the room with her, crisscrossing from time to time to a specific shelf in order to show her a rare or interesting volume. "Is there really a secret staircase?" she asked.

"There is. But first, allow me to show you the orrery. We're quite proud of it here."

"Please."

The orrery was at the far end of the library in an alcove built to display the device, a moving mechanical model of the solar system that included all the planets with any moons that attended them. Beside it stood a celestial globe, but for now, she could only stare at the orrery. It was magnificent. The base of the orrery was a freestanding piece of carved cherry into which had been set a gold plate that housed the clockwork that moved the planets and the moon. A gold ball represented the sun; the moon was a sphere of half ivory, half jet; and the other planets and moons were likewise various gemstones or other semiprecious materials.

"It's beautiful," she whispered.

"Yes, it surely is." He took a step forward. "This one works by means of a key." Fenris set off the mechanism, and, with a whirr of parts and gears, the planets and their moons began to move. Eugenia watched, transfixed.

She drew in a breath and waited for her emotions to settle. She didn't want him to think she was overcome. "I could watch this all day."

"It is wonderful to see in motion, isn't it?"

"One feels very small indeed, imaging all this above and around us." She gave him a quick glance, and was relieved to see he was intently watching the orrery. If he thought her maudlin, she couldn't tell.

"Indeed." She felt a tug on her heart at his reverent reply. Like her, he was fascinated by the device. She looked away because she did not want to admire him, or find him attractive, nor admit he had any qood qualities.

"If I came to live in your library, I'd stand right here for hours and hours and never move except to wind the mechanism."

He walked to the other side of the orrery. "You are welcome to, of course."

"Might I have tea once in a while?" They got on well, she had to admit that. He amused her, dash his soul. When he smiled at that, she added, "Or am I to have only wine and that rare bone on which to gnaw?"

He didn't look away from the orrery. "Tea as well, if you insist."

"I do." She clasped her hands behind her back and rocked back on her heels. "I am a greedy guest."

"It's not so much to ask. Tea, wine, and bones to chew on." After a bit, he reached down and pressed a switch that stopped the motion. His reserve returned, and Eugenia wondered if she'd offended him. Lord, but he reminded her of his father now, the way he'd seemed when she and Hester had been here for dinner. All stern eyes and uncharitable expression. Perhaps he'd had enough of entertaining her. He lifted his gaze and their eyes locked. "I'm not often here, but I'll tell Camber and the staff."

"Don't you live here?" They looked at each other from separate sides of the solar system. Considering how passionately she disliked the man, she was aware, now, just how little she knew about him. How strange that she should be curious to know more. Stranger still that she should feel that frisson of interest. She did, though.

He shrugged, and she found herself unable to read his expression. And here she'd fancied she would always know his feelings about her. "Bouverie is my father's home."

"Yours as well."

He seemed both a stranger to her and a man she knew well, and that, too, was odd and unexpected, and it made her question whether she'd been fair to him. Not about what he'd done in the past, but about what he was now.

He continued to watch her, and she felt another shiver in reaction. "I keep quarters elsewhere that are less formal and more to my liking."

She put a hand on the celestial globe and gave it a turn. Yes, a man like him would need privacy. "Bachelor quarters, you mean."

"As I am a bachelor, I suppose so." He joined her on her side of the solar system. "I like to think I've moved beyond the sort of apartments you mean. I have a house on Upper Brook Street."

"Upper Brook Street?" He meant nothing by standing so close. If that was so, why was she so horribly aware of him?

"Mm."

"You could walk to Hyde Park from there." The chill that pervaded most of Bouverie seemed to have lodged in Eugenia's bones, and she shivered.

"I often do. Cold?" He stood so close. Too close. "Or did someone just walk over your grave?"

She brought her shawl over her shoulders. "Mountjoy says I'm always complaining it's never warm enough."

"And I never can convince Camber that we Talbot men seem not to feel the cold as others do." He held out a hand, and she happened to tilt her head at just the right time such that their gazes locked. He wasn't a boy; not that he'd ever been. He was a grown man, and she could not stop thinking about what that meant. That Fenris should be a man, with a man's needs and appetites. He held her gaze. "Come, I'll show you the secret passage."

"Is there one?"

"I told you there was."

"Men say all manner of things."

"Allow me to prove it, then." He put a hand to her back, and the contact sent a disturbing shiver through her. Not from cold, this time, but because of him. Lord Fenris. Thank goodness, she thought, that he did not notice. He guided her to one of the staircases where the carpet that covered most of the floor ended and exposed a rim of polished oak floor. There were two upholstered chairs here, as well as a desk, behind which were yet more shelves of books. Twenty thousand volumes. There were probably more books than that here.

Fenris stepped up to one of the shelves, and Eugenia moved with him, intensely curious. She studied the wall for any sign of a doorway. She pointed to one of the shelves. "Is this it?"

"No. Here." He rested a hand on a set of shelves that looked no different from the others.

She moved in for a closer look. "It's cleverly hidden. I don't see anything at all."

He made room for her, and she stood beside him while she examined the shelf. "As a boy, I often used this passage to confound my nurse regarding my whereabouts." He lit a lantern on the table and picked it up. "I suspect now that she was humoring me. The longtime staff is aware of the location of all the secret rooms and passages."

She touched a spot on the rim of the shelf that seemed to her to be a slightly lighter shade than the surrounding wood. Nothing happened. What he'd just said penetrated and she looked at him. "There's more than one?"

"The house is riddled with them." He pressed a carved spot on the other side from where she stood. There was a hollow click, and an entire section of shelf swung out. Their eyes met, and once again she had that odd impression of him as a stranger and someone familiar to her. He held the door and gestured. "Shall we explore?"

Not for the world would she refuse such an invitation. "Oh yes, let's."

Fenris closed the secret door after them. If not for the lantern, they would have been in pitch dark. As it was, she could see the walls were carved with columns intended to look like tree trunks. The floor was bare plank. The ceiling was carved with leaves and branches, and even birds and other small animals.

She stood in the passageway and turned in a circle. "You must have been in raptures as a boy, having such a hideaway as this." She, as Fenris well knew, had been raised by a maternal aunt and uncle. On a farm her eldest brother had, until the lawyers found him, fully expected to take over one day. The house she'd grown up in had a mere seven rooms, without a single inch of gilt wood and not even one single secret passage or hidden room.

"I was."

"I wish I'd lived here when I was a girl." She took a step forward and looked around again. "Think of all the adventures one could have in a house like this."

He took her hand. "Come. I'll show you the Turkish bath. It's quite beautiful."

"A Turkish bath?" She did not pull away from him. "Yes, I should like to see that. Nigel went to the Levant after he finished at Oxford. He wrote us the most wonderful letters of his adventures. Robert went, too, when he was young. I suppose you know that."

"Yes."

"He gave me his journals to read. Sometimes he'd read passages to me. They were wonderful. I feel as if I've been there myself." She hesitated because it occurred to her that perhaps she ought not talk about Robert, and just when had she begun to care about his feelings? "Have you been to the Levant?"

"When I was a young man, yes. But my grandfather had the bath installed here after he visited Anatolia. Long before I was born." Still holding her hand, he walked the corridor without hesitation. They passed three steep and narrow staircases leading higher and lower into the house. There were two branches of the corridor he ignored. At the end of the passageway, he took a set of stairs down and then a second until they reached a doorway that opened into a small woodpaneled cabinet. He closed the door after them. The opening vanished into the scrollwork that decorated the walls there.

He waited while she examined the area of the wall they'd just come through. "Here. This leaf here. Do you see?" He reached around her to press a spot on the wall. After the click, he pushed and the outline of the doorway appeared. "So you can make your escape if need be."

Eugenia laughed. "What a grand adventure this is."

"Onward then?"

"Yes." She followed him out of the cabinet and into a corridor. From there, he opened a door that took them into a tiled room with a portal at the other side. The ceilings were high and arched, and everywhere she looked were beautiful Arabian patterns set in tile. The air here was warmer than upstairs, and there was almost no sound but what noise they made.

"The baths haven't been used since my grandfather passed. I'm told he returned from his travels with a Turkman servant who'd been employed in a private home with baths in a similar arrangement to this."

She touched the tiles, cool underneath her fingers. "Why not? You have this magnificent place and you've never had a bath here yourself?"

"I have."

Eugenia looked at him over her shoulder. He tipped his head to one side.

"When I was a boy. My grandfather brought me here. We used the bath, and it was really quite the most splendid immersion of my young life." He held up the lantern and adjusted the screen to widen the glow.

She took a few more steps inside. "How old were you?"

"Ten, I think. The Turkman scrubbed me within an inch of my life, but the warm water afterward? Bliss." He picked up the lantern and crossed the room so as to enter a second, larger room with empty scalloped fountains set into the wall and three empty pools.

She absorbed the austere beauty and tried to imagine what it must have looked like when the pools were filled and the fountains working. "This is marvelous. Simply marvelous."

"It is. And how relaxing to soak in the water after that scrubbing. In here"—they passed into a third room—"we were dried off with the softest towels you can imagine. Our skin was rubbed with oil, our hair combed. I don't think I was ever so clean and presentable in all my days before or since."

Eugenia pictured not a boy, but a grown-up Fenris. Naked. Which was not a proper place for her thoughts to wander. "Why doesn't your father use the baths? Or you, for that matter?"

Rather than answer, he walked her out of this last room and into another corridor with the same ornate scrollwork in the tiles. The decor, she supposed, was after the Ottoman fashion.

"After our bath, we took tea in here." He opened another door and held it for her. This room, like the corridor, had intricate scrollwork and lattices in the shape of inverted teardrops. "I'm told it's copied after a salon in the sultan's palace in Constantinople. I was served tea. My grandfather had coffee and let me try it."

"And?"

He grinned, and there was nothing austere at all about his smile. She shivered inside, in a hot, disturbing way that did not feel at all proper. Not for her. Not for a widow who still missed her husband. Not for a man she'd disliked for so long. "I discovered Turkish coffee was not then to my taste."

"I expect not." There was, incongruously, a gold-framed painting of a spaniel hanging on the wall. She stood before it, head tilted. There was something off about the painting, but she couldn't decide what it was. The dog did not seem to properly fit on the canvas. She couldn't help the impression that the animal might actually slide off the canvas and onto the floor.

He pointed at the nameplate affixed to the bottom center of the frame. "Delilah. My grandfather's favorite bitch."

She tried looking at the painting from the corner of her eye. "She's lovely."

"You are entitled to your opinion."

"Thank you."

Fenris crossed his arms over his chest and leaned against the wall by the painting. She had the eerie sense that the dog's eyes followed him. "Camber—my grandfather, that is—fancied himself an artist. As you can see from his effort, it was mere fancy."

She craned her neck and squinted.

"I'm afraid, Mrs. Bryant, that there is no angle from which this picture improves."

Fenris was right. The painting did not improve at any angle she could see. "Perhaps oils were not his medium."

"Assuredly not."

She was entranced by the thought of a not very talented duke taking the time and effort required of an oil painting, all to preserve the likeness of a beloved dog. "Why does no one use these rooms?"

"My father disapproves."

"Of what?" She looked around. She knew the long estrangement between Fenris and Lily had begun with the previous Camber. She knew as well that Lily's suspicions of Fenris had proved unfounded. For the first time, she wondered if Fenris didn't deserve a great deal of credit for refusing to continue two generations of resentment. "Of anything exotic or not English?"

"He's not quite that bad. But not so far from that, either." He moved to the doorway and put a hand on the jamb, which was not the usual shape but, rather, had a pointed top with rounded sides that sloped toward the more usual, to her, straight-edged door shape. "I don't wish to shock you."

She gave him a quick look and saw the gleam in his eyes. "There's a scandal involved in these rooms, isn't there?"

Fenris nodded, and she couldn't help a smile. "This is vastly more amusing than listening to Hester and your father discuss the proper composting of manure. Please do shock me. I won't tell a soul, I promise."

"On your honor?"

She placed a hand over her heart. "Yes, Fenris. On my honor."

"Very well, then. Prepare to be shocked to your very proper toes."

"Go on."

"My grandfather is reputed to have engaged in immoral conduct in these rooms. Camber, the current one, was furious when he learned my grandfather had brought me here for any reason. My father was certain I'd witnessed one of Grandfather's orgies and that I was corrupted for life."

"Orgies." She looked around the room. "Under the

watchful eye of Delilah? No, this does not seem an orgy sort of room. It's rather a pleasant room. I don't believe you, sir."

"Not here. In the Turkish room."

"The Turkish room."

"It would be wicked of me to show you." A smile flickered at the edges of his mouth, and then his gaze landed on her rather than their surroundings. Another image flashed through her head. His pale brown eyes locking with hers after he'd come, his arms tight around her. A ridiculous and personally humiliating mental slip. He was laughing, though. Or nearly so. Taunting her with that sly smile. Daring her.

"I feel I can withstand the shock."

"If you're sure."

"I am."

He picked up the lantern again and headed for the door. "Have you a vinaigrette on hand in the event your delicate sensibilities are offended?"

She snorted and felt very wicked, which was, she imagined, precisely what he intended. "Lead on."

With a hand on another door, he said, "I've seen the bills for the construction of this room. No expense was spared. I daresay that's the real reason for Camber's objection."

Eugenia put her palm to his chest and pushed her fingers off that broad and solid expanse. He didn't move. "You, sir, are an awful tease. There weren't any orgies, were there?"

He did not open the door. "There were."

"You were ten. Honestly. How would you know? No one would tell a ten-year-old about orgies."

"As Miss Rendell would undoubtedly point out, I did not remain ten." Fenris opened the door, and they went in. He set the lantern on a low table. "Voilà. My grandfather's folly."

The Turkish room was a quite large square with a divan constructed along most of three sides of the walls. The chimney glass stretched from the fireplace mantel to the ceiling. The fireplace had been carved in an Ottoman motif, with the same exquisite scrollwork and curlicues worked into the tiles around it. Crimson velvet curtains with gold tasseled ties draped along the walls between the mirrored walls, single pieces of glass that must have cost the sky.

Hands on her hips, she surveyed the room. "A bit ornate for my tastes. But I fail to see what's so wicked about this. Why do you call it his folly?"

"The expense, for one."

"Yes. I can see that."

Fenris set a hand to the small of her back and walked her along the perimeter of the divan. There were two other doors, one of them covered, like the walls, with mirror glass. Satin-covered pillows remained on the divan as if awaiting the sultan.

"And the other?" She glanced at him. "Reason you say this is his folly?"

He stopped in front of one of the curtained sections where, instead of a fancifully decorated and gilded wall, there was a door, gilt of course, like every other surface here that was not mirrored. "It's said my grandfather brought the women through here." He turned just his head toward her, watching her. "I don't know if it's true, but the passage behind this door does lead to the street behind Bouverie." He touched the gilt-covered door. "It would have been easy enough to arrange for a certain sort of female to arrive without disturbing the household. Without anyone but a trusted servant or two knowing any better."

"Oh. That sort of folly."

He smiled at her, and there was something deep and intimate in his smile. "A den of iniquity, I fear."

"The things you men do baffle me." She frowned at the door, but all she could think about was the parade of women who must have come through that doorway. He'd said it was his grandfather who'd arranged for orgies, but in her imagination it was Fenris she saw surrounded by a dozen naked women. She turned away, disturbed and unsettled as she walked to the divan. "May I?"

"Please." He gestured for her to sit, which she did.

She smoothed her hands on the divan. "This is quite comfortable."

"It is." He crossed his arms over his chest and stood by the door, legs apart, like some ancient Turkish potentate. He had the prettiest eyes, didn't he? He grinned, and that fanciful thought flew from her head. He was only Fenris now, a man she might actually come to like. "I confess, Ginny, I'm equally baffled by you women."

"You? Baffled by women? Which sort of women?" She waved a hand at the room in general and laughed at him. "The sort who come through doors like that or the sort who don't?"

"Both sorts." He leaned against the door. What a delightfully wicked smile, and how very handsome he was. "With the former, of course, one has the advantage of prior agreement as to the term of relations. A few hours. The course of an evening." He gestured. "The acquaintance is over."

She looked around the room. "You could never bring the other sort to a place like this."

"I don't see why that should be so." She wasn't looking at him, but she heard his voice change and take on a silky tone. "After all, I've brought you here."

She looked at him. "That's different."

"In what way?"

"We know each other."

He held her gaze, and her belly did a slow flip. "Not as I'd like."

Eugenia blinked. He did not mean that as she'd initially taken it. He couldn't have meant *know* in the carnal sense. The man, with his infernal good looks and tales of wicked orgies, had sparked her body to life. He'd reminded her she missed the physical intimacy of her marriage, and that was quite apart from the way she missed Robert. She missed Robert with her heart, but her body missed being touched, and there were times, she had to admit, when she thought any man's touch would do. Even Fenris's.

Especially Fenris's.

She cleared her throat. A proper woman would leave. "You never did tell me how you know there were orgies here."

"Servants gossip." He cocked his head in that infuriating way.

"Not just that."

He shrugged and gave the floor a long look before he returned his attention to her. There was something wicked in his eyes. Lust. That was lust in those lovely brown eyes of his. "I've seen the bills."

"Oh." She breathed in and found herself struggling not to laugh when she realized she wasn't mistaken about his desire. "Oh. You wicked man."

"What?" He leaned against the wall again and, without looking, fiddled with the curtain that partially hid the door.

"You've brought women here, haven't you?"

Fenris pretended to be fascinated by the ceiling.

She followed his look then stared, as engaged with the view as he apparently was. The ceiling here was lower than one generally encountered in a house like Bouverie. With her neck still craned, she gazed upward at her face, and the contrast between the aquamarine silk of the divan and the rose pink of her afternoon frock. "Why," she slowly asked, "are there mirrors on the ceiling?"

"My dear woman." Fenris snorted, and she looked at him. He grinned. "Why do you think?"

"Well it can't be for the light—" Oh, good God. She covered her face with one hand. She honestly didn't know whether to laugh or be thoroughly ashamed of herself for thinking, once again, of Fenris with a dozen naked women. Laughter won out.

Fenris left his place against the wall and sat beside her on the divan, his weight on one hand propped behind him. She peered at him through her spread-out fingers but continued to smile because she couldn't stop herself. He'd brought women here. He had. And he must have, had to have, looked at the reflections all around him. Including those reflections in the ceiling glass. Which meant he'd been on his back. She lowered her hands at last. "I'm not all that ignorant, I promise you."

He smirked, and then his smile softened. "A woman's skin kissed in the candlelight? A dance of veils?"

She dropped back on the divan, her feet still on the floor, and stared at her reflected face. "Gah. What a dunce you must think me." She turned her head to look at him. "How many women? Not just one, surely."

"Three or four. Half a dozen."

"Liar."

"There might have been more." Fenris turned and bent over her, his hand now propped up on her other side. "Don't look at me," he said. "Look in the glass."

"Why?" But she did, and she saw bits of her gown and her face over his shoulder, but mostly his broad back, and his dark hair. Her breath hitched. She was wracked with a longing to be touched. More than that. To be filled.

"That's what they saw."

"The women you brought here?"

"Mm. What women?"

"The dozen you brought here, obviously." She fisted her hands at her sides because she had the most horrible urge to see her spread-out fingers pale against the dark material that covered his shoulders.

He laughed and moved closer until he was practically on top of her. She ought to move, to push him away. She didn't. He lowered his head until his breath fell warm on her neck. "There. Are you looking, Ginny? You have only to imagine yourself naked in my arms to know exactly what happened here."

"Fenris."

"At such a moment," he whispered in her ear, and Lord, but that sound was nothing but soft and secret silk against her senses, "I would expect you to call me Fox. It's what my intimates call me."

She didn't move. Or push him away. Or make any sort of protest. And there inevitably came the moment when they both understood a line had been crossed.

Fox kissed the side of her throat.

Chapter Six

His senses narrowed to just Eugenia and him. Aside from his physical reactions, what loomed large in his mind was that their relationship had just utterly changed. He'd succeeded during the time she'd been in London, not easily, though, in smoothing away her abrasive dislike of him. But this? This changed everything and he was half-mad with lust and desire, and something else he did not know how to name. This was Ginny. In his arms, beneath him. His mouth against her soft, soft skin.

What he knew was this: his touch was a lover's caress, and she understood that very well. The very mouth that had once mortally insulted her now brought them together. His entire body was in sensual overload; on the edge of too much even as just this was in no way enough for him. He kissed her throat again.

Always, whatever happened here or afterward, there would be this between them. He did not want to ruin a moment so filled with sexual possibility and could not bear the thought that he might not have what he desired more than his own life.

The sheer effrontery of what he'd done astonished him. He should not have dared such boldness with her. He knew better than to impose himself on a woman who did not care for him. Yet here she was in his arms, with him wanting more than a single kiss, however tender, however sweet. Not enough. Never enough. The power of his desire for her terrified him.

He was very much aware that she wasn't screaming murder or pushing him away. He was also aware that he was practically lying on top of her, pinning her with his weight, and that it was possible she was too horrified, or even too afraid, to object. Just as he was about to roll away, one of her hands left the divan and settled butterfly-like on the back of his shoulder.

Not pushing him away. Drawing him closer.

How quickly the world changed again. That touch was an invitation, and he meant to accept whatever she offered him.

He shifted so he was directly over her. If only they were naked, Jesus, he'd be sliding into her right now. Fucking her here in the bloody abandoned Turkish room, site of his grandfather's sexual excesses and a few of his own. He kissed his way up her throat, slow kisses, tender kisses, a drag of his mouth toward her jaw. Somehow, he ended with one of his arms curled around the side of her head, exerting just the slightest pressure so that he could reach more of her neck.

Sweet, tender, fuckable Ginny.

All this time he'd thought of her as a tall woman. Substantial, because to him she'd always been larger than life. More real. Happier than other people. More vivid than any woman he'd ever known. Her body beneath his was slender, almost slight, but Lord, the curves. She smelled good. The taste of her spread over his tongue, and, just once, he nipped her skin. He reached the underside of her jaw and planted a slow kiss there, and then discovered his other hand had been wandering, too.

Eugenia's leg was slender, firm, and aside from putting

himself inside her, there wasn't much he'd like more than to have his palm on her bare skin, sliding along her skin from calf to knee to thigh . . . How far? How far did he dare take this with all the history between them?

As damn far as he could manage, because what if she came to her senses and remembered how much she disliked him?

A quick look to the side, and he could see their reflection in the mirrored walls. Her curls were a flash of gold. He buried his fingers in her hair just to see the contrast between the pale gold and his hand. He raised his head enough to see her eyes were closed, her lips parted. The loveliest sight he'd ever seen.

Half a second later, her eyes fluttered open and focused on him with frank lust. His breath caught, and his cock came to full life.

Whatever spell this was, let it never be broken.

He pulled himself up those last few inches and took her mouth the way he'd been imagining since just about the day he first saw her. He did. Oh, yes, he did. Her mouth opened under his, and her invitation— he knew damn well this wasn't capitulation—was not one he considered declining.

She kissed him back.

The meeting of their mouths was instantly carnal, desperately so on his part. She had no trouble keeping up; neither of them were sexual innocents. He set his forearms above her shoulders and let the weight of his pelvis sink onto her.

Her fingers twined in his hair as they continued like this, so close to out of control and headed for dangerous shores. Oh, but he craved this, touching her with his hands and his mouth. His body quivered with need, and, for pity's sake, he felt like some green boy, on the edge of disgracing himself. He pulled away enough to slide his lips downward in that so-intimate contact with her skin, and then to her arm below the short sleeve of her gown. The tender underside first, the inside of her elbow, down to her wrist, and all the while, his hips pressed against hers. He rocked once because he was hard now, and he was feeling a very male imperative to thrust. His other hand trailed across her upper body, fingers sweeping over her skin.

He lifted his head, staring at the mirrored walls at their reflected image. "Look, Ginny."

She turned her head, and once he knew she'd looked and seen, he came back over her, taking her head between his hands and holding her in place while he kissed her throat again. He slipped deeper into the urgency of his arousal when she answered the pressure of his hips with a slow roll of her pelvis. The contact pulled a groan from him. He continued the pressure of his hips against hers. He put his mouth by her ear. "Beautiful, Ginny. Lovely."

"Fenris." His name was half groan, half plea as she brought him closer.

With what felt like the last of his restraint, he lifted his head. Some little part of the fog of his passion lifted. "Not here." He understood this might be his only chance for coitus with her, but he wanted more. More than once. He didn't want her to hate him or resent him afterward. "God, Ginny, not a quick fuck."

She looked at him with eyes drugged with passion. "Why not?"

The question stunned him to silence. *Why not?*

She slipped her hand between them and her fingers stroked the length of him from base to tip. Her fingers curled around him as best she could with his trousers impeding her access. "Why not, Fenris?"

He drew a ragged breath. His thoughts were on a fast descent to incoherent. "Camber will be looking for us before long."

"Then why not quick?" Her fingers stayed on him, and her eyes, so full of desire, Jesus, he might give in just to have that passion right now. "I miss feeling like this."

That was it for him. "Why the bloody hell not?"

While her fingers tightened around his prick, her other hand, the one on his shoulder, drew him closer. His eyes were nearly closed, but not quite, and he saw what she hadn't meant for him to see. He touched two fingers to her cheek, making sure with the touch that she did not turn her head from him. "Ginny, this should not make you grieve. What makes you so sad?"

"Nothing," she whispered. She lifted her hips, arching against him.

"Not nothing. Tell me." He kissed her once. Hard. He pulled back just enough to say, "Whatever you say, I'll still fuck you. But I want the truth before I do."

"I miss Robert." She blinked rapidly and touched his lips, a finger laid across his mouth. "I'm sorry. Sorry to say something like that when we are—like this."

His heart broke again, and as he gazed at her, he gave up the very last of his reserve with her. "What do you need? Tell me, and it's yours."

"You. This." She squeezed him. "You, desperate for me. Helpless with want. Touching me."

"You have that." His words ended on a sharp gasp because her first finger reached the head of his cock and swept over the tip, and Jesus, she knew what she was about.

"Is it too wicked of me to say I want to see you when you spend?"

The heat in her eyes nearly stopped his heart. He held his breath while a dozen thoughts and ideas whirled around in his head. Nothing ventured, nothing gained. "In you?"

She shook her head.

"Is that all you want?" he asked. "To bring me?"

She nodded, and the way she looked at him, with frank lust, about ended him right there.

"Just my cock?"

"Yes. Just that." Her fingers moved again, this time finding the buttons of his trousers, and he, he assisted with the venture of unfastening him. He threw back his head when she drew him out, and then she curled her fingers around his sac. Bliss.

"Do what you will, dear Ginny."

They ended up with him leaning back, his weight on both forearms supporting him. He stared at her fingers around him. She knew what to do and did it very well, thank you. He managed a steadying breath. "You have good hands."

A smile flashed on her mouth. "Thank you, my lord."

"Under the circumstances, I give you leave to call me Fox."

She trailed her fingertips along his member, then circled him, pressing her palm against his shaft and sliding her hand up. "Dare I be so familiar?"

"Madam, your hand is on my cock."

"And what a lovely cock it is."

He gasped and felt himself slipping away. "Any liberty you like. I warn you, I won't last long."

"Very well. Fox." She understood precisely the pressure and rhythm he needed, and before long, the power of speech was no longer his.

He let his head drop back. There was almost nowhere he could look where he did not have some reflected angle of her or of her and his sex. He arched his pelvis toward her, and that brought him along even faster. Too fast. Rushing headlong toward completion. He didn't even care that he was about to spend on his clothes. But she wasn't as far gone as he, for she fished his handkerchief from his coat pocket.

His state of arousal moved quickly to the crisis point, and she, plainly anticipating just how badly he'd want to be inside her, tightened her fingers and quickened the rhythm of her strokes. He came, hard and fast, and, as he discovered only afterward, she used his handkerchief to save him from having to hie off to his rooms for a change of clothes.

She leaned close. "Thank you, Fox."

He worked at recovering his breath and wits. He had to blink once or twice in order to focus his eyes. "Thank *you*." She'd damn near killed him. He reached for a curl that had come free of her hairpins and tucked it behind her ear. He'd longed for just this with Eugenia, and he'd got his wish. Perversely, his anxiety about what would happen between them was now a thousand times worse. His lack of restraint might well have ruined everything. He was no more certain of winning her heart than he had ever been. Less, actually.

"It was my pleasure." She smiled, and Eugenia was just so pretty when she smiled like that.

"Did you like that?"

"I did." Her smile was too sweet to bear. "I watched you in the glass."

"Us." He swept back that same curl. "You watched us."

"Yes, Fox. Us."

He sat up enough to cup his hand over the back of her head and bring her down to him so he could kiss her. He captured her mouth in a kiss that was all tongue and strongly suggested she was not repelled by him or what they'd done. They were both a little out of breath when he released her. "I like my sex hard. It needn't be that way between us, of course. But I want to fuck you, and I would like it very much if it was hard and fast and both of us naked. Do you mind me telling you so crudely?" She shook her head. "Good. I like that, too." He kissed her again. "I know it's unfair you've not had pleasure."

"I did."

"Well." He couldn't help a smile. "I believe you've paid me a bigger compliment than I deserve, for I'm sure I'm the only one who came."

She shook her head ruefully, but she was smiling, thank God.

"Soon, Ginny. I want to take you there with me next time."

She tidied his clothes for him, and what she thought of that revelation about him, that he could speak to her using such words and brazenly promise her satisfaction, he had no idea. "We ought to get back, don't you think?"

Chapter Seven

A week later. No. 6 Spring Street.

EUGENIA ADJUSTED HER MEDALLION AND WONDERED if she ought to change the ribbon it hung from. "What do you think, Martine? Is this the right blue? Look in the box and see if there isn't a better blue than this."

Her maid stood behind her, examining Eugenia's reflection in the glass. "You look lovely, milady. And the ribbon is perfect."

"Perhaps we ought to do something different with my hair." She touched the fall of curls around her forehead. "I wish I had darker hair and that it didn't curl so."

Martine laughed. "Milady, half the ladies in London wish they had hair your color and the curls as well."

She sighed and poked at her hair. She didn't need curling papers; that was true. "I always wanted dark hair like Mountjoy's. So much more dramatic."

Someone tapped on the door and called out, "Milady?"

"Yes?" She reseated the comb in her hair. She knew she wasn't anywhere near as beautiful as Lily, but she had something, and now that she was back in colors, she could wear rich shades in combinations that complemented her so often lamented coloring. Martine was right. She might have grown up wishing for Mountjoy's dark hair, but her blond hair and blue eyes were the fashion, and that was something, to find one's looks fashionable through no effort at all.

One of the upstairs maids opened the door. "His grace the Duke of Camber and Lord Fenris are downstairs for you, milady."

"Thank you." She didn't dare turn around and let anyone see the color in her cheeks. That was the problem with having such fair skin. She had mixed feelings about seeing him again. Half the time she was ashamed of herself for what had happened at Bouverie, and the rest of the time she wanted the sex he'd warned her he liked. She wanted his cock in her hands, in her mouth, and inside her. All the pleasure with no risk to her heart.

She touched her hair comb once more. Fenris, that horrible, awful man, made her pulse race. "Have you told Miss Rendell they're here?"

"I'm on my way to her now, milady."

"Excellent. Thank you." She took a deep breath and turned away from her image in the mirror. Whatever the state of things between her and Fenris, driving out with him and Camber was nothing short of a triumph. All London would see Hester and who she was with. After all, what greater proof of social acceptance was there than to be seen with those two men, riding in Camber's new landau? "My cloak, Martine?" She half turned on her chair as she called to the maid who was on her way to tell Hester that Camber and Fenris were here. "Sally, please tell them I'll be down shortly."

Sally curtseyed. "Yes, milady."

Martine fetched Eugenia's cloak, helped her into it, and brushed off every last speck of lint or dirt. Eugenia stayed motionless during the process. She would be serene, she decided. Perhaps even a bit icy, lest Fenris get the idea that she was prepared to enter into an affair with him. She wasn't, she'd decided. Nothing formal. Nothing he could control. If she did take him to bed, it would be on her terms. Not his.

"Thank you, Martine." She waited while her maid finished with three more swipes of the lint brush before she went to Hester's room. She wasn't much surprised that Hester was nowhere near dressed. One gown lay abandoned on the bed. One of the upstairs maids held another, while Hester's maid shook out the skirts of yet a third. Hester herself sat at a desk writing out something in a notebook, wearing only stays and her chemise.

"Lady Eugenia, good afternoon." She pointed at one of the two potted plants sitting atop the desk. One was in a blue pot. The one she indicated was in a white pot with a red and gold Chinese dragon painted on the side. "How would you describe the color of those leaves?"

There were dozens of leaves, all no more than the size of her fingernail. They formed a domed shape that rose some two inches above the pot at the center and high point. "Green."

"Yes, but what color of green? Would you say the leaves are dark, medium dark, medium, or pale?"

She faced the maid. "Has she decided what gown to wear?"

The maid curtseyed and held up the gown in her hands while pointing to another on the bed. "This blue or the citrine, milady."

"I think we must call this a lighter medium green, not now pale." Hester wrote something in her notebook.

Eugenia tapped Hester's shoulder. "My dear, Camber and Fenris are here. You must get dressed."

"I am dressed." She looked at her lap. "Oh. Well, I thought I was."

Eugenia waved to Hester's maid. "She's wearing the blue."

Hester sat sideways on the chair. "Have I a gown that color of green?" She pointed at the potted plant on the desk.

"I don't know. Do you? Does she?"

The maid returned to the wardrobe and brought out a green muslin.

Hester squinted. "Is that a good match, do you think? I don't think so. It's not the right sort of green."

"Why does it matter? You will look very pretty in that frock. Or the blue one."

"Because it would be so very amusing to tell Camber that the leaves of his violet are exactly the color of my gown." She half stood and stared at the pot, then at the gown. "That green is too pale."

"The citrine gown, then."

Hester shrugged. "If there isn't a green like that, it makes no difference to me. Pity. I would have loved to see his face."

Eugenia took the pen from Hester's hand and put it away. She also capped the ink. "Do get dressed, Hester. Now. Two very handsome gentlemen are waiting for you. Wear the citrine."

"Citrine." She squinted at the bed. "It's inaccurate to call it citrine when the color of the stone naturally varies. As well call it topaz. Or amethyst, for that matter."

"I'll entertain them while you finish dressing." Eugenia sent a stern look in the maid's direction. "I shall see you downstairs shortly."

Camber stood when she came into the parlor. Fenris was already standing, but Eugenia made a point of barely glancing at him. Which felt wrong now. He wasn't her enemy anymore. She still did not like him the way she liked Lily or any of her friends, but he wasn't an enemy. Just a man with whom she'd been horribly, wonderfully indiscreet.

Camber straightened his coat and after that touched his hand to his cravat. The thought that he might have taken especial care with his appearance, or that he might be worried about how he looked, startled her. Ridiculous, of course. The duke of Camber was surely not a vain man.

When she'd curtseyed, he took her hand, but his eyes darted past her shoulder. "Lady Eugenia. Good afternoon. Is Miss Rendell coming?"

"Hester will be down shortly."

"Excellent." Camber promptly lapsed into stony silence.

Fenris had so far kept his distance. Whether that was out of respect, or regret, or plain indifference, she didn't know. No matter the answer, he impinged on her senses with such force that she could not keep from glancing at him. His gaze met hers, and she was instantly a complete muddle of emotions. She put an end to the tortured silence and curtseyed to the man. "My lord."

Fox. His intimates called him Fox, after that ridiculous extra name of his. She'd called him that herself.

He nodded curtly, hands clasped behind his back. Not for her life could she dislodge her recollection of their reflected images; his head tipped back, mouth tense. His prick velvet hard in her hand. She'd never forget the way he'd given himself up to her, the way he'd pulsed in her hand. The scent. The sound of his groan as he came.

"Good afternoon, Mrs. Bryant." Despite his formal greeting, there was an uncertainty about him that made her think he did not intend to deal a deliberate insult. Quite the opposite, actually. She rather thought he was trying hard not to offend her by presuming anything. Was it possible he was as unsettled as she about what had happened?

"My lord." Weak at the knees for no good reason, and with no control of her wayward thoughts, she sank to a chair and stared at her feet until she'd gathered her wits.

What had happened between them was madness. Really, nothing more than the result of her slow return from the dark, dark time after Robert's death. During her marriage she'd enjoyed the physical intimacy. Was it so surprising that she missed that? She'd grown used to having a man's arms around her at night, someone to steal a kiss from her during the day, or send her a lingering glance that promised passion. She desperately missed those moments of intimacy, and Fenris, well, he'd just happened to be there when she was weak. That was all. Nothing more complicated than that.

She looked up and found both men staring at her. Fenris cocked his head in a silent inquiry. No one would believe she'd been in his arms. Or that she'd done . . . what she had. No one. Everyone knew their history of mutual dislike.

"As I said, Miss Rendell should be down shortly." She bit her lower lip. What would it be like if she took him to bed? The fact that she could entertain such a thought shook her deeply. It could happen. If she wanted it to. Heavens. Would she like that hard, quick fuck he wanted? She'd lost her mind. Then and now. Her and Fenris? Unthinkable. Impossible. Exhilarating. "She's very much looking forward to the outing. As am I."

"Yes."

"The fog's lifted just in time," Camber said into the silence that followed. "We'll be able to see the street, eh, Fenris?"

"Most fortunate," the man replied.

She wanted to touch him again.

At last, Hester appeared, an ermine muff dangling from one hand. She wore the citrine frock and, well. There was a great deal to be said for the way the bodice contained her bosom. Yellow silk roses were pinned in her dark hair, and, honestly, Hester looked very well so long as one did not examine the back of her frock. She'd gone and tacked the pale yellow ribbon to the back of her skirt, with much the same unfortunate effect as before. Hester did not like the way ribbons flapped in the breeze, she'd once explained when Eugenia demanded to know why she continued to ruin the line of her gowns with those careless stitches.

Camber stepped forward and gave Hester a sweeping bow. "Miss Rendell. How lovely you look."

"Your grace." She bent a knee.

"Shall we?" Fenris gestured to the door at the same time he offered his arm to Eugenia. She rose—thank goodness she could stand without trembling—and put her hand on his sleeve.

Fenris walked slowly so that Camber and Hester would get far enough ahead for him to lean to her and say in a deliberately provocative manner, "Is something the matter?"

"No, nothing." She was lying, and they both knew it. "Why do you ask?"

"You looked . . . stricken a moment ago. You're not ill, are you?"

"I enjoy perfect health, my lord." She adjusted her cloak and kept her hands at her side as they walked out. At the door, Camber collected his coat and hat. He did not look at her or at his son. No, he was all eyes for Hester, who was at present engaged with buttoning her coat. She was off one button. Eugenia would have gone to her to avert at least that disaster of fashion, but Camber stepped forward and rebuttoned her coat. All very avuncular, of course. The entire time he was fixing her coat, they continued their discussion of the best method of dividing bulbs.

Fenris kept his hands clasped behind his back, his hat in one hand. She stopped walking.

He looked back at her, glanced at Camber and Hester, then walked back to her. "Ginny?"

"You shouldn't call me that."

"They won't overhear." Ahead of them, the butler opened the front door. Camber and Hester walked out. Momentarily alone with her, Fenris bent close. "You have but to say the word. Come to Bouverie. The staff knows you have leave to visit the library. You can find the Turkish room from there, I daresay."

She didn't have words. Only a muddle of emotions. And lust.

"We can have that quick fuck any time you like. Consider me at your service."

Hester appeared in the doorway. "Lady Eugenia?"

"On our way, Miss Rendell." Fenris gave a glance toward the door. "Sorry to keep you waiting."

"Awful man," Eugenia murmured.

He smiled slowly and gave her his arm. "Yes. But I think you like that about me."

Outside a glossy red landau waited at the curb, a liveried coachman in the driver's box. The Camber coat of arms was emblazoned on the sides in gold, blue, and silver. A matched pair of charcoal black geldings was hitched to the landau.

The groom bent to put down the step and took over at the door after Fenris himself assisted Hester then her to the forward-facing seat. Eugenia maintained a bland smile as she placed her fingers on Fenris's hand. She would absolutely not engage in an affair with the man. Impossible. Wasn't it?

Once she was seated beside Hester, she smoothed a gloved hand over the black leather seats and then along the lacquered wood, shining ebony, crimson, and gold. The duke's landau was as sumptuous inside as out.

Camber climbed in and sat opposite Hester. Fenris, still on the walk, at last put on his hat and sat opposite Eugenia. Hester beamed at her. The only fault in the otherwise wholly satisfactory seating arrangements was that she was facing Lord Fenris, and how could she look at the man without thinking of all the things they hadn't done?

He watched her, Fenris did, with a lazy, sleepy stare that made her think of sex.

Perhaps she ought to find out what he would be like in bed.

Chapter Eight

BEFORE THE CARRIAGE MOVED ONTO SPRING STREET, Hester pulled a notebook from inside her muff. She held it up for Camber's inspection. "I have been keeping meticulous records. You?"

The duke produced a similar notebook. "Did you think I would not?"

Eugenia slumped a little on her seat, biting back a groan with more effort than she liked. How was Hester to find a suitable husband if at every free moment she was talking about soil and sunlight and the exact shade of green one ought to assign to a leaf?

"Never doubted it," Hester said.

The groom climbed into position at the back of the landau, resplendent in his livery, but Fenris signaled the driver to stay. "Mrs. Bryant, do you get travel sick?"

"No." She refused to think about him in the Turkish room. "Why?"

He tapped his father on the shoulder. "Camber, please take Mrs. Bryant's seat." He held out a hand. "Mrs. Bryant?" His eyes held hers. Honestly, he had the most beautiful brown eyes. "It's easier this way. One of them will fall off the seat trying to see the other's notes."

He was right. And it would be Hester who'd end up in a heap on the floor of the landau. She put her hand on his and the exchange of places was made. Hester and Camber immediately set to comparing pages of their notebooks. Hester produced a tiny pencil, and she and the duke took turns amending their pages.

So immersed were the two in their mutual plant-madness that the rim of Camber's beaver hat touched the edge of Hester's bonnet, which, she now saw, had been put on haphazardly. The bow was the sort that ought to be tied at the side of one's cheek, but Hester had managed, somehow, to tie hers under her chin. One of the ends of the ribbon was, therefore, a good deal longer than the other.

The carriage headed off, and Eugenia tried, she really did, to be unaware of Fenris beside her. She sat straight and clutched the side of the carriage to prevent her shoulder from touching his. Or their legs from touching. He crowded her on the seat. Not deliberately, she didn't think.

Refusing to touch him even incidentally only intensified his effect on her. She watched the houses they passed, counting doors and posts. Anything to keep from looking at Fenris and thinking improper thoughts. None of that helped. She could not stop the recollection of her glimpse of his strong thighs and the flat plane of his belly. His prick, heavens, she adored his prick. Thinking of him made her blood heat.

Since Robert's death, she'd drifted through life, unable to feel deeply about anything. Fenris, of all people, had proved she was not dead to sensation. God help her, in his arms she had felt alive for the first time since Robert died. She wanted that again: And more. She did not dare look at him. He would know. His father would see, and he'd guess, and that could only lead to disaster. She counted windows and attempted to calculate the tax.

As Camber had intimated earlier, the early fog had dissipated and turned a gloomy morning into a pleasant day. There was enough sun to counteract the chill of the wind as they drove toward Rotten Row. It wasn't long before the traffic slowed them considerably. The landau, in all its glossy red and gold, worked into the line of carriages. This proved easier than one might imagine since a duke, it turned out, took precedence in traffic, too.

Hester and Camber at last put away their notebooks, and to Eugenia's delight, Hester waved to an acquaintance. Eugenia confined herself to sedate nods as befit her status as a matronly chaperone. No one, but no one, would guess she'd brought the Marquess of Fenris to orgasm. That was her private secret.

There were, naturally, many greetings to Camber and Fenris. Endless greetings, actually. The landau didn't advance more than three or four yards without someone hailing one or both of the men. It seemed to Eugenia that half the members of the current Cabinet paid Fenris and Camber their respects. There were women, too. Innumerable women, most of them strikingly beautiful or handsome. The Duke of Camber and his son were both vital, handsome men. Indeed, one could hardly forget that fact, what with all the languishing looks and bold flirtations that flew the way of the two men. Fenris accepted all that as his due, while Camber, when he noticed, acknowledged nothing.

Hester and the duke returned to their notebooks, oblivious to the surroundings. "You've drawn a quite accurate leaf, your grace. Remarkable." She looked into the duke's face, a plain woman, no one could say otherwise, and yet so earnest and animated by her shared passion with Camber that she was transformed. Where on earth were all the suitable young gentleman botanists? "What would you say to coloring them? Watercolors would do, I think, don't you? I ought to have thought of that before now."

"Watercolors." Camber nodded. The light emphasized the strong resemblance between father and son. No wonder so many women fluttered their eyes at the duke. "Yes. Yes, quite so. An excellent idea, Miss Rendell. Have I told you about my attempt to breed a yellow rose?"

"No, but I should love to hear. Have you had any success?"

Eugenia groaned, and Fenris reached for her hand and

gave it a squeeze. She risked a look at him and was encouraged to find no trace of smug self-possession on his face. If anything, he looked amused by his father.

She leaned toward him, their shoulders just touching. "Her mother will want to know who's paid attention to her." She had touched his body, she'd watched him spend, seen, heard, and tasted him, and there was in her a longing to feel that again, the response of her body to a man she found physically beautiful. "She'll want to know with whom she's danced, the balls and routs and fetes I've taken her to. What, she will ask me, has my daughter done while she is in London, costing our family a small fortune? And I shall be forced to tell her about the dirt. I shall have to tell her that I may not be able to prevent her from living in the conservatory at Bouverie."

"You might," Fenris said, "mention only that the Duke of Camber and his son accompanied you to Hyde Park."

"And when she returns home with nothing but tales of her adventures with violets and a dozen notebooks of test results?"

"There will by then be watercolors. A very ladylike accomplishment." His hand remained curled around hers. "I recommend that in your next letter you boast of her artistry."

"A delay of the inevitable. Eventually Mrs. Rendell will learn how badly I've failed with Hester."

"Miss Rendell is not without admirers." Fenris glanced at Hester, and Eugenia took in the line of his jaw and the curve of his mouth, and she had never been so viscerally aware that any man was so thoroughly male to her female. "Surely that has not escaped your notice?"

"Do you think so?"

"Yes."

At that moment, Hester looked away from the notebooks to wave at Miss Smith, riding a bay mare and looking very smart in a blue riding habit and a tall cap with a ribbon that tied at her jaw. Miss Smith lifted her crop in greeting. No gentleman could fail to note her figure, and the color in her cheeks was quite appealing. Hester's figure was far better than Miss Smith's.

"Hester?" Eugenia said.

"Yes?"

"Do you ride?"

"I do."

Eugenia beamed at her. "Then we ought to go riding here one day. What do you say to that?"

"I haven't a horse."

She would not fail Hester. By whatever means necessary, Eugenia was determined to put Hester in the company of a gentleman who was worthy of her. "Neither have I, but we can hire them."

Camber snorted. "Hire a horse? My dear Miss Rendell, I think not. You'll ride something from our stables. The boy will manage it."

Fenris nodded. "Certainly, Camber."

"Well, then." Eugenia lifted a hand and was shocked to discover Fenris still held her fingers. How odd that she would have forgotten and that it felt so comfortable to have him do so. She allowed her arm to drift back to her lap and hoped no one had noticed. "Thank you, your grace. That's very kind of you."

Hester gave a careless shrug. "Exercise is always beneficial. But I warn you, I'm a poor horsewoman."

"Hard to believe that." Camber patted Hester's shoulder. "You're such a capable girl."

"Oh, it's true. I've fallen off six horses. Charles says I ought never to ride a horse younger than twenty years. Lord Fenris, have you a twenty-year-old nag?"

"Not in London. But I'll see what can be managed."

Hester leaned over the side of the carriage and clapped a hand on her bonnet when the growing breeze threatened to dislodge it. "Miss Smith." She waved at the other woman. Camber's attention followed her. "Good afternoon. Lady Eugenia says we ought to ride in Hyde Park one of these days. If I do, I should very much like a whip like yours. Will you send me the name of the shop where you acquired it?"

This was duly agreed to, after which Hester sat back and Eugenia enjoyed all of thirty seconds with the belief that she'd managed a miracle in getting Hester to think of anything to do with society and finding a husband.

Still with her hand on her bonnet, Hester grinned. "Your grace, did you notice the tassel on the end of Miss Smith's riding whip?"

"I fear not, my dear."

"It was green." She leaned against the seat, and Eugenia thought she looked very well in her citrine gown. The long end of the ribbon of her bonnet flapped in the now brisk wind. "The exact green of the leaves of your violets this morning. I think it would be useful for me to have a great many things that are green. For the sake of comparison, you understand."

A gust of wind blew through the park, cold and quite strong. The poorly tied bow of Hester's bonnet came undone, and the entire thing went sailing into the air, ribbons fluttering. This event did not go unnoticed. At least a dozen of the gentlemen on horseback whooped as the wind whisked Hester's bonnet higher into the air. They raced after the bonnet, which continued to swoop and dip like some sort of demented, airborne ship. Those not in pursuit laid wagers on who would capture it.

Lord Aigen turned out to be the victor in the bonnet race. He brought back the hat, accepting all the accolades due him in the form of congratulations and hearty slaps on the back. Before he turned it over to Hester, he did his best to reattach the silk roses dangling off the side. While he did this, money changed hands among the spectators. At least once, a breeze threatened to send Hester's bonnet on another sailing adventure. All the ladies were either resecuring their own hats and bonnets or holding them down until they could be refastened.

Eugenia put a gloved hand on the carriage door, and called to him. "Congratulations, Lord Aigen. Excellent riding, sir." Which, indeed, it had been. He'd used his height to advantage in nearly standing up in the saddle to snatch the bonnet from the air.

Aigen urged his horse toward the landau. The men exchanged greetings, and only then did Aigen extend the bonnet to Hester. "I take it this is yours?"

"Yes. Thank you, my lord." Hester stretched out a hand

for her bonnet, but Aigen wasn't yet close enough for her to take it from him. His eyes took in Hester's bosom.

Aigen smoothed his free hand along his chest, apparently not realizing he was crushing Hester's bonnet with the other, and shifted his gaze to Eugenia. "Lady Eugenia. You're a sight for this Scotsman's eyes."

Hester wriggled her fingers but got Aigen's attention only when she leaned farther over the side of the landau. The man stared, once again transfixed by her bosom, which, owing to her leaning so deeply toward him was rather more on display than was best for anyone. "My bonnet, sir?"

Aigen pressed his hand to his heart and, to his credit, lifted his eyes to Hester's face. He used his thighs to move his horse even with the landau. Whatever one might wish to say about his fascination with Hester's bosom, one could not fault his riding. "Ah yes, Miss Rendell. Your wayward bonnet. Sailing away to foreign parts. Rescued now, by my own hand." He waved the bonnet.

Eugenia laughed. "Thank you, Lord Aigen."

"I am moved, my dear ladies, to compose an extempore poem in honor of your beauty."

Fenris dropped his head to hide a groan. Camber glared.

"Go on," Hester said. "I should like to hear you. I enjoy poetry."

Aigen threw out a hand. The one with the bonnet. The ribbons snapped in the breeze. "To the fair Lady Eugenia and Miss Rendell, whose only faults are that you are not Scots."

"Only one?" Hester laughed. "I am relieved."

He winked at her. "You are a star for which . . ." His Scots accent thickened, and it was actually rather charming. The landau moved forward, and when Aigen caught up, he again put a hand over his heart. He cleared his throat and gazed at her and Hester. ". . . a star for which the sky cries— er . . . weeps at its loss."

Fenris snorted and earned a gimlet stare from Aigen. Hester giggled.

She couldn't blame Fenris for that because, well, the verse was perfectly dreadful. But she nevertheless gave him a surreptitious push. If Aigen amused Hester, that ought to be encouraged. She couldn't think of another man Hester had found amusing. Lord Aigen, come to think of it, was precisely the sort of man she hoped Hester would fall in love with. Handsome, intelligent, and in possession of a title. He could hardly be more perfect. She beamed at the man.

"A tear of silver dropped o'er the velvet linens of the firmament."

"What the deuce is he babbling about?" Camber scowled. "Velvet what?"

Hester, of course, listened with perfect sincerity.

Aigen was undeterred by Camber's scornful gaze. Nor by the glare sent his way by Fenris. His speech was now so thick with the Highlands he was nearly impossible to understand. "Soft to earth, to take its place among men and moss. She walks now among us. Oh, beauteous star with amber'd scent."

At least, that's what it sounded like. Those last few words might actually have been Gaelic.

Eugenia laughed in delight. "Thank you, my lord. That was lovely."

Hester clapped her hands. "Bravo, my lord. Bravo!" She put her other hand on the top of the carriage door. Aigen's gaze dropped again, then guiltily lifted. "I very much like the notion of being a beauteous star. Well done, sir."

"You're welcome, Miss Rendell." Briefly, he made cow's eyes at her bosom again. "Stargazing is my newest passion."

Fenris murmured, "There once was a lady from Perth—"

Eugenia kicked the side of his boot. Fortunately, they were saved from more poetry because the landau moved forward again and the sheer number of vehicles made it too dangerous for a man on horseback to come close.

"Well." Hester sat back. "I rather liked his poem, didn't you, Lady Eugenia?"

"Oh, yes."

"I should have liked to have my bonnet returned, though."

"I'll buy you a new one," Camber said.

"Thank you." She gave the duke a smile. "That's very sweet of you. But not necessary."

If only, Eugenia thought, Hester would smile like that at eligible gentlemen.

Fenris coughed once. "Eventually, Miss Rendell, he'll recall the need. If he doesn't, why, then, I'll remind him he's no need for a bonnet."

"Thank you, sir." Hester looked behind them, staring after Lord Aigen. "I only hope he doesn't lose it." She turned around. "Is he a careless sort of man, your friend?"

"Not very." Fenris spoke just on the edge of curtness. "I'll speak with him and make sure he returns your bonnet." Then he dipped his head and said, with a rather deft imitation of Aigen's burr, "Oh, beauteous star."

"You are too kind, sir."

Camber snorted, and then he and Hester were back to talking about plants.

Eugenia peeked at Fenris from under her lashes. "A lady from Perth?"

He was all innocence as he murmured, "She had a regrettable birth—Ouch."

She removed her foot from Fenris's toe and met his stare. The edge of his mouth twitched. "The weather is fine, don't you agree, my lord?"

"Quite," Fenris replied. "If one has the proper footwear."

They were next hailed by Lady Tyghe, riding in a gleaming black phaeton driven by Lord Baring. "Good afternoon." She nodded gracefully to them. "How lovely to see you out and about, your grace." Camber returned her nod. "My dear Fenris. Oh, do stop, Baring. I shan't fall." Lord Baring kept his arm around Lady Tyghe's waist. "Several of us thought we'd leave this crush and walk for a while." She glanced at each of them in turn. "Would you care to join us? It would be so lovely if you did."

This was quickly agreed to. Lady Tyghe sat back and gazed at Fenris with a secretive smile that sent a shock of awareness through Eugenia.

Fenris and Lady Tyghe were lovers.

Chapter Nine

BLAST. BLOODY, BLOODY BLAST.

Fox continued in his annoyance when Sarah's too-intimate smile broadened to include his father. Eugenia had noticed and had drawn all the correct and appropriate conclusions about the nature of his relationship with Sarah. He unbuttoned his greatcoat, put out at Sarah's social clumsiness. But then, he suspected she'd not been clumsy at all.

She was beautiful. Beautiful still. He had, for a short while during their affair, been convinced he was in love with her. He'd made a young man's mistake of confusing sexual compatibility for a deeper emotion. Thank God she had not been in love with him, or they'd have ruined both their lives. He'd proposed to her, a green boy, to a widow six years his elder. Twice on bended knee. He had in the years since found himself grateful to her for refusing him. They did not suit. She'd known it, and had been as gentle with him as she could.

Over the years, they'd resumed a friendship that from time to time involved intimacy of the physical sort. Their last such encounter had been over a year ago. He was beyond irritated that she'd had the bad form to behave as she had just now. If she meant to make Lord Baring jealous, she was about to discover he would not accommodate her.

Eugenia sat stiff as a board with a smile pasted on her face that did not fool him for a moment. Even if she hadn't tugged her hand free from his, he'd have known she was hurt. Jealous? God, if that was all, he'd count himself lucky, for that was something he could remedy between them. But if she had concluded his past with a woman who behaved as badly as Sarah just had was a reflection on his character? That would be much, much harder to overcome.

Whatever was happening between him and Eugenia was too new for him to fully understand. Too new to name. Far, far too fragile. They were barely friends and not yet lovers. If Sarah had just spoiled all that for him, she would find him an unforgiving sort.

Fox, like Eugenia, retreated into a facsimile of nonchalance when in reality he was angry and bothered and anxious. This might well have set him back an incalculable amount, for up to this point, discounting certain events at Bouverie, which, to his mind, had been unexpected, magnificent, and disastrous all at once, he'd been doing quite well with Eugenia. He had worked hard to prove he had changed. He wasn't her enemy. And now? Sarah, blast her, had just exploded all his efforts into dust, and he wanted to shout his frustration to the heavens.

The coachman directed the landau out of the line of carriages and headed the vehicle away from the most crowded portion of the park. They turned down the side road where Lady Tyghe had told them her party would be waiting. Fox tapped on the back of the driver's seat. What he must do was continue as he had, as if nothing at all had changed. Eugenia would eventually realize he was not responsible for Sarah's behavior. "This will do."

The driver brought the landau to the curb. Fox reached over and opened the door almost before they'd stopped and certainly before the groom had jumped down from the back. He pushed down the step himself and stood on the walk with a hand extended. Camber put a hand to the back of Eugenia's elbow as she rose and placed her hand on Fox's.

Not since he was a boy had he waited with such awful tension to see what a woman would do. Join someone else? Hang back and allow him to escort her? Ignore him entirely? That last, unfortunately, and just as crushing now as when he was a boy scorned by the object of his affections.

As Eugenia stepped down, she lifted her hand to shade her face against the sun. Fox resisted the urge to look. He already knew Sarah and the others were a few yards down the path, and that Aigen, the bloody bonnet rescuer, was among them. Eugenia walked a short distance from the landau. He steeled himself to calm while he assisted Miss Rendell from the carriage, too. She caught her foot in the hem of her gown on the step to the curb, and, had he not still had her hand, she might well have pitched headlong to the ground. God help him, he wanted to turn around and see if Eugenia appreciated his rescue of Miss Rendell. He didn't dare.

He held the carriage door for his father, too, and watched as he and Miss Rendell headed toward Eugenia and the others, both walking with their hands clasped behind their backs. His father took notice of so few people, and made friends of even fewer. How strange to see Camber make a friend of Miss Rendell. Or was it Miss Rendell who'd managed to make a friend of Camber?

On the path ahead, Eugenia fell in step with them and provided Fox the answer he'd hoped not to have. Damn. Damn, damn, and damn again. She did not look back or slow down or wait for him. With a sigh, he started after them.

The necessary introductions were made when they reached Sarah and her companions. Where was the line he must toe with respect to Sarah? Too warm toward her, and Eugenia would believe he was still Sarah's lover. Too cold, and he ran the same risk. He settled, in the end, on making it plain he and Baring were on easy terms. That fact must prove Sarah was no longer a lover of his.

As he walked, with nothing much to say to anyone, Miss Rendell was greeted enthusiastically by three young ladies her age. As far as he could tell, Hester Rendell had skipped those typically young and excitable years. She was head and shoulders more mature than any of these young women. Miss Rendell gestured to his father, and to his astonishment, Camber went to her side. She drew her arm through the duke's, and he patted her arm. He'd long suspected his father had wanted a daughter of his own. Here was proof.

Farther along the path, one of the fawning puppies who made up Sarah's group strolled beside Eugenia. Before his eyes Aigen very neatly cut out the boy and took Eugenia's arm. The man knew Mountjoy, Fox told himself. Of course he would pay his respects to Mountjoy's sister. Aigen now walked with his head bent toward Eugenia in a far too confidential manner. She laughed at something he said to her. He hoped to God it wasn't more poetry. Fox closed his eyes and stopped walking. He would not succumb to mindless jealousy. He would not. And had.

He opened his eyes and saw nothing had changed. His father and Miss Rendell remained deep in conversation. Aigen and Eugenia continued to walk arm in arm. Jesus, he wasn't fit company for anyone. God knows in his petulant mood he'd end up convincing Eugenia he despised her, after all. He stayed where he was, far behind the others and taking a vicious satisfaction in doing so. He didn't start walking again until he was quite alone. He concentrated on the scenery and landscaping, aware he was behaving badly, that he had no excuse for feeling as he did, and that there was every chance his mood would degenerate.

He would not stare. Not at them or at anyone. Eugenia could do as she liked. She was entitled to make friends. She deserved to have them. Nevertheless, as he walked, he plotted how he would get her alone and when he had, what words, tone, and expression he would use to explain about Sarah and make sure Eugenia understood his ties to the woman were those of the past. He drifted into a remembrance of Ginny's hand around his cock, of her in his arms, of kissing her and of her kissing him back. So lost had he become in his thoughts that he actually achieved his goal of not watching Eugenia.

When he looked up again, Aigen had left Eugenia and was now walking beside Miss Rendell. She wore her bonnet again, though from where Fox was, it looked a bit bedraggled. His father continued on her other side.

Eugenia, he now saw, walked by herself. Slowly. Behind Miss Rendell, Aigen, and his father. This was his chance. He caught up to her and captured her arm before she could walk away. Every bit of his measured and supremely logical explanation about Sarah scattered to the wind. "Lady Tyghe is an old friend. Nothing more."

She smiled, and he knew he'd given everything away and for no benefit at all. The curve of her mouth was at least a century distant. "I don't know why you feel compelled to tell me something like that." A person could die from such deadly sweetness. "I'm glad she's your particular friend."

"Don't pretend," he said. "It's unbecoming of you."

Her eyes opened wider. "It's not as if you can't have a mistress. Gentlemen like you do that sort of thing."

"She is not my mistress."

Her response to that was a disbelieving snort. "It's no business of mine, sir."

"She is not currently my mistress." That earned him another stare. "Years ago, yes. I don't deny that. And even then I don't believe she would have been classified as my mistress. I did not keep her. Am I to be judged as harshly as that, Ginny? It's unfair. I don't judge you that way." He frowned and stopped walking. So did she. The hole he was digging was getting deeper. "We ought not to be talking about such things. It's not proper."

"You brought it up, not I."

To hell with it. There was a large chestnut tree not far off the path, and he moved them there, under the shade of the branches and out of sight of the others. He held her upper arms. "Look at me, Ginny. Look." He waited for her blue, blue eyes to meet his. "I never took her to Bouverie. Or to

Upper Brook Street. She had, still has, I imagine, her own house. True, we had passionate relations for a time. We were intimates exactly as you imagine. I was impossibly young." Not a single word came out as planned. "You know what I was like then, for pity's sake. She was beautiful, and that's all I wanted in a woman. I know it's callow, but then I was a callow youth. We were lovers. I bought her fine jewelry, paid her expenses, and then . . . we ended. Years ago."

She was almost, but not quite, laughing at him. "As I said, it's none of my business."

"I don't know how to make you understand. I'm not proper enough for you, of that I am aware, but I shan't pretend to be what I'm not. What I am not, is that woman's lover. Once, yes, but not now." He drew in a breath. "That is to say, yes. It is very much your business. She's using me to get at Lord Baring. There's nothing more going on than that." He brought her closer, his heart pounding in his chest. "You and I are not done. Not by a long shot. Do you think I would settle for anyone but you after you—" A polite word escaped him, and while he struggled for one that was not crude, she took a step away and he was forced to release her. "That. What you and I did."

She glanced down the path where they could still see the others, including Camber and Miss Rendell. Sarah and Baring, too. He moved them out of sight of them, deeper into the shadows provided by the tree. "That should not have happened. The Turkish room."

"Why not? Look at me, Ginny. Why not?"

"You know exactly why." She did look at him, and his heart constricted at her bland expression. Then, her cheeks flushed pink, and he grabbed her gloved hand and held on so she wouldn't walk away.

"I'm sure I don't know why, Ginny. Will you tell me?" His fingers tightened around hers, and he tugged on her hand until she had no choice but to come nearer. "Let's not talk about sin, if that's what you mean, but of unhappiness and pleasure. Once, you were a woman who laughed and smiled so often it was a joy to be near you. You loved life." Emotion spiraled through him, all the reasons he'd been so attracted to her, and it killed him to think he'd met the right woman, the only woman for him, and he'd been too full of himself not to ruin everything. "It's why men fell in love with you. Why Robert loved you. You've lost that. I think it happened when you lost Robert, and I'm sorry. So sorry he's gone." He pulled her close because he could not bear to see her grief. "Don't cry, Ginny, please. Please don't." He slid an arm around her waist. "I want to see that joy in you again. When I saw you at Bitterward." He shook his head, relieved, selfishly relieved, that she had herself under control. "You were so altered."

"I'm older now." Oh God, her voice was barren and he didn't know what to do to help her find her joy in life. "Wiser. Not a girl anymore. What young person, gentleman or lady, does not eventually learn to behave with less exuberance?"

"Most of us do, I suppose." He put a hand to her chin and brought her face back to his. "Robert loved the joy in you." He hesitated and almost didn't continue. But he did. "As did I, and when you and I were at Bouverie, in the library and again in that damned Turkish room, I saw that spark again. I felt it and it burned me to my core. You laughed, Ginny. You were alive, and I would sell my soul a dozen times and then a dozen times more to make that happen again."

"You mustn't say that."

He'd already taken exactly the wrong tack with her, but it was too late to correct course. She moved away from him, not far, but he still raised his voice. "I can't be Robert. I'm not him."

She stayed with her back partially turned away.

He went on in a softer tone. "I never was and never could be, but if you and I can find pleasure together, if I've found a way to make you love life again, I ask you, why should we not?"

She faced him and let out a breath. "Because."

He cocked his head, and he could see she was irritated by that. "Because?"

"Because you are Fenris."

"That's no good reason. Why else?" He took her by the shoulders again and turned them so her back was to the tree. He leaned near and nearer yet, and his heart raced. He wanted her to kiss him. He wanted her to cling to him and believe he would do everything in his power to make her life happier. He continued to look at her, waiting for her to say something. His very life might end right here.

She didn't say a word. Didn't move. Not away from him. Not toward him.

He bent closer, and while he wondered if madness had taken him over, his lips brushed hers, and he had never in his life been more terrified of the consequences of rejection. She stood frozen. He kissed her again, lightly. Gently. In the back of his mind, he thought, *such a soft and tender mouth*. He wanted, he desired, her mouth on his prick. God strike him dead for it, he did. While he breathed in the scent of her, he cupped a hand to her nape and brought her toward him, and she allowed him to kiss her again.

He drew back slightly, and he could have sworn she whispered his name.

Fox.

Then he brushed his mouth over hers again, just as tenderly as before, and something in his chest gave way because he'd wanted her for so long, knowing, believing there was no hope whatever and here she was, allowing this impropriety. His silent declaration of desire. He fit his mouth over hers and kissed her more insistently. He adjusted his arms around her, and so did she, and he nipped at her lower lip and then it was like before. Hot. Out of control. Their kiss became a prelude to much, much more.

Her breath hitched, and the fact that she was responding to him was miraculous. She parted her lips under his, and she pressed herself against him while they kissed like that. He did his best to keep himself under some kind of control. In the back of his mind, he understood they were in public and if they were to be discovered like this, the only possible result was scandal.

Eyes closed, she drew back, though he did not let go of her, and he assessed his state, which was just as madly aroused as before. Then she looked at him, brow furrowed. "I do not understand how or why you make me feel this way. It makes no sense when I dislike you so much. I've always disliked you."

"You don't know me. Not the man I became. Don't think about why you once hated me." He tightened his embrace, nearly helpless with his desire for her. "Think about how I make you feel now. Think, if you like, for it's true, that you're fortunate I'm not taking you up against the damned tree because I owe you a quick fuck."

"You're awful."

"I know. Kiss me again?" He braced his forearms on the tree trunk, above her shoulders, and leaned forward. "I promise I shan't be offended if you do."

"I didn't kiss you."

"No?"

She grabbed the lapels of his coat and leaned her forehead against his chest. "I can't think when you're this close. I say and do the most shocking things."

He brought down a hand again and stroked her cheek. "Perhaps this is no great help, but I think you should do those shocking things more often."

Chapter Ten

Two weeks later. 11 Cambridge Terrace.

At half past midnight, Fox knocked at Aigen's door. For longer than ought to be the case, he waited on the steps, cold fog sinking into his bones. There were lights burning upstairs, so he knew the man was home. Eventually, the door opened and Aigen's butler admitted him. Since Fox was a frequent caller, all he needed to do was hand over his hat and coat and drop a coin into the man's hand.

"In his bedchamber, milord."

"Thank you." He knew the way, for he and Aigen spent many a night in long conversation here. He headed up the stairs.

Aigen he found in his shirtsleeves, sitting at a secretary with pen in hand and paper before him. He blotted the page when Fox leaned against the doorjamb. "Good night, Fox."

"Were you not going to admit me?"

Aigen sighed. "I thought about it."

"It's bloody cold out there." Normally, they got on comfortably. Tonight, however, Aigen did not rise to greet him. He stayed at the desk, quiet for the moment. Fox headed for the side table. They spent enough time together, either here or at Upper Brook Street, that they never stood on ceremony. "Whisky?" he asked, aware of Aigen's loyalty to his country's drink. He had his own private preference as well.

But tonight Aigen tapped the end of his pen on the desktop. "There's a port breathing, if you don't mind. Over there."

"Not at all." Fox poured them both three fingers and took one of the glasses to Aigen. He lifted his and crossed half the distance of the room so that he stood nearer the fire. A line of porcelain and brass chimney ornaments, horses mostly, lined the mantel. "To good friends."

Aigen nodded. "To good friends."

When they'd drunk, Fox turned a chair to face the secretary where Aigen still sat. "I haven't come too late, have I?"

"Too late for?"

"At night, Aigen."

"You haven't." He leaned a forearm on the writing surface, and some of the tension went out of him. But not all. "I've had another letter from the family rock pile, and it's put me in a temper."

"What malady does he have this time?"

"Chilblains. And gout. Something else painfully mysterious and likely fatal. Dead in a fortnight, he says, though I'm not to rush home on his account. He's sent me the name of the stone carver he wants to chisel his headstone."

Aigen's grandfather, the possessor of one of the last of the Scottish dukedoms outside of Argyll's holdings, had been dying of some disease or other for the last twenty years. The man was eighty-one, had outlived three wives and four sons, and had never once set foot out of the Highlands. "I thought you Scots were hardier fare."

"He'll outlive me—I own it."

"Unlikely," he said softly.

"If he doesn't, I'll be saddled with that damned dukedom, and I'll go bankrupt. I've seen the way he lives. Hasn't two pennies to rub together but what I send him." Aigen had inherited a decent fortune from his mother's family, monies he'd immediately put in the five percents and in a ship sailing to the Orient that came home with a decent enough cargo to give Aigen relief from his most pressing debts. He downed half his port. "Now that he's dying for certain, he says he's given up on my marrying a female Scot." Aigen glanced in Fox's direction, a crooked smile on his mouth. "He must really be ill."

"I'm sorry if that's so."

He put a hand on the letter he'd been writing. "He's ordered me to find a rich Sassenach wife while I'm here in London. Bring her home to meet him before he's off to lecture his Maker about all He's done wrong."

Fox chuckled. "All that in a fortnight?"

Aigen exaggerated his accent. "I'm to show the poor English lass all the riches the clan can offer. The Highlands—now there's beauty, I won't gainsay him that—and the castle falling down around his head. Our heads."

Fox returned to the sideboard to fetch the decanter. He brought it to Aigen and refilled both their glasses. "It's fortunate I came tonight, if only to rescue you from self-pity. Poor fellow, Aigen, to inherit a dukedom and your family's honor. Even if it is a Scots one."

"I like being Aigen. It suits me."

"You're suited to more."

He bowed his head and grabbed his hair with both hands. "God, a wife. The worst of it is I was thinking of it even before I got his damned letter."

"There are worse fates than to marry a fine woman."

Aigen turned his head to him. "How would you know? You haven't a wife."

"Not yet."

"Which one should I choose, Fox? Who do I take home to the old man before it's too late?"

"Anyone you like." *Save one, damn it. Anyone save one.* "The woman you find most suitable."

Aigen took a long drink from his goblet. "There's one who interests me. It's odd the way she stays in my thoughts. Never thought that would happen."

"Only one?"

"You know who."

"Do I?"

Aigen let out a breath. "I've always admired the women you do. We've similar tastes. So I ask you, shall I ask Mountjoy's sister if she'd like to live in a Scottish rock pile one day?"

His heart stilled. He'd hoped things hadn't come to such a pass. "Why her?"

"A sad and lovely woman, Lady Eugenia."

"Yes."

"I see her at parties with that handsome girl she's got with her. Trying so hard to find her a husband when it's clear as day the girl's not interested in anyone. Not even me, Fox."

"Miss Rendell."

"Yes, Miss Rendell. I don't know why you two don't get on."

"Miss Rendell and I get on splendidly."

"Lady Eugenia. You ought to get on better with her. Why don't you?"

"Are you in love with her?"

Aigen sipped his port before he answered. "I wouldn't mind spending the rest of my life making her smile."

"Miss Rendell would suit you well."

Aigen nodded, but not in agreement with Fox's pointed suggestion. His friend slouched on his chair. "Doesn't give a fig what anyone thinks of her, does she?"

"No."

"A bit young, only not. Not a beauty, yet she is."

"A fair assessment."

Aigen stared at his port and after a bit of searching in the contents, took another swallow. "What brings you here, if I might ask?" There was only the faintest burr in his words. "Besides my wine cellar."

"What else but a woman?" Fox, once again seated, stared into his port, too, aware that he might leave here having ended another friendship because of a woman. Again. He did not want to lose Aigen's friendship. Leisurely, he took a sip. It was an excellent port.

"If you've come to speak out of turn about Lady Eugenia, I warn you I'll not listen to you."

"Not out of turn."

"No?" Aigen tapped his finger on the tabletop. "Is there something I should know, then?"

"Yes." Fox sighed. "When I was young and stupid—"

"When were you ever young? You've been old since the day you were born."

"Young *and* stupid." He lifted his glass in a mock toast and let irony invest his words. "I became unduly attached to a woman I believed was in no way my equal in rank or character. Naturally, I refused to accept that a man such as I could form a connection with a girl like her."

"Bloody fool."

"Yes."

Aigen pushed his port to the far side of the desk. He turned on his chair to face Fox. "Was the woman's name, by any chance under the stars, as melodic to the ears as, say, Eugenia?"

Fox set his forearms on his thighs and stared at Aigen. "My friend Robert was already falling in love with her. And she with him, it turned out." He shook his head. "They met, and I never once thought anything could come of it. She was fresh from the country, all life and passion, not an ounce of decorum."

"Not proper enough for the bloody Marquess of Fenris."

He laughed. "Not by half."

"Her damned brother a farmer, too." He tapped his fingers in a slow tattoo. "Used to be a farmer, though, isn't that right?"

He waved that off. "My esteemed father had nothing kind to say about Mountjoy. Or his two siblings."

"You didn't have to listen to him."

"I was yet several months away from that insight." He lifted his glass to the lamplight. "They got on, Robert and her. I couldn't understand how any two people could be so different yet feel they had anything in common. They recognized something in each other. And I said to myself, how could *she* recognize anything about the fire that burns in Robert Bryant? I wish you'd met him. You'd have liked him better than you like me." He shook his head. He keenly felt the difference between the green boy he'd been then and the man he was now. "They were meant for each other. Everyone saw it. Even I saw, though I refused to accept it until it was too late."

"Her husband, you mean."

"At that time, her future husband, but yes. I kept telling myself she wasn't worthy of him. Not brilliant Robert. What woman could ever be worthy of him? She'd make fun of his deformity, I thought, his strange habits and mental flights—his genius told in his manner. He'd impale himself on her beauty and her joy of life and never recover when he learned she didn't love him, or worse, that she was not the sort of woman with whom he could remain in love once he saw her for what she was. How could he be truly in love when she couldn't possibly love him?"

"Bloody, bloody fool."

He shook his head, still with his thoughts and soul in a past he could do nothing to change. "She never thought of him as a cripple. She never noticed, or if she did, she didn't care. Not in the least."

"She wouldn't."

"As I say, I was young and stupid then. I saw her shortly after he died, and she was wracked. Even I, fool that I am, could see his death had destroyed her."

Aigen pushed his glass in a circle on the desktop. "She loved him. I never met the man. Never saw them together." He let out a breath. "I hardly know her, but I know that much about her. She still loves him, you know that, I hope."

"I was wrong." He shrugged. "About a great many things. My grandfather—he was alive in those days—he and my father both disliked her. They disliked her elder brother, too, and I blindly adopted that opinion as my own. How could any present or future Duke of Camber be wrong?"

"Stupid of you." What hung in the air now was what

Aigen hadn't said. That he'd not be that stupid. He'd not make that severe a mistake with a woman like Eugenia.

"I discouraged Robert. I did everything in my power to stop him marrying so far beneath what I thought he deserved, and it broke us apart. He never spoke to me again. Never mind that for now, I told myself. For I'll be there when he learns the truth about her. I'll not say a word against her when that happens. I would offer up my friendship and everything would be the way it was before." He touched a fist to his heart. "But I'd hate her, you see, for breaking him."

"Which she never did."

"I resented her because once she met Robert, she never cared for me. Not for me. Not for my rank. Not for anything. And everyone cared for me. Why wouldn't they? Why wouldn't she, too?"

"I'm sorry."

Fox sighed and thought of Robert and how bitterly he missed their friendship. "They were fortunate to have what time they did. I heard from others now and again, when someone forgot or didn't know we'd once been close, that Robert was happy. I chanced to see his mother before she passed, and she told me she thanked God every day for bringing Eugenia into Robert's life."

"And?"

"And, I do as well. She made him happy, and I was wrong. In every respect. About them. About Robert. And about her."

"Does she know any of this?"

"She knows I nearly convinced Robert to break it off. She knows I thought her beneath him and unworthy."

Aigen leaned forward. "No wonder she dislikes you."

"I was a fool then." He leaned across the space between them and grabbed the bottle of port to refill his glass. "I'm not now." He refilled Aigen's glass, too. "The woman you marry will be fortunate indeed." He set the bottle of port on the floor by his chair and lifted his glass. "I mean that sincerely. Whether it's Miss Rendell or some other woman."

Aigen draped an arm along the top of his chair and

grinned at him. "Fox. Fox, my stupid friend. Does she know how you feel now? To the point, does it matter?"

He gave Aigen a look that conveyed his opinion of that question. "If I told her now, she'd never believe me." He stood. "I don't want to drive another friendship to ruin over a woman."

Aigen shrugged. "Then don't. That seems easy enough."

"I will if it comes to that."

"That's alarming." Aigen kept his good humor but there was a tension now.

"You've called at Spring Street."

"Several times. As you know, Lady Eugenia is working diligently to find a husband for Miss Rendell. She entertains a great deal. You might try calling on her yourself, you know."

"I know why you feel about her as it seems you do. I even know why she'd admire and respect you."

"Thank you. I think." Aigen lifted his eyebrows. "Am I meant to be flattered?"

"You and I, we have a great deal in common. I don't like many people, but I consider you a friend."

Aigen's smile hinted at an internal irony. "If you had a sister, I swear to you I'd marry her in an instant. But you haven't."

"You don't need to marry for money."

"No." Aigen flashed a more natural smile. "But it never hurts to have more, does it? Mountjoy is deep in the pockets. Besides, my grandfather has ordered me to marry a rich English girl. What choice do I have when he's only days left to live?" He picked up his port while Fox chuckled. "She'd be a good choice for me, Mountjoy's sister. Young but not wet behind the ears. A pretty woman with the mettle to face down the laird of the castle." He laughed. "Truth is, I wouldn't have to pretend to fall in love with her."

And that, Fox thought, was exactly why he was here. "Don't let things get that far."

He hefted his glass and set it down untouched. "And if it's too late?"

He met Aigen's gaze. "Is it?"

"I wonder," Aigen said after too long a silence, "where that leaves us if it is."

"Fair warning." He sighed and leapt into the abyss. "I have business that will take me out of London for a week or two. I hope not much longer."

Aigen understood that perfectly. "Bad luck for you."

"The timing is particularly poor, I admit." He smiled. "Thus, I have come here to drink your port and tell you bluntly that I am no longer young and stupid, and I won't step aside this time."

Chapter Eleven

Six days later. The Italian Opera.

THE BACK OF EUGENIA'S NECK PRICKLED WHEN someone entered the Duke of Camber's box at the Italian Opera. Earlier in the day, a footman had delivered Camber's invitation, and of course—of course—she and Hester had accepted. He hadn't merely sent them tickets to a production of *Don Giovanni*, which tickets he included with the delivery of his invitation—the tickets alone would have been triumph enough—but Camber himself had engaged to escort them.

As it happened, that evening both the House of Lords and the House of Commons sat late, such that Eugenia and Hester took their own carriage to the Haymarket. Shortly after they'd taken seats in the box with Camber's other guests, Parliament had finished its business for the night and the men who'd been delayed made their appearances. Camber arrived half an hour after the start of the opera.

The duke sat beside Hester, and that choice, for there were two other seats open, did not go unremarked by anyone with a view of the box. Opera glasses everywhere flashed. As usual, the two had endless notes to exchange about violets and soil and pollination and something about dividing roots and southern exposures. Frankly, when they got started, Eugenia stopped listening. Lord Monson arrived next, and he took the seat beside his wife, leaving the only open seat the one to Eugenia's left. Camber's box was in one of the two columns of boxes set directly on the left side of the deep stage, mirrored by the two columns on the opposite side. Prime seating. It was far easier to see the boxes across from them than it was to see the actors. Which was, come to think of it, the entire point.

Another person came in, and Eugenia turned with everyone else to see who it was. She expected Aigen and it wasn't him.

Her heart stuttered. Even in the dimness of the box, she recognized the man's silhouette immediately. Not Aigen. Fenris. He'd been away from London these last several days, attending to business on his father's behalf, so Camber had told them. She hadn't known he'd returned. She hadn't allowed herself to admit she cared. He was back from wherever he'd been, and she sat in her seat and the evening was no longer ordinary. She tried to settle herself, to regain the feelings she'd always had about Fenris. That he was a cold, unpleasant man who could hardly dislike her more than she disliked him. She couldn't. No matter what she told herself, from the moment he walked in, she felt as if the floor had fallen away.

He made his way toward the front of the box and greeted his father and Hester with a nod. Lady Monson received a kiss on the cheek. The point of attending the opera, as Eugenia well knew, was not so much enjoyment of the performance, but to see and be seen. At the moment, Fenris was making sure he was seen. He put a hand on Lord Monson's shoulder and said a word or two to the man. He had yet to glance in her direction.

Why should he? They weren't friends, precisely. They weren't lovers, either. Not really. Not proper lovers, at any rate. But he'd been away for days, and so much had happened between them before he left. Though she understood he was trying not to make himself hateful to her, the uncertainty of where they stood and what she felt was going to drive her mad. The leap of her pulse at his entrance lingered still, and what was she to conclude from that?

"Ah," said Lord Monson, lifting his opera glasses and contorting his upper body to survey the stage. "The Incomparable appears?"

Fenris laughed.

Lady Monson elbowed her husband, and that made Eugenia stare at Fenris. As usual, his expression gave nothing away. The Incomparable? She'd heard that sobriquet thrown in Fenris's direction before, Dinwitty Lane chief among those making the reference.

Camber harrumphed, but he, too, trained his opera glasses on the stage. Eugenia twisted about to see for herself. On stage, a dance sequence had just ended, and the ballet girls in their shockingly short gowns were now gracefully turning and leaping with tiny cat steps toward the exits. Catcalls from the pit and the very upper boxes where the public was jammed in tight filled the air. There were calls as well from the boxes that contained the very best of London society. Not one of the ballet girls, that she could tell, appeared aware of the hundreds of men and gentlemen ogling them.

Fenris remained standing. There was only one available seat in the box now, and it was beside her, inconveniently situated next to the wall. Her reticule happened to occupy the chair. She expected that Fenris, if he stayed, would rather remain on his feet than sit beside her where one's view of the stage and the Incomparable, whom she now suspected was quite possibly an actual mistress as opposed to a former lover of his, would be restricted.

The singing resumed. With the ballet girls and the Incomparable no longer on stage, the catcalls died away. Fenris continued greeting the others in the box. He lingered over each of the women. Eugenia was the only person he did not approach, and she was by turns relieved and in despair because of it.

When he was done making sure everyone in the auditorium saw him, he took a step back and looked idly around the box. Eugenia watched him from the corner of her eye.

She would be as calm and sedate as he was. If life was about to murder him, he looked so bored, then she would give that same impression. He held the brim of his hat in both hands and leaned his shoulders against the opposite wall, resplendent in trousers, a dark coat, a saffron waistcoat, and a cravat that tread at the edge of too plain.

During one of his disinterested, sweeping glances around the box, his gaze landed on her. Unfortunately, at the same time she'd just risked a full-on glance in his direction. Caught. She didn't smile or nod or give any sign that she saw him. She did not wish to be reminded of how she had behaved with him, or for him to think she recalled even a second of that time. If he didn't care, then neither did she.

Their gazes locked. My God, one look at him and she was breathless with the impact. She remembered the thrill of his embrace. Touching him. His arms around her. His mouth covering hers. The weight of his body on hers.

Fenris didn't acknowledge her smile, but neither did he look away. Beast. Now they were in a contest to see who would give in first. Slowly, insultingly, he dropped his attention below her chin. She ought to be offended, but she wasn't. Butterflies took flight in her stomach again.

God help her, she knew in her soul that Fenris would be magnificent in bed. Would it be so awful to enjoy him for that?

Eugenia faced forward and pretended to be absorbed by the production, though she had a good view of only the front of the stage. Let him stand there and expire of boredom while he tried to disconcert her. On the stage, the tenor launched into an aria. A ripple of anticipation flowed through the auditorium as male attention once again focused on the stage. Eugenia craned her neck and saw that, yes, the ballet girls were back. Fenris moved to get a better view of the stage, then stepped away from his vantage point. He bent over Mrs. Gloster's hand, facing toward the front of the box so that Eugenia, had she been looking at him directly rather than twisted about and from the corner of her eye, would have had an excellent view of his face. He kissed the air over

Mrs. Gloster's gloved hand and exchanged a murmured greeting with the woman. The man was too charming for his own good. He straightened again and glanced toward the exit. Would he stay? Or did he mean to leave? He did not continue on his way out.

She consulted her program, but her skin prickled with the awareness that he'd looked at the empty chair beside her. The only available seat in the box. She did not want him to sit beside her. Did she? Her pulse raced. Fenris, however, did not move. The chair was lacking. Or was the problem the woman he would have to sit beside?

Hester straightened on her seat, leaning toward the duke. The two were whispering again, and for the merest instant she mistook the way the duke listened to Hester for something more than avuncular sentiment. He might be Fenris's father, but Camber was no white-haired old man. She gave herself a mental shake. He smiled more around Hester and paid her more attention than any other woman, but Camber was more than twice Hester's age, for heaven's sake. All they ever talked about was plants and experiments. Horticulture was not the language of amour. If they'd been talking poetry or art, she might have reason to worry, but no one succumbed to love over botany. Plain as anything, Camber thought of Hester as the daughter he'd never had. Fenris had her seeing intrigue everywhere.

Fenris had left Mrs. Gloster and was now moving behind her row of seats. Her nape itched even more. She stared straight ahead. He was here. Back from wherever he'd been, and she could not stop the frisson of arousal that slid down her spine. He worked his way to the end of the row until he was directly behind her, leaning against the wall again so as not to block the view of the people behind her.

She no longer heard the opera. Nor did she hear Hester and Camber whispering. Fenris's presence was a weight, a breath of air across the back of her neck. As if he'd touched her, when he hadn't. He bent and rested his hand lightly on her shoulder. Since he'd taken off his gloves, his bare fingers touched her skin. She steeled herself. She was not going to let him guess how she reacted to his presence.

"Pardon me, Mrs. Bryant. May I sit?"

She wanted to tell him no.

"Certainly, my lord." She picked up her reticule and moved to the chair by the wall, leaving her seat for Fenris, and him with a place beside Hester.

From here, her view of the stage was reduced to a slice of the very top of the stage. She could see nothing of the scenery unless she leaned over the railing and craned her neck. She could, however, see directly into the box on the opposite side of the auditorium, and that proved a welcome distraction. Two of the occupants had opera glasses trained on their box, and one of the two men was Mr. Dinwitty Lane.

Fenris took the seat she'd vacated and immediately turned to Hester. Eugenia put down her opera glasses and contented herself with staring at the occupants of the box across the way. Mr. Lane had his glasses trained on Hester.

"Miss Rendell," Fenris said in a melting voice. How could she have forgotten how entrancing his voice could be? The huskiness was really just patently unfair. A man could seduce a woman with just that voice alone. "How lovely you look this evening."

Hester smiled at him, but it was plain her thoughts remained with whatever she and Camber had been discussing. "Thank you, and good evening to you, my lord. I hope you're well."

"I am. You? Experiments going well?"

Hester nodded with more enthusiasm than she ought to have shown. "We are gathering our data. It's crucial, you know, that we take exact measurements. Is that not so, your grace?"

"It is."

"Since your father is an accomplished artist, we are not merely taking daily sketches of our respective plants. We paint them."

"Brilliant idea of hers," Camber said. "Takes extra time but well worth it when we examine and compare past data."

"We do not know if the watercolors are stable. We have added to our record keeping in case they're not."

Eugenia did not understand their captivation with documenting the daily growth of their plants. She'd once made the mistake of asking, and Hester had obliged with an answer so long and detailed she was cross-eyed and suffering from a megrim by the time the explanation was over. Horticulture and botany were not subjects that fascinated her.

Camber shifted on his seat in order to get a different view of the stage, but then, no, his opera glasses remained on his lap. It was impossible not to think that here sat a man who had the ear of the government, whose single word could and did decide a man's fate. His patronage might secure one for life; his disapprobation could lead to personal, social, or even financial ruin. And he spent his leisure hours with Hester or painting watercolors of the leaves of a violet.

The second intermission arrived, along with louder conversation as people left their seats and headed for the saloons and foyers where they might be seen even more openly by people of fashion. "Tell us, Miss Rendell," Fenris said, tilting his head to include his father in the remark, "are you enjoying the performance?"

Hester clasped her hands on her lap and gave Fenris and Camber a warm smile. The duke patted her hand. "Yes, my lord, very much. And I wish to say, your grace, how much I appreciate you inviting us. You were kind to think of us."

"Not at all," Camber said.

"I find the tenor to be quite talented." Fenris leaned an elbow on the back of his seat, and, honestly, could any man be as carelessly handsome as him? "What do you think, Miss Rendell?"

Hester glanced at the bit of the stage visible from their seats. There was just now nothing to see but empty stage. Since she'd spent most of the performance whispering back and forth with Camber, Eugenia thought it likely Hester had no idea what the tenor had sounded like. "I like his singing very much."

Fenris had his back some three-quarters to Eugenia, but he turned his head to look at her. The floor fell away again, all because his gaze swept over her. She stilled, afraid he'd guess her attraction to him and think that it meant more than it did. "What do you think, Mrs. Bryant? Do you agree with Miss Rendell?"

"I am quite enjoying the performance." She snapped open her fan. This was too much. How was she to deal with this man when he so strongly disrupted her peace of mind? One look at his lovely brown eyes and she was cast back to the Turkish room, and, God help her, she did not regret what had happened there. Something flickered in his eyes, and she was as filled with doubt as ever. "I beg your pardon. I desperately need a breath of air. I shan't be long."

"Shall I escort you?" Fenris spoke in so offhand a manner she wondered if he even meant it. She looked away. No, she thought. No, he did not. And yet, a voice in the back of her mind whispered otherwise. Across the way, Lane trained his glasses on them. Hadn't the man something better to do than spy on innocent operagoers?

"Will you come along, Hester?" Eugenia asked.

"If you like."

Camber put his hand over Hester's. "I should like to continue our discussion." He looked to Eugenia. "Do you mind if we do? I shan't let her out of my sight. I promise you that."

"Not at all, your grace." More than anything she wanted to be away from Fenris and his disturbing presence. If she left Hester with the Duke of Camber, in his own box in the company of Lord and Lady Monson, Mrs. Gloster, and everyone in the auditorium, what could be improper about that?

As she rose to make her way out of the box, her forgotten reticule slipped from her lap and landed on the floor with a soft clink of the contents. She bent to retrieve it. At the very same time, so did Lord Fenris. Their fingers met.

The medallion Lily had given her swung out. By some perverse jest from the heavens, the ribbon from which it was suspended tangled around a button of Fenris's coat. Momentarily unable to straighten, she was close enough to smell his cologne. The scent reminded her of his mouth on hers, the silk of his hair beneath her fingers. The sound he made when he came.

Fenris made a sound that was a combination of sigh and grunt. "Mrs. Bryant. A moment—"

In such dim and close quarters, Eugenia had little room to maneuver. Unable to see the details of the way in which the ribbon had entangled with his coat, she tugged on the medallion. His lapel flapped toward her.

"Mrs. Bryant—" His head bobbed when she tugged again, and, to her utter horror, her bosom ended up at his eye level.

"Oh dear," Hester said.

Eugenia lifted a hand to forestall the possibility of Hester's assistance.

Fenris put a hand on her shoulder and squeezed. "Please remain still a moment, Mrs. Bryant, I can just—"

This was worse than overhearing Fenris calling her a blowsy girl. Worse by far because she knew she would be laughed at again. She did not want to be this close to him. Not now. Not ever again. Nor did she wish to be the object of everyone's amusement. She gave the ribbon another tug. Fenris's upper torso hitched toward her, and he let out a hard breath.

"The deuce?" she heard Camber say.

"Mrs. Bryant." Fenris's gaze landed on her breasts. The man was unabashedly staring, and it made her dizzy, anxious, and embarrassed all at the same time. "A moment. Please."

"Pull on it," Camber said.

Fenris lifted his eyes to hers, and he was trying not to laugh. He whispered, "Yes, please. But not here, darling Ginny."

He might find this amusing, but the laughter was at her expense because he was Fenris and no one ever laughed at Fenris. Her stomach twisted into a painful knot. She had been the object of his derision before and the thought of enduring that again made her ill. "I hate you," she whispered back.

She yanked on the ribbon, and her medallion came free with more force than expected. Fenris's button arced through the air as she straightened at last. The button hit her shoulder and tumbled down. Into her décolletage.

For one long, awkward moment, no one said anything.

She was aware, horribly aware, of the quiet in Camber's box and distant laughter from Lane's box. Had that awful man seen what had happened? He couldn't have. Could he? The knot in her stomach pulled tighter than ever.

He had. She knew in her soul he had. What else would so amuse Lane and his friends? She remembered, with crystal clarity, all the awful things Fenris had said about her and how happily people had repeated his words to her. She had no polish, a bit dull, and less than attractive, unless one liked a healthy, blowsy sort of girl. She didn't care how vociferously Fenris now denied he'd meant those words. He'd said them, and no one, no one who had been in London at the time, had forgotten.

Fenris held out a hand. "My button, if you please?"

Eugenia smiled sweetly. Poisonously sweetly, she hoped. He only had the upper hand in this acquaintance if she ceded it to him, and she wouldn't. Fenris stood with his back to the stage, hands behind his back, blocking, she realized, any view of her retrieving his button from her bosom. For that, she was grateful. She fished it out and he took it, taking care to hide the exchange from the curious in other boxes. The button stayed on his palm long enough for her to see it was gold and engraved with the family crest. Then he closed his fingers around it and dropped it into a pocket.

From across the stage someone shouted out, "Have you rescued the demmed thing yourself, Fenris?"

She closed her eyes and schooled herself. There was no reason to believe the remark was a comment upon that button, but it was, and she knew, when she opened her eyes, that everyone else within earshot knew it, too. She was as cool as ice. A veritable iceberg. "Hester, do keep Lord Fenris and his father company."

"Yes, Lady Eugenia."

She edged around her chair and exited to the corridor, crowded with people on their way to visit acquaintances or headed for refreshments in one of the saloons or to the retiring rooms, and she joined the river of people. She didn't care where she went as long as she was anywhere but that dratted box. Halfway down the corridor, she stopped under a pool of light from a chandelier and pretended to adjust her gloves. She had no doubt that before the evening was done the story of her and Lord Fenris's button would be on everyone's lips, blown all out of proportion, and with her made ridiculous once again.

Eugenia was aware she was sulking and did not like it in herself. But right now she hated Fenris. She really did. She hated that she'd made a fool of herself with him, and she hated that she wanted to blame him for what had happened in Camber's box when the fault was hers. If she'd allowed him to untangle the ribbon, his button would have stayed attached to his coat.

She tucked herself into a corner and watched people stroll past while she attempted to reconcile herself with the fact that her resentment of Fenris was, in this case, misplaced. Ladies in full evening dress and gentlemen in their most splendid clothes passed by her corner. She admired the jewels on display and wished she had more of her own. Robert had bought her hair combs shortly after they were married, and his combs were in her hair. She had only one ring, and no pearls, no rope of gold beads. No diamonds or rubies. No brooches or earrings. She had only her medallion, which, so far, had brought her not even one perfect lover. Where was the legion of adoring men the medallion's reputed magic was to have falling at her feet, begging for the joy of a single glance from her?

As she stood tucked into the corner, she became aware that she, too, was being watched. More than one gentleman slowed and stared at her as he passed. How many of them had already heard about Fenris and the button? She made sure to look away. She smoothed her hand along her arm and took her time refastening the tiny pearl buttons of her glove. She had to because her fingers trembled.

From somewhere in the crowd, she heard the words *fished his button from her bodice*. Oh, Lord. Her humiliation was complete, and she had only herself to blame. The knowledge made her memory of that awful man's smirk as he took the button from her palm even sharper. Her fault or not, a part of her wished she'd thrown that button in his face.

Gradually, the number of people in the corridor decreased. It was near time for her to return to the box. She didn't want to. She fiddled with her gloves some more. Another gentleman slowed as he walked past where she stood, continued on, then, to her surprise, returned. Eugenia looked steadfastly away. She did not know him.

He bowed to her, and his gaze seemed stuck on her bosom. Lovely. Imagining buttons down there? "Excellent performance tonight, don't you agree? Mozart. Quite the fellow." He aped playing the violin and then fingers moving over a keyboard. "The composer. Wrote the music?"

She did not answer. It was shocking, to be honest, to find herself addressed at all, let alone so familiarly, by a man she did not know.

"Have you hired a box for the evening, ma'am? It can easily get too warm with everyone packed in and every seat occupied." He took a step closer. The way he eyed her bosom made her hate Fenris even more. This was his fault. Why couldn't he have stayed where he was and allowed her to pick up her reticule without assistance? If he had, none of this would have happened. She wouldn't be standing here alone. The stranger came closer. Much too close, and he was smiling at her in a way that made her stomach curl. "One needs to come outside just to breathe, yes?"

She maintained her chilly expression. Surely, he would accept the hint and go on his way. He didn't, though. Instead, he practically sneered at her.

"Come now, even the meanest commodity may speak to a gentleman, if only to settle on terms."

She sucked in a breath, and her stomach dived to the floor. This horrible man had mistaken her for a courtesan.

His gaze swept from her head to her toes and back. "You would enjoy my company. I assure you."

Eugenia tried to walk away, but he blocked her with the simple tactic of taking a half step in whichever direction she went. "Sir," she ground out. "Let me pass."

"Mrs. Bryant?"

Chapter Twelve

FOX CLENCHED HIS HANDS WHEN HE GOT CLOSE enough to see the man who had accosted Eugenia. This was no polite encounter between opera patrons, that was plain. Eugenia was frightened, and the man who had her cornered was leering at her. Until now, he'd thought the adage about anger boiling one's blood had overstated the case. It did not. That aphorism perfectly described his reaction. He was taken aback by the ferocity of his need to protect her from the oaf blocking her way. Through violent means if necessary.

He lengthened his stride, ready and willing to lay hands on the man. Eugenia's head whipped in his direction, and her eyes, wide and so ethereally blue, fixed on him with nothing in them but relief. The man accosting Eugenia leaned only his torso away from her when Fox approached. Why her reaction hadn't cured the fool of his mistake about her gentility mystified him.

"Mrs. Bryant." He needed every ounce of restraint he possessed to maintain an even tone.

She practically lunged toward him, which she was able

to do only because at last the other man took a step back. "Fenris." Her voice shook. "There you are. At last."

For a moment, there was no sign that the stranger recognized her greeting of him as a title of nobility rather than a Christian name or surname. Then the fellow's eyes went wide. Fox took Eugenia's hand in his and kissed the air above her fingers when it was all he could do not to grab the bloody interloper by the coat and throw him into Kingdom Come. Eugenia's arm trembled.

"Fenris." The man's voice cracked at the last syllable.

Fox gave him a cool look.

"Lord Fenris?" He was either drunk or a fool or both. "The Duke of Camber's son?"

With Eugenia's hand still in his, he stood straight. He did not often find that he wanted or needed to impress upon someone the particulars of his rank. Most people knew who he was, and he'd found there was usually little to be gained from the crudeness of insisting on his privileges. Right now, he wanted to grind this man into an acknowledgment. "Yes."

"Well, well, well." The ass looked at Eugenia then at him. He grinned. "Quite a victory for any woman to tempt you from the Incomparable."

Though he itched to use his fists, instead, he addressed Eugenia. "Lady Eugenia. My apologies for being gone longer than I intended. I should never have left your side."

The other man blanched.

Point made.

The stranger was not drunk enough to be insensible to the magnitude of his error, it seemed. Inebriation, however, in no way excused his behavior. Fox looked away from Eugenia and held the man's gaze.

Her fingers tightened around his. "I confess, my lord, I was beginning to worry."

Pale now, the stranger bowed uneasily and said, "Forgive me, my lord. My lady."

Eugenia kept a glacial silence.

"I was mistaken in . . . That is—"

Fox maintained eye contact. How satisfying it would be

to put a fist in his face. His hand twitched. "If you do not make yourself scarce, sir, I shan't answer to the consequences."

"Indeed, sir. Indeed. Apologies. A thousand of them. So sorry to have intruded." He bowed once, then again and made a swift and inelegant departure.

When the fool was gone, Fox continued to hold Eugenia's hand. His anger—not at her—did not diminish. It was all he could do to refrain from pulling her into his arms. "Did he harm you?"

She shook her head, then managed to speak. "No."

"Miss Rendell was concerned by your absence." He was careful to keep a hint of disinterest in his voice. If he had learned anything about Eugenia in the time she'd unbent enough to remain in his presence, it was that she did not take kindly to gentlemen who treated her as if she were mentally incapable. Robert would have taught her to expect that sort of respect from a man who cared for her. "She insisted I find you and bring you back."

She licked her lips. "A moment, if you don't mind."

"Of course not."

Just when Fox believed he might actually convince her to return with him, Lane and his usual companions came around the corner from the direction of their box. The men slowed when they recognized him, and Fox did not think he mistook the malicious gleam in Lane's eye.

Several of the men leaned in to whisper to one another. They slowly walked by, pretending they'd not noticed him. Someone in the middle of the group said *I'd fetch a button from that bosom.*

Fox's anger boiled over. He whirled toward the men, and if not for Eugenia grabbing his arm, he would have launched himself at Lane and his cronies. "Don't. Please. You'll only make it worse."

Lane stopped walking. "My dear Fox."

"You haven't leave to call me that."

Lane's gaze moved between him and Eugenia. "What fascinating company you keep." He made Eugenia an elaborate bow. "Always a delight to see you. Indeed, as others have been so moved to poetry, so am I in your presence. I daresay I'm a better poet than any Scotsman. Hark." He glanced upward, pointing a finger toward the heavens. "She shames the sun, fired o'er with beauty, No man alive resists his duty, to die so sweetly for her eyes, we are gluttons—"

One of the men behind him finished the line sotto voce. "For lost buttons."

Fox clenched a fist. Jesus. What a debacle.

Eugenia smiled. "Why, thank you, Mr. Lane. What delightful verses. Your poetical talent is unbounded." Her fingers tightened on his arm, but she spoke in a pleasant tone that robbed Lane of the delight of seeing his barbs strike home. "You ought to call on us at Spring Street so that we may hear more of your remarkable verses."

Dinwitty bowed again. "Ma'am. Thank you."

Fox speared Lane with a glare that made the man blanch. He wanted to thrash someone, by God. Dinwitty Lane would do as well as anyone.

"I do hope you continue to enjoy the performance." She curtseyed to him. "Good night, sir." While Lane and his friends moved on, she adjusted her gloves.

Fox counted to ten before he spoke in order to be sure he could address her calmly. "You invited him to call?"

"I prefer to keep my enemies close." Her enemies, naturally, included him, and he saw quite clearly she intended that missile for him, too.

"Damn you," he said in a low voice.

She pressed her mouth tightly closed. "Go away."

"As if I'd leave you open to another improper advance. Or untoward remarks by lobster-brained fools." He clapped a hand on the back of his neck, but too late now. The acerbic words were spoken. "Ginny." He drew a breath. "Ginny, my dear heart. There are times you try me beyond my capacity to behave." He inclined his head. "No excuse, I know. My apologies."

She meant to object, he knew it, but all she did was press her lips together and stare at the place where his coat was missing a button. The fabric had torn. "Thank you," she said in a voice so soft he barely heard. "For convincing that man to let me alone."

"You are welcome." He watched her expression shut down. "Ginny," he said. "My love." Her eyes lifted to his, shocked. Well. He didn't care. He truly didn't. "You cannot wander the halls by yourself."

"I am aware."

He forced himself to relax enough that he did not speak more curtly than was wise. "Allow me to escort you back to Camber's box."

"So everyone may wonder what you found while you had your hand down my gown?"

He stiffened. "No such thing happened. Everyone in the box knows it. Camber, Miss Rendell, Lord and Lady Monson. Everyone who was there knows. Including you."

"What does it matter when Mr. Lane spouts poetry to the contrary?"

"No one takes Lane seriously."

"Yes they do. You know they do. Who do you think they'll believe?" He could tell she was fighting tears. He, in return, fought the urge to take her in his arms. She'd never allow it, for one thing. "You know nothing of the power of rumor." Her eyes were a common enough blue, but the fact was he'd always thought they were pretty. Striking in their shape and intensity. She'd always had a way of looking at a man as if she saw through all his pretenses.

"I do, Ginny." This was his doing, her fear of gossip. He'd give anything if that weren't the case. "I promise you, I do."

"If I'd known you'd be here, I would have declined Camber's offer of tickets."

"You wouldn't have."

"I only wanted Hester to be seen in his box." Her lower lip trembled. "She's a wonderful girl, and if there was even one man with half a brain in his head in this awful town she'd be engaged to be married already. But no one sees that about her. She's amusing and generous and kind and intelligent and there's not a better person alive than Hester."

"I daresay my father is aware of that."

"As if that makes any difference. He's not a suitor, Fenris. It's the men your age who won't see."

"I think you're mistaken."

"And now that business with the button. I've only made everything worse." She looked away, a hand pressed to her cheek. "I want to go home. Please take me home, Fox."

He touched her arm. "Come now, what will people say if you don't return?"

"I don't care."

"Will you deprive that plant-mad girl of the opportunity to discuss botany with my father? Never." He adopted a jovial expression. "Confess it, tonight you were hoping—"

Her chin lifted. "Dreading."

"—I would arrive and save you from listening to their interminable conversation about budding and fertilizer and the dangers of overwatering."

Her eyes flashed. Disagreeing with him agreed with her. "Your father has been perfectly delightful tonight. I think it's charming the way he humors Hester."

"Humors her?" He threw a hand into the air, and though he knew better than to let his emotions get the better of him, that's what happened. "You willfully misunderstand, Ginny."

She gave him an icy stare. "I certainly do not."

"He's enamored of her, for God's sake. He's bloody well making a fool of himself over a girl who dreams of root systems. Are you blind?"

"No, I am not. And no, he isn't." She inched away from him. "Enamored of her, I mean. Or making a fool of himself. That's nonsense. He's your *father*. He's the Duke of Camber."

"For pity's sake, woman."

She drew herself up with an astonishing primness. "She's the daughter he's always wanted."

"Good God. You can't be serious."

"I think the attention he pays her is sweet. There's no romance, Fenris. That's absurd. He doesn't see her that way."

"Every man alive thinks about the women he meets in a carnal way."

"He's old enough to be her father."

"I assure you, Camber has thought it about Miss Rendell."

She crossed her arms underneath her bosom, still with her chin lifted. "Have you?"

"Of course."

Her eyes widened.

"On a purely theoretical level, of course, but I assure you I have had such thoughts."

Her cheeks turned pink. "Even if I grant you that, *she* does not think it. As far as I can tell she does not think about any man that way. That's the problem. She simply refuses to think of any man as someone she might marry." She gave him a look of part speculation and part exasperation. "Though she did once remark that she finds you handsome."

"Don't throw her in my way." He shook his head. He'd not stand for that. Not from her. "Don't think it. Don't dream of it. It won't work."

"She'd do very well for you."

"I don't require any assistance, thank you, in finding a wife."

The corridor continued to slowly empty of people. Not a crush anymore. Only a crowd. Her mouth firmed. "You can avoid my deadly aim with Hester simply by failing to appear in our path." She tugged on her gloves. "How odd that such a tactic would not occur to you. It's not so hard to avoid matchmaking mamas, after all. You've been doing it successfully for years."

"I fully intend to be married."

Her eyes flashed again. "Here. Since you won't allow someone to introduce you to a lovely, sweet, intelligent, and worthy girl you don't in any way deserve." She drew off the medallion she wore and pressed it into his hand, closing his fingers over it. "You need this more than I do."

He opened his fingers and stared at the carved face of

Cupid on this side. He turned it over. A bow and arrow. How precious. "You're right. Quite right. I am in sore need of such magic as this is said to possess."

"I am happy to be of assistance, my lord."

Danger lurked in the treacle of her reply, and he decided to meet that head-on. He gave her a bow that reeked of irony. "Thank you. You are too, too kind."

"I hope it works for you better than it has for me."

While she watched, he discarded the ribbon and attached the medallion to his watch chain to hang beside the fob he already wore. "There."

"You'll be married before the New Year. Congratulations."

"I don't see why not." He patted the medallion and grinned at her. "I expect now I'll be trampled by hordes of suitable candidates for my heart."

"Your barren heart."

He tapped the left side of his chest. "I'll miss the echo when I've found my heart's desire."

Her mouth quivered, and she glanced away. "Stop it."

"Whatever do you mean?"

"Don't amuse me. It spoils my mood." When she looked back, her attention skipped to the lapel of his coat.

Fox touched the place where his button ought to have been. "Are you happy? I have several engagements tonight, and now I must rearrange everything in order to return home and change. There. Does that sufficiently darken your mood?"

Her splendid bosom heaved, just the once, alas. Her expression softened and became, dare he think it, contrite. "Yes. Very much, sir. I am sorry for the loss of your button."

"I should hope so." He tugged on his coat. "It's ruined."

"It was my fault."

"Does it hurt much to admit your fault?"

"Yes. It does. Awful man." She held out a hand. "Give it to me."

"My coat? No. Why?"

"Everyone who sees you will think the button is still down my bodice or believe it's true how you retrieved it." She opened her reticule and took out a tortoiseshell etui. "I'll sew the thing back on myself. God forbid you should be even a minute late to your engagement with incomparably pretty ballet girls."

"Ballet girls?" His heart fell, since not for a moment did he suppose her use of that particular description was anything but deliberate.

She closed her fingers around the box and met his gaze. "I know what a serious matter your social calendar is when there are ballet girls involved."

"I'm sure I don't know what you mean."

"I've been married. I know perfectly well what men do with women." She flushed, because, yes, as she'd amply proved with him and appeared now to be recalling, she did know a thing or two.

He let out a breath. "Ginny. I do not have a mistress. Not Lady Tyghe and not an Italian ballet dancer, either."

"Not even an incomparable one?"

"Not presently."

She gave him a skeptical look. "But you did once."

"I did." He sighed. "She was extremely beautiful, I don't deny that. I suppose she still is, but beauty is not enough to continue in a relationship. Not for me, at any rate." He cocked his head. "Why so curious?"

"I'm not." Her cheeks pinked up again. "It's just that everyone talks about her as if she's some sort of prize, and you were the winner."

He touched the underside of her chin. "What do you want to know about us?"

"Nothing."

"Her name is Addolorata."

She firmed her mouth in an obvious attempt to stop herself from smiling. "Did you call her Addy?"

If she was amused, so be it. He knew an opportunity when one presented itself. "I called her darling."

"*Darling.*" She looked around, but there was no one near

enough to overhear. The corridor was all but empty. "I shall never be able to hear that word again without thinking of you and Addolorata."

"Indeed? I shan't be able to use that word without thinking of you."

Her mouth twitched, and he was struck by what he could only call lust. "Don't be wicked."

"Why not?"

She met his eyes, and for a heartbeat, he had no breath. "Because it's not proper."

"What would be proper enough for you?"

She sent him a killing look.

What wouldn't he give to die in her arms again? "Come now, you must admit that is a legitimate worry on my part. Both in general and in the specific. I ought to know what I am to call you."

"What about 'my lady'?"

He feigned astonishment. "Do you mean to tell me that when I am in the throes of passion with you, you would prefer I call out, 'my lady'? You should have told me that."

"Throes of passion." Her eyebrows drew together. She held up a hand. She was laughing, and the joyous sound made his heart swell. "You really can't call me *darling*. I'm sorry, but I'm likely to assume you mean your incomparable Addolorata. No, you'll have to cry out, 'my love' or perhaps 'goddess.'"

"Goddess?"

"Yes." She smiled, and that nearly killed him, too. "You'll think so, I promise you."

"I don't doubt that." He turned so they faced each other. She was still smiling. "I'll call you Ginny."

"No one calls me that."

"All the better." He wanted her so badly, he ached. "I won't worry that I've reminded you of some other lover."

"Enough of this, Fenris." She looked around again. "You ought to behave."

"I don't see why. You like me best when I don't."

She wriggled her fingers at him. "The button."

"As you command." He reached into his pocket for it. "You carry needle and thread, do you?"

Her expression suggested she did not think much of his intellect. "Half the women in London carry needle and thread. A lady never knows when she might find herself, or another, in need of a repair. Mind you, the thread won't be a perfect match, but it will do so that you may continue your evening uninterrupted without resorting to blaming me for your imperfection." She pointed to a bench on the opposite side of the corridor.

"We ought to go to one of the saloons. We'll be more comfortable there." He didn't give her a chance to object. He simply took her arm and started walking. "I'll buy you some refreshment while you atone for the error of your ways."

Chapter Thirteen

HE WAS ALONE WITH EUGENIA, IF NOT LITERALLY, then at least in possession of her undivided attention, and that was progress on a scale he hadn't dreamed of making with her in a public place. They did not speak while he escorted her to one of the smaller public rooms on the second floor. A few patrons walked the corridors, and as they passed one of the larger saloons, he saw that a good many more people of quality remained ensconced there rather than in the auditorium.

Eugenia kept her hand on his arm, and he, so daring of him, placed his hand over hers while they walked. Their encounter with that fool in the corridor and with Dinwitty Lane had, he felt, changed yet again the tenor of their relations. He reminded himself that where she was concerned, nothing was assured. But he still felt as if he had a claim on her that he had not had before.

Her opera gown was white silk with an overdress of blue that was cut away and swept back to just above the level of her knees. In the back, the blue material flowed into a modest train, though she was still required to lift it, from time to time. She hadn't Miss Rendell's bounty, but her bosom was well curved. Without her medallion, she lacked jewelry around her throat, and that, oddly enough, only emphasized her bosom. She'd never been one to wear jewels; even tonight, at an event at which a woman often wore her best pieces, she wore only a pair of hair combs. It would be, he reflected, his pleasure to buy her jewels. One day, God willing, that would be appropriate.

He saw her to a seat in one of the smaller saloons, at a plush bench with a table drawn near, then ordered a coffee for himself and a chocolate for her.

He rejoined her, sitting beside her on the bench. Close, but not too close. He wanted to take her somewhere private, an inn, a hotel, his own home on Upper Brook Street, the Turkish room at Bouverie, if she could be convinced of that, and then prove the spark between them could be fanned into fire.

While they waited for one of the footmen to bring their refreshments, she took out her tortoiseshell etui and deftly threaded a needle with dark thread. He had the rare luxury of watching her without having to hide that he was doing so. Though he'd been attracted to her from the day he first saw her, maturity and experience of life had only improved her looks. He'd been such a bloody damned fool about her.

"This won't take long." She tied a knot in the end of the thread. A footman brought the coffee and the chocolate, which she eyed when the servant placed it on their table. She waited until the man, having pocketed the coin Fox gave him, departed.

"Is something amiss?" He crossed one leg over the other and stretched his arm along the back of their seat. Her gown molded her bosom, and he was viciously aware of her size and shape. God, what he would do if they were alone now, and she was naked.

She sniffed. "I only drink chocolate in the morning."

"You can make an exception." Must he always take the wrong tack with her? Because, of course, his high-handed reply brought a familiar stiffness to her demeanor. He wondered if he did such things because he enjoyed maneuvering himself into a position of dominance over her. He did like winning. He expected to win, and he worked hard to make sure he did so more often than not. With her, perhaps he did enjoy the way she refused to give over to him. A worthy opponent made victory the sweeter.

"Chocolate in the evening makes me ill." She drew his cup toward her. "I'd rather have coffee. Do you mind?"

"I do." That response he made with full knowledge of the effect it would have on her. Which was to bristle at him, eyes flashing. He schooled himself to stillness, but when she looked at him like that he wanted to put her on her back and fuck her until neither of them could breathe.

"You should have asked me what I wanted." She pushed her chocolate to him before she picked up his coffee and drank from it. "Mm. This is excellent."

"The part of the man does not suit you." He couldn't help provoking her, but what else could he do? He knew damned well that if he attempted a traditional courtship, she'd resist with all her considerable will. She'd turn to someone like Aigen purely to provoke him.

She made a face. Eugenia, it seemed to him, delighted in provoking him. "I am an independent woman now. I play whatever part I wish."

"Do you think so?"

"Why not?" She returned him a serene gaze. He rather thought she'd learned that particular reaction from Miss Rendell. "If I prefer to choose my own beverages according to what *I* should like at the time, then I shall, and you cannot gainsay me."

He contemplated taking the coffee back and placing his mouth exactly where hers had been. She'd probably pour the chocolate on his head if he did that. "I see all now."

"At last." She drank more coffee. His coffee.

"My mistake with you from the start was a failure to treat you as if you were a man."

"One mistake among many." Her white cashmere shawl draped down to her elbows, so carelessly sensual. He wanted to kiss her from her shoulders to the tops of her gloves, and then peel off the gloves and kiss his way down to her fingertips.

"First you take my coffee, next you'll demand a cigar and a bottle of gin."

"Why shouldn't I?" She lifted her chin. "Perhaps I shall. A little blue ruin in the evening might be just the thing."

"It would serve you right if I got you drunk and took scandalous advantage."

She stared at him, wide-eyed, then burst out laughing and dropped the needle on her lap. While she searched for and found it, she said, "Dear Lord, you can be amusing when you wish."

"I am a man of varied talents, as you will discover." Besides the two of them, there was hardly anyone left in the saloon. Servants, an old man who'd fallen asleep in a chair by the fire, and two other gentlemen. Not of the Ton, he thought. The next act must have already started. He plucked at the tear in his coat. "Speaking of your feminine accomplishments?"

"I'll have to repair the hole first." She squinted at his lapel, glanced at him, then looked back at his coat. "I won't darn it tightly. That way your valet can easily pick out this thread and use a better one."

"Perhaps I'll just buy a new coat." The last remaining gentlemen paid up and walked out of the saloon, leaving them with the servants and snoring old man.

"Wasteful of you." She took one more sip of his coffee before she scooted close enough to slip her hand underneath his lapel. He uncrossed his legs and turned his torso toward her. "Keep your head back."

"Anything you desire of me, darling." His position, quite happily, as it turned out, gave him additional opportunity to study her bosom. She hadn't an extravagant shape, but the curve of her breasts was in no way inadequate, and he was a man who did like a woman's breasts. Notwithstanding his appreciation of her in evening dress, he wanted to see her nude, to hold her naked in his arms—if they were in the

Turkish room at Bouverie, all the better—and suckle and lick and discover where she was most sensitive. Did she prefer a gentle touch? Did she mind a rougher hand? God help him if she did.

He prayed she might like that.

Her needle flashed, and he amused himself with imagining her naked breasts in his hands and mouth and reflected images of him touching her in just that way. While she stitched, he tapped the medallion now hanging from his watch chain with his other fob. "To think such a small thing brought us to this pass."

"What do you mean?" She used a tiny pair of scissors to snip the thread then tied another knot in the thread hanging from the needle.

He smoothed a finger over the surface. The metal was warm. "This. Cousin Lily's medallion. The magic drew me out of Camber's box in time to prevent you from a very uncomfortable situation."

Still concentrating on her needlework, she didn't look up, but he saw her forehead crease. "The magic isn't protective." He could see a smile curving her mouth. "The medallion brings lovers together, as you well know."

Fox took a moment before he replied. "I believe that was my point. I wonder how soon you'll be inexorably drawn to me. Again."

She continued to sew. "I fear it's broken or has lost its magic. I've worn it diligently and slept with it beneath my pillow, yet I've not been thrown together with a gentleman who makes my heart race, met no mysterious strangers. No beaux send me letters declaring their love. No dreams of my future husband."

"What?" He waggled his eyebrows. "The medallion causes you to dream of your future beloved, and you've not once dreamed of me? You're right. The deuced thing is broken."

"My dear man, I don't have dreams about you. I have nightmares."

"You wound me."

She laughed.

"What sort of man could win your heart?" She hesitated, and he cursed his clumsiness because he knew the answer. She had found the man she loved. "Someone like Robert," he said softly. "Honorable. Amiable. Intelligent. A man everyone likes. Never out of sorts. Never cross."

"Not never." She smiled—sadly, he fancied. "But yes, rarely."

"I am sorry for your loss. You know that, I hope."

Eugenia looked away, then back at him, and he saw the sadness there. "He used to leave me notes to find. I never knew where or when, and some he'd hidden weeks or even months before, if he'd tucked them somewhere clever. I'd open a drawer and there'd be a scrap of paper, and he'd have written a poem for me or related his memory of a time I'd made him smile or laugh or weep."

"That sounds like him." He could see Robert penning a note like that, then hiding it for his wife to find some future day.

She went back to sewing. He caught a flash of gold as she held the button to his coat and began to reattach it. One day, he thought. One day, the two of them would once again sit in just such a domestic scene, but in his version of the future they were husband and wife. The image felt so real to him, so inevitable that he had to remind himself no such thing had yet happened. She finished with the button and brought out her tiny scissors again.

"He wouldn't want you to be alone. Robert." He paused until he was certain his voice wouldn't sound thick. "He wouldn't want that for you."

She snipped the thread and sat back, eyeing his coat. She gave his chest a pat, with no thought, sadly, to the intimacy of the gesture. "No."

Impolitic words rose up. *Marry me, Ginny. Marry me, and you won't be alone.* He did not say them.

She sighed. "For a very long time after he died, I thought I'd never love another man."

"And now?" His heart gave a hard thump. Had Aigen pressed his suit with her while he was away?

"I know I'll never love anyone the way I loved Robert." She packed away her sewing kit, and his eyes followed the line of her cheek, the sweep of her throat. With a sideways glance at him, a careless one, she said, "I'd love another man in a different way." She dropped her etui in her reticule before she looked up. "Because he would be a different man, you understand. Not Robert. Someone else, and he would be worthy of me and I worthy of him in an entirely different way."

He saw all his hopes for the future turning to ash, because she wasn't ready to see him as her husband. What if she was thinking of Aigen? "You intend to remarry?"

She gave him a quick grin. "I'd like to." Her smile faded. "In the vaguest sort of way." Her hands fell to her lap and he let out a relieved breath. "I liked being married; I would like that again. But I've no one in mind."

"No?" He heard himself speaking even as a part of him warned him he was making a mistake. Too late. The words he'd held back before flew into the air between them. He took her hand in his. "Then marry me. Marry me, Ginny, and we'll learn how best to love each other."

She folded her hands together, amused, and he didn't know whether to be grateful, insulted, or crushed. "Now, why would I do that?" She touched the medallion hanging from his watch. "You've this now. It's inevitable that you'll find the woman of your heart."

"True."

She touched his other fob, the one he'd already had fastened to his watch, and turned it over. His initials were embroidered on the front of the rectangle. On the other side, the one she was looking at now, appeared the words *With Love*. "I've never seen you without this."

"It was a gift."

"From someone you cared for deeply. Who was she? Not Addolorata, surely. Or was it?"

"My mother." He saw she'd not expected that. "She made

that for me shortly before she passed on. I was quite young at the time. An infant." He touched it, too, and their fingers brushed. "Camber gave it to me when I went away to school."

She looked into his face and, slowly, caressed his cheek. He held his breath. "I wish you wouldn't make it so difficult to dislike you."

This was an evening for indiscretion, for more impolitic words spilled from him. "Come back to Bouverie with me. We'll visit the Turkish room and finish what we began."

"I'd best get back to Hester."

He tightened his fingers around hers. "Then, meet me there after this interminable opera is over."

"Fenris."

"I'll give you a key."

Chapter Fourteen

❧

As she followed Fenris back to Camber's box, Eugenia lost her hold on the edge of her shawl and had to twist back to catch the trailing end. By the time she'd done that, she had to hurry to catch him up and then walk faster than she liked to keep pace with his determined stride. She took two steps to every one of his. "Fenris."

"Don't call me that." The words were sharp enough to cut. "To you, when we are alone, I am Fox."

She put a hand on his arm and pulled. "My lord."

He whirled on her. "What?"

She took a breath, and his eyes flicked to her bosom. She did not want him to be angry with her, but she wasn't about to dance to his tune, either. "Please slow down."

He stared at her, hostile, and she glared back, breathing with her mouth open. He flushed. "Forgive me." He started walking again, more slowly this time.

"Why are you angry? Because I won't do that with you?"

"I am not angry." He stopped walking and briefly closed his eyes. When he opened them, he spoke softly and without directly meeting her gaze. "I never say the right thing to you. I, who've never failed to seduce any woman I choose, never say what I ought where you are concerned."

After a moment spent unable to parse out what he meant, she frowned hard. "I suspect your powers of seduction are rarely tested."

He glanced at her, and that was uncertainty she saw in his gaze. One of the candles in the wall sconce guttered out and left them in a dimmer light. "Is that a compliment or an insult?"

"Both." She touched the button she'd reattached to his coat and wished she understood him better. She wished never to have to guess what he was thinking.

"You prove my point. You say you want a proper man— some vague fellow who meets some even vaguer standard, one I'll warrant you couldn't articulate for all the gold in Christendom." His eyes darkened, and what she saw there made her think of mirrored rooms and wicked, wicked pleasure. "But, darling Ginny, you respond best to me when I'm not proper enough. By God, you do. Don't deny it."

She didn't dare answer. She was very much afraid he was right. She didn't want him to be, but he was.

He let out an exasperated sound. "Would you come away with me if Miss Rendell weren't here?"

"You're impossible." She dropped his arm and walked away. He followed. How had things got so out of her control? "We aren't lovers, you and I."

He came even with her and stopped her with an arm to her elbow. All her butterflies came back. "With all due respect, that's a lie."

"There is a difference between a single past encounter and a mutual expectation of future ones."

He snorted.

Eugenia plucked at her shawl. She was out of her depth here. "I can't be your lover."

"Why?"

"Because I couldn't love you." The wall behind him was white, but fingers from all the hands that had touched the surface had left smudges on that expanse of paint.

"How do you know?"

They were at the stairs that led to the entrance to Camber's box, and she headed up them. Fenris took two steps up to her one, turned, and blocked her way. Remarkably, nothing changed in his expression. He seemed as calm, and two breaths from bored, as ever, but he bit off the syllables of her name. "Mrs. Bryant. How do you know?"

She hoped by all that was holy he couldn't tell she was taken aback, both at what she'd said and by his reaction to it. Somewhere along the way, she'd lost the keen edge of her dislike. He'd defended Hester against Dinwitty Lane. He'd made her laugh. Even tonight. When he came into a room, every man but him disappeared. "I know it. That's all."

"You think I still hold you in contempt."

"No, I don't." She tried to walk past him but he stopped her with just the sound of his voice.

"For God's sake, Ginny." He kept one hand on the wall, but his fingers curled into a fist. "You were married to my best friend, the finest man I've ever known." Anger crept into his dark and velvet words. "Do you really think I could despise the woman he loved?"

She regarded him in silence. He waited her out, waited for some acknowledgment of that confession. What was she to say to that after so many years of resenting him for the awful things he'd said about her? "I don't know what you felt then. I know only what you said. But that does not signify. It doesn't. I'm not that young girl. You're not that young man. That's all past now. They were your words, and I didn't know the man who said them any more than you knew the girl you said them about." She went around him and started up the stairs.

He grabbed her arm and joined her on the step. Every bit of the charm he'd shown earlier was gone. "I do not despise you. You do know that, don't you?"

She stared directly into his face. She wasn't afraid of him, not at all, and she might have been of another man. "Listen to us. Fox. This is ridiculous. Let's not fight. All that's in the past. It hardly matters anymore."

"Agreed."

She didn't trust his quick assent, but she summoned a smile anyway. "Excellent."

"Yes." He came down one step. "And given that, why can't we be lovers in the present?"

For a moment, words failed her completely and all she managed to say was, "Because."

"Why, Ginny?"

She plucked out some of the very few emotions she did understand among all those swirling in her. "I would feel as if I were betraying Robert. That's why."

"Us being lovers betrays Robert? But not your remarrying some vague, dull fellow?"

"I don't know you. I don't know you at all. Not really."

He moved closer, effectively pinning her to the wall unless she chose to push him. She didn't, though. Why not? Why on earth not? "What do you want to know about me?"

"I won't be bullied."

"Bullied? Hardly. I've asked a fair question. What do you want to know about me? Besides that I adore your hand on my cock?" He leaned closer. "God, Ginny, don't do this. Don't push me away just because you're afraid of what you'll feel."

She tugged her arm free and moved briskly up the stairs to the next corridor. He caught up, and she hurried toward the entrance to the box. In two long strides he was in front of her again. "Whatever you want. It's yours."

"Fenris. Don't."

"Let's go somewhere private, you and I." His eyes pinned her again. He lifted a hand, and she was momentarily breathless with the possibility that he would touch her, and why would she feel like that? She was mad to care an atom for Fenris. Mad, mad, mad.

"You wouldn't fall in love with me. You know you wouldn't." The walls she'd constructed to contain her opinion of him continued their slow erosion, and she was helpless to stop it from happening.

He shook his head, smiling. "No, my darling Ginny, I

wouldn't fall in love with you. It's too late to worry about the barren landscape of my heart. I'm already in love with you."

"You aren't."

"Ginny." He used that dark silk voice, and chills raced up and down her spine from all that she heard in the way her name left his mouth.

"It's too soon for me. I can't fall in love yet. Not with you."

"Why not me?"

"Not with anyone."

He backed away, but he was still watching her. Too carefully, she thought, and it was flattering and appalling to think why. "What are we to do? You and I?"

"Return to our seats and enjoy the rest of the performance?"

"Very well." He shoved his hands in his pockets and leaned a shoulder against the wall. He sent a lopsided grin her way. Her heart eased at the sight. She didn't want him to be angry with her. "Or, we could stay here."

"No, we couldn't."

He looked around. "I have been admiring this corridor. The stairs are of an extraordinary craftsmanship." That made her laugh, and he continued to grin at her. "If this fine corridor is not to your taste, come away with me." He tipped his head her direction. "I'll take you someplace wicked. Indulge your every whim."

"Be serious."

"I am." He pulled his hands free of his pockets. "If the Turkish room is out of the question, then I'll take you to Upper Brook Street."

"Not now." She walked past him, hardly able to believe she wasn't sending him away, set down. "For heaven's sake. Not here and not now."

"Later, then," he said, joining her.

"Are you mad?"

"An evening between gentlemen, my word of honor on it. I'll give you whisky, blue ruin if you prefer. We'll smoke cigars, talk about the races, and lay wagers we can't afford to pay."

"You're impossible."

"No. I'm irresistible."

"You're not." She looked at him sideways. He was right, blast him. He was irresistible.

"I am. You can play the man's part with me. Until I take you to bed, that is."

She stifled a laugh. "Honestly."

"Do you like to have your ears kissed? The back of your neck?"

"If we were lovers, it wouldn't last."

His eyes twinkled with good humor. "My stamina is legendary."

"Behave."

"I'd rather not."

"Look at the evidence. Whatever happens, one of us will spoil it."

This time, he rolled his eyes. "Propriety never works with you. Make no mistake, Ginny, I mean to get you naked and on your back. Your hands and knees, too. Astride me. Up against the wall." She clapped her hands over her ears for all the good it did. "You'll know something about me that's real and true before we do all that and more. I mean to have you screaming my name without any of that vagueness you talked about. You'll know exactly and precisely who's bringing you to pleasure."

"Stop. You're impossible."

A gentleman came around the corner, heading for the stairs to the upper boxes. Fenris took a step back, which was an uncomfortable reminder that he had been standing too near. And of how strongly she'd responded to his being so close. When the man was out of sight, Fenris moved to her side, and she couldn't feel the floor beneath her feet anymore. "Come away with me."

Her mouth opened, but no words came out. She'd never heard a man speak as if the words themselves were made of passion, but that was what she felt as Fenris spoke to her now, and that, that shocked her to her toes.

"Can you feel it? The heat? The desire between us? The air between us threatens to combust. I want more of that, don't you? I want that fire between us. Don't deny what you felt with me before. Don't pretend you don't want to know where that sort of desire will lead us."

Her stomach took flight. Which was absolutely unaccountable. He tapped a finger against the wall. She leaned closer to him, and his eyes flicked to hers, not a careless look at all. The intensity shook her, touched her in a way that made her heart roll over in her chest.

He grabbed her upper arm and pulled her toward him. "I want that quick fuck. And a long, slow one, if you'll have that, too."

If any other man had said such a thing to her, she would have slapped him or simply frozen him into silence. She stared at him longer than was polite, and he stayed where he was, eyes fixed on her. He clenched his jaw. They were close enough to the stage that she could hear conversation from the auditorium and the sound of music. He released her and put a hand on the wall above her shoulder. "I'm good at fucking, as you will discover."

She stared at him. "Yes. I'm sure you are."

"I'll make you feel. I'll tell you secrets about me. Things I've told no one else. Have I shocked you?"

"No." Her breath caught in her throat, and she was horrifically aroused.

The tension left his upper body, and he pushed off the wall, though he stayed close to her. He smiled like a cat that had got the cream. "I apologize if I've offended you."

"I don't know if you have." She tilted her chin. "I don't understand you."

"You don't want to like me, I know, but perhaps"—his fingers swooped in to brush the side of her head, just one hand, and just the lightest of touches—"perhaps you should stop trying so hard to dislike me."

Chapter Fifteen

Two days later. After dinner at the home of Lord and Lady Baring.

TONIGHT, EUGENIA HAD MANAGED THE MINOR miracle of getting Hester dressed and away from her violets early enough that they had not arrived appallingly late for dinner, as was the usual case with their engagements. At the moment, Hester was taking her turn at the piano. She sat with a graceless plop and kicked at the hem of her gown so as to touch the pedal with her slipper. Edward Fraser, Lady Baring's second eldest son, a naval lieutenant home on leave, sat beside Hester with a good deal more grace, his hands poised over the keys. Lady Baring, as it happened, stood beside Eugenia.

Dinner was long over, yet people continued to arrive and crowd Lady Baring's saloon. Unexpectedly, the back of Eugenia's neck prickled with awareness. She ignored her goose-pimpling flesh and forced herself to pay attention to Lady Baring while keeping an eye on Hester. She resisted the urge to lay a hand on her nape.

A commotion interrupted Hester and Lieutenant Fraser as they were beginning to play. Edward nudged Hester just in time, and they sat a moment, waiting for the butler to announce the newest arrivals. Eugenia turned to look when Hester beamed.

Camber. And Fenris. She ought to have known. The duke stood just inside the door, surveying the room. When he saw Hester, he brightened. Fenris stood beside him, his hands clasped behind his back, eyes sweeping the room. Eugenia knew precisely the moment when he saw her. Her breath hitched.

The announcements were made and the commotion attending the appearance of Camber and Fenris died down. At the piano, Hester said, "Ready?"

Lieutenant Fraser nodded and the two launched into Johann Christian Bach's four-handed Sonata in F major. Conversation slowly stopped as Baring's guests realized they were hearing something extraordinary. Hester sparkled, and Lieutenant Fraser more than kept up his part. Their fingers flew along the keys, and their bodies moved in concert with the demands of the piece, leaning together, moving away, crossing arms over the keyboard.

Lady Baring said with a touch more surprise than she ought to have, "Heavens. She's quite good."

"Yes." Eugenia couldn't have been any prouder than if she'd been Hester's mother. "So is your son."

"We've missed his playing while he's been to sea."

When the two were done with their musical selection, they sat with their hands above the keys, looking at each other, both with broad smiles as they took in the enthusiastic applause and requests for an encore. Lieutenant Fraser helped Hester to her feet so they could acknowledge the accolades. He held her hand while she curtseyed, and he bowed, and they grinned at each other. Hester's smile transformed her in that way that made her looks immaterial to anyone who was paying attention. This, this was why Eugenia had been so certain of Hester's eventual success. For all her modest looks, Hester absolutely shone. How could anyone fail to love her?

The lieutenant lifted Hester's hand and bowed over it again. It seemed at last that someone had noticed.

Lady Baring snapped open her fan. Her attention was on her son and Hester. "Her father knows Camber, is that not right? A longtime friend of the family, I'm told."

"Yes. Her brother and Lord Fenris are friends, as well."

"And she has your friendship."

"She does."

"A connection to two dukes." Lady Baring continued her thoughtful consideration of Hester. "Her mother, I understand, is one of the Gloucester Percys."

"Yes."

"A lovely girl in her way." She glanced at Eugenia. "Our Edward would be quite a catch for her."

Eugenia acknowledged that with a curtsey. "That's so. But he'd be fortunate to have her, Lady Baring."

"She's made a bit of a splash. A girl of such talents, and Miss Rendell is—" She pursed her lips.

"Unique?"

"Yes." Lady Baring smiled, and to Eugenia's great relief, there was warmth there. "Precisely my thought."

"Your son is very handsome. And accomplished."

"He's his father's good looks." Lady Baring tapped her fan on Eugenia's arm and smiled. "It's time he settled down."

Hester was now on the opposite side of the room, not far from where Fenris stood with Lord Aigen. She had a knack, Hester did, for making a friend of everyone, and she was doing so now. A dozen men and several young ladies surrounded her, including Dinwitty Lane. Baring's eldest son was among them, too, doing his best to cut out his brother. She couldn't help thinking that Hester and Baring's eldest would be quite a match.

As she watched Hester, she saw Lady Tyghe cross the room toward Fenris. Their greeting, when it occurred, was polite. Lady Tyghe was just the sort of beauty she'd always thought a man like Fenris best appreciated. He'd never have called that beautiful, languid woman blowsy.

"Shall I speak to Edward?" Lady Baring tapped Eugenia's arm again. "A hint or two might not be amiss."

Across the room, Lady Tyghe practically draped herself

on Fenris. He did not look pleased. "I'm not sure it's wise when they've only just met."

"I think it would do no harm to let him know we approve of her."

"I'll defer to your judgment, Lady Baring." Camber was now heading in Hester's direction, and Eugenia's heart sank at the thought of the two of them doing nothing but talking of plants. Somehow, she didn't think Lieutenant Fraser would find the subject fascinating.

Lady Baring's attention moved past her. "She is a favorite of Camber's, isn't she?"

"Like a daughter to him." Eugenia gave Lady Baring a broad smile. "It's really very sweet."

"Yes." Lady Baring turned her head, and Eugenia followed her look. Lord Aigen and Fenris were heading their way. She did not see Lady Tyghe, and found she was inordinately pleased by that. Lady Baring offered her hand to Fenris when the two men arrived.

Aigen grinned when Fenris had done bowing over her hand. "The two most beautiful women in London." He bowed over Lady Baring's hand, too. "You are radiant this evening. And here is the lovely Lady Eugenia." Aigen clapped Fenris on the back. "Confess the truth, Fenris, have you ever seen two such beautiful women?"

"I daresay I have not."

"Good evening, my lords." Eugenia smoothed her skirts because it gave her an excuse to look away from Fenris. When she finished, however, Fenris was holding out his hand to her.

Instinctively she put her fingers on his. Because that was what a lady did when a gentleman greeted her. Because this was Fenris and she liked him better than was safe. Her reaction to the contact was immediate. A shiver shot through her and whirled in her belly before it settled in the vicinity of her knees. He tightened his fingers around hers.

Lady Baring looked from Fenris to her. "Lord Aigen," she said. "I'm quite parched. Will you take me to fetch a glass of orgeat?"

"Delighted." Aigen bowed.

"It's been lovely speaking with you, Lady Eugenia." Lady Baring extended a hand to Aigen. "Shall we?"

Lady Baring's departure left Eugenia and Fenris in a silence that was not as awkward as it ought to have been considering the way her pulse raced. She drew her hand from his and waved her fan underneath her chin. Would she really agree to become his lover? The thought took her breath. "Lady Baring thinks her son ought to marry Hester."

"Does she?" His eyes stayed on her, and she lost herself in them.

Good Lord, she couldn't even recall what she had been about to say, and she only just managed to stop herself from telling him his eyes were the prettiest she'd ever seen on a man.

He cocked his head. "It's too warm here. Don't you agree?"

He took her arm and led her toward one of the exits. "I would not mind a breath of fresh air."

They ended up outside where a terrace led to a modest lawn. Much smaller than the one at Bouverie. Fenris leaned against the low wall that marked the boundary between the terrace and the lawn. He studied her.

She folded her fan and let it dangle from her wrist.

"What?" Fenris asked.

Eugenia closed her eyes and tried to make sense of her feelings. She failed. Her emotions were a jumble that left her uncertain about everything. She touched her chest. "I don't know what's wrong with me."

"There's nothing wrong with you." He spoke in a low voice, the one that always sent a shiver down her spine, but it was the kindness with which he spoke that brought a lump to her throat.

"I've been in a fog for so long, Fenris. I didn't feel anything, and now I do and it's your fault. I don't know if I want this. I don't like you. You know I don't." She lifted her hands in a gesture of futility. "I used to not like you."

"I am aware."

"I never felt this way about Robert. I mean, I did at the start, when I wasn't sure how he felt about me, but I was never uncertain about my feelings, only about his. I never teetered between hating him and liking him. Never once. I dislike this ambiguity. Intensely."

He tipped his head to one side and smiled. "Come get drunk with me."

"Don't laugh at me."

"I'm not laughing at you."

"You are."

"Believe me, it's at my own expense."

"It's absurd. The two of us."

He held out a hand. "Come here."

She went to him. When she was close enough, she touched the medallion he now wore as a fob. "All the young ladies sighed when you came in. They adore you."

"The stampede has begun." He tapped the medallion. "It looks well enough here, don't you think? Aigen is mad with envy." He tugged on her hand and brought her close. Too close. "I think of you whenever I see it."

She propped a hand on his chest and pushed away. "Impossible man."

"That's so." He let her go. "Make whatever excuse you need to take your leave and see Hester home," he said. "I'll wait for you at the mews behind your house."

Her breath caught in her throat and ruined her attempt at nonchalance. "Why?"

"Why do you think? We're going to get drunk together and tell each other our deepest, darkest secrets."

Chapter Sixteen

Four hours later. No. 25 Upper Brook Street.

"THIS ISN'T BOUVERIE."

"No. It's not." Fox dug the key from his pocket but kept his other hand at Eugenia's back. As if that would keep her from changing her mind. She touched the numbers painted on the wall beside the door. He closed his fingers around the key. "The Dukes of Camber own the whole of this street and the six or seven surrounding streets. Eight years ago, the yearly lease came up here, and rather than negotiate with another tenant, I took this house myself."

"For your bachelor quarters."

"For an escape from Bouverie."

"Why?"

"Bouverie reminds me too much of my father." He put the key in the lock. "Every time I step foot in the place, I feel the weight of centuries of expectations." He opened the door and held it open for her. "At times, it's more than I care to deal with."

His butler, Golde, kept candles burning in the chandelier in the entrance to the town house, so the foyer was softly lit. Exactly as he preferred. Light reflected off the crystal drops in the chandelier, from the gilt frame of the mirror across from the door, and from the mirror itself. As he turned from the door, he stole a glance at Eugenia. His heart skipped a beat.

This was his home, and Ginny was here. Against all reason and decency, she was here with him. He had every bad intention in the world so long as it sped them toward the moment when she agreed to marry him. When he had, at last, convinced her that her feelings were safe in his keeping.

Without giving voice to those thoughts, he escorted her to his study and lit candles before he crossed to the sidebar. Eugenia stood in the center of the room, her cloak drawn tight around her, candlelight flickering off her hair. He'd imagined this several times, being alone with her, though most often those dreams had a bedroom as the setting. He found the bottle he was looking for and turned back. "If we're going to get drunk, whisky's as good a way to go as any."

"If you say so." She slipped off her cloak and draped it over a chair.

"I do." He studied her while he opened the whisky. "I can take you home if you'd rather."

She shook her head.

"Good." He opened one of the cabinet doors and found several bottles of wine on their sides. But it was glasses he was after. "Here we are." He retrieved two tumblers from the back of an upper cabinet and splashed two fingers into one and half that amount in the other. "Aigen gave this to me. From the Wateresk distillery in the Grampian Mountains." He crossed the room to hand the smaller portion to her. "Have you been drunk before?"

"Tipsy once. On wine. But not drunk."

"Ah. A virgin. Not to worry, I've experience with virgins."

She turned pink, but she laughed just as he'd hoped she would.

"We'll go slowly." He smiled down at her, and he thought

she was the most alluring woman he'd ever known. "I promise it won't hurt a bit."

"Men always say that to girls." She glanced into her glass. "They always lie."

"We're a sorry lot, we men. A sip, Ginny. Like so." He demonstrated what he meant and waited for her to try.

She did, but too much for someone who had no experience with drinking. Her eyes went wide, and she coughed. "Goodness. I don't think I like it."

"Try again. A very small sip this time." Her eyes were a pure, clear blue. This close to her, he could see her lashes were longer than they looked because the tips were so pale. He lifted his glass. "To my bloody father."

"Don't curse."

"We're drinking together. I'll curse if I like." He lifted his glass to her. "So should you."

"I couldn't."

He took a slow sip of his whisky, and she did the same, a wisely smaller one than before. "Better?"

She stared at the whisky. "Yes, actually."

"Good." He took her hand and walked with her to the fireplace. Here, in his home, the servants were instructed not to let the fires go out when he was in London. Still with her hand in his, he put a foot on the grate. "What do you think? Of the whisky."

They remained silent while she drank what was left in her glass. He'd not given her much. She tipped the glass and watched the few remaining drops pool. "The taste grows on you."

"It does."

She shook her head. "I don't think I'm drunk."

"Not yet." Fox let go of her hand to fetch the whisky bottle and pour another finger into her tumbler. He added more to his and set the bottle on the mantel. He didn't intend to drink much. He needed a clear head. Wanted a clear head, at any rate. "Shall we sit?" He gestured toward the velvet sofa that faced the fire. She frowned in that direction.

"My lovely, darling Ginny, come sit. You can't be comfortable standing. Nor warm enough, either."

She sat primly on the sofa, not quite in the center.

"Shall I put more coal on the fire?"

"Please." While he did that she lifted her face to the ceiling. "This is a very masculine room."

He finished with the fire and walked to the sofa, bringing the whisky bottle with him. "It is. But then, this is my private office, and I am a man."

She lowered her chin, and he dragged his eyes upward just in time. Her gown barely exposed her upper shoulders, but there was more than a hint of an inviting roundness of bosom. He did like a woman with an inviting bosom. Everything about her appealed to him. Always had. He stared into his tumbler. He could see parts of the ceiling reflected in his glass as well as orange lights from the fire.

"You said you'd take scandalous advantage of me."

He looked at her, and he could see all her doubt and worry, and it made his heart clench. "Do you want me to?"

Her smile faded. "I don't know. I'm here, so I think I must." She shook her head. "I don't want to think anymore. It only makes me feel sad."

Fox put the bottle and his half-empty glass on a table beside the sofa. "I'm happy to oblige you."

"Tell me a secret." She met his gaze. "Something shocking."

"I still want that quick fuck."

A smile flashed over her face. "That's not a secret. I'm not shocked, either."

"Others would be shocked if they knew I was saying such things to you."

"True. But you might as well tell me the weather is cold. Come now, Fenris. Tell me something that will shock me."

"Very well." He searched her face. "I've not been to bed with a woman for nearly a year. Not since before I went to see you at Bitterward."

"To see me?" She waved a hand at him. "You never did. You came to Bitterward to propose to Lily."

Here he was, alone with a woman he desired, and he was practically paralyzed by the possibility that he'd do something to scare her off. "Did I?"

She took another sip of her drink. A bigger one than the others she'd taken. "I think I like whisky."

"You like excellent whisky."

"Yes. I think I do." She slipped her feet out of her shoes and curled her legs underneath her. She lifted her eyes to his, and he did like the way she smiled at him. "Have you got a cheroot?"

"I have."

"You promised me, after all."

"I did."

She held out a hand and wriggled her fingers. "You men smoke and drink when you're alone together."

"Among other things."

"Robert said you talked politics and mathematics."

"He and I did."

She settled more comfortably on the sofa. "Once, though, he admitted you talk about disreputable subjects, too. Ballet girls and courtesans and ladies you wish were not ladies." She gave him a sideways look. "The Incomparable and the like."

"The Incomparable has had her congé from me for some time." He went to the desk drawer where he was fairly certain he had a cheroot. After a moment's search, he found an ebony socket, and in another moment, one cheroot tucked away in a different drawer. "I've only the one here. I've more in my private quarters. I can fetch them if you like."

She let her head fall back on the sofa. "I don't mind sharing. If you don't."

"I don't." He returned to the fireplace and lit the cigar from a taper. He nodded at her, cheroot in hand, and sent a stream of smoke toward the ceiling. After a bit, she held out a hand. "Fenris."

"Fox." He cocked his head. "When we are private."

"You said you'd teach me to smoke. Was that a lie?"

"Never." He sat beside her on the sofa and handed her

the cheroot. He did not let go, however. "Have you smoked before?"

"Twice a virgin."

He laughed at that, and so did she.

"I believe I'm drunk enough to try." Still with her head on the sofa, she blinked at him. "How does one know if one is drunk?"

"Are you feeling relaxed? That the world is a pleasant place?"

"Yes." Her gaze turned inward. "Yes, I believe so."

"I'd say you are likely mildly inebriated." With his other hand, he reached for her whisky. "Let it settle on you for a bit. If you get too drunk, too fast, you won't remember tomorrow that you've seen me naked."

Her mouth twitched. "I have not."

"Not yet." He let go of the cigar. "You shall, Ginny. I promise. Don't try to inhale your first time."

"Overbearing man." She nodded. She put the socket to her mouth, inhaled, and promptly choked.

"I told you not to inhale." He reached across her for the cigar and took it. "As with anything worth doing, practice is required." He inhaled and blew out a smoke ring. They watched it slowly expand and then vanish.

"That's very nice." She took the cigar from him and, this time, took only a puff that she immediately let out. "Observe," she said, waving the cigar. "I've made a smoke cloud better than yours. Mine hasn't a hole in the middle."

"Talented woman."

"I am. Very talented." She stretched out her arm and picked up her whisky, which he had set on a table on his other side. She was, he assumed, unaware that her bosom pressed against him while she did so. She straightened and took a drink. "Did you see the way Dinwitty Lane was looking at Hester this evening?"

"Not especially." Christ, he was randy as hell, seeing her with a cigar in one hand and a glass of whisky in the other. "I did see him staring at you, though."

"Wondering about buttons I expect."

He threw back his head and laughed. "He's jealous he's not had his hand down your dress."

"Neither have you."

"No, but he doesn't know that."

She looked at him over the rim of the tumbler and blinked once before wrinkling her nose in dismissal. "Lady Baring thinks Hester should marry her son Edward. Lieutenant Fraser."

"Not a bad match, I'd say."

She put the cheroot to her lips again with no better result than before. When she'd finished coughing, she blinked several times. "She offered to speak to her son. The lieutenant. But I think it's because her eldest was interested, too."

"I don't want to talk about Miss Rendell."

"She could fall in love with you, you know. If you tried even a little bit."

He took her whisky from her again. "No more for a bit."

"Why?"

"Because I intend to take advantage of you, and I can't if you have any more to drink."

She made a face at him. "Don't treat me as if I'm a child and you're a nurse insisting I eat my peas properly."

"I have always liked peas."

"Turnips, then."

He shifted on the sofa so he faced her and draped an arm along the top. "I especially like turnips."

"There must be some vegetable you don't like. I'm that one."

"I was a perfect child in every way and ate every vegetable ever to be put on my plate."

She let out a breath. "Lord, you would be. You're perfect in every way."

"As I mean for you to discover."

"You know what I mean. We do not have a pleasant history, you and I."

"I beg to differ. Our recent history is very pleasant indeed."

"I'm going to start calling you the Incorrigible."

"If you like."

She took another drag on the cigar, drew too much, and set off coughing. "Heavens, this thing is vile." She sat up, head down while she waited for her lung spasms to subside. "You take it."

He did so and stood to toss the thing into the fire. When he rejoined Eugenia, he sat closer to her than before.

"You've not told me a single secret about you." She shook a finger at him.

"I told you I'd not been intimate with a woman since before Bitterward. That's a secret only we two know."

"That's a lie."

"It isn't."

"What do you call what happened in the Turkish room?"

"I call it damned arousing." He drank half his whisky and then the rest and wished he had more. "I don't understand why I've remained so besotted with you over the years. But I have done so, and here you are, Ginny, in my private home. Quite alone and just drunk enough that you haven't slapped me."

"I don't like you," she whispered. "Not even a little."

"I know." He lowered his head to hers, and he thought, *To hell with decency. And to bloody hell with caution.* "Isn't it delicious this way?"

Chapter Seventeen

❧❧

EUGENIA HELD FENRIS'S GAZE BECAUSE SHE'D COM-
pletely lost her mental footing. His arm looped around her
shoulders, warm and insistent, and he sat so close their tor-
sos nearly touched.

Fenris had always been fastidious about his dress. It was
a habit he shared, unknowingly, with his cousin Lily. Always
perfectly put together. One didn't have to like the man to
appreciate his looks. He was a long-legged specimen, taller
than average with dark hair that flirted with being brown.
For so slender a man, he was impressively broad through
the shoulders. His light brown eyes were heavily lashed. His
mouth was, she noticed yet again, surprisingly tender.

He did kiss well, didn't he? She couldn't forget that about
him. Their position was intimate. When had he moved so
close to her? Her stomach dove when she understood he
meant to kiss her. Again. Without them being in the heat of
mad passion.

"Ginny." His hand slid around her waist and settled into
the small of her back.

"My lord?"

"Mm?" His fingers angled downward. "If you're not going to call me the Incorrigible, then call me Fox."

"Are you drunk?"

"No."

"Then what are you doing?" His palm pressed against her, and she swayed toward him.

"In the main," he said with that infuriating calm of his, "I am wondering what you would do if I stripped naked right now."

She blinked. "Why would you do that?"

"For a quick fuck."

"Oh yes. I remember that."

"And then a long, hard one."

"Incorrigible."

"You said you'd not seen me naked. I said I'd remedy that." He shrugged in a way that belied the subject. "What would you do with me if I were naked?" He lowered his head and kissed the top of her shoulder. "What about desire?" he murmured. "And the heat of your dislike of me?"

She pressed her hands on his shoulders and managed to put a few scant inches between them, and then she wondered why she'd done that when his lips on her skin felt so lovely.

His mouth left her shoulder, and he lifted his head just enough to look at her. Her skin tingled where his lips had been. He'd managed to bring her closer again. This time he kissed the side of her throat. And she let him. She wasn't dizzy, not exactly, but she wasn't entirely herself. The whisky had relaxed her, but she did not feel in the least addled. Merely that the world was a very pleasant place. He nipped her earlobe, then drew back to look into her eyes. The backs of her legs went a bit wobbly. How did he do that?

"Shall I tell you another secret?"

She laughed. "Do, please."

"I've never been intimate with a woman who professes to dislike me."

"Well. Why would you be?"

"Indeed. It occurs, however, that there is much to say for strong passions in the bedroom." He curled a lock of her hair around his finger. "What would happen, Ginny, if we did this deliberately? No blaming the heat of the moment. We simply decide that we will enjoy each other? Physically. And learn where your dislike of me takes us."

Once again, he'd snatched the world out from under her. "We are in your study. Not your bedroom."

"Ginny, my dearest, we can indulge anywhere we find a few moments of privacy." He dipped his head again and pressed his mouth to the top of her shoulder. "I assure you, we are very private here. But would it not be novel for us to do this here?"

"Strictly speaking, it would be novel for us to do this anywhere but the Turkish room at Bouverie."

"You're right, of course. My excuse is that I am drunk."

"You are not."

"Not with drink. With desire. For you."

"Oh, for pity's sake." She turned toward him, sitting so she could put her folded arms atop the sofa and her chin atop her arms. "Not even a turnip would believe that."

"Mm. My delectable little root vegetable." He mirrored her position on the sofa, except that he had only one arm on the sofa. The other was on her hip. "Let's formalize our serendipitous and mutual physical lusts."

She squinted at him. He looked perfectly serious. "Formalize."

"Yes."

"Are you asking me to become your mistress?"

"I can't keep you. Not in the usual sense. Your brother would have my head. We'd agree to exclusivity, naturally." He slid his hand over the curve of her hip and then to her flank. It felt lovely and wicked all at the same time. She gave him a lazy smile, but at the edges of everything, she smoldered.

"Are you teasing me?"

"No." His hand wandered again, this time along the neckline of her gown where it showed above her folded arms. "There seems little point in offering you a house, though I will buy you one if you like. You could tell your brother you leased the house from a fool who didn't ask a decent rent of you. But I'd have the deed made over to your name. I'd keep a key for as long as you and I last. You could change the locks whenever you like."

"You're serious." She felt she was mentally three steps behind him, but she was floating, rather deliciously, and so decided she didn't care.

His eyes snapped to hers, alert instead of that lovely, sleepy honey brown. "If all I can have from you is an affair, I would certainly agree to a formal arrangement, yes." He touched her cheek with the backs of his fingers. "And if all I may have is the shameful advantage I take of you tonight, I'll have that, too."

She smiled again. "There's something wrong with that. I just can't think what. Aside from my not liking you, I mean."

"Understood. I'm not sure I understand entirely, either. Whatever happens, I hope you know it doesn't mean you don't love Robert anymore." He trailed his index finger downward over the curve of her breast. A shiver followed in the wake of his moving finger.

"I'll always love him."

"As you should." He reached for the whisky and their glasses again and poured them both more. When she'd taken hers from him, he lifted his glass. "To Robert. The best man I never knew."

She tapped her glass to his and drank. Afterward, his gaze locked with hers and for a moment all the air vanished. She'd been a married woman and she knew full well what that look meant. Her body responded.

He put down his glass. "Come to bed with me, Ginny. For the night. A week. A year. For as long as it takes you to decide if you really do hate me."

"What possible reason would I have to accept such a proposition from you, of all men?"

"I can think of several." His hand was back at her hip, then lower, to her calf.

She could scarcely breathe and tried to cover by taking

a sip of whisky. She must be drunk, she thought. Why else would she enjoy this state of arousal? Why else would she flirt with him like this, not anywhere near safe. And yet with him, she could be whatever she wanted. "Name one."

"Revenge." There was no other description for his smile but silky. "Imagine, my dear Ginny, bringing me to my knees. Using me as well or as badly as you wish. Breaking my heart, even."

She snorted and with the hand holding her tumbler tapped his chest where his heart ought to be. "There's a block of ice in there, Fenris. Not a heart."

"Melting what chip of ice resides in its place, then." He leaned away from her long enough to pick up his glass. He took two swallows then regarded her with a look that sent a chill down her spine. "You might find sex, deliberate sex, I mean, with a man you hate to be . . . stimulating."

She gripped the top of the sofa with one hand. When he used that voice, she couldn't help but think he must be right. "Do you think so?"

"Think of the power you'd have over me. All the ways you might make me pay for my wrongs against you."

"Fenris. Fox." One more drink of whisky. Still holding her glass, she stuck out a finger and jabbed him in the center of his chest. Lord, but he felt solid. "Poor, deluded vegetable lover. The only proper formal arrangement you could offer this turnip is marriage. And neither of us want that. Can you imagine?"

He didn't laugh. Or scowl. Or do any of the things she expected. He returned to his position that was far too close to her, and this time, his hand curled around her ankle. The air went away again. "I disagree. Shall I prove it?"

Which did he mean? Did he disagree there was only one formal arrangement he could offer or was he disagreeing that he didn't want to marry her? She searched his face for the answer and did not find it. "Proof. Yes, in a case like this, proof is called for."

His hand glided up her stocking to her garter. She gasped when the tips of his fingers brushed over her skin.

"Good, yes?"

She stared into her glass and saw it was empty. Now how had that happened? "May I have more whisky?"

He took her empty glass and set it aside. He stretched for his glass, looked at what was left, and drank half. "You may have the rest of mine."

"The world is still pleasant, Fox."

"I agree." He gave her a quick smile. "Let's keep it that way for a while yet."

She took a sip, a properly small sip from his glass. His hand remained beneath her skirts, and now, his clever, agile fingers were well past her garter.

"Lean back," he whispered, and she did, settling into the corner of the sofa. He followed so that the distance between them did not change. "Still relaxed?"

She nodded. Lord, his fingers reached her thigh, and she was going to melt.

"Ginny. My turnip. Like so." He nudged her, and she parted her legs in response. He cupped the back of her neck, and his other hand slid along the folds of her sex, stroking so she could barely think or breathe. She could feel, though. Every shiver. It had been so long since she'd been touched like this, brought to the very edge of orgasm. He drew his other hand down her arm. He took away her glass and she was glad to have it gone from her hands. "Spend the night with me, Eugenia."

"Will I see you naked?"

He smiled that secret, dark, and wicked grin. "Yes."

Chapter Eighteen

FOX DID NOT ENTIRELY RELAX UNTIL HE CLOSED THE
door to his private apartments with Eugenia still at his side.
Not entirely sober, but not drunk, thank God. He lit the
candles in the girandole while they waited for Golde to
arrive with the repast he'd ordered. He kept an eye on Eugenia, who walked around the anteroom to his bedchamber.
On the walls were several of the paintings he'd bought over
the years, by artists who were not necessarily well-known
but whose work he liked. She paused by each one.

He'd hardly put away the flint when Golde tapped on the
door. Since Fox did not think it proper to have female servants, given this was a bachelor establishment, Golde pre-
sided over a staff of men. There weren't many. His personal
chef and two footmen, one of whom doubled as a groom, a
kitchen boy. His valet, of course, would be summoned from
Bouverie. In the morning, he'd see about sending for a girl
who could do for Eugenia.

"Milord," Golde said with a bow. He gestured, and both
footmen entered with the various parts of their meal. His
butler had found somewhere a vase of white roses, just

moments, it seemed, from being too old, and these he placed in the center of the table once the tablecloth was laid. While the two footmen arranged the table, Golde went about the business of preparing the room, lighting more candles, bringing up the fire here. The butler disappeared into the bedroom where he would turn down the bed, ensure the linens would be warm, and light a few more candles than when Fox came here without a companion. These days, that was always the case.

Fox stayed by the fireplace while she inspected the room and his servants laid out the table. He'd always admired the way she moved, and even with the whisky she'd consumed, she moved gracefully.

Golde came back from the bedroom to put the finishing touches on the arrangement of the food. He opened the wine, a '75 Burgundy, to let it breathe. On his way out, he drew the curtains. Shadows deepened with the silence.

He and Eugenia were alone. In his private quarters. He locked the door, and when he turned around from that, Eugenia faced him. She held one end of her shawl, a fringed silk that draped over her arm and dangled to the floor. "I take it," she said with a sideways look at him, "that this is where you come when you wish to be improper."

He returned to the fire and set one foot on the grate. "This is the place to which I retire when I wish to be private."

"With a woman."

"No." He shook his head. "Rarely. And not since before my visit to your brother's house." He was capable of charm, he knew that. He had learned to be charming in order to counter his father's brusqueness. He'd spent years mending fences and rebuilding bridges destroyed by his father's vitriol once he'd become man enough to understand the damage Camber had done all those years and days past when he'd been so angry at his sister marrying Lily's father. No more the damage he himself had done during the time he'd slavishly adopted his father's prejudices.

"Did you bring Lady Tyghe here?"

"I did not then have this house, so no." He moved away

from the fireplace. "I've brought relatively few women here. There are other locations that accommodate one's fleeting interest in a woman. If I were to be interested in pursuing someone for more than an evening, there are arrangements that can be made that do not involve my home."

"I'm sure." She looked around one more time. "It's a very nice home," she said. "It suits you." She cocked her head at the painting she'd stopped before, then at him. "And reveals you."

He nodded. He did like the way she looked at him with such an assessing glance. She saw him. The man, not Fenris, the heir to a dukedom. "The monstrosity that is Bouverie represents my family honor."

"I like Bouverie. You don't?"

"It is my father's home. My grandfather's home, the home of all men who have been Camber."

"I don't find it monstrous."

"Though one day that frigid set of bones will be mine, I cannot look forward to it. But here?" He gestured. "Here you may find my heart."

"There's no denying your good taste."

"I'm glad you think so." He wanted very much to go to her, pull the pins from her hair, and thread his fingers through those thick straw-colored tresses.

Still with the end of her shawl dangling, she moved to the next painting, one of his favorites. She stood facing it. "Is this from Anatolia?"

"Persia. A depiction of the Festival of Fire." Sumptuously dressed Persians danced outdoors, to a tune played by musicians at the outer edge of the gathered people. The top and sides of the painting were of an inverted teardrop-shaped window, intricately decorated, and painted in exquisite detail. In looking on the painting it was as if you were yourself in the center of that window, watching the musicians and dancers outside.

"It's very old, isn't it?" She looked at him over her shoulder. "The painting, I mean. The colors are just lovely."

"It is."

She returned to her study.

"Above all else," he said softly, "my staff is discreet."

After a bit, she faced him again. "Nothing less for you."

"Not if they wish to remain in my employ or get a character from me if they should leave." He walked to the table and surveyed the repast of fruit, cheese, thinly sliced beef, quail, bread already sliced, and, in a welcome touch, a plate of marzipan, another of sweetmeats, and a bowl of candied almonds. He made a note to give the entire staff a bonus. "Would you like some wine with our meal? It's an excellent vintage."

"Yes, thank you." She joined him at the table, standing, as he did. She touched the flowers. One of the petals drifted to the table.

"Not so potent as the whisky." He poured two glasses of the Burgundy and handed one to her. Before she accepted the goblet, she draped her shawl over a chair. She sipped so small an amount he doubted she tasted it. He busied himself with selecting a plate of food for her. He added a section of orange then ate one himself. It was still cold from the ice it had been sitting on in the larder. The fruit was sweet, and, without much thought, he took another and held it to her lips. "Taste."

She put down her wine, untouched but for that one sip, and did. She ate it slowly, half the slice, then the other, eyes closed, and one hand just under her mouth to catch the juice until she'd swallowed the last bit. Her eyes opened. The tips of her eyelashes were blonder than her hair, her irises blue as the sky. "Mm. That was delicious."

"So, my dear Ginny."

She didn't need him to say more. Her cheeks pinked up. "Give me a little more whisky first."

He laughed, at his expense, not hers. "I am too full of myself tonight."

"That's always so."

"Boiled too long in the wine of my self-importance."

"Boiled, you say?" She laughed softly. "It's not fair to

amuse me so. How can I hate you when you make me laugh?"

"I use every weapon to hand." He waited until her attention returned to him. "It's a rare vintage, Ginny. A lesser man than I would be drunk on it."

"I've not given you leave to call me Ginny."

"Your point?"

"None, I suppose. An observation is all."

"I've learned that if I do not take what I want, I am not likely to get what I want." She made a face at him, and his mouth twitched up. "Besides, it's what your friends call you. Lily calls you that."

"Yes, but you and I, we're not friends."

"No." He slid an arm around her waist and brought her close. "Not friends at all."

Her hand got in between them, but instead of pushing him away, she ran her fingers down his waistcoat and past the waist of his trousers until her palm curved over his not entirely soft sex. With her hand firmly covering him, he was getting harder by the moment. She pressed lightly, and two of her fingers swept over his balls.

"Mm. God, I do love your cock."

He let out a slow breath, as soft as he could, but there was no hiding his reaction from her. Then he ruined the illusion of his self-possession by sucking in a breath when her fingers moved over the top of his cock.

"It *is* very large." She leaned against him, and when was it, exactly, that he'd lost control of the encounter?

Eyes closed as he savored her handling of him, he pressed his hips forward. "Ginny—"

"Don't call me that."

"Ginny, my love." He opened his eyes and stared into hers. She lifted her chin. "I'm going to put that inside your naked body, and you will scream my name before I'm done."

"I won't."

He absolutely refused to smile. It was a near thing, though, stopping himself from that. "Several times, in fact."

"Never."

He brought her hard against his body. His senses were completely overrun. She was smiling at him, a smug, private knowing smile. She smelled like orange water. Common everyday orange water, and the scent was driving him mad. He lowered his head and kissed her. Hard and fast, mouth open, not waiting to ease her along to kisses that invaded her mouth. He started there. Taking her mouth.

She did her share of taking, damn her. When he pulled back, they were both breathing hard.

He held her by the shoulders. "I like a woman who wants to be fucked hard, and not necessarily in a bed. I like a woman on top and when she's on her knees and I'm behind her. Or up against a wall."

"A wall? You've done that?" She stared into his face, eyes wide, and he kissed her again. A little slower, but no less carnally. The woman still had her hand on his sex.

"Yes." He permitted himself one very tiny smile. "Have you?"

She let the hand that wasn't on his cock fall away from his shoulder. She leaned toward the table and with her bare fingers picked up and rolled a slice of roast beef. She ate slowly. When she was done she wiped her hand on a napkin. "That's none of your business."

Fox returned her wayward hand to his cock, and got a smug look in return. Followed by another stroke along his length. "I'm happy to close any and all gaps in your sensual experience."

She made a face at him.

"Now, perhaps?"

"You're being crude on purpose."

"If I were being crude, Ginny, I would have told you I want to fuck you against the wall right now. If I were being crude, I'd ask you if you know that if you were to shave the hair on your quim, your newly bare skin would be unbearably soft. And then I'd demand that you do so before our next fuck."

"Is that so?"

"Yes." He pushed his pelvis forward and was amply rewarded for his crudity. "If you were to do such a thing, I would write my name there, above your slit, in purple ink."

"Your entire name?" Her eyes opened wide, but her innocence was disingenuous. He had not ever been this aroused in his life, he was certain of it. "My lord, I don't think there's room there for all those names."

"I would write *Fox*, and when the ink was dry, I'd put your back against the wall there—" He nodded in the direction of the door. "I'd lift you up, and I'd push inside you, and you, my dearest Ginny, would be wet for me, and I'd take you hard and fast."

"I think you're all talk."

He leaned in and nipped the side of her throat. "Imp."

"Incorrigible."

"Oh yes. I'm a hard case."

While he drew a hand down the curve of her back she said, "Do you even have purple ink?"

Chapter Nineteen

"IDLE CURIOSITY?" HIS HEART LURCHED ALONG WITH parts south. "Or something else?"

Her smile was secret, unreadable, and it put an ocean's distance between them. "What would I write on your noble skin, I wonder? In purple ink."

He laughed, looking at her, drinking in the sight of her, hardly able to believe she was here with him and following him down indecent paths. No matter what she was thinking about him or feeling about him, she was here. In his house. In his private rooms. "*Where* is more my concern."

"Just above, I think." She cupped him again. "Perhaps I'd draw a picture."

He stood his ground, and the tension between them filled the room. His prick was now at painfully full attention. "Your name would suffice."

She put her free hand in the center of his chest and pushed. "Get your purple ink, my lord."

His mind filled with images of him with his hand over her freshly shaved mons, and he forgot how to breathe. She gave him another push, and he took a step back. Not very far, though. "A pen, as well?" he asked.

"What did I say?" Eugenia tapped his chest again.

"The ink." Fox took a backward step, toward his bed-chamber. "Which, I feel I ought to point out, is useless without a pen."

She tapped her chin. "A pen, too, sir."

"Your wish is my command." But as he retreated, he grabbed her hand and brought her along.

"I'm hungry," she said, looking back at the table with the food Golde had laid out for them.

He stopped. "Take the plate, then."

She picked up not the food he'd assembled for her but the plate of marzipan.

And then, there they were. In his bedroom with the fire just warm enough and the candlelight casting a glow that did not reach all the shadows. He took her hand and walked her to the desk. He retrieved his bottle of purple ink from the drawer where he'd stashed it the day the gift had been delivered to him. He held it up with a flourish. "Behold."

Eugenia moved to the side of the desk, set down the marzipan, and leaned her forearms on top of the desk. "Lady Tyghe gave you this, didn't she?"

"Mm. Arrived last week as I recall."

She licked her lips and considered the ink he held. "Unopened, I see."

"I'd not thought I'd ever have a use for it." He put down the ink and opened the drawer that contained his quills. He fished out a scrap of blotting paper as well. Would she really? Would Eugenia Hampton Bryant, who had every reason to dislike him, do this and more with him?

"Are you going to tell her that you've used her ink?"

Supplies in hand, he faced her. His attention went to her bosom and lingered. He imagined his hands covering her bare breasts. Such charming curves. He wanted her naked in his arms. Now. Ten minutes ago. A year ago. "What do you suppose?"

"Not." Eugenia considered the candies on the plate. "She's not as stupid as she pretends. Am I right?"

"No. She's not."

She grinned. "Purple ink is a gift you are to use for her benefit. To write her poetry and lavish her with compliments."

"Precisely."

She ate a piece of marzipan, and while he watched her, he wondered if Robert had understood the treasure he'd had in his wife. Of course he had. Robert had never been any sort of fool. There had been times when the man's enormous intellect consumed him. Some subject caught his fancy, and he was never satisfied until he had reduced the idea to nothing but bone and gristle. When in the grip of intellectual curiosity he had often been curt to the point of shocking rudeness. Had Robert, with his brilliant mind trapped in a deficient body, been able to satisfy his wife? He saw no sign that he hadn't.

When she was done eating the candy, she smiled. Slowly. Wickedly. Hers was not the smile of a woman who did not understand the pleasures of the body. They had managed, those two. Imperfect Robert and perfect, happy Eugenia.

She held out a hand for the pen and ink, and he handed them to her. Was she really going to be so bold? "If you'll just remove your britches. And lie down on the bed, there."

"I warn you, you cannot help but see my nether regions." He was jealous of a dead man. The man who'd been his closest friend until he'd ruined it.

She gazed at him without smiling. "I've seen your parts."

"By God, you have. But that was in the heat of passion. This is different. There is a certain intimacy gained once a man allows a woman a close acquaintance with his parts."

"Yes." Her tongue came out and ran the length of her bottom lip, and he was instantly thinking of her mouth on him. "That's so."

He let the silence build, and while he did, she licked the residue of the candy from her fingers. He removed his watch, taking a moment to touch the medallion hanging from the chain. Quickly, he stripped down to his shirt. The clothes he removed, he threw over the back of a chair. Boots next. Then his breeches. He'd always believed in being master of himself, and that meant being master of his body, too. He worked himself hard to maintain that physical control. Clad in only his shirt, he sat on his bed, pushing himself back until he was on the piled-up pillows. He crossed his arms behind his head.

Eugenia put the supplies on the nightstand by the bed: ink, pen, and the bit of blotting paper he'd taken out. She sat on the edge of the mattress. His cock was hard, tenting his shirt. The idea of her writing on his bare skin was titillating, of course. Even more arousing—and he was certain she understood this—was the implied promise that she would allow him to do the same. Or nearly the same. Another night, when they were more familiar, he would shave her and write his name on her.

She drew his shirt up high enough to expose his hip and his sex.

"Have you decided what to write?"

"I believe I have." She turned to the nightstand and opened the ink. She laughed. Giggled, actually. "Oh, my heavens."

"What?"

Her eyes twinkled when she looked at him over her shoulder. "The ink is perfumed. Lilac, if I'm not mistaken."

"Good God."

She dipped the pen in the bottle and returned to him. "Be very still, my lord."

"I've told you before, you have leave to call me Fox."

"Thank you." She put the scrap of blotting paper beside him, then placed one hand on his belly, just to the side of his cock. She bent her head over him. He was, of course, unbearably hard. Her breath warmed his belly and even, once or twice, his cock. He wanted her mouth on him, bringing him.

He tightened the muscles of his stomach when she touched the quill to him. The tip pulled a bit, and he twitched.

"I said be still, Fox."

"My apologies."

She wrote along his midline, from the bottom of his nether hair to the top of his belly so that the letters, whatever they were, would read sideways in the direction of his hip to his armpit. She went back to the ink several times, occasionally pausing to blow on the letters she was writing.

"Four words so far." He struggled not to move.

She touched her tongue to her top lip. " 'I hate the marquess.' "

"Too short. You've written more than that."

" 'Eugenia hates Fox most.' Don't move. I'm almost done." She took the blotting paper by the edges and placed it carefully over his skin. "There."

She removed the paper and twisted her torso to return the pen and blotting paper to the table.

In the meantime, he pulled his shirt out of the way and read, upside down for him, but in a neat, indisputably purple script, the words *For the Lady Eugenia.*

She turned back and smiled at him. "You can't have anyone else until that's gone, you know."

"I don't want another woman."

"You, Fox? You're not so constant, I think." She shook her head. "Robert envied you your ways with women."

"Did he tell you that?" He let go of his shirt, but she grabbed a handful of the fabric and kept it off his belly.

"Don't spoil it so soon," she said.

"Very well." He pulled his shirt over his head and pushed himself to a sitting position, leaning his back against the headboard. He ran a finger along the bottom of the words. "Dry now."

"Is it?"

"You may have it now," he said, looking at her from under his lashes. "As much of it as you like."

Her gaze traveled from his head to his toes and back. "You're an impressive specimen," she said. "Much as it pains me, I must admit I find you physically lovely."

"Come here, Ginny, and let me put this inside you."

She smiled, and it was a lovely, and intensely arousing, sight. "I thought you were going to do that against the wall."

"I am only too willing to oblige you." He pushed off the bed and, taking her by the arm, walked her backward to the door of his room, with her protesting in laughter the entire way. "You're just the right height for this." He put her back to the wall, planted his feet, and gathered handfuls of her skirt. Their eyes locked. "Do you hate me now, Ginny?"

"More than ever."

Her answer sent lust spiraling through him. "Good."

He found the back of her thigh and pulled her leg up. Her breath came hard, and she knew exactly how their bodies ought to fit together because she adjusted herself so that his hard thrust into her was smooth. She tilted back her head and groaned, but he grabbed her chin and said, "Look at me."

She did, defiant. "You won't make me say your name."

"I will, I promise you."

"Never."

He drew back his hips and pushed forward into heat and all that softness, tight around him. Her skirts were in the way, and his fingers dug into the back of her thigh, nearly at her bottom, holding tight, while he pulled the layers of fabric aside. Another thrust, a rock of her hips toward his. Her arms held his shoulders tight.

Freed now of the obstacle of her bunched-up skirts, he slid in farther this time. He used both hands to hold her now. He leaned in and kissed her, hard, with desperation, with lust. He was nothing but his thrusts into her, the slickness of his slide back before he pushed forward again. He circled his hips once, and she moaned. Not his name, just a sound of pleasure, low in her throat.

This was Eugenia in his arms. His prick was inside her, and she had come here to be with him. Like this. Eugenia. The woman he'd loved from the moment he'd heard her laugh. Before he was ready, his body raced toward climax. Close. So close and threatening to consume him.

He pulled out of her and lowered his head while he

concentrated on vanquishing his need to orgasm. It was a near thing. When he looked at her, her defiance was back.

She said, "You're not Robert." Her eyes flashed. "It doesn't matter how good you are with your cock, you'll never be Robert."

Fox released her thigh and turned her around. "No. I am not. Nor do I intend to even attempt to be him."

He worked at the hooks of her frock. He unfastened enough of the hooks to loosen her bodice, and really, women wore far too many clothes. He made short work of the remaining fastenings, and before much longer, she was wearing only her unmentionables, then like him, nothing at all.

Chapter Twenty

EUGENIA WAS SHOCKED TO SILENCE. FIRST, THAT she'd had the bad taste to tell him he was not Robert, a fact of which he was most assuredly aware, second by the rapidity with which he stripped her naked, and third, by the fact that he was so physically magnificent, her body clenched with longing. Sheer animal lust. She'd give nearly anything to touch him. Caress him. Kiss him. Taste him. Drink him in.

She'd never been more than slightly tipsy before, but she wasn't drunk, at least not in the usual way she thought of being inebriated: unable to speak clearly, not in control of her movements, a mind muddled to incoherence. Instead, her emotions lurked just under the surface of her skin and none of them seemed as important as having him inside her.

His body entranced her. All hard muscles and, Lord, his cock was just so lovely. He had surprisingly little hair, and his nipples were darker than she would have supposed. Robert had once mentioned that Fenris was obsessed with his physical conditioning, and the truth of that was quite plain.

His fingers on her were capable of pulling reactions from her she thought had died with her husband. She resonated with the aftereffects of his touch, with a longing for completion that ached. She leaned against the wall and didn't even have the wit to be embarrassed that she was naked—my God, naked!—with Fenris staring at her, so yes, after all, she absolutely must be drunk.

"I want to look at you," she said.

His mouth curved, and he took half a step back. "Very well."

His belly was flat, his legs long. A purple bruise covered part of his upper arm, and with the tip of a finger she traced a circle around the injury. She had to stretch to touch him. "What happened?"

He looked at the bruise. "That? Boxing match."

"Did you win?"

"That was the judgment."

Her eyes traveled down his body. She refused to think of him as Fenris. He was merely a man whose body aroused her and to whom she wished to engage in any number of unspeakable acts. Whatever went on in his head, whether he liked her or disliked her was not presently a concern of hers. His penis remained erect. The purple lettering on his belly remained. *For the Lady Eugenia.* "You didn't finish," she said.

"No."

She lifted her gaze and their eyes locked and she was lost in a haze of honey brown depths and physical desire. And now she saw Fenris standing before her, and she did not have to think of anything but his body and hers and all the ways they fit together.

"But then," he said softly, "I did not finish you, either."

"True."

"Will you allow me to remedy that?"

"I think you'd better." It was as if some other woman were speaking. The words were true. Truer than anything.

He closed the distance between them and put his hands on hers, lifting her arms over her head and pinning them to the wall. His eyes darkened, and she drew in a breath. Slowly, he drew his hands down, along her forearms, to her upper arms, her shoulders, and then, he sank to his knees before her, his hands sliding down her body, over her breasts, down her stomach. His tongue dipped in and out of her navel. He kissed her belly then lower, lower. His fingers pushed through her hair there. "I will write my name here," he said.

"So you say."

"I do say."

She shivered once, right before he put her thigh over his shoulder, and he settled his mouth over her. He kept one palm on the inside of her thigh, but mostly she couldn't think of anything but his mouth on her and the sensations sizzling through her. For three or four minutes, she fought her reaction because in the back of her mind she thought it would serve him right if he didn't get what he was after.

But who, after all, would she be punishing? She wanted that orgasm. She wanted to come.

Besides, the Marquess of Fenris proved himself to be a relentlessly talented man. Her body simply reached a point where denial did not work. All that desire found its way through the breaks in her determination to see him suffer. He pulled her forward without mercy; she slipped under the spell of her own body and her utter dependence on him to, as he'd said, finish her. He made her quite selfish, and when he stopped before she was quite there, she protested.

He gathered her into his arms and kissed her once. "A bed. I want us in bed, Ginny."

"Hurry."

He carried her to his bed, and when he'd put her down, he lay on his side, a palm resting on her upper chest. She would have protested, but the reverent hunger in his eyes as his gaze traveled over her stilled her voice. "Let me look at you," he whispered.

She would have told him no, but his palm glided over her, along the curve of her breast, very lightly, bringing her nipple to a peak just from that slow, deliberate motion. She felt the pull of that all the way to her sex, and that was precisely what she craved from him. He leaned over her and dipped his head to the aching peak of her breast. His tongue flicked out and upward, and she arched with the movement. He sucked, once, his tongue dragging upward, then his mouth, too, releasing her at the last moment to the sudden chill.

Again. Again he repeated his devotion. Recognition that this was Fenris lavishing such intimate attention on her rippled through her, deep and fierce, an undercurrent that heightened her physical response. His hand smoothed down the other side of her body, fingers curving over her hip, around her groin, and then between her legs. His mouth left her breast, and he trailed kisses down her body until he was at her sex again.

And, oh, Lord, he finished her, and though she didn't scream his name, she cried out because she hadn't felt that rise to passion in far, far too long. She didn't care in the least that she was undignified, because the only thing she lived for was what his tongue was doing to her and the sexual peak that was out of reach until it wasn't.

Fenris didn't wait for her to relax or come back to herself. He pulled himself over her and thrust inside her in one smooth stroke, and she rocked her hips toward him because he felt so good inside her. So good. There wasn't any way to describe what he did with his body except to say that he devoted himself to fucking her, and he did it very, very well. Part of her hated him for making her feel like this. She hated him for reminding her that Robert was gone and she could still feel.

At one point, when she was on the edge of tears, she put her hands on either side of his face and said, "You'll never have me. Not ever. No matter how good you are."

He dipped his head and his hips continued the thrust and withdraw, and she thought she might never have experienced anything quite so worth her immortal soul. His breath came hard, but he spoke, low and hard. "Do you think so?"

And he was so smug, so absolutely certain of himself that something inside her snapped. "Yes. I do think so." She put her hands on his shoulders and pushed. His skin was warm underneath her fingers. "On your back, you hateful man."

His smug smile broadened. "Whatever you desire."

When he'd complied, she straddled him and watched his eyes widen. "Did you really think you were going to teach me what this is like?"

"My apologies. School me, then."

"Were you so sure of yourself that you actually thought there wouldn't be things I want from your body?"

"Lord, I hope you do."

She lifted her hips, and he was quick to adjust himself, and the plain truth was that the sensation of his cock entering her at this angle felt better than she would have believed possible. She circled her hips and clenched around him.

Fenris sucked in a sharp breath.

For this moment, their physical joining was about her and her pleasure and making certain the man understood he wasn't going to have the upper hand just because he was Fenris and he lived a charmed and perfect life. She found a rhythm that kept her on the edge, a slow and steady undulation. He set his hands to her hips and left them there, just touching for now. He let her continue to lead them, though from time to time he rocked his hips. His timing was exquisite.

"Beautiful Ginny," he whispered. "Beautiful, beautiful Ginny."

She dragged her eyes open and focused on him, and all she could think was that this was the man who'd tried to destroy her happiness, and here she was. Here they were, and she could take whatever she wanted from him. Anything at all. She took one of his hands and placed it over her breast. He spread his fingers, pressing, cupping, then catching her nipple between his first two fingers. Still rocking her hips, she placed her hand over his and showed him what she wanted. "This," she said.

He complied.

"Yes. God, Fenris, yes."

His other hand slid back to her hip, fingers closing on

her, increasing the motion of their joining. He shifted his hips and slid into her at an angle that sent her out of her mind with passion.

They ended up with him sitting with his back against the headboard and her tight against his lap. His mouth took hers, his hands explored and delved, and he was astonishingly good at finding places that wonderfully concentrated her mind on their bodies. At one point, she tensed her inner muscles once more and he said, "Do that again."

She did.

"I am your slave," he ground out. "More." He got a hand between them and found the exact spot that sent her hurtling away from herself. She came hard, and if she said his name, she didn't care. When she opened her eyes after that, it was to lock gazes with him.

"My turn," he said.

"Yes."

He put her on her back, and she concentrated on his reactions, his breathing, the change in his thrusts into her, and she wound her legs around him and met him, and stroked her fingers down his back, and she could feel the tension in his body. The sex was hard and fast now, and Fenris's breath was hot against her skin, near her ear, along her throat.

She held him as if they really were lovers, and when he came, his shout was half groan. She watched the way his expression changed, that inward look while he was in the grip of his climax. She drank it all in, and a part of her adored this, him coming into her like this, so fierce. And just before he was done, when he'd pumped hard once, buried himself in her, and trembled in her arms, she put her mouth by his ear and whispered, "I hate you, Fenris. I hate you beyond life."

He stayed in her, but pushed up, keeping his weight on his palms to look into her face. He thrust one more time, with a low, soft moan as he shivered. Their mutual stare continued. "I can only think, my darling Ginny, that if you loved me I'd be a dead man right now."

"Awful, awful man," she said.

"You're sublime. I've never had a better fuck."

"Toad."

"Goddess." He withdrew from her and lay on his side again, a hand on her belly.

"You're no god, Fenris."

"I don't have such aspirations." He pressed his mouth to her stomach. "Do you think it will be as good the next time? Because, I tell you, Ginny, my love, I came like a bull."

"The next time?"

"Yes." He drew back and trailed a finger along the midline of her body before he slid off the bed. "Later tonight if possible. Tomorrow. The next day. Next month."

Eugenia frowned at his back as he walked to the table. She hadn't been with a man as perfectly formed as he was, and she decided that she was a fool if she didn't appreciate the beauty of his body. She hadn't ever once thought about the fact that Robert had not been perfect. It hadn't mattered.

He brought back a plate of food, two glasses, and the wine, all of which he set on the table beside the bed. He sat beside her, cross-legged, and fed her another section of orange, then a slice of beef so thin he had to roll it up to bring it to her lips. "This time more than a drop of the wine. It's one of my best."

She sat up enough to take the glass, and while she drank, Fenris lowered his head and took her breast in his mouth. His tongue flicked over her nipple, and then his fingers took the place of his mouth.

"Is St. George's acceptable to you?" he asked.

"St. George's is closer to Spring Street. Besides, I never see you there. That's another reason I go to church there."

"I prefer to get my sermons at St. Paul's, but for our purposes the privacy offered by St. George's will do nicely."

She looked at him over the top of her wineglass. "Our purposes? You and I have no mutual purposes, Fenris."

His fingers got clever again. "I can think of at least one."

"Hush, you. Lord." She gasped. "Incorrigible."

Fenris rolled onto his back, one knee raised. He took her

hand and pressed a kiss to the back of it. "Ginny. I came in you."

Her heart did a peculiar turn in her chest.

He tilted his head on the mattress so he could look at her. "Ginny." He cocked his chin in her direction. "I don't want your brother accusing me of impregnating you and leaving you to bear my bastard. More to the point, he wouldn't permit it."

Eugenia's mouth went dry. "We can't be that unlucky."

He smoothed a hand over her belly. "Suppose we have been? What will happen when your brother discovers that fact? I don't know which of us is the better shot, but I hope to hell it's me."

"Mountjoy wouldn't shoot you."

"If I refused to marry you? Of course he would. And I'd have to let him." He cupped the side of her face and rolled over to pull himself partially over her. "Did you mistake me or my intentions?"

"You said a quick—" She waved her hand.

"I apologize for my coarse language. Perhaps it led you to mistake my intentions, though you're more than intelligent enough to understand. You are the sister of a duke. You can't possibly have thought I would take you to bed even once if I was not prepared to marry you. You can't have thought I would contemplate abandoning you to the possibility of a bastard."

"But—" Her throat closed off.

"But?"

"But, Fenris, I don't love you."

He laughed. "That is no secret."

"It would serve you right if I told you yes."

"I won't press you for an answer now. But be assured, if there are consequences, you and I must be married."

Chapter Twenty-one

❧ ❧

A week later. No. 6 Spring Street.

EUGENIA COUNTED THE DISTANT CHIMES OF THE clock in the front parlor. Two. In the morning. Her body still vibrated with the emotional residue of her dream, and she didn't dare close her eyes lest she fall back into that dreaming despair.

She and Hester had not stayed out late, electing to make an early night of it after a pleasant supper with friends of Hester's father. Not so most of the Ton, who might only now be coming home from the evening's entertainments.

With her arms wrapped tight around her upraised knees, she stared at the folds in the canopy overhead and wondered if the void in her soul that was Robert's absence would ever grow smaller. She'd dreamed about him, so vividly that when she realized what had happened, her heart broke as if she'd only just lost him.

She missed him. She missed his voice and his smile and even the way he scowled when something annoyed him. She missed him telling her about his day and about how his research was going. She missed his kisses and his arms around her at night. She missed the intimacy, the way their bodies pleased in both giving and receiving.

Tears built up, pressing on her. If she stayed in bed, she was doomed to stare at nothing while she wept, and if by some chance she did fall asleep, she'd only dream about Robert again. She could not bear waking up convinced he was still alive. She didn't dare give in to the temptation to hold on to that feeling, to imagine that he was only somewhere else in the house or perhaps visiting friends, and that all she need do was find him again or wait for him to come home and tell her how sorry he was to have left her alone for so long.

But she did. She let her thoughts go back to her life in Exeter because she wanted to feel whole again. She closed her eyes and imagined she was home. Not at Bitterward but in Exeter, and that Robert was just downstairs. All the details of their bedroom were vivid in her mind. Burnt orange walls, that spot on the wall where a candle had fallen and made a black mark before Robert had rescued it. The view of the park to the rear of the house. When Robert came back upstairs, he'd say her name. Touch her shoulder, and she'd turn onto her back and look into his face.

He never came. No matter how ferociously she imagined, Robert would never come to her again.

She slid out of bed and rang for Martine. While she waited, she washed her face. The water in the basin was cold enough to raise goose bumps along her arms. Martine came in wearing one of Eugenia's cast-off cloaks because by now she knew that Eugenia would want to walk. Swiftly. Sometimes for hours before she could stand to return to her empty house. Not empty, for Hester was here, and that helped her loneliness. But Hester wasn't Robert. Even her company didn't fill the numbing emptiness of moments like this.

Wordlessly, Martine arranged Eugenia's still-braided hair in a coil at the back of her head then dressed her in one of the gowns she wore only when she was at home in private. Respectable but hardly fashionable, but then, no one would see her. She put on a pair of half boots and a heavy wool cloak and added a reticule containing enough money to hire a hackney to get home if Martine was too tired.

Martine picked up the lantern she'd brought in with her. "Milady?"

She nodded.

On their way through the foyer, Martine took one of the umbrellas from the stand near the door. One never knew what the London weather would do this time of year.

Shadows lay deep around them as Eugenia strode out, as quickly as she could, and even this rapid pace wasn't enough to take her mind off Robert or the feeling that she had betrayed his memory. At home, they'd often walked out at night to see the stars and talk about whatever struck their fancy. Politics. His research. Poetry. Village gossip; he knew everything that went on. He'd hold her hand, and not just because, with his mismatched gait, he needed to steady himself. He held her hand because he wanted to.

Eugenia kept her hood up because she wished to be invisible. A shadow moving through the city. Martine's boots clicked on the walkway, just behind her. The air was damp and heavy with fog and approaching winter, and that was another reason to be glad of her thick cloak. She stayed to streets still reasonably well lit, but not the most trafficked. Mayfair wasn't large, though, and it was difficult to avoid the main thoroughfares. Indeed, the occasional carriage passed on the street, a gentleman or two on horseback, and once or twice someone on foot.

She walked until she had to open her mouth to breathe, and she could hear Martine breathing, too. Heart pounding from the exertion, she slowed. They were near St. James's Street, so she took the next turn to avoid the area. There'd be too many men leaving one of the various clubs having imbibed too much port with their dinner and cards. But she'd come too close to the part of the street where the clubs were. There were more people here, men who saw her and Martine and mistook their reason for walking out alone.

"Here's a pretty girl," one of them cried. "Let's have a look."

She grabbed Martine's hand and wheeled around, walking rapidly away. They were followed. Heels clacked on the street. They walked more quickly yet. Not quite running but close enough.

"Hold on there," the man shouted, and the slurred, drunken voices of him and his companions were much too close. The men crossed the street. She threw a glance over her shoulder and fear shot through her. One of the men had separated from his companions and was now moments from intercepting her and Martine. "A moment, lovely ladies!"

Martine gasped and, closed umbrella in one hand, grabbed Eugenia's arm and planted herself firmly between Eugenia and their pursuer.

"Mrs. Bryant?" Her name seemed to come from nowhere. A different voice. Not from the man who'd followed them. A voice she recognized.

The man who'd called her name was taller than the other and without the prodigious belly. He left the middle of the street and joined her on the walkway. She recognized his silhouette long before the light from the street lamp identified him to her.

"I'm not mistaken," he said. "It is you."

"Lord Fenris." She curtseyed, aware at the same time of Martine stepping back. She pushed back her hood.

"What are you doing out here at this hour?" He looked down his nose. He wore evening dress. Dark coat, the white of his shirt and cravat against a claret waistcoat. A cream silk scarf peeked from the edges of his greatcoat. "With only your maid? You can't be on your way home, unless you're lost. Are you?"

"No."

His eyebrows rose. "You live several streets in the other direction, I hope you know."

"Yes." Why, why, did she have to be so infernally unlucky as to encounter Fenris?

"Well, then?"

This man had been Robert's friend. He'd sat with her husband, dined with him. He'd had years to know Robert, and she wondered, if she touched his arm or his shoulder and concentrated, would she feel the remnants of Robert's friendship with him? Would her fingers tingle from the contact? "I am walking."

He cocked his head in that annoying way he had but did not immediately ask the question he so obviously wanted to pose to her, which must be something along the lines of was she out of her mind? All he said was, "May I ask why?"

If he'd sounded like his usual pompous, blue-blooded self she'd not have answered him, but his question was soft and careful, and she was not in the correct frame of mind to deal with Lord Fenris or any of her contradictory feelings about him. She wanted that wall back between them because feeling hurt. "I could not sleep."

"An unpleasant affliction." He bowed. "I'm sorry to hear that." He hesitated. Even in the dark she could see the emotions flickering over his face, and none of them were condescending. "Are you well, Mrs. Bryant?"

She hadn't the fortitude to answer him in a way that would not reveal more than she was willing to have him know.

He looked away and then back at her. "Is there anything I can do?"

The question, coming from him, astonished her, but what threatened to bring her to tears was his sincerity. She was in a fragile state indeed if she believed he was sincere about anything but his condescension. No matter what they'd done in private. She swallowed hard and struggled for composure.

"Would you object if I accompany you on your walk?" He waded into the river of silence between them. He looked at the sky. "Early, I suppose, but dark nevertheless. The streets are not as safe as they ought to be. If something happened to you, I don't expect I would long survive the ensuing encounter with your elder brother. I can follow behind you if you prefer to avoid my company."

Lord, it was as if he wasn't really Fenris, but some other man entirely. "I shan't make you walk behind me. Don't be absurd."

He flashed a smile at her before he offered his arm. "I am relieved."

Eugenia started walking again, not as fast as before. Fenris said nothing; he just kept pace with her. Martine stayed behind them.

"I don't think we'll have rain," he said.

"No."

"Nor snow."

"No."

"We're having a mild end to our fall."

"Yes." She looked at him. He was the only person with whom she did not need to pretend she was fine when she wasn't, and just knowing that eased her heart. "Listen to us, talking about the weather like two old tabbies."

"Civilized tabbies, Mrs. Bryant."

The silence came back, and after several minutes of that, she said, "I had a nightmare."

"The normal sort or was it about me?"

"The normal sort." She did not entirely succeed in sounding light or carefree. "I find that a walk is the only thing that settles my nerves."

"I, too, find activity is beneficial when I've not achieved a calm state of mind. I am sorry to hear that your sleep was interrupted in so unpleasant a fashion."

"I dreamed about Robert."

He glanced at her but kept walking.

"I woke up crying. That hasn't happened in months."

"I'm sorry."

"It's odd the way something will make me think of him." She swallowed. He'd known Robert. Before her, they'd been dear friends. "Lately, I'll think, oh, Robert would have liked to know how that vote went, or that's a story he would have loved to hear." She clasped her hands behind her back. "I mean, what you said about Mr. Lane having the brains of a lobster. He would have loved to hear that."

"He always did have a sense of the ludicrous, and Lane is certainly that."

"I fear you made an enemy of him that night."

"As if I hadn't already."

She slowed because she could hear Martine laboring to keep up. Fenris matched her pace. "And the button. Awful as it was, Robert would have laughed so hard."

They seemed to be making a loop around the St. James's area. The occasional carriage rattled by, carrying its passengers home from an evening of dancing and dining.

She glanced at him as they walked, and she had the strangest sensation of unwarranted intimacy. Not the physical kind, but something deeper. She watched him from the side, and he was Lord Fenris just now. Not Fox. And she did not exactly hate him.

"We are almost to St. James's Street." He pointed. "Best if we turn back rather than cross here."

"Are you afraid you'll be seen with me?"

He stopped walking, and his eyes burned into her. "Mrs. Bryant. St. James's Street is not an area where a gentlewoman ought to be. At this hour. Unaccompanied."

As if to prove his point, indistinct but raucous singing from another street became louder. She ignored the noise. "You're with me. Martine is here. It's hardly inappropriate."

Several men appeared at the far corner. They were singing and two or three had an arm slung around a compatriot. A very well-to-do group of young bucks. She wondered what and how much they'd drunk to get themselves in that condition. She even felt superior because she'd drunk whisky and not got herself into such a disgraceful state.

"If we were anywhere but here, I would wholeheartedly agree."

"They're on the other side of the street." She returned her attention to Fenris. "Ignore them. Please. I don't want to return home yet."

One of the members of the inebriated group separated from the others and crossed the street. "Fox?" he called. "Is that you?"

"Damn," Fenris whispered.

The singing stopped in favor of low laughter. The others

followed the first man, and before long, they were close enough for Eugenia to see that the man in the front was none other than the lobster-brained Mr. Dinwitty Lane. His friends gathered behind him.

Fenris pushed her into the shadows and flicked her hood over her head.

"You've female company." Lane walked to within a few feet of Fenris. "Let's see your commodity, shall we? Not the Incomparable, I'll warrant. But someone just as lovely."

Martine took a step forward, umbrella clutched in one hand. She put herself in front of Eugenia, between Mr. Lane and his friends. The men ogled her.

Lane lifted his quizzing glass and examined Martine. "Pretty enough, but I must say, she's not up to your usual standard."

This Fenris did not dignify with an answer, though he had the temerity to put an arm around Martine's waist. Oh, he was a dog. A dog!

"Haggling over price?"

"You've had too much to drink."

"I'm well-to-do, I daresay." The men behind him joined in his laughter. Lane moved his quizzing glass in Eugenia's direction. "What's this? Not one companion but two. Oh, ho, ho." There was just no mistaking the sexual nature of that laugh. He waggled a hand and actually attempted to move past Fenris and Martine. "A blonde? I've always heard you were partial to brunettes."

"Lane, if you value your life, stand aside."

"Let's have a look at her. Is this one up to your standards?"

Martine blocked his way, putting a hand on his chest.

Lane's expression darkened. "I do not suffer whores to touch me without my permission."

Eugenia gasped.

Lane looked Martine up and down again in the most insulting manner possible. "You might do for him, but not for me. I wouldn't give a shilling for you."

"That's enough." Fenris addressed his companions. "Restrain him, or I won't answer to the consequences."

One of the men took that to heart. "Lane, come along. It's not worth it."

Lane, however, gave Martine a push and headed for Eugenia.

Fenris made a rather frightening sound, halfway to a growl, and grabbed Lane by one shoulder and shoved him back. At the same time, Martine bashed the fool over the head with her umbrella. Lane's hat, crushed by the blow, tumbled to the pavement. Amid all this, his companions shouted or laughed. A few called out objections. Someone yelled, "Melee!"

The man who'd tried to call Lane back started for his friend. Too late. Much too late.

An infuriated Lane struck Martine. Fenris roared while Eugenia flew to Martine's side. Lane's eyes widened with recognition. "Lady Eugenia?"

She took Martine's arm. Her maid kept her other hand pressed to her cheek. "Did he injure you?"

"No, milady." But when Eugenia pried Martine's hand from her cheek, she could see the beginnings of a bruise.

She whirled on Lane. "How dare you? How dare you, sir? Have you no decency?"

Lane ignored her. He stared at Fenris, openmouthed. "My God, man, Lady Eugenia? The bitch who threw you over for Robert Bryant?"

The silence that followed chilled Eugenia's blood. Even Lane's companions understood the gravity of that awful quiet. Martine plucked at her arm and pulled her away from Fenris and the others.

Fenris cocked his head in that way he had. The corner of his mouth twitched and then his expression was blank. "You are mistaken in every regard, Lane." He sketched an elaborate bow. In the dim light, it was hard to tell, but she had the impression Lane had gone ashen. His friends remained uncharacteristically silent. "I'll bid you good night. For now." He put his back to Lane and the others. "Mrs. Bryant, I'll see you home."

His voice frightened her, and she didn't understand why. "Thank you, my lord."

Fenris took her arm and headed them in the general direction of Spring Street. She stayed silent, afraid to speak lest he reply in that awful tone he'd used with Dinwitty Lane. They covered the distance between St. James's and Number 6 Spring Street without a single word exchanged.

He went inside with her, and though he left the door to the street open, he took off his hat. "Martine. I need a word in private with Lady Eugenia. Go upstairs. I'll send her to you shortly. If she's not with you in twenty minutes, by all means come fetch her."

Martine curtseyed and left. For a bit, they listened to the sound of her retreating footsteps.

"I suppose," Fenris said, "there's no talking you out of these walks."

"Nothing else helps."

"Have you a pistol? More to the point, if you do, do you know how to shoot?"

"Martine does."

"What kind?"

"What kind? I don't know. About this big." She held her hands some four inches apart.

"Your maid is a frightening woman."

"Yes."

"I doubt you pay her enough." His amusement faded, and it was as if it had never been there. He was again the way he had been with Mr. Lane in those moments of deadly quiet. Cold. Frighteningly remote. "Has she ever fired the weapon? And if she has, did she hit what she was aiming at?"

She waited half a heartbeat then said, "The hole in my dressing table is hardly noticeable. I keep a box of hairpins over it."

Alas, he was not amused. He ran his tongue around the inside of his mouth before he replied. "I'll pick you up at sunrise."

"Sunrise. Why?"

"I'm going to teach you how to shoot a pistol."

"I don't want to get up that early."

"Will you agree to send for me before you go haring off on one of these walks of yours?"

"No."

"Then you'll meet me at sunrise."

"Pistols at dawn?" She was shaking inside, and she did not understand why. She only knew she was filled with dread on his behalf. "How droll."

He froze her blood with an icy stare. "If you don't, I will write to your brother and tell him you've been endangering your life." She believed him. Every word he said. "I will tell him, in no uncertain terms, that you cannot be trusted in London without him or your brother Nigel to look after you."

"Can I shoot you?"

"No."

"Pity."

"Sunrise, Ginny."

Chapter Twenty-two

FOX ARRIVED AT EUGENIA'S TOWN HOUSE AT TEN PAST six in the morning. Sunrise wasn't for another twenty minutes, so the street remained dark. He'd brought the closed carriage, for obvious reasons, and one without a coat of arms that would identify him to any curious observer.

No lights shone from the street-facing town house windows. He thought it unlikely she intended to accompany him on this venture. She hadn't believed he was serious about any of it, and at any rate, she had the right to change her mind about such a reckless endeavor. He himself had had second thoughts, but how could he be the one to back down?

His coachman remained in the driver's seat. Though the hour was early, the street was no longer silent. The carriage itself made soft noises, leather creaking, the springs reacting to shifts in weight, the horses, the groom and coachmen moving in their respective places. The lead horse lifted a shod foot and brought it down on the cobbles with a sharp clap. His groom dismounted; the faint thud of his shoes on the street carried all the way to him inside the carriage.

Fox leaned forward and pulled aside the curtain to signal the man that he wished to stay inside for now.

He'd be turned away at the door. Though he'd feel a fool for being ignored, he was damn well serious about writing to her brother if she refused. If she hated him the rest of his life, he'd still write the letter. While he stewed on his many unpleasant alternatives, he rubbed a finger over the surface of the medallion she'd given him. The motion was soothing. How long should he wait before he pushed the issue or gave up? She might still be sleeping, seeing as she'd not been home long. But that was her fault, wasn't it? Not his.

At half past six, he sent his groom to the door of Mountjoy's town house. The windows remained dark. He actually heard his heart pounding in his ears as he watched from the carriage window, fully expecting the man would return without Eugenia. At the door, his servant hunched his shoulders against the morning chill. The door opened sooner than he expected. A hopeful sign? Or proof that her butler was a light sleeper?

His groom conveyed his reason for disturbing the household at this hour. The man half turned as he swept an arm in the direction of the carriage. And then—

Eugenia appeared in the doorway. Her maid, the redoubtable pistol-carrying, umbrella-wielding Martine, was behind her. He caught a flash of Eugenia's bright blond hair before she flicked up the hood of her cloak and followed his groom down the steps.

Before she reached the street, Fox opened the carriage door and stepped down, hand extended to assist her. She did not greet him. Inside, Fox took the rear-facing seat. Silence fell while his groom secured the door and Martine climbed to a seat on the top of the carriage.

"Good morning, Mrs. Bryant."

She grunted a response.

He tapped a finger on the lid of the box that contained a set of dueling pistols. "I have observed in the course of my life that certain individuals are constitutionally unable to greet the morning with any degree of charity."

She glared at him.

"I presume you are one of those women."

"Mmph."

He raised a hand, palm out. "I won't expect you to speak, then." He stretched out one leg. She was here. With him. He would not have to compose an unpleasant letter to her brother. "You were seventeen when I first saw you."

"Nineteen."

"You looked seventeen to me. At any rate, you were young, and new to London and society."

"Must you really?"

"You are at my mercy." He grinned. "I enjoy mornings."

She glared at him again.

"Naturally, you were the object of much masculine interest being, at one and the same time, the sister of a duke who seemed to have taken control of his estate in formidable fashion, and a young woman of considerable good looks."

"I cannot bear to be lied to." She put a hand to the side of her head. "Particularly before the sun is properly up."

"In the years since, you've settled into yourself and your position in society. Gone is the innocence that marked you at your debut."

"Must you?"

He ignored her tone. "I find you even more desirable now than you were then."

"Stop."

"I only tell you now because you are in no condition to argue with me. By the time you are, it will be too late. I have spoken truth to you."

She leveled him with a glare. "You're blathering on now because if you waited until later, I'd shoot you."

He laughed and thought it a success when she summoned a sneer.

"It's rude to be so cheerful at this hour. You can't have got any more sleep than I."

"I'll not utter another word."

"Thank you."

The carriage continued on to Marylebone, past the demolitions and construction of new streets to the remaining open fields. By then, with dawn giving way to morning, Eugenia seemed marginally more alert and, he hoped, less inclined to her previous poor mood. They left the carriage and walked to an area where they would have a clear enough view that she'd not shoot man or beast except by misfortune or pure luck. Martine followed, in step with his groom. The two servants stopped several feet away.

He intended to see this through exactly as he'd said he would. Since she was determined to continue her late-night walks through Mayfair, she needed to know her way around a weapon. She'd not be the only woman of gentle birth to arm herself.

"We'll begin with a discussion of firearms and safety."

"Sensible." She nodded.

He took out one of the pistols and demonstrated the parts. "Barrel, trigger, pan, grasp, butt. Never aim a weapon at someone you do not intend to shoot, for you never know if the one to handle the weapon before you, or even you yourself, was careless. Or whether you, for a multitude of reasons, do not recollect the state in which you left it."

"Understood."

"Excellent."

She pointed at the pistols. "Those are dueling pistols. Mountjoy gave Nigel a pair when he came of age."

"They are. We'll make do with these until I've had the chance to purchase something suitable for you to carry."

"I'll buy my own, thank you."

"You may do whatever you like. I'd prefer that you defer to my expertise, though. If you don't like what I choose for you, by all means buy another weapon more to your tastes. I hope to God you'll at least consult the gunsmith before you do." Lord, but he sounded an ass. He stopped the words that would have followed and made him sound an even bigger prig than he had already. He took a breath and waited until he was confident he could speak in a manner that wouldn't get her back up. "Allow me to restate. If you'll permit me to purchase something for you, I will be easier in my mind, knowing you've a quality firearm that suits you. You may reimburse me for the expense if you like."

"Send me the bill."

"I shall. Now, I'll demonstrate." He went through the steps to load the pistol slowly enough for her to see what he was doing. "You'll load the other later. In the meantime, a few rules to keep us all safe. Muzzle pointing upward at all times." He demonstrated. "Do not cock the weapon until you're ready to fire. If at a shooting match you hold the pistol any way but muzzle up while someone, such as my groom there is doing, sets up or marks a target, you'll be disqualified. Moreover, God will send you to hell for endangering life and limb. It is an inviolate rule. Is that clear, Ginny?"

"Do not call me that. Only my intimates may call me Ginny. And you, sir, are not an intimate."

"I beg to differ. Any woman who's made me come is an intimate. You were very good at it, by the way."

She gaped at him, cheeks deliciously pink, and he pretended not to notice. But he did. He surely did. He managed, though only just, not to laugh. Plainly, morning was not the time to trust to her good humor.

The targets were set now, a thin square of wood on a post with a paper target on the front. Without speaking or assisting, he watched her load the other pistol. She did well, with only a hesitation or two about how to proceed, and one pause for a question to him. When she was done, she pointed the pistol muzzle skyward.

"Unload."

She did so.

"Now load again." This time she performed the steps without questions and with fewer hesitations. He had her load and unload twice more and ended quite satisfied with her progress. With her beside him, holding the pistol in the prescribed manner, he confirmed that Martine and his groom were well away from the area and that no animals or other people had wandered into range. "Ready?"

She nodded.

"When dueling you'll wish to turn your torso like so." He stood sideways, his left arm at his side, his right holding the pistol muzzle to the sky. "So as to minimize the target you present." He leveled his forearm and sited the target.

"Any of several instinctive reactions will spoil your shot. Closing one or both eyes is one. Don't laugh. Most beginners do. Another is jerking or recoiling of the head or upper body. That will pull your shot wide. Consider the pistol an extension of yourself." He relaxed. "Deliberate and cool. Cock the trigger." He stopped talking so she would hear the sound. "Use your right eye. Site your target down the barrel thus. There will be noise and recoil. Depress the trigger. Like so."

He fired and hit his target dead center.

"It's very loud."

"Yes." Fox put down the pistol while his groom trotted out with a set of paper plugs and a pencil to mark the shots on the reverse of the target. Only when the servant was out of range did Fenris hand her the other pistol. "Check its condition. Is it loaded?"

She did, with little hesitation. "No, sir."

"Aim, as I showed you. I brought the smallest dueling pistols I have, but you'd do better with something smaller and lighter yet. The Manton brothers will have something more suitable for you than these." He stood to one side of her and adjusted her grip on the pistol, then stepped back. "Fire."

"It isn't loaded."

"Fire so that you understand what pressure to apply to the trigger. The recoil will be different when you shoot in earnest, of course. Imagining the gun is merely an additional length of your arm."

She lifted her chin and did as he'd demonstrated. She pressed the trigger and the barrel of the pistol twitched. "Ah. Yes, I see what you mean."

"Again."

She'd already reset her feet. He crossed his arms over his chest and watched her. He liked her determination, the way she concentrated and even took a moment to settle her breathing. She sited and dry fired several more times in succession.

"I believe you're ready for a live shot. You'll need a great deal of practice at this. It's critical that you perform every step precisely, and for God's sake, remember that a loaded weapon is designed to kill. It does that very well."

"Yes. Yes, that's so." She spoke quite genuinely. Dare he think her morning mood was fading? "I do thank you for the reminder."

He collected the various parts from her as she completed the process. Soon enough he stood behind her, watching as she held the pistol muzzle upward and confirmed the area was clear. She set her feet, aimed, then reset. The muzzle wavered, and she reset her position again. Then, just as he'd shown her, she fired.

Off to the side, Martine applauded. With the muzzle of the pistol pointed to the sky, Eugenia stared at the target. "Not a bull's-eye."

"No."

"*You* had a bull's-eye."

"I was not firing a weapon for the first time. You did very well for a virgin."

Her shoulders shook with her laughter. "Have you no shame, sir?"

"None at all. Do you think you can do that again?"

She made a face at the target. His groom was already halfway there with the paper and pencil. "Do you mean miss the center?"

"Your first shot hit the target inside the outer circle. Most people firing a gun for the first time are fortunate to hit the target at all."

She squared her shoulders, so obviously insulted that he could not help a smile. "You think it was a fluke."

"For you to make a more than decent shot your first time is something to be proud of. I doubt your maid hit the target the first time she fired a pistol."

"It wasn't a fluke."

"Madam." He crossed his arms over his chest. "You have fired a pistol precisely once in your life. That is hardly a sufficient number of shots to give you status as a markswoman."

"I'll have you know I aimed carefully." She eyed the target. "Exactly as you instructed. Deliberately and coolly."

"We'll soon know if it's a repeatable event." As soon as

his groom was off their makeshift range, he picked up the other pistol, loaded it, and took his shot. The report disturbed a flock of crows. The birds launched into the air, cawing.

She eyed the target. "A bull's-eye."

"Breaks your heart, does it?" The crows, still calling to one another, resettled.

"Never."

He pulled the muzzle up while the groom went out to mark his shot. "I've fired this pistol more than once."

"Are you considered a marksman?"

"With all humility, I am considered one of the finest shooters in London."

"One of." She looked at him thoughtfully. He was tempted to lean down and kiss her, but he didn't dare. Not with Martine watching and quite likely armed. "Who's a better shot than you?"

He shrugged. "With a pistol like this? Or just shooting in general?"

"Like this."

"One or two men, perhaps."

"Is Dinwitty Lane one of them?"

"Yes."

"I thought he might be."

"A step back, Ginny. You're over the line."

She looked down, saw that she was, and repositioned herself. She set her feet, sited, and fired. He was not astonished when she hit the target again. "Better," she said. "But not a bull's-eye."

Six more rounds proved her talent was no fluke. She simply did not miss the target. Her worst shot hit the edge of the paper, and two struck just inside the inner ring. He judged them done for the morning when he noticed her surreptitiously shaking her right arm.

They cleaned the pistols on the field, and when they were done with that and on their way to his carriage, he said, "If you should encounter Mr. Lane on one of those nighttime walks of yours, I expect you or Martine to shoot him."

Chapter Twenty-three

❧❦

The following morning. Bouverie.

EUGENIA TURNED FROM THE WINDOW WHEN FENRIS came into the parlor from a door other than the one she'd come through. In a house built on the scale of Bouverie, this could not possibly be the best parlor. It wasn't nearly grand enough. It had the advantage of intimacy, simply on account of its size, which was smaller than the other parlors she'd seen on previous visits.

The predominant colors were cream and pale gray and very much suited her mood. The chimney was carved wood, the mantel squared off and narrow, with chimney glass that went only halfway to the ceiling. A slate gray fringed drapery filled the gap between the ceiling and the glass. Ten wooden chairs lined the walls, and there was but one table and that in the center of the room. She'd elected not to sit. The windows, high and narrow, overlooked a side street where the world was almost entirely gray with fog. Today they might well have rain. Perhaps snow.

"Mrs. Bryant." Fenris bowed to her. She had the impression, based on no more evidence than a slight disarrangement of his hair, that he had dressed hastily. "It's fortunate you found me here."

"I would have tracked you down, wherever you went to ground."

He glanced at the table, empty of anything but a rather ugly blue and white vase. "You have no refreshments." This appeared to surprise him. "Shall I call for tea? Cider? A bite to eat?"

"Thank you, but no. It's too early for that."

The corner of his mouth twitched, and he adjusted his coat. "To what do I owe the honor of your visit at such an hour of the morning?"

If she'd had Martine's umbrella, she would have hit him with it. He deserved it. "You know very well why I am here."

He approached her but stopped short of coming close enough to touch her. "I fear I don't."

"The entire city is talking. Did you think I would not hear?"

"Whatever do you mean?"

"There must have been fifty people who left their cards with me just this morning, at an ungodly hour, I might add. My poor butler is exhausted." She shivered and kept her shawl close around her, for the room was cold.

"Come closer to the fire." He gestured. "Please."

She stayed where she was. Once again, she had that sense that the world was falling away from her.

"If you don't," he said with a sigh, "I'll have no choice but to build up the fire to prevent you from catching a chill. In a fortnight's time Camber will have discovered the shortage in coal, and task some poor young maid with the waste. She will be discharged through no fault of her own. I shall then be obliged to find her another position and half of London will think it's because I've had my way with her."

"Do you mean to say such a rumor would bother you?"

"It would." His eyes landed on her with no sign of humor. "Particularly because I don't fuck my servants."

"But you would me?"

"Yes." He spoke curtly, but she was not going to be intimidated by him. Let him glower and try to shock her with crude language as much as he liked. "And very well, too, I hope you'll agree."

She walked to the fire and stood with her hands out. "Next time I call, I'll bring my own coal, and we'll have a cozy visit."

Fenris laughed, but she didn't think she was imagining he wasn't entirely at ease. And no wonder. "Woolen stockings are a great help." He moved to her side, a polite distance between them. She shot him a look. He wore tan breeches, a forest green coat and a gold waistcoat with a damask pattern worked in the same color thread—the embroidery was exemplary—and Hessians with tassels. Practically gaudy for him. Lily's medallion hung from his watch chain. When she lifted her chin, she found him watching her. "Why have you come?" he asked.

"Don't let's play games."

He shrugged. "As you wish."

She was not about to back down or slink away without having carried out the task that had brought her here. "You can't honestly intend to duel Mr. Lane."

Fenris did not react, and that in itself told too much. "I don't know what you mean."

She clapped her hands slowly. "Bravo, my lord. Bravo. The very incarnation of confusion stands before me."

"Thank you." He bowed with all intended irony, she was sure. "I assure you, however, I am indeed confused."

"Lord Aigen has already called on Mr. Lane on your behalf."

"Has he? I wonder why."

"You know he has. Are you mad?" She took a step toward him. Lord, the havoc this man played with her emotions, from the moment she'd heard of the challenge to right now. "No one will believe there's anything illicit between us. There's no reason to meet anyone at dawn tomorrow or any other day."

"People will believe anything if it is sufficiently salacious or scandalous. If I do nothing, our affair—"

"There is no affair."

"—is all but fact. That's hardly the point, whether we are having an affair or not. Lane and his cronies will talk, and it won't matter if it's lies or pure truth." He shook his head. "You, of all people, should know that. We ought to be married immediately."

"No."

"He insulted you." His low voice sent a shiver down her spine, and her throat thickened. She had to stop herself from begging him not to meet Lane. How had this happened to her, that she was in the middle of something so unbelievably asinine and deadly? "He used an epithet that no gentleman should ever use against a lady. I won't let that go unanswered. Nor will I allow anyone to think I would compromise you."

She moved away from the fire and instantly regretted it. "They won't. No one will think that of you."

"It wasn't just Lane who saw us and heard what was said."

"But I don't care!" She took a step forward and stopped herself. She could hardly speak, but she forced out words thick with incipient tears. "Fenris. I don't care."

"I do. Someone must protect my reputation." He leaned against the table with the ugly vase. "If you won't, then I fear it's up to me."

She glared at him, unamused and angry. "Ought I to send Hester to throw a glove in his face and inform him I'll meet him at dawn?"

"Miss Rendell would certainly run circles around the fool."

"Pistols at twenty paces, sir."

"Choice of weapon is his."

"I don't see why." She let out a frustrated breath. "Honestly, Fenris. He didn't insult you."

"No?" He pushed off the table and strode to her. "Then you have a peculiar recollection of the events of that night. I clearly recall that he implied I was a sexual intimate of both you *and* your maid." He was closer than she'd thought, close enough that if she'd wanted, she could have touched her medallion, now the only fob hanging from his watch chain.

"I wasn't insulted."

"You ought to have been."

"Why?"

He pretended astonishment. "Am I to understand that you'd be willing to engage in an affair with me? We needn't ask your maid to join us. Unless?" He waggled his eyebrows.

"My God, are you ever serious?"

He touched the medallion, rubbing it between thumb and forefinger. "Far too often."

"There's no need for violence; that's all I came here to say." This wasn't going at all how she planned. "Isn't this sort of thing usually avoided by an apology?"

His smile faded. "I don't intend to apologize."

"Don't be dense. I mean Mr. Lane. It seems to me a part of Lord Aigen's duty to you in such a matter is to convince the offending party to apologize."

"Ginny. My dear." He pressed a hand to his heart, and she could have screamed, she was so frustrated by his cavalier attitude. "Is it possible you're frightened for my safety? I'm touched."

"Hardly." He was constantly shifting the conversation from where she meant it to be. She put a hand on the table and immediately removed it because her fingers trembled. Fenris believed his honor and hers were at stake, and, with a sinking heart, she realized there was a vanishing small hope that he would back out. "Yes, of course I am. Fenris, please. I don't want to be the woman responsible for the death of Camber's heir."

"That is unlikely." He remained close. Close enough for her to touch. She had to put her hands behind her back to keep herself from throwing her arms around him. Hysteria would not help her cause.

She took a steadying breath. "You're awfully sure of yourself."

He lifted a hand. "I am reckoned an excellent shot."

"Mr. Lane can shoot the face from the Jack of Clubs." She pressed her lips together before continuing. "Several people were only too pleased to share that fact with me.

You said yourself he's an excellent shot, so don't deny the danger."

"Shooting a living man is substantially different than murdering the Jack of Clubs."

"What if you're killed? What then?"

He walked to the fireplace and stood by the screen, hands extended to a fire that could easily have been mistaken for one that had been banked for the night. "In such a case, my poor father will have to find a woman to provide him with another son. It's not my fault he was so shortsighted as to fail to sire more than one son capable of stepping into his shoes. Or mine."

"Oh, for pity's sake, Fox." She set a hand on the table again, but made a fist so he wouldn't see her trembling. "Why are you treating this as if it's a joke? If you die, your father might never recover from the loss. How can you be so cold and unfeeling?"

He glanced at her then back to the fire, and she didn't imagine the flash of disappointment she saw in his eyes. "I was raised to it."

"Don't," she said. He made such a jumble of her emotions she hardly knew how to put words to her intentions, and now she was feeling both foolish and inarticulate. "Don't do this."

"Defend my honor? And yours? I'd not ask you such a thing."

She had no answer for the bitterness of his reply except for the shameful thickness that crept into her words. "You could be killed."

Fenris kept his back to her. "I might only be wounded, you know." When he moved, he turned only his head. He smiled though his eyes were bitter. "Think of that."

"Be serious."

"Never more, Mrs. Bryant. There are other advantages to this duel you've overlooked."

"Is that so?"

He faced her again, with a smile as cold and brittle as ice. "You might bring the very intriguing Miss Rendell along to help you nurse me back to health. What better way for a couple to discover they are destined lovers but for one of them to be brought back from the brink of death?"

Eugenia deliberately misunderstood him. "You don't deserve Hester."

He fingered the medallion again. "Doubtless so. But then I am not in love with her, so my heart is safe from her. If I were in love with her, I promise you, I would do all within my power to make sure I did deserve her."

Eugenia went still. She did not want to hear him. She did not wish to understand what he was telling her. "Duels are illegal."

"They are." He walked away from the fireplace.

"There. You see?"

"Not at all. What is your point?"

She wanted to stomp her foot, she really and truly did. "Dueling is illegal. That is my point."

"Are you accusing me of intending to engage in an illegal activity?" He laid a hand over his heart, and this time there was a hint of a genuine smile on his face. "I am shocked. Shocked, I tell you."

"You cannot meet Mr. Lane."

"If only he were easier to avoid."

She took a step forward and was struck by an overwhelming sense of intimacy that extended beyond the impact he had on her senses. She had been to bed with this man. She'd touched him, kissed him, caressed him, and she had, for God's sake, written her name on his belly in purple, scented ink, and he had convinced her he adored her for all her boldness. "Fox. Please."

He took her hand in his. "Your concern is all a man hopes for from the woman whose honor he will defend on what may be the last day of his life." All trace of a grin vanished from his face, but she did not trust him in the least. "Will you give me a kiss so that if I am mortally wounded I will have the sweet taste of your lips as my dying memory?"

"I am not amused." She tugged on her hand, but he didn't release her. "I'm not."

He put his other hand to her back, between her shoulder

blades. An erotic shock ran through her. Her arousal so stunned her that she stared into his face, unable to marshal coherent thought for several seconds. She wanted to go to bed with him again.

His head dipped to hers, and still she did not move. Not an inch. When his lips brushed hers, she steeled herself against a desire to throw her arms around him and not let go.

When he kissed her, she could barely stop the tears that burned in her eyes, or hold back the sobs building in her chest. He could not meet Lane. He couldn't. She stepped forward, into his embrace, and told herself this was nothing but animal lust between them. She was overreacting because of all the horrible things she'd been imagining since she heard the first rumor of a duel. His hand settled into the small of her back, and he let go of her hand to hold the back of her head.

Her breasts felt heavy, there was a flutter in her belly, and, God help her, all the sensation in her body seemed to relocate between her legs. His mouth was astonishingly tender. So tender. As the contact between them continued, her desperate state seemed to transfer to him, for his tenderness turned carnal. His tongue swept into her mouth, and, ninny that she was, she answered his invitation. Fox kissed her as if he could barely control himself, and how could she not respond to that when she was mad with lust?

He ended the kiss, and all she could think was *no, don't let this end yet*. He drew in a breath, a gasp, really, and his arms stayed around her though it made no sense to her at all that he would react this way.

"Don't be angry." His words were low. "Please don't be angry."

"I'm not angry." She only wished she knew what she was. If not angry, then perplexed. Yes. That. But how was she to account for the giddiness? The quiver in her belly? The trembling knees? She drew in a breath. Let it out. Then another until she felt she had all those wild emotions under control.

A wry smile twisted his lips. "Perhaps you are overcome with desire?"

She shook her head. "I don't know. No. Of course not."

His eyebrows shot up. "You destroy me."

"The only thing I know is that this is madness. Us. We are madness together."

"Sweet madness, surely."

"We were mad, the both of us. At Upper Brook Street and just now." She moved away from him, to the window where the fog continued to block the view. She was bereft.

"At least now I go to my doom knowing the delight of our mutual madness."

She whirled, her skirts whisking around her ankles. "If you're killed, will that help anything?"

"It would prevent me from living with the dishonor."

"Fenris."

He gazed at her. "Fox."

"I'll never understand you men."

"I rarely feel I understand women."

"Please. Is this really necessary? A duel."

He shrugged. "I will be astonished if Mr. Lane does not deliver an apology before the night is out."

"If he doesn't?"

"Then I will meet him tomorrow morning and hope that I am the better marksman. Regardless—unless I am killed, of course—you and I will have to be married."

"Still you make light of this?"

"Not in the least. Marry me, and I can go to my fate knowing there is a chance I've left a son behind to carry on another generation in direct descent from the very first Camber to grace this earth."

"I am at a loss. You cannot be reasoned with."

"At the moment, I feel I am entitled to that sentiment more than you."

"Good day, then." She headed for the door but halfway there, turned back. "I don't wish for you to be killed on my account. If you believe nothing else I've said, believe that."

He gave an ironic smile. "We make progress, then. I'll call on you tomorrow. Unless I am dead, in which case, I hope you'll find it in you to forgive my absence."

Chapter Twenty-four

EUGENIA SAT UP IN BED, HEAD ON HER KNEES, LISTEN-
ing to the clock chime. One o'clock in the morning. Most
of London was still awake, balls and formal dinners winding
down. Plays, ballets, and operas were over by now. The
Haymarket was probably a crush of people and carriages,
all going nowhere quickly.

All anyone had talked about tonight was the rumored
duel between Fenris and Dinwitty Lane. The rumor transformed constantly. The duel was over a slight to a woman,
variously whispered to be Lady Tyghe, a ballet girl, an
actress, a German countess who wasn't even in London, and
a certain Miss R. There were three Miss Rs in Town this
short season, only two of whom were considered likely candidates for such an argument. Hester was not one of them.

According to another version, Fenris and Lane had quar-
reled over a horse, with the usual inability of some people
to refrain from jokes in very poor taste. The irony was that
the version that said she was responsible for the argument
was universally dismissed as absurd. Which it ought to be.
With every iteration, every ridiculous rendition, with every

rumor shockingly close to accurate or nowhere near the truth, Eugenia's stomach had twisted into a tighter knot.

She rang for Martine, and her maid came in, a cloak over her arm and the gun Fenris had sent to her in the other. The maid handed her the pistol. "Thank you."

Once she'd determined the weapon was loaded, they left and were outside in the cold night air of Mayfair by half past one. While they walked, Eugenia told herself they weren't deliberately walking in the direction of Bouverie, and that even if they happened to pass near the house, she wouldn't stop. She couldn't possibly call at this time of night, and besides, Fenris wasn't likely to be there. He'd be at Upper Brook Street, wouldn't he? More to the point, whether he was at Bouverie or Upper Brook Street, he was unlikely to be outside on a path that could possibly intersect with hers.

Ten minutes later, she and Martine crossed to the street that paralleled the west side of Bouverie. Fog swirled around the building's upper stories and in the street, too. The damp air carried the scent and sting of smoke from all the chimneys. Only a few lights were on upstairs; the servants' quarters. Fewer lights burned in the windows of the middle floors. Camber, she wondered? Or was Fenris home?

Was the marquess pacing his room somewhere inside there, fretting over the events to come in just a few short hours? Was he lounging in his club or reveling in the arms of a mistress? She ignored the sound of someone walking on the close that ran between this street and the one parallel. A single person, walking quickly. She remembered her gun almost too late. She slipped her hand into her pocket and wondered if she'd be able to shoot a living person.

Martine faced away, umbrella at the ready. The back of Eugenia's neck prickled, and she waited to see who was heading toward the street where she and Martine stood. A shape emerged from the fog, a man in a greatcoat and a hat. A gentleman, she thought. Too slender to be Dinwitty Lane, whom she would be only too happy to wound just now.

He slowed when he saw them, then walked slower still. Martine slid her other hand into the pocket of her cloak and moved so that she continued to face the man as he approached. The turned-up collar of his greatcoat made him hardly more than shadow. Then he took off his hat and bowed. "Another night unable to sleep, Mrs. Bryant?"

Her heart jolted.

Fenris. Of course it was Fenris, for she was cursed. *Blessed*, said a voice in her head. Lucky beyond belief. She must be, for she never met anyone but Fenris out here. "How could I sleep tonight, of all nights?"

"I know your maid is aiming a gun at my heart. You, madam, had damn well better be armed."

She showed him her pistol and, at his satisfied nod, dropped it into her pocket.

He went to her, and Martine simply faded from Eugenia's notice. He stood too close to her, gazing into her face, and it was as if there were an invisible connection between them, drawing them together. This was inevitable, their meeting. Destined, and she wasn't going to resist. He tipped his head in the direction of Bouverie. "Come with me?"

She moved with the pressure of his hand on the back of her elbow. They crossed the street to Bouverie where he opened a side gate that admitted them to the grounds. To their left was the mews, a stretch of buildings that ran the length of the street that backed Bouverie. Not a single light in the windows that she could see. He put a key to the lock of a door toward the rear portion of the house. He held the door for her and Martine.

Inside the small foyer, Fenris stripped off his gloves and stuffed them in the pockets of his greatcoat. With a quirk of a smile in her direction, he blew on his fingers a few times, then turned up the lantern that had been left on a table near the door. There was a candle there as well. He lit it.

The foyer was plain, with a plank floor, a table, and plaster walls painted white. Directly across from the door by which they'd entered, a staircase led upward into dark. To the left, more stairs led down. Fenris put a coin in Martine's hand before he handed her the candle. "You'll find your way below?"

Martine curtseyed. "My lord."

"Tell Mrs. Harrison she's to look after you. Ring for her if you need anything."

She glanced at Eugenia, questioning with a look. Silence settled between the three of them, and in the quiet, Eugenia considered the fact that Fenris ought to have taken them to the front door so that he could be said to be officially at home and entertaining a caller. But he hadn't. He'd brought them in clandestinely, through this private entrance that was not the servants' entry. Martine waited for Eugenia to agree with this dismissal of her or else signal that she ought to stay. All three of them waited.

"I'll send for you when you're needed, Martine." Eugenia nodded at the down staircase, and Martine lifted the candle and disappeared.

Still wearing his hat and coat, Fenris took the lantern in one hand and Eugenia's hand in the other. She still wore her gloves, yet the contact felt intimate.

As she climbed the stairs, she told herself there needn't be anything improper about this. He might be taking her to a parlor to lecture her on her habit of late-night walks. He might. And even if he were thinking of something else, she was not obliged to do anything she didn't want to do.

They ascended two flights of stairs, past what would be the floor containing the public rooms of parlors, saloons, dining rooms, and the like. They exited to a back corridor with a plain rug and the same white plaster walls as in the little foyer. He stopped at a wooden door, also quite plain and unpainted, and lifted the latch. He went in only far enough to hold the door open for her.

She entered a withdrawing room that was clearly a part of the main house, designed as a place for the staff to stage service of meals. The walls were lilac, and there was a domed ceiling with white scalloped decorations. Behind her, the door they'd come through clicked shut.

"I did not intend to stay the night here." Fenris crossed the withdrawing room and opened another door, which he held for her as well. She found herself in a bedchamber. Oh,

Lord. She struggled to separate the implications of this from her sense that anything that happened, from the moment he'd emerged from the fog, was inevitable. She was swept up, carried along. She had known all along that they would meet and end up here.

With only the lantern, the room was quite dim. She could make out the shadows of furniture, bed, chairs, tables, and the glow of the fire. Fenris came in after her and put the lantern on a desk painted gold. Across the way, a door opened.

"Milord?"

"I won't be going to Upper Brook Street after all." Fenris walked in front of Eugenia. "You needn't stay close. I'll ring for you when I need you."

"Milord." The dark form that was Fenris's servant bowed once and withdrew.

How quiet the house was. The usual creaks and pops one heard. The low hiss from the fireplace. She stared at her feet, but the urge to watch Fenris overwhelmed her. He slipped out of his coat. He draped that over a chair and put his hat on the seat. While he did this, Eugenia's pulse raced. He went to her, that same unfathomable expression on his face, and, after unfastening the frog that closed her cloak, put the first two fingers of his hand to the side of her face. His skin lay cool against her heated cheek.

She licked her lips. "If you have another engagement . . ."

"Not until morning." He put his hands on her shoulders, underneath her cloak, and slid them forward until her cloak slipped off. He caught the garment just in time and folded that over the chair, too.

"You can't mean to go through with this." She swallowed. With every sweep of his gaze over her, she lost another shred of hope that she would tell him no and save herself. He'd bespelled her somehow, and the thing of it was, she didn't want to come out from under it. "Your appointment, I mean."

His eyebrows lifted. "With Mr. Lane? I do."

"This morning, you said he'd apologize."

"I don't believe I said precisely that, but nevertheless, he has refused to do so." He shrugged one shoulder. "One finds it necessary to take a stand in such circumstances."

He couldn't die. It would be her fault if he were killed, and Lily would never forgive her. "Don't." She clutched his arm. "Please don't."

"Don't what?" He rested his hands on her shoulders, mostly on her gown, but his thumbs swept over the bare skin above her collar. Part of her wanted to believe he had no improper intentions, but in the end, she wasn't a fool. There was nothing proper at all about her being here. In his room. She was alone with a man she wanted desperately to dislike. And didn't. She was going to repeat every mistake she'd ever made that had given him power over her feelings.

"Don't be a fool. Don't get yourself killed on my account."

He moved behind her, and when she would have faced him, he put his hands on her shoulders again. "No. Stay like that."

She did. Lord help her, she did. Because surely Fenris, of all men, could not hurt her any worse than what Robert's death had done. Could not. Her stomach dropped, then soared and dropped again when he unhooked the first fastening of her gown. Then the second, and she really couldn't believe how badly she wanted this to happen.

"Have I told you I'm glad you're wearing colors again?" His voice came soft and low in her ear. Once, just once while he found and unfastened all the ties and hooks and ribbons of her clothes, he pressed his mouth to her shoulder, and the shock of that warm and intimate contact weakened her knees.

When the time came, he draped her gown over the chair, and then her stays and petticoat. She'd already stepped out of the sensible half boots she'd worn. Had she really done that on her own? She anticipated his hands on her, touching those places that made her melt. Once again she was wracked with desire.

He stood behind her and gathered two handfuls of her

chemise, and she drew in a breath as the fabric slid up her body, over her head, and then, simply, off. He rested his palms on her shoulder, then smoothed a hand along her arm while he breathed the words, "Such beauty. You humble me, Ginny."

That moving arm circled her waist, forearm resting on her bare skin, drawing her back against his front. His other arm he wrapped loosely around her very upper chest. He angled his lower hand to her hip while he drew the other downward and around the outside of her breast.

How long had she felt herself separate from people? As if there were a barrier between her and anyone else, that everyone was real and vital except her. Fenris had come inside that barrier once already, and he would do so again tonight. His hands on her, those whispered words brought him into a world she had, for too long, inhabited alone. Tonight, here, with him, she would once again feel, really, truly feel like a living, breathing animal.

He kissed the side of her neck. His fingers moved again, cupping her breast now, plucking, a caress that drew longing from her. He dropped to his knees and his hands glided around her, downward. So tender, so unerringly finding places where the lightest touch of his fingertips made her shiver with longing.

He removed her garters and stockings, and when she was absolutely bare, he turned her around. Still on his knees he kissed the top of each of her thighs, hands cupping her bottom, then moving around her hips and down. His fingers slid lightly, so lightly between her thighs. "Lovely Ginny."

Butterflies took flight in her belly, and she looked down, her hands resting lightly on his head. Fenris. A man she had hated for years. His hair was silk against her fingers, thick locks of dark, dark brown settling around her hand and fingers. She was hardly able to believe she felt like this, when for such a long time after Robert's death she'd thought those feelings had died with him.

This was Fenris, the Marquess of Fenris, on his knees before her, worshipping her with his hands, his mouth, his eyes and breath. He ran his palms from her legs to her hips and up her back as far as he could reach, and desire snaked through her, twisting her emotions and then pushing out everything but him and what he made her feel.

At last, though, he rose and took her face between his hands and kissed her, openmouthed from the start, savagely even, a deliberate taking of her, a prelude to what would come. Tongues touched, entwined, their breath mingled, and his hands cupped her face. He was breathing faster when, at last, he pulled away from her. He took her hand and guided her to his bed, a monstrous canopied four-poster.

He said, "Lie down. I want to look at you."

He undressed while she did that. Boots, stockings, his coat and waistcoat. He let them drop where he stood. She caught a flash of the medallion when he put his watch on the chair. Very quickly he stripped himself of everything, and Eugenia's breath caught, because physically he was shockingly perfect. Sleekly muscled, just as she remembered, and, yes, absolutely as large everywhere. Lord. His cock was erect, and she had an intense longing to touch him, all the girth and inches of him.

From the bed, she held out a hand. "Come here."

"Ginny," he whispered as he joined her.

He came over her with no preamble. He nudged a thigh between her legs, and she adjusted. From the very first push of him inside her, she groaned. Her passage was wet for him, ready for his entry, aching for him, and this was a thousand times more intense than before. Pure joy flashed through her. Perfect. So simple, to feel *this* way, to accept a man inside her.

He groaned when he was as far inside her as it seemed possible for him to be, stretching her, filling her, and this was what she'd wanted all those lonely years since Robert. She missed this, a man's body, his sex inside her, pushing. Thrusting, then the delicious slide away. She missed knowing she was adored.

"God, Ginny, my God, you take my breath." Eyes locked

with hers, he withdrew all but the head of his cock, then pushed forward again, slowly this time, and he fit so perfectly. She tipped her hips toward him, and he put his hands on either side of her, lifting up enough to see her, and the rhythm began.

Every stroke delicious, the roughness of his thigh against hers, the slide of his belly against hers, skin to skin. The hitch in his breath and hers. His thrusts were harder now, as hard and as rough as before, and she found she did like that. She lost herself to the pitch of her body, the call of her climax, met that, her arms tight around him, palming his backside, feeling the flex and release of his muscles. He was good at this, she realized. Taking a woman. Practiced.

Well. Thank God, for that.

At one point, he paused and took a steadying breath. His eyes drooped half closed, and she had one leg drawn up, and she arched against him, pressing herself to him, and he stared into her face, shook his head once, and grabbed her wrists, pinning them to the mattress above her shoulders, and he pumped hard against her forward push. He put a hand on her breast and curled the other around her head, and he rolled his hips and hit a spot inside that shattered her.

"Yes," she heard him say. "Yes."

She was brought to a point where the pleasure reached such a peak she couldn't move, could hardly breathe, and only moments after she had breath in her lungs, he hit that spot in her, no accident then, and she came apart all over again. He gave her the space of a breath or two to come down before he shifted his weight to one forearm, nearly on his side, and cupped her bottom, bringing her harder forward. The rhythm continued, faster now. Urgent.

They reached a point where she knew he was close, and so was she, again. His eyes, at this moment, were unfocused, lips parted, and then he whispered to himself, urgent and with shorter and shorter breaths. "Ginny, Jesus, oh, God."

He threw back his head and let out a low moan as he pressed hard into her. His arms shook and he lowered himself onto her, hips still hard against her, still pushing forward, head to her shoulder, and she held him while he finished.

When, later, he withdrew from her, he breathed her name again, and for some reason she couldn't speak for fear she'd cry.

They began again with him exploring her body, his cock soft, and she touched him, too. Eventually, he grinned at her and the light in his eyes was so very smug when he put her on her back and he entered her again. Different this time than before. More desperate now, so that neither of them had time to think. He was rougher than he had been, and that made her smile, because if he thought to master her like this, he was mistaken. She wanted this from him.

She turned her head and bit his upper arm, not hard, but enough that he felt it, and he shouted out. She wound her fingers into his hair until he forced her hands away and spread her arms wide and pinned her. Very different this time, his taking possession of her like this, with both of them aware that she'd both invited him and brought him with her.

"I don't want to bruise you," he said.

"I don't care."

He bent his head to her breast, his fingers tight around her arms, and closed his teeth on her nipple, enough that she sucked in a breath and then went over the edge without him. The finish this time was sweeter, but no less intense. They lay together for a time, limbs entangled.

"Ginny." He drew a strand of her hair away from her face. "I have to send you home now."

Chapter Twenty-five

※※

EUGENIA AND HESTER WERE IMMEDIATELY SUR-
rounded when they arrived at Hyde Park shortly before
noon. It was their habit on days she and Hester were not at
home to walk to the park before making calls. It had been
her thought that getting out of the house would take her
mind off the fact that she'd heard nothing from Fenris. Nothing but the most awful silence.

A friend of Hester's, a Miss Lynd, drew them into the
midst of a crowd that quickly grew larger and included both
genders, though most everyone was Hester's age or younger.
Lieutenant Fraser was among the gentlemen, with his elder
brother, too.

"Have you heard?" Miss Lynd put a hand on Hester's arm.

Hester smiled, but Eugenia's heart fell to her toes in a
premonition of disaster. "Heard what?"

"Everyone's talking about it." She fanned the air with a
hand.

"About what?"

"Dinwitty Lane and the Marquess of Fenris dueled this
morning."

"Dueled?" Hester shot a worried look at Eugenia. Though her stomach clenched, this was not the news she'd dreaded hearing. The fact of the duel was nothing. "Heavens, why?"

There was a great deal of talking at once with interruptions and fevered speech from the crowd around her and Hester. She saw Lieutenant Fraser pushing his way toward them. Toward Hester.

"Mr. Ellington said Mr. Lane insulted Miss Reade."

"No, no, it was Miss Rosalyn."

"No it wasn't. It was—"

"Fenris insulted Miss Repton—"

"They argued over a horse, is what I heard."

"—a Miss R at any rate."

"No one's seen Mr. Lane."

"Oh, dear," Hester said. The crowd around them grew thicker.

"Or Lord Fenris. Has he called on you, Miss Rendell?"

"No." Hester turned her head this way and that. Baring's eldest managed to reach Hester before his brother. "Do you think he would? Why?"

"Well he would, on account of Lady Eugenia. She's a connection of his, after all."

"No. Not that I know. Camber's not said a word to me." Hester turned to Eugenia, eyes wide and concerned. "Surely, Lord Fenris would call to let you know all is well, wouldn't he, Lady Eugenia?"

Before she could formulate a response to that, more opinions were offered. Lieutenant Fraser inserted himself between his brother and Hester.

Someone said, "My brother says he wasn't at his office at Westminster."

"They had an engagement today, and he was not there. He never misses appointments."

"His secretary claimed he did not know where Lord Fenris was."

Speculation continued in this manner with stories about other duels interspersed with appeals to Eugenia for any scrap of information, since, after all, Fenris's cousin was her sister-in-law. There was nothing she dared offer, no knowledge she could share. Silence seemed by far the safest response.

A young man came blowing up to the group, out of breath as he greeted the others. Lieutenant Fraser put his arm around Hester's waist. Silence fell. "I've just come from St. James's Street."

"What?"

"Pray tell, what have you heard?"

He took off his hat and put it over his heart. "There were bets at White's that Lane would kill Fenris at five to one odds." He waited for the gasps to subside. "Three to one Fenris would be wounded." He looked around the gathering, expression grave. Eugenia's heart stopped beating. "I'm told someone's just paid out fifteen thousand pounds."

Hester frowned. "For which wager?"

The young man's gaze settled on Hester and with apparent reluctance he said, "That Lane would kill Lord Fenris."

One of the young ladies let out a shrill scream that descended into tears. "No, no. Not him." She swooned and was only just caught by one of the men. Amid the rush to restore the girl to her senses, Eugenia stood immobile, numb to all reaction. Baring's heir stood beside Hester and had bent to whisper in her ear.

Her heart beat once, but surely never would again. This was Robert's death all over again, with her not where she ought to be and having to hear the news from strangers.

"Three thousand pounds?" Hester tapped a foot. She gave Lieutenant Fraser a push. His brother, too. No one was listening to her. That girl, whoever she was, continued to sob as if she had a right to such heartbreak. "That seems a great deal of money to wager on something so uncertain. Even if you'd win fifteen thousand."

"Wait! Wait! Wait!" The gentleman who'd brought the news lifted his hands and obtained enough silence to be heard over a raft of desolate young ladies. "At Brooks's they're saying it's Lane who was killed, and that Fenris is even now on his way to the Continent."

Conversation, if at that point it could be called any such thing, degraded into babble. Eugenia worked her way free of the crowd, leaving Hester to the cluster of young men and ladies. She found a place in the shade of an ash tree, and there she stood attempting to make sense of her feelings. Of course she did not wish for Fenris to have been killed or injured or, God forbid, be on his way to Italy or Prussia or some such nation. Or for Lane to have been killed, for that matter. She did not want anyone to be injured. But that sentiment did not explain the fact that, for a moment, her heart had stopped beating, or that she'd thought, *not again.*

A commotion near the street distracted her. Lord Aigen this time. The gathered crowd saw him, and even before he dismounted he was mobbed, absolutely mobbed. A woman near him cried out, a high, keening sound that struck cold fear into her heart. Eugenia's knees turned to water.

She started toward the others, meaning to rescue Hester, but Aigen, standing at the curb, scanned the throng, searching for someone. Baring's sons remained with Hester. When Aigen saw her, he nodded without his usual smile. Just a single motion of his head to signal that he hoped to speak to her as privately as possible in this public place. Her stomach clenched with dread, and she squeezed her closed parasol in one hand. She leaned against the tree, not out of sight of the crowd, but far from its siege. Even she, in her state of shock, knew she ought to stay where she was. Aigen would come to her with his news.

By the time Aigen arrived, she was composed, though, as she discovered, she could barely speak. "Fenris?"

"Is very much alive."

"Oh, thank God," she whispered. Aigen held her elbow, and she leaned into that firm grip. "Mr. Lane?"

He looked over his shoulder to be sure they'd not be overheard. "Under a surgeon's care."

She drew in a breath. "How badly was he injured?"

"Worried for his health, are you?"

"One needn't like a man to hope he's not been killed or badly injured."

"True." He considered her. "You don't seem the sort of woman to involve herself with the likes of that fool."

"I didn't."

Aigen straightened. "Fenris sent his personal surgeon to him. I'm told it's not considered serious. Missed his heart, but one never knows with a wound of any sort. Infection is always a risk."

Eugenia looked at him from under her lashes. "But Fenris is unharmed? You're certain?"

He nodded. "He is keeping private for the moment."

"Packing in the event a removal to the Continent seems wise?"

He laughed as if he found that amusing, the sort of thing one might say in jest rather than all earnestness. "Aye." He plucked a leaf from over his head and leaned his shoulders against the tree, holding the leaf by the stem. "He said Lane insulted you in some way. Don't worry. Fenris did not share the particulars with me."

She said nothing.

He examined his leaf for a while, then looked at her sideways. A breeze stirred the leaves overhead. The shifting light glinted off Aigen's hair and brought out bronze streaks in the darker brown. He shook his head to knock back the hair that fell over his forehead. "I know all about Lane and his behavior at Mrs. Wilson's and elsewhere. I hope you know it's like Fenris to step in and object to ill treatment of anyone."

"Is it?"

"It is." He watched her long enough that she felt her cheeks warm. "I consider him a good friend. Do you? Or has he sent me on a fool's errand?"

She opened her mouth to reply, then didn't.

"Go on," he said. He tapped the top of her head with his leaf. "Say what's whirling around there in your head."

"He's exasperating. Fenris is. Is he really uninjured?"

"Yes." He laughed. "Have you a message for him? Not that he sent me here for that, you understand, but since he asked me to put your mind at ease, I thought you might have a word or two for him."

She shook her head, but when Aigen shrugged and moved away from the tree trunk, she said, "Yes. I do."

"I am at your service."

"Tell him I said he's a fool."

Chapter Twenty-six

⊷⊶

Ten days later. No. 6 Spring Street.

"Ah," someone said from the doorway to the front parlor where Eugenia sat with Hester. This was their day to receive calls, and the parlor was crowded with visitors. Footmen worked their way through the room, silently picking up abandoned plates and cups, cleaning up spills, and bringing in refreshments as required.

She recognized the voice before she saw who it was. Lord Aigen's brogue was familiar everywhere. "There she is," the man said when he stepped into the room. Like the other gentlemen, he held his hat and riding whip under one arm. "And the other delightful young lady as well. Miss Rendell, good afternoon."

Hester beamed at him. Eugenia counted herself lucky that she had convinced Hester she could not go to Bouverie until after they received calls. Lieutenant Fraser was here, and Eugenia was beginning to have high hopes for him and Hester.

"Lord Aigen." Eugenia offered him her hand. "Good afternoon." He bowed over her hand with more charm than any man ought to have. There was a reason he was a favorite of the ladies.

He released her and turned to Hester, with, she rather thought, even more charm than he had shown her. "Miss Rendell." He pressed a hand to his heart. "So very lovely. I hope I've found you in good health."

Hester smiled, and Aigen's eyes widened. "Yes, my lord, thank you. And you? Are you well today?"

"I am at this precise moment quite excellent. As what man would not be in the company of two such women as you and the charming Lady Eugenia?"

He glanced at the sofa across from her and Hester where Lieutenant Fraser sat. One look was all Aigen needed. The lieutenant jumped to his feet. With a bow, he nodded to Hester. "Miss Rendell, I hope I will see you again soon."

Aigen took the man's place while Hester extended a hand as if she were a queen. The two young women at the other end of the sofa where Aigen now sat whispered to each other. One of them turned bright red.

"Thank you, sir," Hester said. Eugenia nudged her. "You'll call again, I hope?"

He bowed. "I shall."

She nudged Hester again. Hester cleared her throat. "That will be delightful."

Lieutenant Fraser bowed. When he'd made his departure, Aigen whistled a brief tune and said, "How much longer is he in London? Sailors are so rarely home, you know. I'm surprised he's not shipped off already."

"I'm sure I don't know," Eugenia said.

"I think . . ." Aigen rose. "Well, well, well. The devil."

Eugenia followed his gaze and saw that none other than Dinwitty Lane had just come in. He'd come alone; not a single one of his toadying followers was with him. He stood straight, but she thought he looked pale and drawn. She put a hand on Aigen's arm. "I invited him, my lord. To prove that enemies can be forgiven. I'm glad to see he's healing well."

"Healing?" Aigen shook his head in exaggerated puzzlement. "Don't know what you mean. As you can see, he is in peak form."

That, Eugenia understood, was how these things were done. Neither Fenris nor Lane could admit they'd dueled or that the rumor was that Lane's injury was such that Fenris had found it politic to be away from London for a time. Aigen wasn't likely to say differently, nor anyone else with knowledge of the affair. "I see that now. The error was mine."

"An easy mistake to make." Aigen looked away from Lane. "You won't be insulted, will you, Lady Eugenia, if I tell you Fenris is a bloody damn hero?"

She blinked at him. "A hero? What for?"

"For defending a woman's honor, that's why."

Mr. Lane made his way to her and Hester. He bowed, slowly and with some stiffness, when he reached them. "Ma'am. Miss Rendell."

Eugenia took his hand and pressed it. She *had* invited him. And she did mean to turn the other cheek if that meant an end to gossip about anything Lane might once have said. She would be forever grateful to him for not dying. "Mr. Lane. Thank you so much for your visit. Would you care to sit?"

He nodded, and she made room for him on the sofa. He sat carefully and without moving his left arm. "Hester, be so kind as to fetch Mr. Lane a bite of something, won't you?"

A few moments later, Hester returned with a plate of cold meat and sugared biscuits. A footman behind her held a tray with a cup of tea, which, at Hester's nod, he placed on the table beside Mr. Lane.

"Thank you, Miss Rendell." With his right hand, he reached for the plate she'd brought him. "How kind of you."

Hester brought a chair and sat on it. "A fine day, don't you think, sir?"

"Yes, Miss Rendell. It is." Lane swallowed a bite of ham.

Everyone ignored Aigen and his glower.

"May I say, Miss Rendell, that you look particularly well today?"

She beamed at him, and Lane blinked several times. "Thank you."

He cleared his throat. "Perhaps you'll play the pianoforte for us? I heard you at Lord Baring's. Do you sing?"

"Not well."

"I like to sing."

Aigen snorted, but Hester's attention remained focused on Lane. "Do you, Mr. Lane?"

Lane ate a biscuit. "I like songs about hunting."

"I see. Yes, they have an appeal."

"Military songs. Anything with brave men marching off to battle."

Hester continued beaming at him. "What about songs with strong women? Do you like those?" He dusted off his hand and Hester passed him his tea. "Sugar or milk?"

"Plain is fine, Miss Rendell. Thank you. I like those songs, too, strong women, but not the ones where everyone dies."

"Do you know, Mr. Lane, I quite agree."

"What about you, Lady Eugenia?" Lane still held his tea. He looked unsettled. Not surprising with Lord Aigen glaring at him, but Eugenia had seen similar reactions from men as they realized just how badly they'd underestimated Hester. "Do you like the songs where the ladies die for love?" He flushed, and his embarrassment was nearly charming.

She sent a warning glance in Aigen's direction and was rewarded with a wink and silence. She returned her attention to Lane. "Like you, I prefer songs in which people live happily ever after."

Conversation rose and fell, and for some time afterward, people departed and arrived and new groups formed. Lane, with his injury, kept his place on the sofa. This, she thought, was what it was like to be a social success. An endless stream of callers, lovely, eligible men like Lord Aigen calling and paying compliments, gentlemen reciting poetry, and dozens of young ladies eager to be friends or already among Hester's friends. Watching Hester charm Dinwitty Lane was something, too.

She fixed the moment in memory. She intended to describe the scene to Mrs. Rendell in some detail since it was her daughter who was at the center of it and managing London and the Ton with a cooler head than Eugenia had possessed at her age. She would not mention that Hester still spent more time with the plants at Bouverie than at parties.

Another lull in the conversation lasted long enough that Eugenia turned around to find the cause. Lord Fenris stood in the doorway with his father. As was the fiction required of these visits, which was that they were to be so short that gentlemen callers need not bother to hand over hats or riding whips, Fenris and Camber held both items in hand. In addition, though, Camber held a small bouquet of tiny purple flowers.

The two men started across the room. Even as she recognized the importance of Camber being here, Eugenia's heart thumped against her ribs for private reasons. The least of them was wondering what would happen when Fenris and Lane were face-to-face. She and Fenris had not seen each other since the night before the duel, and his familiar cold and condescending expression tied her into knots.

How could he be so cool when she could think only of whispers shared in the dark and her desperate desire for him? He was well. He was unhurt, and in seeing him she realized she'd not entirely believed he'd not been injured.

And then, there they were. Camber and Fenris, standing before her and Hester with Dinwitty Lane now white as chalk and dead silent. Eugenia was very much aware that all eyes were on them. The Duke of Camber did not often make morning calls. Add in a looming confrontation between Fenris and Lane and no wonder the room had gone silent. Camber greeted her and then Hester, and she was grateful indeed for the attention the duke lavished on Hester as she craned her neck to see the flowers Camber held.

"Mrs. Bryant . . ." Fenris held her gaze, paying no attention, for now, to Mr. Lane.

"My lord?" They were interrupted before either of them could say more.

A man whose name she did not immediately recall put an overly hearty hand on Fenris's shoulder. "A word," he said, attempting to lead Fenris away from Mr. Lane. "If I might, about your recent speech in the Commons?"

Fenris slid away from him and bowed. "May I find you later? Or call on me at Westminster tomorrow at eleven. Tell my secretary you've an appointment with me." His lips curved. "I assure you, it will be kept."

The man bowed and, with an anxious look at Mr. Lane, retreated.

Fenris bowed. "Mr. Lane."

Everyone in the room held their breaths.

Lane nodded. "My lord."

"I hope you're well today."

"Fit as a fiddle." He pointed to his now empty plate. "Ought to have one of those sugar biscuits, Fox. They're excellent."

"Thank you for the recommendation."

Fenris looked at Eugenia again, and she wished more intensely than ever in her life that she possessed the power to read minds. "Mrs. Bryant, I—"

"Surprised to see you here, Fox." Lord Aigen clapped him on the back. "Stopping by for the famous hospitality, no doubt." He bowed to the duke. "Your grace. Have you a favorite in the Garrie race tomorrow?"

Lane snorted. "Portland's gelding will win the day."

"Aye, I agree with you, Lane." Aigen kept his grin. "I'm sorry we can't wager on it, for I'd like to take some coin from you."

Camber's eyes sparked. "Win by a length."

"That much?" Lane brushed the tip of a thumb over his lower lip. "No. Can't happen. Not with Viceroy in the field."

"Care to wager on it?" The duke locked his hands behind his back.

"Indeed, your grace, I do."

Fenris returned his attention to Eugenia, and as the discussion of racing continued, he wrapped his fingers around the underside of her forearm and brought her to her feet.

"What's this?" Lane said. "Are you taking her away?"

"Only for a moment." She could not look away from Fenris. Nor, it seemed, could he look away from her. "I'd like some of those biscuits Mr. Lane so enjoyed."

Camber gave his son a sharp look. He still held the flowers in one hand. "I was about to ask Mrs. Bryant and Miss Rendell if they'd walk out with me later this afternoon or the next. I thought they might like to visit Ackermann's."

Eugenia curtseyed. "That sounds lovely, your grace. You're kind to think of us."

"Not at all."

Hester plucked at the duke's sleeve. "Camber." She went on tiptoe to look at the flowers he held. "Are those *your* violets?"

"Indeed, they are, Miss Rendell." Camber held out the flowers and, with a bow worthy of a courtier, presented them to her.

She took them and examined them with a gimlet eye. "Excellent scent. Good color. Large blossoms perfectly formed." She lifted her head. "Precisely as your sketches and paintings depicted them. Ought you to have cut them?"

"Not from our experimental set, but they are from Bouverie."

"They're very pretty." She bent over the flowers and breathed in. "I do love violets."

"I thought you might like to wear them in your hair." The duke coughed. "You modern young ladies still do that sort of thing, don't you? Put flowers in your hair? I know the girls did in my day. Very pretty."

"Of course they do, Camber." Fenris let go of Eugenia's arm, put aside his hat and riding whip, and took Hester's violets. He held them beside the curls arranged atop her head. "Yes, I think this will do quite nicely. Have you any spare hairpins, Miss Rendell?" He took the pins Hester hastily pulled from her dark curls. "Thank you. A moment if you please. Don't fidget."

"No, sir." Hester watched Camber during the process, with one of her serene smiles on her lips.

Fenris fastened the violets in her hair and stepped back. "What do you think, Mrs. Bryant? Camber? Does she not look lovely?"

Lane cleared his throat. "The very picture of beauty."

"Look in the glass," Eugenia said.

She did and touched the violets gently. When she returned, she smiled in a way that made Fenris cock his head. Lane and Camber, too.

"Very pretty, Miss Rendell," Aigen said.

"No one's ever given me flowers before." She took Camber's hand in hers and pressed it. "Thank you, your grace. I'm sure I must have the most beautifully arranged coiffure of anyone in the room. In all of London, I daresay. There's no one with violets as lovely as these."

Camber coughed again, and Eugenia wondered if it was possible that Fenris was right, and his father was enamored of Hester. He couldn't be. He thought of Hester as a girl. The daughter he'd never had. Didn't he?

"Shall I crystallize them, Lady Eugenia? I've been meaning to make a chimney ornament for you." She sent a glance in the direction of the fireplace. "They would make us a lovely reminder of Camber. And Bouverie, of course. Don't you agree?"

"Yes."

Fenris retook Eugenia's arm and walked her away while his father and the others stayed with Hester. He'd retrieved his hat and riding whip and now had them tucked under his arm. Near the door, he drew a bouquet of white violets from his pocket. "I'm afraid they're a poor second to Camber's specimens, but on our way here, we passed a girl selling them, and I thought if Camber was to bring flowers for Miss Rendell, then you ought to have them, too. A gift from me. Or a peace offering if you're still angry with me."

"I'm not angry." She took them from him, absurdly touched by his gesture. "Thank you. They're lovely." Flowers. Such a small thing, really. A penny or two spent, but he'd thought of her.

He stayed near her. "I chose the white violets because

they made me think of you. Delicate. Not the usual sort at all."

"Really." She gave a laugh. "You'll turn my head with talk like that."

He fingered one of the blossoms. "A lovely color for you, with that hint of purple here at the center. You ought to have a gown just this color." Lightly, he touched her fingers. "I'd insist you put these in your hair, too, but Hester ought to have her moment, I think."

He looked in the direction of the corridor. "Come away so I can kiss you, Ginny."

"Stop trying to distract me from properly thanking you."

"I'd never distract you from that."

She brought the violets up to inhale the scent. "Incorrigible. That's what you are. They smell so lovely."

"I think of you often." He tugged on her elbow.

"Stop. I'll laugh at you and everyone will wonder what you've done."

"Let them." They ended up staring at each other, caught, the both of them. "Ginny." His soft voice sent a shiver down her spine.

She broke the rather terrible silence. "I was terrified. Terrified something awful had happened." The words came out too quickly, and she hurried to cover the emotion. "I mean to say I'm glad you weren't hurt."

"I confess I share the sentiment." Such a noncommittal reply.

"I'm glad everything's come right."

"You think it has?"

Her heart turned over, and she gave in to the mass of insecurity that roiled inside her. "Let's us make the best of this, Fenris, shall we?"

He gazed at her. "The best of what?"

"This. Everything. You and Mr. Lane. All the gossip. What else would I mean?"

He cocked his head. "A man who's had to face the prospect of death finds himself with a different perspective of what's worthy of his attention."

"I'm sure."

He lowered his voice. "Being with you is worth any cost. Any price."

"I've not asked you for anything." Her pulse thumped in her ears.

His mouth turned up at the corners. "Ask. I'll give you anything you like. My fortune."

She rolled her eyes at him.

"My collection of dueling pistols."

"I'll gladly take those from you."

"My name."

Panic filled her. She lifted the flowers. "I have these."

"My heart?"

"Fenris, no." She patted his chest, and was horrified to find she had to blink away tears. "You don't want that."

"The question is what you want." The light in his eyes flattened, and she hated that she'd made that happen. "We must talk. You know we must."

"Not here. Someplace quieter."

"Where, then?"

She sighed. "There's a parlor in the back of the house."

Chapter Twenty-seven

❦

EUGENIA TOLD HERSELF THAT THIS TIME SHE WOULD not lose her head. There was nothing of substance between her and Fenris. Nothing that would sustain a relationship of any meaning. Quite the opposite. What they'd shared was purely physical. They were lovers, nothing more. She did not have a heart to give him.

As they walked to the parlor she meant, her body felt light as air. The slightest breath would blow her off her feet. Noise from the front parlor receded as she walked, and she had the odd conviction she was entering a different world.

The back portion of the town house was almost eerily quiet. Fenris walked silently behind her, but when she reached the parlor, he moved past her to open the door. He closed it after them. The room wasn't large, so once they'd stepped inside, her heart banging against her chest, because Fenris always did that to her, they were hardly ten feet apart. She was safe now, but she soon would not be. Not with Fenris looking at her with that dark and brooding gaze.

She tucked his violets into her bosom because she didn't know what else to do with them, and instantly wished she hadn't, for his gaze dipped downward. There were six chairs here, all of them set with their backs against the wall, waiting for someone to move them to some convenient and agreeable place. A scarlet velvet sofa faced the fireplace. She thought about sitting there, but in the end, she didn't. If she stayed on her feet there was a chance she'd not give in to him. Her sewing was here, on the floor beside the sofa, as well as a wooden frame that held her embroidery work. On a table was a stack of books from the subscription library. She and Hester took turns reading them when they did not have an engagement outside the house.

"Do sit." Fenris gestured.

"I'd rather stand, I think. My lord." She lifted her eyes to him and, as always, meeting his gaze only reminded her how physically lovely he was. Her belly tugged at her. He moved between the sofa and the fireplace. Heavens, but he was a lovely man. But what he wanted from her, she could not give. She'd loved once. She'd loved Robert so deeply his death had destroyed her, and she could not face that again. That kind of love was not safe, and she knew that's what Fenris wanted from her.

He let out a short breath. "I think we can be less formal than that with each other, don't you? Fenris will do if you can't bring yourself to call me Fox when we are in private."

His acerbic reply irritated her enough that a similar note crept into her voice. She wasn't perfect. She wasn't the creature he'd obviously built up in his mind over the years. The paragon Robert had loved. Well, she wasn't a paragon, and Robert had known it. "Was there something you needed to say to me?"

"Yes." He glanced past her shoulder to the door. "Please make sure it's locked."

She did turn back to the door, and she did turn the key in the lock.

"Thank you."

Eugenia crossed the room but stopped short of where he was standing at the fireplace. "Yes?"

He put his hat and whip on the mantel. "I know it's early yet, but have you anything to tell me?" He spoke in a low voice. Politic of him. She trusted her staff not to listen at the door, but there was no sense taking a risk that anyone, someone else's servant, one of her guests, even, might eavesdrop.

"I thought the point of dragging me away from my guests was that you had something to say to me."

"We ought to be married." He let out an exasperated breath and set a fisted hand on the mantel. "You know. You know."

"What do I know?"

"Ginny. My God, Ginny. I did nothing to prevent a child." His eyes darkened. "I don't regret it, don't think for a moment I do. I'd not change anything about that."

Why, Eugenia wondered, was there never a sinkhole when one needed one? Right now, she wished intensely for the ground to swallow her up. And it didn't.

"I understand your feelings for me are not what either of us might wish, but surely you understand me. I took no precautions. Did you?"

She couldn't speak. Such things were done, but she didn't know the methods herself. Or, rather, she'd heard things, but she would have had to ask for the details of what to do. Martine, mostly likely, would know, but Eugenia hadn't asked her or anyone else.

"I've a right to know, too, if you suspect you might be with child by me."

This was a serious matter. The most serious of her life. "Yes, you do."

"Well?"

She moved behind the sofa, her hands on the carved arch of the back. "Not yet. That is, I'm not certain. As you said, it's early."

"Not certain is not the same as no."

She couldn't meet his gaze any longer so she stared at the rosette carved in the wood along the back of the sofa. That she was having this conversation with Fenris was incomprehensible. Nothing in her view of what her life was to be like had prepared her for this. She was Eugenia Hampton Bryant. A widow who had once married and lost the love of her life. She was sister to a duke. Her life was otherwise unexceptional. Events flowed around her, never distinguishing her. She had friends she liked and some she loved. She had family she adored and a life that had no drama. No excitement. Not the slightest risk of scandal. Until Fenris.

"In a few days, I think." She rubbed her palm across her forehead and wished herself anywhere but here.

"Ginny," he said softly. "Are you saying your courses are late?"

"I don't know." She glanced at him, expecting he'd be as horrified as she was at the possibility. But his expression was, as was so often the case with him, unreadable. "I've never been . . . regular. I'm sorry."

"Don't apologize."

She didn't say anything to that. Her chest was tight, because now that he was forcing her to confront their situation, her situation, she couldn't entirely keep back the panic. "I never meant to trap you."

"Don't look so terrified. I am prepared to marry you whether you are certain or not."

"No." She shook her head. "No. You mustn't marry without love."

"Yours or mine?"

"Either. There's a woman out there for you." She swallowed hard. "I'm sorry. So sorry to think I might take that from you. You deserve to be loved." She only just kept back a sob. "I cannot love you as you deserve."

"Well, then." He remained by the fire. The chimney glass, which stretched the width of the mantel and the height of the wall, reflected his back from the shoulders up. "We shall have to be patient awhile longer."

She looked at the door. The real world was out there, and she did not want to rejoin it.

"Don't go yet," he said.

"We'll be missed."

"If you go out there now, someone is sure to ask you why you've been crying."

"I haven't been." She blinked and was mortified to feel tears slide down her cheek. Not many, but enough.

He went to her and put his handkerchief in her hand. "Stay here a moment. Until the horror passes and you've forgotten, for now, that you might be forced to marry me."

"God, Fenris." She crushed his handkerchief in a fist. "Must you speak so bluntly?"

He did not immediately reply. "We may find it necessary to make the best of things. A child out of wedlock would destroy us both." He touched a finger to her chin. "You know that."

"Yes. I know."

"Ginny." He shook his head and lowered his voice, though there was no one in the room. "We could elope. We needn't tell anyone what we've done."

She gaped at him. "We can't."

"We're of age, you and I. Mountjoy's permission, while desirable, is not required. Nor is my father's. We'll marry and say nothing until circumstances force us to reveal what we've done. Who knows but that as time passes, you might learn you like me better than you do at present."

"I don't see why I wouldn't. I don't hate you anymore."

"Progress."

"It isn't love."

"Have I asked for that? If you are with child, we have some time before we'd need to confess the sin of a clandestine marriage."

"That's absurd." She pressed his handkerchief to her eyes. "What if I'm not? We'd be married. A divorce or annulment would be a worse scandal than a secret marriage. And that's supposing you could get one."

"No divorce. No annulment." He hesitated, and she had the impression that he discarded several thoughts before settling on what to say. "If we don't marry, and there's a child, the damage to Hester's reputation might well be irreparable."

"We can't marry in secret."

"I don't see why not." He shrugged. "I leave the choice to you."

"I've never been able to deceive Mountjoy. He'll know. He'll take one look at me and know."

"Then we'll tell him." He reached for her hand, and she let him take it.

"Tell him what? That we must marry?"

"I'll tell him I love you."

"God, Fenris, no. No lies. Please. Besides, he wouldn't believe you."

She could see him try not to scowl and fail at it. "Why do you persist in coloring my every remark with the worst possible intent?"

"I promise you, Mountjoy will know if you lie to him. You can't tell him that. No one will believe it."

"I'll tell him the truth, then."

She sat down hard on one of the chairs. For several seconds she stared at her lap. "One duel is more than enough."

When she looked up their gazes locked. "Lord, Ginny, how late are you?"

She swallowed hard, got up and paced to the sofa, and stared at one of the carved roses again. "Not very."

"Not very? Marriages are made on less certainty than that."

She pressed a finger on each of the petals of the rose in turn. "I'm sure I'm not. I mean to say, I'd feel something if I were, and I don't."

Fenris strode away. She presumed he was headed toward the door. Thank God for that, for she did not want him to see her break down. But he didn't proceed to the door. No, he stopped near her. Behind her. "Ginny," he said.

She jumped, because he was much closer than she expected. And now the chimney glass reflected back her face and his. Objectively, they made a handsome couple. Him with his dark hair and hers so pale in comparison. If one knew nothing about them, one might think they suited.

"I beg your pardon." His voice was soft. Too soft. "I did not intend to startle you."

She watched him in the glass. He was a man of great physical presence. "It's nothing. It's just I never thought I'd be in such a predicament as this."

"Why won't you look at me?"

Eugenia turned around. "There." She lifted her chin so she could look him in the face. "Better?"

"Yes." But now it was his turn to look away. He touched the carved rose. "How many petals?"

"I'm sure I don't know."

"Yes you do. You were counting." He lifted his head again and held her gaze. She'd rather have died than looked away from him when he so plainly meant to challenge her.

"Thirteen." She turned sideways to him and swept a finger over the wood. One of the servants must have built up the fire, for the room felt unnaturally warm to her.

Fenris cocked his head. "Thirteen, you say? That seems an unlucky number. Are you sure you counted right?"

"Of course I did." She seized on the change of subject. Anything but the possibility that he'd gotten her with child. That she'd been so stupid, so ignorant as to allow that to happen between them. Mountjoy would guess. He would, and she didn't want him to think so ill of her.

"I wonder why the man who carved this wasn't more careful."

Thirteen petals. She counted again to be sure. "There's no pride in workmanship these days."

Fenris laughed and, blast him, she smiled back. He didn't seem upset, and that was something. He wasn't blaming her for this. He never would, either. No matter what happened.

In the space between breaths, her body provided a forceful reminder of how attractive a man he was. "I'll write Mountjoy and tell him the piece must be replaced."

"Why? You might call in a carpenter and have the carving altered. Remove a petal from here. Or here." He pointed in turn.

She leaned a hip against the sofa and crossed her arms underneath her bosom. The moment seemed so normal. Why, she couldn't be pregnant. Not after so few encounters. Such things happened, yes, but not to her. Not to men like Fenris.

His attention dipped, oh so briefly, and it was as if he'd physically touched her, leaving behind nothing but heat. "That won't alter the fact that the piece was carved with a thirteen-petaled rose."

"I suppose you're right." He was standing near enough now that his shoulder brushed hers. Purely accidental, but with the contact, her awareness of him as a thoroughly male man blossomed. "Shall we burn it at the stake?"

She laughed, and his eyes, his beautiful, soulful eyes, darkened. Desire slithered through her. She refused to acknowledge the reaction, but that didn't change the fact of her experience. "I wonder how bad the case is?" She touched the carved wood. What if they had been unlucky? Knowing Fenris would marry her mattered more than she could say. "How many thirteen-petaled roses are carved onto this sofa?"

"Thirteen?"

"Heaven help us if that's so." She summoned a smile, but it felt as pale as the violets he'd given her.

"Should we count them?"

Eugenia shook her head. "Too dangerous. Thirteen. Unlucky number."

He nodded gravely and stroked his chin. "Might we omit the number? Skip from twelve to fourteen, for example. Or invent a number. Huberteen, perhaps?"

"Huberteen." She smiled in spite of everything. "Would that mean huber takes the place of three?" She counted roses carved into the left side of the sofa. ". . . two, huber, four, five . . ."

He put his hand over hers and pressed gently down. Her pulse jumped. She didn't dare move for fear she would betray herself to him. "Don't tempt fate, Ginny. Not again with all those unlucky flowers."

The moment her reply formed in her brain, the ill-advised words left her mouth. She wanted them back, but she'd let them free and they hung in the air, accusing her of unintended meaning. "I never took you for a superstitious man."

He touched his medallion, rubbing a finger over the metal surface. "That proves how little you know me." He took the disc between thumb and forefinger. "I believe utterly in the power of this, for example. If I believe in that, why shouldn't I believe in the possibility of ill luck if we discover there are thirteen thirteen-petaled roses carved into this sofa?"

"My point precisely." A wave of disbelief crashed over her, panicking her. She *was* late, just not very. It wasn't unusual for her, and she hadn't any symptoms at all. Pregnant women fainted, didn't they? They were ill in the morning. "It's too dangerous to proceed."

Fenris gave her another long look. "Think of all the ill luck that must have befallen the previous Dukes of Mountjoy."

"What ill luck?" One of his fingers moved over the hand he'd trapped on the top of the sofa, caressing her first finger. "After all, the title did not die out. And Mountjoy found Lily." While she was trying to put her world right again, he set his hands on either side of her face. "I'd say that's good luck, wouldn't you?"

"Ginny," he whispered.

From the moment he said her name like that, with such longing, she was lost.

"Lily married the man she ought to have."

She fisted her hands at her sides. "You deserve the same. Marriage to a woman who loves you."

"My dear." He smiled, laughter threatening there. "I deserve you. What's more, I believe you deserve me."

Then he kissed her.

At first he was gentle. Tender, even. Hardly the sort of kiss that might happen between lovers, which they were not. Her body betrayed her. She opened her mouth under his, and his kiss turned carnal. Sinful. Soul-stealing because, Lord, he kissed as if he thought she were the most desirable woman alive, and how could any woman resist that?

She swayed toward him as desire engulfed her. They ended up with him sitting on the sofa and with her straddling his thighs. The back of his head rested on the sofa, and his hands were underneath her skirts, lifting them, and then, heavens, his fingers were so clever. She braced her hands on either side of his head, and they kissed some more and then she drew away, and she said, "We can't. Fenris, we can't."

"I want inside you." He briefly closed his eyes. "I'll withdraw." He slid one hand to her bottom, and from the movement of his other hand she guessed, correctly, it turned out, that he was freeing himself from his breeches, because a moment later, he drew her forward and his cock was at her entrance. "Yes?"

His eyes were so beautiful, glazed with lust. For her. She put her forearms on his shoulders and sank down. She fell into his lovely eyes, and he pushed up, filling her, making himself fit. She drew breath. Nothing, nothing was as sweet as his cock inside her.

"Jesus." He threw his head back. "What you do to me."

Her world became nothing but the physical sensation of his sex filling her. At one point, he put his hands on her hips and took control of the tempo. A slower motion that brought her deliciously, perilously close to orgasm. He was so good at this, and if she'd possessed the power of speech just now, she might have told him so. But all she could do was clutch the top of the sofa and match each thrust and withdrawal.

There came a point when she rocked forward, and his mouth opened on a groan that pulled at every sensitive point in her body. His next thrust was deeper and slow and exquisite, and her desire gave way to raw need. She reveled in what was now a brutal shove inside her.

He slid to the edge of the sofa, and she made some incoherent sound of protest until she realized he was getting them both onto the floor. The moment her back landed on the Kidderminster carpet, his weight was planted on his hands, above her shoulders, and he flexed his pelvis forward and her body poised on the edge of orgasm.

She couldn't think of anything but him and the fit of his body to hers. She held him tight, bent her knees, and his next thrust went deeper yet. She was afraid she would never reach the peak. Fenris slowed, and she held him tight, and he said, "Ginny."

She opened her eyes and saw him over her and my God, he was inside her and her body was rushing madly toward heaven. Fenris was inside her. "Please. Fox. Please."

"Ginny. I—"

"I don't care," she said, because at that moment she didn't. When he withdrew completely she sobbed once, pure frustration.

"I can't come in you again, for God's sake."

"I hate you." He was right. She knew it, but it didn't change her physical frustration.

"Tut-tut. I shan't leave you unsatisfied."

He slid down and put his mouth on her, and within seconds she was right there again, her body hovering at complete destruction, and he was going to take her away from everything but her body, her reaction, and oh, God, he did. He did, and she stayed there at the very peak for longer than she would have believed possible.

Somehow, when the pure selfish loss of herself began to recede, her befuddled mind managed to recall that he had not had any completion. Not fair. Not fair when he'd brought her such physical joy. She pushed his shoulders, and he obligingly slid away from her, on his back, one arm over his eyes, the other gripping his still erect cock.

"Poor, poor man." She sat at his side, gaze on his pelvis. He lifted his arm and watched her until she pushed away his hand and curled her fingers around him. "I suppose your lovers tell you all the time how beautiful your cock is."

"No."

"Liar."

"I pay them to say such things—Ginny." He sucked in a breath.

"You don't pay me, so I assure you they mean it."

"Do you?"

"Yes."

"I seem to recall, my dear, that you are good with your hands."

"Am I?"

"Refresh both our recollections if you're not certain. Put some detail in the vagueness of your recall."

She bent over him and took his prick in her mouth. That was wonderful, hearing him groan, the feel of his hands cradling her head and then the arch of his hips and his push forward, the pulse of his cock when he came. Salty tang. The tremble of his hands on her head.

When he was done, when she'd taken her time looking at him and remembering that he was as beautiful here as everywhere else, she sat back, her fingers still lightly around his member, softening now that he'd released. "I want to do that again."

Fenris opened his eyes, and there was a wicked gleam there amid the languor of his repletion. "You have only to tell me," he said. "And I will oblige you at any moment of the day or night."

Chapter Twenty-eight

Three days later. The home of Admiral and Mrs. Padget.

AT THE PARLOR DOOR, FOX KEPT WALKING AND, ALAS, spouting nonsense at Eugenia. He'd not heard from her since that afternoon at Spring Street, and he was in a dark mood. Now he was here, as was Eugenia, and his mood was not appreciatively different despite his having her in front of him. He stopped himself from saying something monumentally unwise and instead settled on the inane. "Admiral Paget has a collection of carvings you might like to see. They're quite beautiful. Come with me, Ginny."

He was overcome with the sinking conviction that his success with other women was all illusion, a conclusion he'd drawn about himself that sprang from his position and status and not any innate charm. Eugenia had been heinously accurate when she'd suggested to him that his vaunted powers of seduction had never been tested.

She studied the hallway decor, and his doubts deepened. He stopped walking, and that made her give him an inquiring look. The usual pull of his attraction to her kept him witless. From somewhere in the depths of his brain, he found words.

"You will also have the opportunity to tell me what mischief Lane has caused you now."

She shot him a wide-eyed glance over her shoulder. That was panic there.

"I saw you speaking to him just now. You did not look happy. Nor did he. I'll shoot him dead this time if he's insulted you again." Completely the wrong thing to say, since if Lane had done so, she'd hardly tell him now that he'd threatened murder.

At least now she was looking at him. "It was nothing."

"Don't lie."

She faced him, and a hundred different reactions passed over her face, but the final one was exasperation. "All right then. I'll tell you."

"Do."

"He asked me to marry him."

"What?"

"Thank you." Her reply was overtly accusing. He deserved it.

"Was he serious?"

"Yes." She plucked at her skirt. "He was very sweet about it. He said he'd already been all the way to Bitterward and back to talk to Mountjoy."

"Oh, for God's sake." The parlor door was open, and he had the presence of mind to head them in that direction. Inside, Eugenia slowed and then took her arm away from him. The room was empty. He closed the door.

"No doubt I'll have a letter from Mountjoy soon," she said.

"You didn't tell that fool yes, did you?"

She went to a display cabinet near a heavy mahogany desk. He followed, and at the last moment she turned. Her skirts whipped around her legs. "How could I? Under the circumstances?"

"If circumstances were different, would you have accepted him?"

She crossed her arms underneath her bosom. "I don't know. I'd want to know him better."

"That lobster-headed dunce?"

She examined the desk, to hide a smile, he hoped. "Well. I don't think he's quite as dull a boy as I've assumed."

"Indeed."

"He began by asking me if I was in love with you."

His brain emptied of rational thought. And, it would seem, circumspection. "You told him you were not."

She quirked her eyebrows at him.

"You did, or he'd not have offered for you. Not even Lane would propose to a woman who's just told him she loves someone else."

"He's not stupid, but he isn't very bright."

"Do you love me?"

She gazed at him, mouth open and at such a loss for words that he took pity on her. In a way. He closed the distance between them and put his hands on either side of her face. He tipped her head back and lowered his mouth to hers.

He kissed her. While he did so, he told himself there was no bigger fool than him right now. That he'd better make love to her now because he might never get the chance again. He did not want to one day be on his deathbed thinking of this moment and wishing he'd kissed her one last time before she ground his heart to dust. He did not want to spend the rest of his life wondering what would have happened or if he could have turned her opinion of him. If there came a time when he did give up his suit as hopeless, he wanted to be sure he'd done all that he could to make his case to her.

She didn't push him away, so he kept kissing her until he realized she wasn't kissing him back. He drew back and focused on her mouth at first, so kissable. Eventually he looked at her face. Her eyes were open wide, and he could not for his life tell whether the anger he saw there would win out over the desire.

"Honestly. You're not to be borne."

"You can't marry Lane."

"I know that." She put her hand on the fall of his breeches, and to his delight, while she smiled so very smugly, she curled her fingers around his mostly erect cock, which, being a dutiful sort of male member, came to greater attention. He sucked in a breath, and her eyes went just that much wider.

"Fox," she said softly. "What am I to do with you?"

His good sense vanished, but then he hadn't started this encounter with much. He pushed his pelvis forward and covered one of her hands with one of his, and then he kissed her again while she pressed against him, pushing up and then down, and she was the one to work her hand to the side and unfasten one of his buttons. Another button and another, and, God yes, she slipped her hand underneath the flap and found her way past his smallclothes.

What was left of his mind melted away.

He kissed her again and, still kissing her, spun them both toward the desk, and then he came close to saying a word that wasn't proper at all, because the damned door had come open. He broke away from her and strode to the door. He closed and locked it this time, and she was still there, standing in front of the desk looking lost. Her gaze swept over him, over the disarrangement of his trousers, and that was quite enough for him and any hope of sanity.

In three steps, he crossed to her, and he pushed aside the blotter and the sextant on the desk. She made no protest. Not a single word did she utter. No objection. He turned back to her, grabbed her around the waist, and lifted her onto the desktop. Lust burned through him. Selfish, selfish lust. Whatever was going through her head right now, he didn't intend to waste his chances.

Her eyes were wide open, her lips parted, and he fell into her eyes and drowned. She leaned forward and kissed him hard, and now both of them were lost to each other. He gathered handfuls of her frock and stepped between her spread legs. He slid his hands along the tops of her thighs and turned his fingers inward. Warmth, there, between her legs, the slickness of her arousal. He got a hand behind her and pulled her forward, to the very edge of the desk.

With the froth of her skirts and petticoat around them both, he unfastened enough buttons of his breeches to free himself completely. With one long, fast stroke, he was inside her. He shouted, a raw sound, incoherent. The breath left his lungs. Every damn time it was like this with her.

The sound that came from her as he seated himself was part moan, part groan, and she said, "God, yes. Fox."

Some part of his brain told him he ought to slow down, but she had one arm thrown around his shoulders and her other hand propped up on the desk, her thighs tight around his hips, and she pushed toward him with her hand on the desk and met his second thrust and the third, and all the ones after that, too.

He had one hand on the desktop, too, the other around her bare thigh, and he tried to time his strokes but he couldn't think of anything but the clench of her around him, all that softness and the slickness as he moved in her, and he was going to come very soon. He would have worried about that, about coming far too soon, but he did manage to angle himself just right and she came apart in his arms. The sight and feel of her climax set him off. Not that he would have lasted much longer in any event. He withdrew just in time.

"Ginny." He had just enough presence of mind not to shout, but it was a near thing. In his last coherent moment, he was shaken to his core by the knowledge that this was Eugenia, that she was as taken away by this as he was, falling with him, too, and it just wasn't possible that she did not feel something for him. His climax hit, shook him out, and by all rights ought to have killed him. How he managed to stay on his feet afterward remained a mystery.

When he opened his eyes, he found her gazing at him, and if he'd possessed the power of speech, he would have told her he'd never seen a lovelier sight, never felt that sex was worth all the mess and emotion until now.

They were quite close; her arm remained around his shoulder, his fingers still spread out and gripping her thigh. She had her hand around him, and he pushed forward one more time and savored the shiver of orgasm that lingered. He kissed her again, slowly this time, and she kissed him back, reluctantly, he fancied, but then she wasn't the sort of woman to deny what they'd just done.

He fished out his spare handkerchief and cleaned up as much of the mess as he could, and while he did that, he slid a finger along her nether lips, then two, over the nub there. Her head dropped back, and he felt her contract.

"I can't," she said, whispered, murmured. Moaned.

"I think you can." And he brought her again, very quickly, her with both hands propped on the desk, and at least this time he had mental acuity enough to enjoy watching her. His first handkerchief did the rest of its duty.

Slowly, she opened her eyes. "We're both mad. Mad."

"Not madness," he said. "I want to do this again, Ginny. Don't you?"

"No."

He slid two fingers inside her. Despite that he was standing between her legs, despite that he had his fingers inside her, despite that she'd come apart with him, he was wracked with doubt. She'd submitted to him, yet he was no closer to what he wanted than ever.

"Fox, God."

He stroked inside her with his fingers.

"I think it's best if we pretend this never happened."

"When I'm done bringing you again, you may pretend all you like." He slid his fingers along her. "But not until then."

Bring her he did, and if they'd been anywhere a man could decently make love, he'd have put Ginny flat on her back and done so again and again until his cock refused to rise. But alas, they were not any such place, and it was bad of them to behave like this in their host's home. They righted their clothes, helping each other.

At the door, both of them with their clothes arranged, hair smoothed back, and all the outward signs of illicit sex brushed or cleaned away, he paused. "I'll escort you and Miss Rendell home." He lifted a hand. "Pray do not argue."

As it happened, it was a good thing he'd insisted, for the smell of smoke was thick in the air even before his carriage arrived at Mountjoy's town house. He brought the horses to a halt. The scene was chaos, with men shouting and the staff and residents of nearby homes clogging the streets, some in varying states of dress.

Men stripped to their shirtsleeves formed a line, passing buckets to one another or manning the fire engine, taking turns at the pump. The entire staff of Number 6 was outside on the street, some of them with only their coats over their nightclothes, because it was Mountjoy's town house that was burning.

He turned to the two women, both of them white-faced with shock. "I'll take you to Bouverie."

Chapter Twenty-nine

❧❦

Two days later. Bouverie.

IT WAS PAST NINE IN THE EVENING BY THE TIME EUGE-
nia came home—not home, for the town house was currently
uninhabitable, but to Bouverie, where she and Hester were
staying until repairs to the Spring Street town house were
completed. She was exhausted, physically and mentally,
having spent the day and a good portion of the evening going
through the contents of the house with some of the staff to
compile an inventory of what had been destroyed or dam-
aged and to recover what necessary day-to-day items they
could.

She'd been to Mountjoy's banker and received funds sufficient to assist the staff in replacing lost possessions and to
find lodgings for the staff that had nowhere to go until the
house was repaired. She nodded to the Bouverie butler and
headed upstairs. Her intent was to return to the room she'd
been given, undress, and fall directly into bed. Her feet took
her in a completely different direction. *Only a few steps
more*, she thought when she reached the corridor that led to
Fenris's quarters. A few steps more, and she would see him.
She didn't know why that seemed imperative to her, but it

did. He would be true. Truthful with her. He would listen to her and not just *tut-tut, don't worry your pretty head* the way Mountjoy's banker had done, for example.

When she stood before his closed door, her hand poised to knock, the sheer lunacy of what she was doing washed through her. She froze. Her body felt as if it did not belong to her. She ought not be here.

And yet she knocked.

The door swung open in response, though there was no reply to her knock. There were lights inside. She whispered, "Hullo?" and told herself she'd escaped a situation she ought never to have considered getting into in the first place.

Then she heard distant voices and recognized the cadence of Fenris's speech, the dark and honeyed timbre of his voice. He really could not help the way he sounded. She took a step inside, still with that sensation of her body not belonging to her. Some other woman was walking into a gentleman's private apartments. Alone. Eugenia Hampton Bryant would never do such a thing.

She found herself in an anteroom, though not the one she'd been in before. That one she'd reached through the back stairs. Like everything in Bouverie, this room imposed. Here was wealth, it said. Position. Nobility.

Faint light shone from the bedchamber, and she, acting on instinct alone, on selfish desire, if she were to be truthful, followed that inviting glow. No one was in the bedchamber, though the fire was up and there was a glass of some liquor on the table. The door on the opposite side of the room was half open.

She crossed the floor, moved past the four-poster, and stopped just before the doorway. From inside that room, water sloshed. Warm, wet air wafted over her. With a finger, she pushed the door. It swung smoothly open onto a gentleman's dressing room.

Fenris was there, and she watched his head swivel toward the door as it opened. His valet stood at the far side of a copper bathtub, a towel stretched in his arms. The servant looked away from his employer to the door, eyes wide, but

Eugenia hardly cared, for Fenris was on his feet, obviously seconds away from stepping out of his bath. He was naked. Water dripped off his body and his hair was wet and slicked back from his face. Shadows flickered over him.

He faced her and cocked his head, silent. Offended? Annoyed? Angry?

Eugenia was mortally aware of the impropriety, but then she was already compromised. His valet knew she'd been here before.

He stepped out of the tub onto the tiled floor around the bath. Water dripped to the floor. He reached behind him for an edge of the towel his valet held. "What's happened?"

"I've just come from Spring Street."

"Only now?" He lifted an arm to keep the towel from dragging through the water and bent at the waist to rub his hair. When he straightened, he said, "You've had a long day, then."

"Milord." His valet came around the tub, reaching for the towel. If Eugenia's presence here scandalized him, you'd not know from the man's expression or voice, other than that vague annoyance that Fenris seemed to wish to dry himself. The servant took the towel and went to work rubbing away the water that clung to Fenris.

"It was awful," she said. To her horror, her voice broke.

Fenris waved off his valet and crossed to Eugenia. He put his arms around her and drew her against him. "Tell me." His chin rested on the back of her shoulder. "Have you lost much?"

"Everything smells like smoke and ashes." She put her arms around his shoulders and held tight. "The kitchen is mostly gone, and the entire below stairs is nothing but standing water. There's a great gaping hole in the ceiling of the back study. Mountjoy trusted me to take care of things and—"

"Hush, my dear." His arms tightened around her, and it felt good to have him close, to feel that for this moment, at least, she wasn't alone to deal with the ashes of the house. "Hush."

She put her head on his chest and sniffled.

"Good God, don't cry. I cannot give you a handkerchief just now."

She clung to him, tears pooling in her eyes and her trying to keep him from guessing how close she was to giving in to tears anyway. "I'll manage," she said. "I know I'll manage."

"Of course you shall. You're a capable woman." He lifted his head and addressed his valet. "My robe, if you will, then you may go. Thank you. I'll ring if I need you."

"Milord."

He loosened an arm, and she stepped away while his valet helped him into a thick silk robe with as much aplomb as he would have if his employer weren't standing naked in front of a woman to whom he was not married. His valet vanished through a back door. Fenris belted the robe and held out his arms. "Come."

Ginny walked into his embrace again. "What if Hester had been home?"

"She wasn't."

"That's not the point. She might have been."

He drew her close. "You might have been home. Both of you. If I hadn't delayed you, you might have been home when the fire broke out. I've been thanking Almighty God since then that you weren't."

"Mountjoy's going to come to Town to deal with this."

He put his hands on her shoulders and pushed her torso back so he could look into her face. "Now there is disaster." His mouth curved, and he chucked her under her chin. "Your brother will likely find a way to blame me for this. I'll need you to protect me from him."

"Oh, he won't, and you know it."

He was smiling still, though only just. "And he'd certainly have found a way to take a pound of my flesh if you'd been injured."

She put a hand on his chest and pushed. He didn't move, and after a bit, she didn't want him to. His skin was warm, soft over the muscles. He had a new bruise from his boxing, smaller than the faded one from before.

"So, yes, thank God you and Hester were not at home." He slung an arm around her shoulder and headed for the bedchamber. On the way, he picked up the lantern and closed the door behind them. "Something to drink?"

"No, thank you."

"You don't mind, do you, if I finish mine?"

"No."

He set the lantern on a table and picked up his abandoned drink. He curled his fingers around the glass. "Do you know what happened? How the fire started?"

His hair was standing every which way, and she couldn't help herself. She went to him and combed her fingers through his hair. "There, now at least it lies straight."

"Thank you." She would have stepped back, but he caught her hand and held on. "Tell me everything, Ginny."

"A curtain in one of the servants' rooms caught fire. The footman had the window open, he says, because he likes the cold air, and there must have been a breeze."

He sipped his drink and tugged on her hand. "Do you know if Mountjoy has insurance? Sit down."

"Not yet." She liked the closeness, the warmth of his body. "I don't know about insurance. Mountjoy is a cautious, prudent sort. I'd not be surprised if he did."

"How much have you lost?"

"The back study I think must be considered a complete loss. The top floor where the fire started, as well. I'm not sure about below stairs." She sighed. "Hester and I may need new clothes. I'm not convinced the smell of smoke can ever be got out of what I was able to retrieve. I've made a list of everything. Mountjoy will need it when he comes."

"My poor, dear Ginny. So efficient. You are a treasure. I hope your brother knows that. He doesn't, I'm sure. He takes you for granted." He pulled her against him, one arm around her shoulder. She felt him kiss the top of her head. "I'm glad you're here."

"Thank goodness, else we'd be on the street." Eugenia breathed in. His skin smelled very faintly of the scent he used—lemon, she thought.

"Hardly. But I meant here." He emptied his glass and set it down. "In this particular spot. My room." He kissed her forehead. "In my arms."

She rested her cheek against his chest. "I don't understand this. This compulsion I have about you."

"I've the same one about you."

"I don't like you."

"Ah, ah. You do not hate me."

"Incorrigible, that's what you are."

Still with his head bowed over her, he murmured, "I know."

She frowned, though he could not see her, and put her hands on the knot of the tie that held his robe closed. "Just awful," she whispered.

He drew in a breath, and she unfastened the sash. The two ends dropped, and the robe parted. She took a step back and Fenris allowed his arm to slide off her shoulder. She pressed her hand to his chest, then the other. "Your skin is warm."

"I like a hot bath."

She moved her hands to the sides of his chest. "You make me weak. My knees weak. You are . . ." She briefly closed her eyes. ". . . so lovely to look at."

"Lovely to touch?"

Without taking her eyes off him and his now insistent erection, she nodded. "Very."

"Please." He spread his hands wide. "Indulge any whim you may have."

She licked her lips and leaned in to kiss his chest, then came closer to kiss the side of his jaw. She trailed her other hand down to curl her hand around his member, then lower to his sac.

"What a stimulating whim."

"Your cock is marvelous." She tightened her fingers around him and drew her hand up. "I adore touching you. This." She gently squeezed him. "This is the part of you I like best."

"A sentiment I share. Ah." He swallowed. "Pray continue."

"Should I?"

"You must." Light danced in his eyes. "I don't wish to deprive you of any joy you might get from such touching of my person."

"I don't think it's joy."

"Such a disappointment. But go on. Somehow I'll bear up."

"You make me think the most disgraceful thoughts. It's appalling."

"Disgraceful?" He pushed his hips forward. "Best tell me what you mean by that."

She looked between them at her hand around his cock and at the pale skin of his belly. He was thick and hard. "I want to kiss you."

"There?"

"Yes."

"That *is* disgraceful. I think you should."

She lifted her head and found him watching her.

He tipped his head, and his expression was a delicious mix of anticipation and amusement. "Incorrigible, aren't I, allowing you to debauch me like this." He curled his hand around hers. "Shall I stand or sit?"

"You're quite tall. Sit, I think."

Fenris moved back when she released him and left only to fetch a chair to place before the fire. He added half a scuttle's worth of coals before he sat, his robe untied and open. Eugenia knelt between his spread legs. She was thrilled. Aroused. On fire.

He put his hands on her head, exerting just the slightest pressure to prevent her from bending over him just yet. "Do you really enjoy this, or is it something you tolerate because you know I like it?"

"I adore it."

"That's wicked of you."

"It is."

"Yet another horror for me to endure." He touched her cheek and drew in a long breath. "Do your worst."

She did. Her very, very worst. The moment her mouth

touched him, he whispered her name. He felt wonderful, tasted wonderful. His every groan wound her lust for him tighter. Right now, she was the one with the power, she was in control of his pleasure, and she did so want to see that he reached that place where only sexual release mattered.

Her own arousal intensified as she took him deeper. His hands tightened on her head and by the end, when she knew she'd brought him nearer to climax, he'd moved to the edge of the chair. They found a rhythm between strokes of her tongue, her palm moving along his shaft, the pulls of her mouth on him and the forward rock of his hips. Not rocking anymore, a thrust.

She swept her fingers down to caress his sac and press that spot just behind his penis, and he shouted. His cock throbbed in her mouth, and she relaxed and took him as deep as possible.

He kept his hands on her head when she sat back. Slowly, his eyes focused.

"When I have my brain back in my head, I'm going to take you to the Turkish room, strip us both naked, and fuck you senseless."

Chapter Thirty

~❧❧~

Later that week.

As Eugenia fell into sleep, she slid her hand beneath her pillow to smooth the medallion. It wasn't there because Fenris had it. How odd that she still had the habit. She hadn't yet told Lily that she'd given the medallion to Fenris. Guiltily, she realized she'd never told Fenris he was to sleep with the medallion under his pillow. Even without actually being able to touch the medallion, every night she indulged in the opportunity to think of the people she loved. Her brothers. Lily. Her late parents, and the aunt and uncle who had raised her and her brothers. Inevitably she thought of Robert. He was gone, so unfairly gone before his time. In her final moments of wakefulness, she could hold him in her heart and imagine he was smiling at her from heaven.

She fell into a deep and vivid dream.

She stood in a bedroom she didn't recognize, wearing a gown of blue silk worked with vertical stripes of roses in pale gray. Delicate lace dripped from the cuffs. A few inches above the wrists were bright red ribbons. A costume of some sort, her dreaming mind informed her. Well, yes, naturally, a costume. The Duke of Camber was holding a masquerade in a week's time, and the affair was the talk of London. She and Hester had yet to settle on what costumes to wear.

In her dream, she didn't recognize where she was, yet she felt she knew the room well. The room lights were low, with only a girandole on one wall, its three candles angled toward the chimney glass so the light was reflected back. Several chimney ornaments sat on the carved marble mantel: a brass fiddler, a porcelain Chinese dragon, a bit of moss that Hester had crystallized.

A door opened, and a man entered. Not Robert. Whoever he was, he locked the door before he walked from the shadows by the door to the lighted center of the room.

"Ginny," Fox said.

He walked to her, stopping behind her, and then slowly drew a finger along the top of her shoulder. When she was with Fox, the loneliness she'd lived with for so long always faded away, and she was at peace. In the wake of his touch, devastating arousal rippled through her. She trembled with it, burned with it while he removed the pins from her hair and drew his fingers through it until it fell soft about her shoulders. He brought her hair over her shoulder and planted a kiss on the shoulder he'd bared.

Eugenia drew in a breath that trembled.

"Sweet Ginny," he whispered. "Sweet, sweet Ginny."

Deftly, he unfastened the back of her costume, and then, as was the nature of dreams, she was nude, and he was running his hands over her body, and he proved himself familiar with each and every sensitive place. She was going up in flames.

He carried her to the bed, and when he joined her there, he, too, was in his bare skin. She turned on her side and rested a hand on his upper chest, savoring the peace that came with his company. Eyes closed, she touched him, and he stirred.

She opened her eyes, met the lovely golden brown of his eyes, then, with a smile, looked him over as boldly as he ever looked at her. His body took her breath. Sleek muscled chest from driving and boxing, legs formed by riding, flat belly. Tight nipples. She kissed one, then the other and smoothed her palm along his torso down to his flank. Such warm skin. She wanted so much to taste him. To hear him moan.

And then. Yes, then, his beautiful cock. She shifted down, fingers curled around him, and he drew a sharp breath when she brought her hand up, then down. She took her time touching him, adoring his body, and eventually, she moved over him and he put his hands to her hips.

"Beautiful, lovely Ginny." The slide of his cock into her left her breathless. Every nerve in her body was concentrated there. Fenris pushed his pelvis toward her and they began a slow and gentle lovemaking until slow wasn't enough. She wanted him driving into her the way he liked to do. That mastery of her that stopped her thinking of anything but the two of them. And then, and then, when she'd lost herself, well, then she took control of her pleasure. And his. She wanted to lose her mind that way again. Safe in his arms.

He did bring her peace. And she did lose herself in this.

Lord, he did, and it was wonderful. He moved them so she was on her back with his body over hers, his hand above her shoulders, and he slid into her again, moving with all the untempered passion she needed from him. All the while Fenris whispered that he loved her beyond life, and she listened to those words. She felt them and felt the echo of them as she left the dream for sleep.

The effect of that odd dream lingered at the edges of her mind when Martine brought in her morning chocolate. She took the cup and inhaled the scent. "Thank you."

"Milady." She dropped a quick curtsey. "Miss Rendell wishes to know if today you and she might explore the attic."

"Mm." She swallowed a mouthful of chocolate. It had been Fenris's idea that they go through some of the attic trunks here to see if they might find anything they could easily work into costumes. With so many gowns urgently needed to replace what had been ruined in the fire, costumes landed far down on the list of priorities. Remaking something from the attics of Bouverie was the expedient solution. "Yes, yes, indeed. As soon as we've had breakfast."

Less than an hour later, she and Hester were in the north attic with Martine and two of the footmen. The previous afternoon, Fenris had produced a very long inventory of the several attics in Bouverie and handed it over with a request that anything that looked useless be discarded or sorted out for the housekeeper to decide what might be repaired or donated. It was the least she could do.

The footmen instantly made themselves useful moving furniture to get to the trunks in the back of the space.

The first two trunks contained old linens and moth-eaten blankets. Eugenia had those set aside for the housekeeper to decide what would be given to the ragman. There was an empty garderobe with a broken door, easily fixed by a competent carpenter. She made a note of that, too.

Perhaps an hour later, Eugenia's list was going on a third page, and fully half the items they'd examined so far were stacked to one side for further disposition. Hester wiped a cobweb off the lid of yet another trunk. "Oh. Lady Eugenia, do come see."

The trunk she'd just inventoried was full of books and pamphlets from a hundred years ago. She closed the lid and joined Hester. Clothes and linens packed in tissue paper filled the trunk Hester had just opened. She closed the lid and one of the footmen moved it aside for them. In short order they found another two trunks of clothes.

She had the footmen bring the trunks of clothes downstairs to the small parlor where they'd be away from the dust. There, she and Hester sat on the floor before the first trunk. The top garment was a gown from at least fifty years ago. She held it up. One of Fenris's relatives had worn this. She looked inside the trunk and found that all the required linens and undergarments had been included, from petticoats to gloves, stockings, shift, and even carefully wrapped red-heeled shoes with gold buckles.

Hester reached in and took out several linen chemises,

each one beautifully embroidered with a monogram and the crest of the Dukes of Camber.

As Hester rummaged in the contents again, a flash of blue caught Eugenia's attention. "What's that?"

"This?"

"No. The blue there. Underneath." With Hester's assistance, she brought out a frock of a medium blue silk. She spread it over her lap and brushed her fingers over the material with its vertical pattern of stripes formed of gray roses and garlands. Not exactly like the gown in her dream, but so eerily similar that she shivered.

Hester leaned in to have a better look. "What a pretty fabric."

Eugenia held up the material. The hem was soiled in places, and there was a stain on one of the sleeves, but other than those defects the material was in quite good condition. "Yes. Very pretty."

"Whoever wore that was a healthy woman." Indeed, the dress would have been worn by a woman much rounder than Eugenia. "That blue would be lovely on you. It's your color." Hester fingered the soiled sleeve. "We could add some lace to hide the stain. Perhaps sew on some ribbon?"

She fingered the material. The scent of lavender wafted to her. "Last night I dreamt I wore a dress just like this. With the loveliest lace you can imagine at the sleeves."

"If you dreamed of it, then you must wear this, Lady Eugenia. There's no question that you must. And look. What do you think of this?" Hester held up a gown of red and gold stripes. "This will do for me."

"It is pretty."

She brought the fabric close to her face. "Red looks well on me, don't you agree?"

"Yes. It surely does flatter you. Lieutenant Fraser will be sure to admire you." She waited for Hester to acknowledge that, but she didn't.

Instead, Hester said, "I can make a matching domino."

Eugenia tried again. "Or his eldest brother?"

"Who? Oh. Not him."

"You prefer Lieutenant Fraser?"

"I don't prefer anyone."

"At all?"

Hester laid the red and gold gown over her lap and stroked the material. "I'll be a lovely shepherdess in this."

"Indeed, Hester."

"Do you think the duke will recognize me?" Hester glanced away, but not so soon Eugenia didn't see Hester's wistful expression.

"I'm sure your costume will be most clever." She folded the blue gown over her arm and tried to analyze the sudden pinch in her heart. Was it possible Hester had misunderstood Camber's attentions to her? "Do you want the duke to recognize you?"

"You'll be so lovely in a costume made from this." Hester leaned over and stroked the gown Eugenia held. "You'll be the most beautiful woman at the masquerade."

"My dear girl." With a glance to be sure they were alone, she took Hester's hand. "If something were the matter, you'd tell me, wouldn't you?"

After a too-long hesitation, Hester nodded.

"And?"

Her mouth turned stubborn. "I won't marry any of Lord Baring's sons, and so I told Camber."

"Camber? Did he attempt to advise you, then?" Hester nodded to that. "What did he say?"

Hester swiped at her cheek.

Eugenia reached for her hand, holding it between hers. "Did you quarrel with him?"

She sat up straight. "First when he told me I ought to marry Lieutenant Fraser. Again when he said I should marry Lord Fenris."

"Fenris?"

"As if he would. As if I wanted to." All brisk motions, Hester folded the red and gold gown. "I told him I wouldn't marry his son for love nor money." She lifted her eyes, and Eugenia could see her anger and hurt. "Pray don't take offense, Lady Eugenia. I've never been in love before, and

I fear I'm not handling it well. I didn't think being in love would be so . . . difficult to endure."

Eugenia sat back and wondered what she might dare to say. Hester wasn't the usual sort of young lady, but unrequited love was an unhappy experience. "The duke," she said carefully, "is considerably older than you."

"I am aware." Her mouth firmed. "However, I fail to see why that matters."

"How much can you have in common with a man so much your elder?"

"Lord Fenris doesn't care an inch about plants. He's bored silly ten seconds into any discussion about plant propagation."

"He has other qualities." When Hester didn't say anything in response, she sighed. "Has the duke given you any reason to think he might return your feelings?"

"No. He's been kind and generous, but nothing more. And, I daresay, tolerant of me." Hester folded the gown. "I can't help how I feel, Lady Eugenia. I don't want Lord Fenris. Or Lord Aigen or anyone related to Lord Baring. He's not the curmudgeon everyone says, you know."

"The duke."

"Yes," Hester said. She sniffed once and dashed a finger beneath her eye. "I don't know how I fell in love with him. I didn't mean to. Did you mean to fall in love with Robert?"

"No. It just happened."

"For you both."

Eugenia nodded.

"I'd never even thought about being in love until the day I realized what had happened to me." She shrugged. "It's a pity. I do wish he'd stop telling me I am a sweet young woman. I'm not, you know."

"One day, Hester, someone will love you just as you are." Eugenia couldn't help wondering what Fenris would think.

Chapter Thirty-one

A week later. Bouverie.

FOX STRAIGHTENED FROM HIS SLOUCH AGAINST THE wall the moment Eugenia walked into the ballroom. Her costume, a Turkish robe of sorts made of sumptuous blue silk worked with stripes of gray, seemed familiar to him even though he knew he'd never seen her wearing it. She turned to respond to someone's query of her, and then he remembered why her costume was familiar. From one of his dreams.

At his side, Aigen bestirred himself, too. "That's Lady Eugenia? In the blue?"

"Yes."

He looked at her from under lidded eyes. "Well, well, well. A vision, to be sure."

"Yes."

"And Miss Rendell, in the stripes?"

"Yes."

Miss Rendell was dressed as a shepherdess in a gown of sumptuous red and gold stripes. She held a crook in one hand and had arranged her hair high on her head, with garlands of flowers throughout. Aigen was right. Miss Rendell was very pretty.

Fox gestured. Over the blue and gray garment, Eugenia wore a short-waisted jacket of the same fabric but trimmed with wide bands of gold. Pearls and gems, one presumed they were paste, glittered on the jacket. A sash of gray and gold encircled Eugenia's natural waist. The look, given the present fashion, was shockingly revealing of her figure. Her slippers curled up at the toes, and she wore a gold turban, set back to reveal some of her bright gold hair. Her domino was blue, gold, and gray. She looked delectable.

His father approached the two women, greeted them, and walked them both away from the crowd at the entrance, Eugenia on one arm, Miss Rendell on the other. After all his trying and failing to prove to Eugenia that he was a better man than he had been, he had no more ways to prove himself. He would never succeed with her, and she would never love him. The knowledge hollowed him out.

For the next several minutes it was possible for him to watch Eugenia as his father introduced the women to friends and political cronies, many of them Cabinet ministers and sitting peers. Eventually, though, he joined his father to pay his respects to them and offer to fetch them both a glass of lemonade. Going on three weeks since she'd told him she was late, and not a word one way or another. He lost sight of Eugenia after that, though on one occasion he saw her dancing with Aigen and another time with Lord Baring. Miss Rendell had a constant stream of admirers, including both of Baring's sons.

Some two hours later, he was standing by one of the exits in no better mood than before. He'd tried ignoring Eugenia, but that was no good. He always knew when she was near, and if he scanned the crowd for any reason, he always ended up hoping for a glimpse of her. She'd become a habit with him.

He watched her emerge from the crowd and head his direction. He could have moved. Walked away. He didn't.

White chalk from the ballroom floor dusted the underside of her curled-toe slippers. She didn't see him at first, but when she did, she halted, expression uncertain. He waited to see whether she would speak to him or move on. Her cheeks were flushed with color, and he supposed she'd been dancing, since a set had just ended. Just when he thought she would move on without acknowledging him, she gave him a brilliant smile. Appalling what a smile from her did for his mood.

"Is that you, Lord Fenris?"

He gave her an elaborate bow. He was dressed as a cavalier, in boots, spurs, cape, and loose-fitting trousers. He'd elected to leave off a wig to emulate the then fashion for long curls. Other than that, his costume was as accurate as any other here. "At your service, fair maiden."

She smiled. Desire left him as helpless as ever with her. Not only desire. A part of his heart would always belong to her. "Monsieur."

"Enjoying yourself, I hope?"

"Yes, very much." She walked to him. A rope of pearls draped around her throat. Had Robert given them to her? Had she fastened them on tonight, thinking of the man she loved? He wanted her to love him, but her heart had already been taken up by Robert. She would never have room for him, and he was going to have to accept that. "You make a handsome cavalier."

"Thank you. May I say the same about you?" He forced a grin, because she expected that of him, that he would be agreeable at all times. "Substituting lovely sultana for handsome cavalier, of course."

"I've been wondering where you were. I didn't see you dancing. All the ladies were wondering why."

"Here and there. About. I saw you dancing with Aigen."

"Yes."

"And with Dinwitty Lane. Did he propose again?"

She narrowed her eyes at him. "You aren't having a good time?"

"I don't care for parties."

"Yes, you do."

With those words ended the brief improvement in his mood. "My mistake. I adore parties."

"You're being difficult on purpose." She continued in a soft voice. "Don't."

"Yes, I am being difficult." He gave her costume another long examination. When he looked up from what was an inappropriately intense study of her figure, Eugenia's gaze on him was steady. He didn't look away. The air between them felt decidedly close. She could fuck him as if no other man would do, but she couldn't love him.

"I'm doing my best with you, you know." She took a half step toward him, then stopped. "It's not easy to change. Mountjoy always said I was stubborn, but I'm trying. I am."

"Your best is very good, Ginny, but no match for me when I am in a mood." He shook his head. She was going to fall in love with some other man. He'd let her use him, willingly, and what she'd learned from him was not that he loved her, but that she could break away from her widowhood and be happy. "Forgive me. I'm not fit company for you."

"Has something happened?"

"Nothing you would care to hear about." He took a step toward her, close enough to touch her pearls. "I've never seen these before. Did Robert give them to you?"

"They're Hester's. She lent them to me."

Thank God. "I'd give you pearls if you let me."

"I'd not accept them from you."

"Why not? They'd be a gift freely given."

"You know very well why not."

"I want you to have something to remember me by."

She studied him, and he didn't like at all that he felt she was seeing more than he wanted. "What's got into you tonight?"

He made an impatient gesture. "I am in a mood, that's all. Forgive me. I don't mean to be cross with you." He touched the pearls she wore. She lifted her chin, and they stood there with him thinking thoughts he shouldn't. "Diamonds, I think, is what I ought to buy you." He let his hand fall away.

"Nothing so extravagant."

"Would you marry Aigen if he asked?"

"I don't know him well enough to answer you. And if I

did, I don't believe I'd tell you." She gave a tiny shake of her head. "Robert is gone. But you're right; he wouldn't have wanted me to stop living." She licked her lips. "I did for a while. For too long, but then you know that. You've helped me see that."

He didn't look away from her.

"Sometimes, when I'm with you, I feel . . ."

"Vexed?"

"Yes." Her quick smile flashed over her face. "Exasperated, too. But you make me laugh. You do. It never lasts, you know it doesn't. We don't suit at all, but I want to thank you. For making me remember what it's like to be happy."

Jesus, she might as well tell him she'd already given her heart elsewhere. "Oh, Ginny. You break me."

"I'm sorry if I do." She touched his arm. "I don't mean to hurt you."

And there they were again, with the world closing in around them in that heavenly way that only happened with her. He cocked his head, and when she didn't speak or move, he held out his hand in invitation. "A last time for us?"

She didn't deny that. Nor tell him she had good news or disastrous news. All she did was place her fingers on his hand, and he led her out of the ballroom. They might have been going anywhere perfectly proper. The card rooms were down the corridor in this direction. As were two saloons opened up for those looking for conversation away from the dancing. But he did not take her any of those places. He took her to the office he kept at Bouverie, a floor above the ballroom and tucked away in a corner that, during the day, had a view of a small garden. His spurs jingled as he walked, her hand in his.

In his office, he brought her inside, then closed and locked the door. The servants had strict instructions to keep the fire going so the room was not frigid, thank God. The curtains were drawn for the night and the only light came from the banked fire. He pulled off his gloves and shoved them into the pocket of his coat.

"How can you see in this dark?" Eugenia said in a low voice.

The room was pitch-black, but he knew his office and the arrangement of its furniture. He drew her to him, sliding an arm around her waist. "Can't see a bloody thing."

"Will you light a candle?" Her hands landed on his chest, resting there lightly. There was amusement in her voice, but tension as well.

"No."

"Why not?"

"Because we're going to do this." He kissed her, and while he did, while she kissed him back, he ran his hands along her sides and then underneath her short jacket and over the curve of her bosom, and she leaned into him, looping her arms around his neck and opening her mouth under his. As mad as he.

He wasn't in a mood for delicacy. Not tonight. Not after watching her dance and wondering what he would do if this man or that was the one she fell in love with instead of with him. She'd danced with Aigen, for pity's sake, when Aigen was a credible threat to any woman's heart. She could do worse than Aigen.

Fox kissed her the way a man kisses a lover, and, by God, she kissed him back. Matters went quickly out of control, not that he'd intended for anything but that to happen. She pressed herself against him and brought his head closer to hers, and she kissed him with all the passion he'd dreamed about with her.

He drew away and led her the five steps to his desk. He moved behind her, with her facing his desk and, at first, with just his hands on her shoulders. She didn't move. This wasn't a flirtation that might lead to more; this was a prelude to sex. He knew it. She knew it.

Fox slid his hands down to her waist, below the short jacket, then below the sash that belted the frock made of the fabric he'd dreamed about. She wore a short corset, but below that was her natural figure. He gathered a handful of her skirts, then another. He pressed his mouth to the back of her neck, the side of her throat, and she let her head fall back to rest against his shoulder.

The silk of her frock and the linen underskirt beneath rustled as he brought the fabric higher. He put his mouth by her ear. "Put your hands on the desk. It's sturdy enough for us, I promise."

She complied, and the position bent her at the hips. He took a step closer, trapping her skirts between them, and slid one hand between her legs, waiting for her to adjust her stance, which she did. He found her slick and hot. He stood with his pelvis against her bottom, slightly bent forward himself in order to reach her. He swept his thumb along the top of her thigh while his fingers delved.

He was hellishly aroused. She drew in a breath and held it, but he waited until she let it out before he caressed her there. He fetched her with a great deal of deliberation. In the dark, he relied on senses other than sight to judge how close she was; the tension in her body, the way her breath shortened, the flesh swelling under his fingertips, and then, as well, her whispered plea for him to bring her release.

In the darkness, her long, low moan was all the more arousing to him. He moved a hand to the middle of her back and exerted a gentle pressure when she would have straightened. With his other hand, he brought her skirts up higher, out of the way. She understood what he intended, for she went quite still while he unfastened the fall of his trousers.

"Yes?" he asked. He asked because he didn't want to be wrong about whether she wanted to do this with him and because, very selfishly, he wanted her to admit she desired him. She did not love him, but by God, she desired him.

"Yes."

He found her entrance and his mind locked out any sensation but her and his cock. He pushed forward, and she pressed her hips back, and his foreskin slid back, and he hadn't intended to slam into her but he did. She made a sound in the back of her throat, a grunt, but then she lowered her head. "My God, Fox."

He hesitated.

"Again." Such a fierce whisper.

So he did, and she braced herself, and when it came right down to it, she set the pace between them, not him. He held her hips with both hands, and she steadied herself against his thrusts. Shoves, really. Hard. Almost as hard as he liked his fucking. Once or twice he had to adjust her skirts to keep them out of the way.

The pressure of her around him, the softness of her, and the friction sent him mad with desire. Taut with it, alive with the joy of having his cock in her. She shifted her hips and pushed out, and he had barely enough presence of mind to think about making sure he responded to what she needed from this. There was a particular angle that made her moan, and he concentrated on that.

So close. He was so close.

He managed to slow things down so he'd last a little longer and found the angle that made her shudder and then cry out, and that pressure was damn near as good for him. At one point, he worked his fingers into her hair, cradling the back of her head while he wound tighter and tighter.

They fell quiet now, the two of them, silent in respect to words, but not for a second was his awareness of her anything but the very reason for his desire. He could barely see in the dark, but it didn't matter. He recognized her in her cries, the sound of her moans. The scent of her perfume and the fever heat that burned through him.

He dropped his torso over her back, hands on the desk outside hers, and she braced herself again as his hips rocked into her, meeting his every thrust into her. Sooner than he would have liked, he reached the point where he was so close to coming that he took over the pace. He pushed back to hold her hips again, tightly now because they were both near to climax.

There was only them in this delicious cover of darkness, and in the next instant there was only his approaching crisis, and, Jesus, her passage was clenching around him, and he shouted something incoherent, and he nearly didn't withdraw in time.

Chapter Thirty-two

The next day.

FOX ARRIVED AT BOUVERIE FROM WESTMINSTER shortly after nine o'clock that night. There was a dusting of snow on the ground, and when the front door closed behind him, he stamped his feet to knock off the ice. He pulled off his gloves and rubbed his hands together, but his fingers stayed cold. The butler took his coat and hat. "Where is everyone?"

"His grace is in his study. Miss Rendell has retired to her room. As has Lady Eugenia, I believe." As he said this, the butler handed him a note, sealed with plain red wax.

"Thank you." He slipped the note into his coat pocket. "Here it is, the last days of the season, and we're all at home." He handed over his gloves. "We're a sorry lot, aren't we?"

"A bit nippy to be out gallivanting, milord."

"I suppose you're right. I've not dined yet. Have a light supper sent to my room?"

"Sir."

As he headed for his room he broke the seal on the note. There was a single sentence:

We must talk.
—Eugenia

With her note in hand, he went first to his room where he opened a carved rosewood box.

His valet came in carrying his robe and a pair of felt slippers, but Fox waved him off. "I may be going out again. I'll need a coat and what have you. I'll carry them with me now, if you don't mind."

"Milord."

Inside the box was the fob his mother had made for him. The edges were worn and there was a stain on a corner. He touched it once before he took out the gold band he kept inside, along with the few other mementos he had of her. He put the ring into his coat pocket.

His valet came back with the requested items. "Thank you. If I'm not back in fifteen minutes, it's because I've gone out. Don't hold my dinner past then. I'll find something to eat later."

"Milord."

With his coat, hat, and gloves in one hand, he went to Eugenia's room. He tapped the back of his knuckles on the door.

She opened the door, and in her eyes he saw an entire universe there, moving according to laws beyond his understanding. She took a deep breath and stepped into the corridor. She closed the door behind her.

"I take it we need the strictest privacy?"

She nodded.

His chest was tight while he walked with her down the stairs to a saloon at the back of the house. If it were daylight, there would be a view of the rear garden. Not much of a sight with the wintery weather of late. At present, the curtains were drawn tight. The fire wasn't even laid, for they'd not used this room so far this season. He put his things on a chair and lit a branch of candles and then another so the room wasn't unbearably dim.

Eugenia walked to the fireplace, but it was cold and barren, not even ashes in the hearth.

"Shall I start a fire?"

She gave a tight shake of her head and picked up a porcelain Buddha sitting on the mantel. Still facing the fireplace and turning the Buddha over and over in her hands, she said, "I've been doing arithmetic all day it seems."

"And?"

She faced him and shrugged. "As I said, I've never been terribly regular."

"Yes." He waited for her to continue.

She let out a quick breath and surveyed the room. She briefly clasped a hand over her mouth, then slid her fingers downward over her lips. "I've been ill. In the morning. Afternoons, sometimes. It started this week."

He had, in the course of his life, dreaded hearing such words from his lovers. He'd not faced those consequences before because he'd been lucky, careful, and circumspect. Now? A mass of emotions burst over him, rained down on him. Part of him was terrified; part of him was overjoyed. He wanted to pick her up and spin her around. He did neither. Nothing, absolutely nothing with her was easy. What he wanted was her to be happy with him. Instead, she held back tears.

She said, "I'm sorry."

He crossed the room and took her hand in his. "I'm not. Nor should you be. No tears. I won't have that, my love." He brought her hand to his mouth and kissed her palm then went down on a knee. "Will you marry me, Ginny?"

· She gazed at him unflinchingly. "Why ask when there's no choice?"

"There are always choices." He kissed the other side of her hand. "Some are harder than others. Not this one. Not for me. Must it be so for you? Marry me. Now. Tonight."

"Tonight?"

"I've a special license."

Her shoulders slumped. "Of course."

"Marry me. Or am I to have your brother's rage heaped upon my hapless self?"

"You know I will."

"Don't be sorry." He stood and pulled her toward him. The satisfaction of knowing he was getting what he wanted was tinged with uneasiness. He wanted her to marry for love, and she wouldn't be. "This was always a possibility. You knew that. As did I."

"And this—"

He kissed her on the mouth. Just once. Not long enough to be crude, but not so short a kiss that she didn't have time to respond to him. He took a breath and stopped. With the tip of his first finger, he smoothed the space between her eyebrows. "I recognize that frown. Stop. You've nothing to worry about. I'll take care of you. You'll want for nothing."

"That isn't the point."

"I won't be the sort of husband who expects his wife to follow him in all things."

She dropped her forehead to his chest. "Don't be so decent." She whispered, "Please, don't. I can't bear it."

He drew a deep breath. "This is what I want."

"And here I thought you were overcome by passion."

"Oh, never doubt that I was. As were you. Several times as I recall." He laughed very softly, but she heard and thumped her fist on his chest.

"Don't make me laugh."

He cupped the back of her head and drew her closer. "I have seen your goodness. Your kindness, your generosity. Your wit. I lust for your independent mind as well as your body." He waited a beat. "There. Does that help?"

His coat muffled her laugh. "Horrible man."

"Yes. Awful. I know. I shall willingly give you all that I possess." The words, which he had intended to sound certain, instead took on a recklessness that threatened to give him away. He could not stop himself. "My heart, too. Have you not yet accepted that you have that?"

She lifted her head. "I know."

"When I am with you, I'm happy. I won't ask you for anything more."

"What about someone who loves you? Someone head over heels in love with you?" She leaned against him, and he slipped an arm around her shoulders. "You should ask for that."

"Robert would be glad to know I will take care of you."

She brushed her fingers over his cheek. "All that and diamonds, too?"

"Yes. All that." He set her back a step. "I'll come with you to fetch your coat."

She closed her eyes, and he could see her trying to hold back tears. "What if I'm wrong? What if I'm not pregnant after all?"

"There's very little in life that's certain. What if the sky falls or the world ends? Suppose tomorrow is Judgment Day?" He allowed his hands to slip off her shoulders. "And then suppose it's not. We can't wait until you're showing, for God's sake. That won't save me from your brother's wrath."

She let out a short laugh.

"Shall I send a servant for your coat or will you want Martine with you?"

"Martine. She's waiting for me."

He picked up his things, blew out the candles, and headed back upstairs. When they reached her room, Martine was in the anteroom dressed to go out. She held Eugenia's coat in her arms. He returned her a considering glance. Of course Eugenia's maid would know her employer's intimate condition. And the man responsible. "I trust you are not presently armed."

She patted the pocket of her coat and gave him a rather vicious smile.

He set down his hat and gloves and put on his coat. "Pray don't shoot me yet."

She returned him an unflinching gaze. "Depends why you're here, milord."

"After you've helped Lady Eugenia with her things,

please go to the mews and ask one of the grooms to bring my carriage, the plain one, to the side street. No livery. Wait for us there."

"Milord."

He put on his gloves. "We'll be there shortly. Thank you, Martine."

Forty minutes later, he stood before the clergyman with Eugenia at his side. Her hand rested atop his raised one as the man read off the words that bound him to Eugenia for as long as he should live. He put his mother's ring on her finger, and moments later, he was a married man.

Whether he would ever have his heart's desire was another matter entirely.

Chapter Thirty-three

❧❧

Later that night.

Not a Hampton. A Bryant no longer. A Talbot.

What on earth had she just done?

God knows she was returning to Bouverie a different woman from the one who'd started out from that labyrinth of a house. No longer Lady Eugenia or Mrs. Bryant. She was a married woman again. To Fenris.

They'd decided, she and Fenris, not to make a formal announcement of their marriage. Camber would be told. Hester. The Bouverie staff. Mountjoy would be told when he arrived in London. She dreaded each and every revelation to come.

Fenris held her hand during the entire drive from the reverend's house to Bouverie. He frequently swept a finger over her wedding band. He didn't let go except to leave the carriage at the side exit of Bouverie. He opened the gate one-handed and then turned the key over to Martine and let her open the side door.

When Martine opened the door for them, he swept Eugenia into his arms and carried her inside. He kissed her once, quickly and on the mouth, before he set her on her feet.

"Well, Lady Fenris." His voice was all smoke and desire, with a large amount of satisfaction thrown into the mix. "Welcome to Bouverie."

Emotion jammed up her throat and kept her from replying. Instead, she rested her head on his chest. What had she done? Nothing but what had to be done.

Still with his arms around her waist, he twisted to look at Martine. "I'll see to her tonight. We'll call if you're needed. Her room."

Her maid bent a knee and headed for the down staircase.

"Martine?" he called after her.

"Milord?"

"Thank you for not shooting me."

"It was a near thing, sir."

He took the candle Martine had left them. With Eugenia's hand in his, he led her upstairs. But not to her room right away. They ended up in the Turkish room where he secured the door. She found herself glad to have a few moments to gather herself. He always knew, didn't he?

"Lady Fenris."

Eugenia shook herself, but her stomach remained firmly lodged somewhere around her toes. She stared into Fenris's face. Her husband's face, and if he hadn't still held her hand, which he did, she might have crumpled to the floor. "What have we done?"

"I'll take that as a rhetorical question." He watched her. Examined her. He could lay her soul bare with his eyes. He stripped off his greatcoat, hat, and gloves, letting them fall to the nearest end of the divan. While she watched, he stripped down to his skin, efficiently and quickly. Naked, he put his hands on his head and slowly ran his fingers back through his hair.

From the moment he'd set his fingers to undo his cravat, Eugenia had stopped thinking about anything but him. The man and his magnificent body and that she was soon going to be able to touch him. Say what you would about her utterly conflicted emotions; there was no denying the physical attraction that sang between them.

He stayed just as he was. Naked. Hands on his head. Erect. And she glanced away to see his body reflected in the glass. Front. Side. Back. The sight was so beautifully erotic she had to close her eyes. She would lose everything if she continued to look at him. Everything.

"What do you see?" he said.

She dragged her eyes open and met his gaze. The sleepiness was gone, replaced by a stark emotion that peeled away her years of resentment and hurt. Gone. Vanished in his eyes. Vanished in the ring he'd put on her finger.

He held out a hand.

"The impossible. I see the impossible." The words came on a breath. He loved her. She saw and could no longer deny it. He loved *her*, and she was humbled that he allowed her to see, even believing she did not return those feelings. "I see forever."

She took a step toward him and put her hand on his. His fingers closed around hers. "What do you see?" She put her other hand on his chest. Palm over his heart. She closed her eyes and let the beat of his heart thrum through her. Slowly, she opened her eyes. "When you look at me? What do you see? For I suspect the woman you see is a stranger to me."

He turned her around, and her coat and bonnet joined the pile of his clothes. He unfastened, as quickly as Martine ever did, the buttons of her gown. She smoothed her skirts.

"I see you."

"My God, Fenris. I married in a muslin gown I wear when I do not expect company."

"You look lovely. Comfortably lovely."

"How could you let me go out like that?"

Slowly, he shook his head. "Madam, I was not about to give you an excuse to change your mind."

To her horror, tears threatened, because he loved her, and she didn't have half his courage. Her eyes burned and not a single word could pass the lump in her throat. With her assistance, he managed the rest of her clothes. He stood behind her when she, too, was stripped to her bare skin. He rested his fingers on her shoulders, dancing the pads from her very upper arms to her throat and back.

Candlelight reflected in the glass a dozen times. She watched him behind her. His head was bowed and a lock of his dark hair had fallen across his forehead. In the glass, the man behind her ran just the tips of his fingers downward, over the curve of the side of her breast.

"Ginny," he said. He wrapped his arms around her, and he rested his chin on top of her head. He slid a hand over her belly and left it there, fingers spread. "Ginny, my love. I'm not sorry at all."

She turned in his arms, and this time, she took his hand and walked backward to the divan. As she lay back, he resisted. Instead, he leaned against the upholstered back of the divan, one knee bent to the ceiling. The view of his cock transfixed her.

He tugged on her hand and straightened his leg. "You may have all of me, madam."

"Might I?"

A sly grin appeared on his mouth as she straddled him. "If you're very, very good, yes."

She lifted her hips and, a hand around his sex, seated herself, slowly. Wonderfully. He sucked in a breath and thrust up against her push down. "Yes." She whispered the word. "Yes. Just so."

"Lovely. You, so lovely." He brushed his fingers over her breast, then down the midline of her body. Once again, he spread his hand wide over her belly.

She brushed back that wayward lock of his hair then kissed him and rocked forward. She tasted his mouth. Took him, drank deep of everything she'd refused to imagine before. One of his hands covered her breast while the other held her bottom, and for a while they made love like this, slowly, with one or the other of them from time to time looking away to watch in the glass.

At one point, his eyes were half closed because he was watching the joining of their bodies, and she stared at his face. He caught his lower lip between his teeth, and she slowed the roll of their hips. She cupped his face between her hands and tilted his head to hers. His gaze flicked up to hers, and something tugged at her chest, a feeling that expanded until it could not be held in and brought a sob rushing out of her.

"My darling Ginny." He looked at her as if she were his world, and her heart clicked into place. Her love for Robert wasn't pushed aside. She would always love Robert, but there was room in her heart for another love.

He made her happy. When that had happened, she didn't know, but she was happy when she was with him. And sometimes, at times like this, she thought that feeling was more than happiness.

She rocked her hips harder, and he responded by grasping her hips and bringing her down harder. His cock went deeper inside her, and she let out a groan. He held her and reversed their positions so that he was on top of her. She brought her hands down and spread her fingers over his backside, knees bent, doing whatever she could to keep their connection.

"I love you, Fox," she said. "I love you madly. Desperately. With all my heart."

"Hush." He pushed up on his palms and stopped moving, even resisting her hands on him urging him to start again. "You needn't say that."

"I take it back." She sucked in a breath and tried to still her arousal. "I don't love you anymore. I did, but not now, you awful man."

He was still hard, but he wasn't moving. "You can't take it back. It's too late. Say it again."

"No. You said you'd bring me here and fuck me senseless, and you haven't. I can't love a man who doesn't keep his word."

His eyes got big and wide and then an evil grin spread over his face. He pushed his hips forward. "That?"

"Fenris."

"Fox," he said, the word harsh against her ear. He moved slowly in her again, but that wasn't what she wanted from him. "Then say that other word that sounds like that." He covered her and, with his weight held on his arms, kissed her, and she kissed him back. He drew away. "Say, 'Fuck me,' Ginny, and I will, as hard as you like."

"As hard as you like?"

"I'm hoping there won't be a difference." He stopped moving.

"God, I hate you."

"Say it." He grabbed her arms and pinned them over her head. "I'd die to hear you say that."

She wrapped her legs around him. "Fuck me, Fox."

And then he did, and held her while he did, and there really did come a point where she lost her mind while he moved in her, hard and fast. He angled himself in her the way he had before, and he was saying that word and others like it, and then he couldn't speak, either, and it was just the two of them. They were slick with sweat, the both of them.

His belly slid over hers, and it wasn't hurting her but she was right there on the edge of discomfort at the very same time her body hurtled toward a climax. He put his mouth by her ear and whispered, "Do you love me now, Ginny?"

She broke. Completely, and then he did, and she held him close, and when she came back to her body, while he was shuddering with his release, she opened her eyes and said, again, "Yes. I do. I love you, Fox."

Chapter Thirty-four

The next morning.

TAP, TAP, TAP.

Fox tightened his arms around Eugenia and ignored the noise. They were in her bed, and he was warm, sexually sated, and very comfortable. He did not want to be any more awake than he was right now.

Tap, tap, tap.

A door opened. He kept his eyes closed.

"Milord?"

He recognized Martine's voice but would have continued to ignore her if not for the thread of tension in her words. Martine had a head on her shoulders. He disengaged himself from Eugenia and rolled over. He kept the sheets up. "Yes?"

"Sir." She gave him a quick curtsey. "The Duke of Mountjoy is here and asking to see you and her ladyship."

"Ah." He looked over at Eugenia, still asleep. "Thank you." Something in Martine's demeanor set off an alarm, and he frowned to himself. "What else? Is Mountjoy angry?"

She hesitated.

"Out with it." Jesus, had Eugenia's brother somehow

found out about the two of them? He didn't know how, but rumor traveled at lightning speed.

"Mr. Hayden says he went to your father's room this morning." Hayden, of course, was his father's valet of the last thirty years. Martine put both her hands over her mouth, and her eyes slid to Eugenia.

Fox sat up, his heart pounding. "What is it, Martine?"

"Below stairs is in an uproar. He's threatening to quit, sir."

Eugenia stirred and rolled over. "What is it? Martine, is that you?"

Fox put a hand on her shoulder. "Your brother is here, so in any event, you will need to get up."

Eugenia took his hand and kissed it. "Good morning to you," she murmured.

He squeezed her shoulder and gave his attention back to Martine. "Why is Hayden threatening to quit?"

"Miss Rendell was there."

"Of course she was," said a sleepy Eugenia. "She's staying here, too."

"No." Martine's eyes went wide, and she took a deep breath. "She was in the duke's bedchamber."

Under the covers, he gripped Eugenia's hand. They were both of them now fully awake. "I presume she and my father were not having tea or a pleasant discussion of botany?"

"No, milord. They were not."

"Oh," Eugenia said, very softly. "Oh, dear."

He hung his head and sighed. "Please send my valet to Camber and tell him—my father, I mean—that I would like to speak to him in his office at his earliest convenience. And, if you would, ask Hayden to attend to me in my rooms. Please tell Mountjoy that I will see him shortly. Shoot whomever you feel needs it. Then you may assist Lady Fenris."

"Milord."

When Martine was gone, Fox gathered Eugenia in his arms. "Whatever you're paying that woman, it's not enough."

"Hester was in your father's room?" She gripped his shoulders.

"So it would seem."

"How am I going to explain this to Hester's mother?"

He kissed her on the mouth. "When you're ready, find your brother. If I'm not with him, then I'm still with Camber."

He slid out of bed and put on enough clothing that he could decently manage the walk to his rooms, carrying his boots and the rest of his clothes. Hayden was there, stone-faced. "Thank you for attending to me," he said. He dropped his clothes onto a chair and held up a hand. "So there is no misinterpretation, the Lady Eugenia and I were married last night. I've sent my man to look after Camber, by the way. I've no idea what's got into my father, but I will deal with that and my wife's brother as soon as I'm washed and decently dressed. Can you manage that or must I pay you your wages now?"

Hayden bowed stiffly, and Fox waited while any number of offended and stubborn emotions flickered over the servant's face. At last, he gave a grudging bow. "My lord."

"Thank you."

Once he was dressed, he headed for his father's study. Halfway there, one of the footmen intercepted him. Fox tried to compose himself. He was tired, having spent much of the night most enjoyably not sleeping, and hungry, and in desperate need of tea. And for God's sake, he was to confront his father about compromising a young woman who had accepted his hospitality. He forced a smile. "Yes?"

"My lord. I beg leave to inform you that his grace requires your presence in the Grand saloon."

"Which bloody duke are we talking about? Camber or Mountjoy?"

The footman took a step back. "Both, my lord."

"I will be there shortly." He took another step down to the first floor then turned back. "Have tea brought there. And chocolate for Lady Fenris." Because Eugenia drank chocolate in the morning and he'd be damned if she missed hers today. "And food. Something light."

"My lord."

The door to the Grand saloon was open. Camber was there. As were Hester and Eugenia, who had, it would seem, dressed with unusual haste. Her eldest brother wore a thunderous expression, to say the least. Mountjoy's wife, Fox's cousin Lily, stood beside him. She was as heart-stoppingly beautiful as ever. There was as well another woman whom he knew he'd met. God help him if he could remember her name. Aigen was there, too, standing with his elbow on the mantel.

Fox composed himself and strode in. "Camber. Mountjoy. What the devil are you doing here, Aigen?"

"You weren't at Upper Brook Street, so I came here. To warn you." He glanced at Eugenia. "But now I'm enjoying meeting your delightful relations. I've been invited to go hunting at Bitterward."

"Warn me about what?"

"Dinwitty Lane is writing poetry to Lady Eugenia. Very bad poetry as he's not a Scotsman, but all the same, I thought you ought to be warned that he's handing out manuscripts to anyone who looks at him sideways."

"Did you bring one with you? No? I'll have to send someone out to fetch me a copy." Fox walked to Lily and took the hand she extended to him. "Cousin Lily. Lovely to see you."

She bent a knee. Her gaze landed on the medallion hanging from his fob, and when she looked up, she looked at Eugenia then gave him one of those smiles that stunned a man who wasn't prepared. Lily was no fool. Mountjoy was damn lucky to have convinced her to marry him. "Well, well, well, my dearest cousin Lord Fenris. I presume congratulations are in order?"

"Yes," he said. "They are, Cousin Lily." Fox held out his hand to Eugenia, and she took it. He brought her close and he felt a certain improper glee when Mountjoy's eyebrows about hit the ceiling. Marriage agreed with Mountjoy. Before he married Lily, the man hadn't known the first thing about how to dress. His cousin had repaired the most glaring of the man's defects.

"Take your hands off my sister, Fenris."

"Your grace. I have the great honor to present Lady Fenris."

Aigen stood straight. "It's true, then?"

Mountjoy looked at Hester and nodded at the girl. "Lady Fenris. Delighted to—"

"Mountjoy, darling man." Lily put a hand on his shoulder and got his attention. "He means Eugenia."

The young woman whose name he could not recall took a step back, trying to remove herself from what was admittedly a private and potentially volatile confrontation between two families that did not have a history of good relations. He remembered the girl now. Caroline Kirk. Eugenia's younger brother, Nigel, had married her eldest sister.

Mountjoy goggled at Lily. "Eugenia hasn't married Fenris."

Fox put an arm around Ginny's waist, and pulled her close. "Last night."

"About time." Aigen didn't speak to anyone in particular.

Eugenia's brother choked. "The devil—"

Lily elbowed him, and Mountjoy closed his mouth. "My dear cousin." Lily curtseyed. "Eugenia. Felicitations. Mountjoy and I are delighted beyond words. And very sorry we did not arrive in time to attend the ceremony."

"Are we?" Mountjoy asked Eugenia.

Fox was aware he was holding his breath.

"Yes." Eugenia rested her head against his shoulder. "We are very sorry you weren't there to share in our happiness."

"Camber," Fox went on. "Forgive me for not having the opportunity to tell you in private." This was a rare moment, him about to take his father to task like this. "But then, I presume you are about to present us with your future wife."

"Yes," Camber said. Good Lord, his father was actually smiling. "Yes, indeed."

"Thank God." Eugenia let out a breath.

Hester clasped her hands to her bosom. "You're not angry, are you? Not terribly, I hope."

"Certainly not." Eugenia moved forward and enveloped Hester in a hug, and there were attempts to explain from his father and Hester but, frankly, none of them went well or made good sense.

The arrival of tea, chocolate, and breakfast made a

welcome interruption. Fox served Eugenia her chocolate personally and received a kiss on the cheek for his trouble. "How sweet of you to remember."

"What the devil is going on, Fenris?" Mountjoy demanded. "I came here because you told me there'd been a fire at Spring Street."

"There was."

"And?"

Fox strode to the table and poured himself a cup of tea. "I'm not going to give a word of explanation until I've had tea and something to eat."

Eugenia took over the tea service and proceeded to get everyone served and seated, and if it hadn't been for Aigen's quick action the silence might have killed them all. Aigen made his way to Fox and thumped him on the shoulder. "Congratulations. You've married above yourself, you scoundrel."

"That I have." He looked over at Eugenia, and her smile made his heart a thousand times too big for his chest.

Lily's gypsy medallion clinked against one of the buttons of Aigen's coat. When Aigen at last released him, Fox touched the bright metal. Was there magic in it? He doubted it, but then again, he was married to the woman he loved. As far as he was concerned, it was all owed to that bit of metal.

On a whim, he removed the medallion from his watch chain and bounced it on his palm. He winked at his wife.

Aigen watched him. "That's a pretty bauble."

"Here, Aigen." He held out his hand, and Aigen took the medallion from him with a puzzled expression. "It's yours now. It will bring you luck in love. Just as it did for me."

"Worked for you, didn't it?"

"It did at that."

"Thank you. I could use that sort of luck." He fastened the medallion to his watch and patted it, then leaned close and said, "Who is that pretty girl over there with your wife?"

"Ah." Fox smiled. "That, my dear friend, is Miss Caroline Kirk."